CW01678209

THE ORANGE HAND

A thriller
by
Tom Bilotta

WH books

WH Books IPB

A thriller by Tom Bilotta

WH BOOKS IPB

Editor: Silvia Penso.
Jacket design by Scott Mc Kenzie.

First English Edition, May 2015
eBook and eMooks®, patent by Tom Bilotta.
Available for any IOS Apple and Android devices.
Download eMooks® for free. App Store and Google Play.
eMooks® by Movie Book S.r.l.

Language:
ENG| ITA

USA | Canada | UK | Italy | Australia | New Zeland

wh-books.com

THIS BOOK IS DEDICATED TO...

My parents.
Raising a child is never easy,
I dare not imagine what raising me must have been!

- Tom Bilotta

eMooks®

READ. LISTEN. AMPLIFY YOUR EMOTIONS.

LISTEN TO THE SOUND OF A BOOK.

Tom Bilotta presents a revolutionary mindset which is likely to change the contemporary publishing industry's face: **eMooks**. A innovative free e-reader system for "movie-ebook", called **eMook**, with the addition of an original soundtrack and sound effects. Available for IOS Apple and Android devices.
The first **eMook** is "Anatole", a thriller jazz story with the addition of an original soundtrack by Alex Fabiani, pianist and composer. **eMook** is the next generation of digital book. **eMooks** is going to change the world of publishing.

SEE MORE HERE: www.emooks.net

SEND HERE YOUR PICTURE OF ISBN CODE FOR A FREE DOWNLOAD: info@emooks.net

Bilotta, Tom.
The Orange Hand | Tom Bilotta

Set in Times New Roman

The Orange Hand

WH Books

FOREWORD

Life is often unkind. It throws you into messy, sickening situations to sort out. How many times have you wished to hide and vanish off the face of the Earth? I am familiar with the feeling and I am sure the same holds true for many of you.
It's like a rabid dog that chews and tears you apart from the inside. And you can't do anything about it, you let it do its thing, you try to shut yourself off, because you know that no-one can truly understand you. But we cannot hide inside ourselves. The building blocks that allow us to rebuild our life are our loved ones – we have to hide with them, inside them. That is the real goal. Anything else is just oblivion.
This book also aims to be a small help for everyone who is trying to overcome a difficult part of their lives but cannot find the strength to do so. Because even when everything seems to be working out for the best, the worst inexorably comes. Likewise, when you are sinking at the bottom, about to drown, life lifts you up and leads you back to shore. Joe Brigati and Paolo Iorio are very similar despite the very different lifes they have lived. Both are looking for rest from their anguish and for redemption from their tragic existences. Their opposite paths will never join, but they are after the same feeling of peace. They will reach it in very different ways. And it will be up to you to choose whose footsteps you will follow in, in your own lives.
Remember, everything can be overcome, even the problems that look unsurmountable. Every peak is far away when we begin our journey, but there is always a path that leads us there. Finding it may not be easy but we will do it with the help of our loved ones.
All this to say that we only live once and that life must be experienced fully. We can't grow tired of listening to this. Bitterness and joys always find a balance in the end. Even for evildoers, because life doesn't spare anyone.

Tom Bilotta

This novel was completed in June 2013

It entered and won the international contest
'***New Authors 2013***' with the temporary title
'Orange Blood Biography'.

- Fiction Crime 'The Hand' (2016-2017 | ShowMedia Production ©)

INTRODUCTION

This book does not aim to take a crack at historiography nor to slander the pharmaceutical industry and the multinational corporations that populate it. Its narrative goals are far from it: the novel intends to entertain the reader with a fast-paced thriller. Its plot is based on a theory I find plausible, that is, that Evil is hidden everywhere, in every place. Evil with a capital 'E', indeed, ruthless and soulless. Fueled by a greed for money and power. This cancer may lurk even in the pharmaceutical industry, a sector that, by its very nature of helping the weak, should be candid and protected. CEOs that only want to make money regardless of people's health. Figures who only care for their own interests and in order to foster them, they sometimes go as far as creating a 'need for meds' from nothing.
Everything revolves around this: our health is an invaluable asset and each one of us needs to take care of it. This balance can, however, be undermined by an unwritten law of marketing: 'if you want to sell and the market has no demand, you have to create it from scratch'.
This is the starting point of this novel. Have you ever stopped to think about all the times we pop a pill at the slightest trace of a symptom? These substances we ingest, are they really useful? What part of their effect is due to the power of suggestion and what part is real? Or is there someone influencing us from the shadows, telling us how to behave? This is advertising at work in the world of drugs. Just imagine the immense profits of such a mind game, which sees us as guinea pigs.
No-one truly knows the real economic advantages of diseases. What if someone chose to put an end to this business? Could you imagine what would happen? The 'strong powers' would do anything to prevent someone or something from thwarting their interests and profits. And those same ruthless men are often in charge of the financial and political world.
The story you are about to read is pure narrative fiction. The plot is all made up, except for the historical facts that lie at its basis. Those are, unfortunately, all real. But then, where does fiction end and what is the truth? Discover it for yourselves.

Happy reading,

The author

I

*"First, you create the product. Then,
on a fake basis, you create a need.
Health is just another way
to make money, maybe the most lucrative
of them all."*

August 22nd, 2012, 11.41PM. Outskirts of San José, a modern dormitory town in Silicon Valley, California. A bunch of buildings owned by multi-billion dollar IT companies and rows of townhouses for their employees, each of them looking like the next one, with a shared backyard and a small swimming pool. In the evening, the place turns into a desert: citizens retreat into their homes to get their rest and after 11PM the town is empty, with the only exceptions of street sweepers and policemen. All that remains is a sad patch of concrete in the middle of the arid terrain at the southern end of the San Francisco Bay Area.
As usual, a *Metropolitan Police* patrol was roaming in search of possible criminals. San José was one of the American cities with the lowest crime rate, a real catch for any policeman, at least until that day. On August 22nd, the reputation of the city was turned upside down, going from being the capital of Silicon Valley, the wonderful, state-of-the-art realm of all things IT, to being the background of a murder.

On that August day, in the isolated parking lot of a *Burger King*, two agents noticed a white car, a Chrysler sedan, with its trunk open. They braked and switched on the light on their car's right side to have a clearer view of the area. A leg was sticking out of the open trunk. On the ground, a small red stain.
Gun in hand, they rushed to the sedan to have a better look. What they saw painted a terrified look on their faces.
In all their career, they had never seen anything like it. Not a soul was around, no killer to be seen, just the corpse of a man about fifty years old, with grizzled hair and a lean physique.

His clothes had been taken off, leaving his naked chest in plain sight. There was, clearly, the intent to create a sort of grim showcase, a remarkable display. And the killer's work stood out: there was a shocking amount of stabbing wounds on the victim's body, nineteen according to their tally, all to the heart, which created a deep gash on the left side of his torso.
“Like a crater carved with a knife”, the coroner's report would later say. On the victim's forehead, written in blood, were the words “DELINQUENT SHAME”, a weird, outdated wording. An orange hand print was also found on the car's side, with further analysis showing that the print belonged to the dead man himself: traces of the same paint were found on his right palm.
The survey was carried out by the district's forensic team. It had been years since their last murder case: in that corner of America, computer forensics are in much higher request and their colleagues were left to rot in their offices, envying their fictional counterparts on TV with their murders and sensational cases. This was their turn to shine.
As they analyzed the crime scene, the forensics team brought to light another detail. In his right hand, same one as the print, the victim was holding a piece of orange paper with the following words: 'Rule number one... Before you create the product and then you get, with fake scientific reasons, the need. Health is a way as any to make money, perhaps the most lucrative... Are your words, son of a bitch!'.
A clunky translation it may have been, the author was certainly no native English speaker and they may have used an automatic translator, but the note's meaning was clear. 'Rule number one... First, you create the product. Then, on a fake basis, you create a need. Health is just another way to make money, maybe the most lucrative of them all... these are your words, you son of a bitch!'
There was no trace of his clothes, just a bloodied lab coat under his body. The car's keys were also missing, and the vehicle had been powered up by reconnecting the wiring, like in the movies. The glove compartment contained a map with a circled area on San Felipe Road, a secondary road that toils up the arid, isolated areas south of the city. The Chrysler came from the Rental Car Garage SJC located in San José's Mineta International airport. According to the database, it had been handed back on the day before the corpse's discovery: August 21st, 11.30 AM.
The city's homicide squad handled the case, but failed to find its culprit as well as answers to so many of its questions. What was the meaning of the place marked on the map they found in the dashboard? The detectives drove

to mile 26 of San Felipe Road, but all they found was a stretch of arid ground, two rocks and a bunch of trees, none of which related to the case.
Had a meeting with the killer been held there? Was it someone the victim knew? The corpse had certainly been brought to that parking lot in San José after the murder. The real scene of the crime was never discovered, just like Mark Bongher's clothes and personal effects were never recovered. The victim's identity came up after a few days afterwards, thanks to a phone call and a cross check of the missing persons database. His wife waited and waited for him to come home in San Francisco, but eventually reported his disappearance.
The case was riddled with holes. Another detail only furthered the mystery: the person who had brought the car back to the garage was no other than the victim himself. But why steal the same car which he had regularly rented up to a few hours earlier?
An investigation was carried out into the man's life, hoping to shed some light on the situation, but even then, the detectives were only led to a dead end. Born in Amsterdam Mark had come to the USA at age eight along with his family. Having graduated with honors at Michigan University, he had moved to California for a job as research scientist: he was project leader at Biotech FourStreet Laboratories Inc., a private biochemical lab in San Francisco. With no criminal record, he had led an irreproachable life. No lovers either, nor enemies on the job. He was affluent and had no vices. Even his children, a ten years old boy and an eight years old girl, were exemplary. The investigators tried to extend their searches to the wife, but that offered no leads either, not even an extra-marital affair. Likewise, the messages left by the killer weren't understood any further. So it came to pass that the Bongher murder was eventually shelved as the isolated act of a sexual maniac, i.e. a case of attempted homosexual rape ended in violence, despite the lack of any evidence that could support that hypothesis as the corpse revealed no relevant bruises nor seminal fluid. The idea was only based on the victim's lack of clothes, anything to avoid closing the investigation without at least a plausible hypothesis. Mary Bongher was thus left without answers.

II

"The beginning of an adventure
can often change the tide
of one's destiny."

The phone rang. I opened my eyes with the same feeling of unease that had marked these last months: I was fatigued and apathetic. I had fallen asleep on the couch again, in the middle of the afternoon. I felt as if my head were being mixed by the barman of the pub across the street: my cocktail was equal parts nausea and headache.
It was already 5 PM, another day I had thrown away. Ever since leaving my job at the newspaper, *Repubblica*, in Milan, my favorite pastimes were watching TV and drinking. I couldn't forgive myself for those recent developments: I had dropped the job of my life for a stupid argument with my boss.
Becoming a journalist had always been my goal, ever since I was a young boy daydreaming about Milan. I sat in my room in Toronto and imagined the town as my grandfather had painted it in the tales he spun on my parents' couch. He had truly known the place in its glory days, when the town under the golden statue of the *Madunina* was like one big neighborhood where everyone knew each other. Now it's a metropolis where it is easier to get to know the pakistani immigrant selling roses at the street corner than a lady across the street.
Depression had filled my brain. With the economic crisis raging on, making ends meet without a job would be no easy task. My funds were about to end and I felt like throwing up at the sole idea of putting up an ad on the internet to look for a job. What a humiliation. What would my former colleagues say if they saw me deliver pizzas? No offense meant to pizza delivery people, of course. But I could never. And what would I say to my parents?
That's the thing with us thirty years old. We're so good at feigning independence, but when push comes to shove, we're inextricably linked to

the thoughts and will of our mother and father. Physically independent we may be, but mentally, not at all. It's like a lasso keeping us at bay wherever we go.
My professional debacle would turn into a veritable family catastrophe, especially considering that my choice in career had been my own idea all along. And I didn't want to hurt my folks like that. They would've wanted me to stay in Canada and work in the family business, the one my father has started as he left Italy. With the sweat of his brow, he had made a new life for himself abroad, a future he could hand over to his children.
I, on the other hand, needed to breathe the air of my homeland. I needed to feel Italian, not Canadian, and most of all, I needed to try my luck as a journalist, my only goal in life. And I made it, by emigrating backwards. Except I was throwing it all away now. But I have a bad attitude and when people can't use their heads and want to force me to do things I don't want to, I flip out. Truth is, I'm too proud, I couldn't have kept working in that office. Better to find something else to do, like writing a book. That was, after all, my first job, which I used to pay for my studies before coming to Italy.

My cellphone's vibrations sadly brought me back to reality. “Andrea office”, read the blinking display. “What does he want now?”, I shouted in my mind and lit up the last remaining red Marlboro from the pack on the living room's table. Come to think of it, I hadn't heard from him in months.
Andrea Marchi was a sweet boy and the manager of an event planning agency in downtown Milan. I had known him for a while, ever since managing editor Alberto Masi had moved me from crime news to the show business. Which is journalistic shorthand for 'you're about to be fired', or rather 'either you get out on your own or we'll take care of it'. Coherently, I could only stand three more months before slamming the door behind me.
Andrea was, at any rate, the only good thing to come out of those crazy days spent between TV starlets and VIPs. The parties he organized were always wicked and theatrical, he knew perfectly well how to let people have fun. Last but not least, we got free drinks at every rendezvous of his.

And I know what you're thinking: "I wonder how many girls you've been with in that environment". "Been with" or, without mincing words, "fucked". Zero. Truth be told, the appeal of the writer, or journalist, has plummeted recently, just like the shares of Lehman Brothers Holdings Inc. which brought the world to its knees.
In the Nineties, all you had to do was flash your journalist badge and the girls, with their eyes wide open, cried "You're a journalist? For real?!? Cool..." It swept them off their feet, to put it mildly.
It's not like that now, and even less so at those slick parties where teenagers only have eyes for the latest reality show star, purported VIP and/or useless TV character.
I have always been in the corner, watching and drinking, a shadow among the shadows.
The phone stopped ringing and I woke up from my reverie as the display lit up again: "You have a new message in your voicemail".
That'll be Andrea, I thought to myself, so I dialed my voicemail to listen to it. "Beep... Beep... Hi Joe, this is urgent, I need to talk to you. Call me asap."
Odd message, what could ever be so urgent after months of silence? I decided not to call him back, nausea took over and I still needed to lie down for some minutes.
At 6 PM, the phone rang again. I opened my eyes and grabbed my iPhone from the table: 'Andrea office', it said again. I had to take the call this time, I couldn't possibly keep on pretending not to hear it. I struggled to conceal the typical voice of someone who was sleeping up to a few seconds earlier: "Hello?"
"Hi Joe, is this a good moment? I was hoping you'd call back."
I could have, yes, but I absolutely didn't want to.
"Sorry, it's just that I've been very busy this past few days", I lied.
He stood silent for a moment in a way that spelled out 'cut the bullshit'.
"I can imagine... anyway, I'm calling you for an urgent business. A friend and client of mine wants to write a book, a biography, and I immediately thought of you, would you be interested in helping her out? After all, now that you're out of a job, it'd be a good way to make some money."
I didn't even bid for time: I sank his offer with a clear "no" and kept up my façade of a tough, busy guy.

"Mmmh... Thanks, but I'm not interested. As I told you, I'm very busy these days and I may be about to go back to Canada."
The lie was clear as day, a child would've seen through it. But pride can lead to abysmal mistakes.
"Listen, you'd really be the right person for this. At least let's meet, let's talk about it. Keep in mind that this contract would be hella sweet, you'd get a load of money!"
"If you say so, let me think about it for a couple of days. I'll let you know."
"Okay, but if you don't call me back, I will. You're not getting outta this!"
The hound hung up with his trademark approving laughter, which echoed in my nausea-addled cranium. I didn't care about any of that and went back to sleep without thinking about it twice, as if the phone call hadn't touched my blurred mind.
From that August afternoon, Andrea started a bona fide harassment campaign toward yours truly. Every day a call, a voicemail. I was being hunted down and I only had one way of putting an end to that psychological torment: accepting a meeting with that client of his.
As bad luck would have it, a few years earlier I'd published a thriller novel: it hadn't been a smashing success, but Andrea's agency had taken care of the launch party for the emerging authors' crime fiction series for my publisher and to him, I had become 'the writer'. Possibly the only writer he ever met in his entire life. And to Andrea, that only meant one thing: profit. I was just a means to an end, but why not.
I didn't dislike the idea – and it's not like I lacked the background. Before coming to Italy, I had dabbled in writing a couple biographies and he knew it. Then my passion for journalism took me over and I dropped out of college to fly from Toronto to Malpensa airport, toward Milan, the city of my parents and of my grandparents. And here I struck gold, getting first into local newspaper *La Gazzetta della Martesana* and then directly to *La Repubblica*. Thanks to two big scoops, I quickly made it to a major national daily newspaper with almost no experience. I had found out a network of gambling houses frequented by bigwigs and, better still, I had uncovered a cocaine trail that went from Bogotà directly to Lombardy, for the enjoyment of Milan's nightlife. A stroke of luck? Maybe. But I never lacked investigative prowess. Nor inventive.

Else it would have been near impossible to land such a job as an Italian Canadian who had just treaded on his ancestors' soil. Everyone thought I had connections, they said that since I was born in Canada, I had no right to have a steady job for an Italian newspaper. Actually, I've always spoken and written to my family in Italian, which I consider my native tongue, while French and English came later, at school. I was way more qualified than some colleagues who could barely string two English words together, the bare minimum to go on holiday abroad. But to all of them, I was the Canadian with connections.

In those days, I travelled Milan on my Vespa, hunting for news, forgetting my previous job as ghostwriter. Now, thanks to Andrea's offer, I could get back on my feet. Many famous freelance writers started out by penning biographies and in all honesty, the 'ghost' part was a good fit for my new, post-sacking looks.
I felt better. Now that Andrea had managed to persuade me, I felt a small boost of energy: that job could work for me and for my mother as well. It would be a passable justification for my dismissal from *Repubblica*. Back in Canada, she was always a very demanding parent. I was a single child and, as often happens, I had the spotlights trained on me. Her expectations were high. She never accepted my choice of dropping out of college to pursue a journalistic career, of abandoning Toronto for Milan at the drop of a hat. “You've got no talent, where do you think you're going?”
I've always been incurably stubborn: when people tell me 'no', it sounds like an exhortation to dive in headfirst regardless. So that's what I did: I packed my luggages, kissed goodbye to mom and dad and left toward my new life in Milan.
Now I would be able to tell mom that, after five years of journalistic activity, I had decided to make it big as a writer: 'no talent', my ass. That problem was over, but it was far from being the only one. My journalist's pride was still wounded and it held me back. I had to figure out how to make my next move. My instinct told me to refuse the offer, considering the job's scarce literary value. With all due respect, Andrea's clients were hardly the intellecual types: TV starlets, soccer players, VIPs and businessmen, typical inhabitants of a world I did not belong to. That kind of people, in all honesty, were better framed by a photo shoot on a gossip

magazine than a biography. But I couldn't be too picky, the crisis was starting to worry me and paying rent had become a nightmare.
I set my instinct and my pride aside. I went back to thinking rationally: I had to accept. I had touched the lowest point in my life, now I could do with new strength to pull myself up again. And Andrea was stretching out his hand.

III

"The sun was at its zenith and Milan's asphalt
was boiling. 'Da Sandro'
was the typical, noisy restaurant
where it's near impossible
to have a chat."

I dialed the number on my phone's screen and held my breath. "Hello?", a weak voice answered on the other end.
"Hi Andrea!"
"I've been waiting for this call for some weeks now. Have you finally made up your mind?"
"Not quite, but I did realize that saying yes would be the only way to make you stop harassing me. Listen, let's meet this week, okay?"
Andrea could hardly mask his enthusiasm: "Okay Joe, sure thing. Is Tuesday okay? I can buy you lunch and we'll talk."
"Fine, let's do this."
"Done deal... let's meet at 1 o'clock at *Da Sandro*. Have a nice day!"
He hung up without waiting for my reply. What an unusually curt call: Andrea always made a point of telling me all his last work projects or indulging in a little gossip about shared acquaintances. But on that day, nothing. Ah well.

The sun was at its zenith and Milan's asphalt was boiling. 'Da Sandro' was the typical, noisy restaurant in Corso Buenos Aires avenue where it's near impossible to have a chat, but the city has a way of getting calmer in August, softer, less hectic. It can, at times, look like a countryside town where the few inhabitants greet each other on the streets. A pleasant feeling, to tell the truth. Finally, a quietened city.
The owner greeted me as I walked in. "Hey, Joe, everything okay? We haven't seen you in a while."
"Hi... Matteo. It's fine, thanks. ...have you seen Andrea?"

In all honesty, I didn't feel like sharing my private business with a stranger, even though I had lunch and dinner there every day when I worked for *Repubblica*.
He answered me from behind the counter: “He's at table 14, down the stairs and to your left.”
That was fine – on a sunny day, eating in a cellar was ideal. But I knew all too well why Andrea had picked that table: the man was cunning and was trying to exhaust me by denying me my cigarette.
I could not understand why he was so obstinate: he wanted me to accept at all costs, with any trick.
I saw him sitting alone at the end of the underground cellar. I came closer.
“Hi Andrea, wouldn't you rather sit outside? It's hot, but at least we'd breathe fresh air.”
“Sit down, Joe. I'm paying, so I pick the table. You'd roast for hours under the sun if it meant getting to smoke a cig.”
I kept my calm, even though it wasn't easy. “Fine, fine, busted. I'm gonna sit down and shut up.”
One of the flaws I hate the most is hypocrisy, but taking too much time to explain an idea comes a close second. Andrea was a champion at this, he would wear you out to get what he wanted. We ordered *spaghetti allo scoglio* and started to talk business.
“As I told you... this client of mine, or rather friend, wants you to write a book. It's a biography, but not her biography – her partner's, a businessman. She's an Argentinian model who lives here in Milan, a lovely girl, and on top of her modeling job, she works as an assistant in a design studio.”
Andrea stopped talking.
“Are you okay? You look pale...”
“Don't worry, keep talking...”

I knew it. It was a shit job. Joe Brigati, from Toronto, after five years of honored investigative journalism in Italy, had hit rock bottom. I thought back to my first jobs in Canada, when I wrote biographies for oddball characters: big, fat immigrants who wanted to boast to friends and relatives. Sadly, I couldn't go back. I would have to deal with the dismal biography of your typical young businessman who lollygags around Milan

on his white Porsche Cayenne, with no regards for speed limits or pedestrians. The kind of character about whom, honestly, nothing can be said. He was no hero and no smart aleck: his business belonged to his father and all he did was inherit it, get all he could from it and bring it to collapse.
"Okay Andrea, I get it. Thanks for the lunch, but I'm not interested. I can't do something like this... just thinking about it makes me want to throw up."
I realized as I spoke that I had turned off my brain for a second. Rationality was being fucked over by pride. I blushed, then paled as I thought about my bank account.
Luckily, he still hadn't given up: "Is that a 'fuck you'? Listen, she's a friend... it's not what you think."
He sipped his wine and then grinned: "You can drop the act, I know for a fact that you spend your days watching satellite TV from your couch. I'm giving you a chance to earn some money and get your name out there. People don't care about you anymore. You're dead to them!"
My heart jumped. That motherfucker got me good. I'd been knocked down from atop my pride and grounded with a single blow.
"How much are we talking about?"
Andrea beat about the question some more before eventually getting to the point: a whopping thirty thousand Euros. A lot of money, especially when compared to a journalist's meager pay. Too much money, maybe, if anyone were to just stop and think about it for a moment. But the crisis was fucking with even the little reasoning I still had in my body.
"Told you, it's an easy-peasy job."
"I hope there's a lot on the character's plate, I have a professional dignity to uphold... understood?"
Andrea gave a hint of a smile, he knew perfectly well that I was bluffing. And he wisely let it pass.
"Don't worry, you won't regret it."
We spent the rest of our lunch making small talk like the old times. Then I dashed off, with the thought that I may truly have reached the bottom of my short, absurd life.

But what could I do? Earning that amount of money would take me a year of hard work. Getting it all in one fell swoop with that job was a precious occasion.

The meeting with the client was set at 12.30 of a warm September Friday, in Milan's outskirts. Summer didn't want to leave and the sultry weather still reigned supreme. More than one week had passed since my meeting with Andrea at *Da Sandro*, ending August and turning the page on a fresh new month.
As usual, timeliness wasn't my forte and I was late, majorly late. I was supposed to meet Andrea at 11.30 and at 11.47 his silhouette appeared from the door of his agency, under Piazza San Babila's colonnades. He was livid.
I parked my Vespa and listened to him utter his rightful complaints: “Fuck you, Joe, how can you always be late? We've gotta dash, Jenny's waiting for us... Come on, get into the car and make it quick!”
The car, a white Mercedes-Benz SLK AMG, was parked in front of him with hazards on. I was delighted to notice that he had parked it smack dab in the middle of a pedestrian crossing, like a true Milanese. At least my delay had done me some good: now I knew that the customer was called Jenny. An exotic name. As he drove, Andrea was uncharacteristically silent.
On top of my delay, he was likely irritated by my choice of clothes: pure Canadian style, Italian origins be damned. After all, while I can fluently speak and write this country's language, I'm no fashion addict, unlike so many of my peers who were born in the capital of fashion. Ever since I was born, I have always had the gall to impose myself, my style.
“You could at least have put on long pants...”
What? Me? I couldn't let it slide. “I don't even know if I'm gonna accept. And I'm gonna get paid for what I write, right? Not for how I dress.”
“You're the same old stubborn mule.”
I didn't answer, but I smiled. I didn't look half bad: a white short-sleeved shirt, short blue pants and light blue loafers. It was, after all, still hot and I had no intention of adapting my style just to cater to some guy or gal. My lean, slightly buff body looked good in short sleeves and pants. I

could've done with a little more tan, but in those days I was just a ghost of myself and my skin tone reflected it.
We were headed toward Milan's Bicocca district, an old industrial zone turned posh meeting place for college students and graduates. Our meeting was set there, in the studio where our model client worked as assistant designer. I noticed with satisfaction that all the people standing outside were dressed in a completely different way than I, wrapped in their suits and ties: I adore being different. Students aside, the streets seemed inhabited by so many mannequins.

We made it to the office's parking lot, inside a red brick building which had been recently modernized. A black Porsche Cayman was parked in plain sight, with hazards on, and in the driver's seat was a young woman of about twenty-five, a brunette wearing gaudy Gucci shades.
"Hi Jenny! Sorry we're late...", Andrea cried as he drove close to her, struggling to stick his head out of the window. His seatbelt was choking him.
After a quick wave of her hand and the shadow of a smile, her Porsche's tires spun on the asphalt. Andrea followed her without a word.
The young woman looked beautiful. I didn't get a very good look at her, to tell the truth, but with those shades, she wasn't lacking in charm. And then I suddenly understood the negative reaction toward my clothes, or rather Andrea's embarrassment at the thought of having me with him. The place of our meeting was a restaurant, which would have been fine, except it was the kind of place where the cover charge alone was like a hundred and fifty Euros. One Michelin star could be seen at the entrance, while in the courtyard, a wedding reception was in its photos/videos phase, or as it were, 'take shoots of the husband before he makes a run for it'.
"You see now why long pants would've been better?"
I nodded. There was, after all, nothing else to say. We were in the only green oasis of Milan's former industrial outskirts and I felt ashamed. A lot, to be honest.
"Jennifer Blasquez, this is Joe... Joe Brigati. He's the writer I told you about. From Canada, but a hundred percent Italian."
Not quite – if anything, I'm of Italian origin but a born and bred Canadian, or 'd.o.c.' as the Italian quality assurance label goes. Andrea probably

wanted to avoid the embarrassment of suggesting a Canadian writer for a book in Italian. I chose not to correct him and offered my hand to the client. “Nice to meet you, Jennifer...”

“Plesure's mine, and call me Jenny. I've heard a lot about you... forgive my accent, I'm Argentinian. You, on the other hand, speak Italian very well.”

Andrea culled that topic before it got out of hand: “Of course Jenny, as I told you, he's Italian... but he lived in Canada for may years.”

Again with that story, I thought to myself.

She smiled, possibly seeing through my embarrassment. She seemed nice, not too much of a snob. That was good news, at least my work would've started on the right foot. Her angelic face, with full lips, was lit up by eyes as blue as gem stones. Her body was thin, fit for a model, and her olive skin gave her a Mediterranean flair. The black sheath dress she was wearing gave her a sexy, elegant flair: all men in the restaurant turned their heads to look at her as she walked past their tables.

She didn't point out my unrefined summer attire and didn't even scoff at my loafers, a staple of the *very nice Canadian style.*

We sat at our table while the newlyweds outside kept on their fake smiles for the photographer, surrounded by confetti and visibly moved relatives. The waiter gave me a look, understandably. Had I been forced to wear a bowtie in summer, I would've also glared at a thirty years old man dressed like a kid. We ordered a fish fry and I started off by setting my boundaries:

“I want to make one thing clear”, I said, quick as a high speed train, “I haven't said yes yet. I want to understand what this is about first, why you want to write this book.”

Jennifer kept her smile on and didn't bat an eyelash, seemingly understanding where my reservations were coming from. “You see, Joe, I imagine this can't look too appealing to you. I assure you there is a reason I want you to write this book, even though I have no obligation to explain it to you. He's the only one who is aware of the real motive.”

Her face turned dark as she stared me right in the eyes: “You are a means to an end, nothing more.”

“Fine, let's start from the beginning, then. Who are we talking about?”

Writing a biography is no easy task. Moreso when it's about someone you have never known, never seen, never even met for one minute. The pieces of information you can collect are often ragged, blurred, and fixing them on paper can be dangerous. There is the risk of telling falsehoods without even realizing it, or of having to make up entire sequences in order to make the narration livelier. It requires a great deal of attention.
The job requires interviewing all the people who have known the subject of your book and collecting all their tales in a notebook or voice recorder. It's not unlike a historiographical analysis, requiring you to turn into archaeologists and delve into your protagonist's past. Or private eyes, one could say.
In this case, the work in front of me set out to be much more straightforward. All I would need to do was interview Jenny or her boyfriend and write it all down.

"As we were saying, who is this about?" My question fell on deaf ears. Jenny shook her head, while Andrea hinted at a sign of disapproval, without looking at me, more interested in his fried fish than in the talk, "My partner."
"Okay, well. I knew that. I meant, what's his name, what does he do in life... just to get a feeling of who we're talking about."
She took a sip of water and gingerly wiped her lips with her napkin. "Joe, you can't know anything about that. At least until you take the job."
I was flabbergasted. Andrea tried to ease the situation with a dash of irony: "I told you this was the job for you. Aren't you a mystery lover?"
He was right, I've always enjoyed mysterious situations. Truth be told, one of the reasons I chose to resign from *Repubblica* was my utter inability to stop getting myself in trouble. I saw conspiracies everywhere, sneaked inside to find out something more and my bosses were tired of cops listing me as 'persona non grata' at any given crime scene.
"My friends, help me out here. How the heck am I supposed to choose whether to take the job if you can tell me nothing?"
"That's the whole point of it. You'll have to write a biography based on the info we'll feed you as you go on", Jenny said with an alluring voice. "Only at the end of it all will you find out who it is that we are talking about."
This didn't make any sense: why keep all this mystery?

"You must understand, Joe, that the main character in this tale is not from Milan. He has lived a complicated life and doesn't like to talk about himself. He's very discreet."
Sure, it's not like I cared much about all that, but the situation was getting increasingly absurd. Why would a discreet person want a book written about themselves?
"It's a present from you, then?"
I looked at Jenny straight in the eyes, as if to look for confirmation with all my strength. She, however, shook her head in reaply.
"Not really. Actually, he's the one who asked me to make arrangements with you. He's in the States for work and doesn't have time to take care of these things, which is why I'm going to take care of this personally..."
I knew I was going to get into so much trouble and that I would regret it big time. But my heart started to race like in the good old days – I was excited.
"Should you take the job, this is the check. Feel free to cash it, it's the total: thirty thousand Euros, so you'll be able to work without a care. I'll be waiting for you at the office next Monday at 9..."
She brushed her silken hair out of her face, got up and waved us a sweet goodbye, then resolutely walked toward the counter to pay for us all.
"Fuck, what a girl!"
"Joe, forget her. She grew up fast, from rags to riches within a few years. And she's the woman of your new boss, after all..."
Andrea gave me a smug look, coughed and kept on talking. "What did I tell you? You can't say no. But be careful, I'm gonna tell you again, that girl is dangerous. Do what they tell you to and nothing more."
Have I already mentioned that I'm stubborn? Maybe I have. It was no accident that Andrea's words soon went forgotten – I could only think about her and the book I would write.
I was undeniably hooked. It may sound strange, with all my earlier reluctance, that looking into that woman's eyes would turn me around. But it wasn't just because of the money, as convincing as it can be. And it wasn't all about Jennifer either, though to be honest that, too, was exciting. The real reason was always the same: my forced stay at home was alienating me. I had almost fallen prey to depression. I couldn't sleep well,

I didn't bathe, didn't eat, didn't want to see anyone. I had fallen into the cracks.
And this was my floater.

IV

"You chose to wait
even though you knew
what that would cause.
The money god corrupted you,
your soul is lost."

Sausalito, a charming seaside town a few miles from the Golden Gate Bridge connecting the Pacific Ocean with San Francisco Bay. It's an elegant place, filled with international brand shops, posh jewelry stores, antique shops dealing in European furniture from the Eighteenth and Nineteenth centuries. It's the American bourgeoisie's favorite place to spend a holiday on the West Coast.
August 24th, 2012, 8.27 AM. Right at the town's entrance, visitors are greeted by a traffic circle painted lilac. It's a unique way to welcome guests, the wisteria matching the wooden sign with the words "Welcome to Sausalito". At night, the festive lights that hang all year long over the narrow streets gently reflected their lights on the sea. Elegance shone through every corner of that enchanted place, with its Yacht Club and attached restaurant facing the water in the middle of the small town, like a king sitting on his throne in the middle of the crown room. On the opposite end, as the waves broke on the rocks by the small port, Angel Island could be seen in the distance. Under the spinnaker's shadow, yachtsmen could admire the monumental villas of the town's rich residents set in the hill's green hues. Classy restaurants delicately dotted the Bay along with the wooden piers, old and restored, which were once used to moor the fishermen's boats. Lastly, lofts abounded: former boat shelters which could be seen from the promenade among the oldest buildings of the sea town. The economic crisis had, sadly, eventually reached this corner of paradise. Many colored signs marked homes for sale: everyone but a wealthy elite was trying to make revenue, but they couldn't find buyers. Many people left, never to return, except for those living in the

southernmost side of town. Houses were made of wood there, not elegant but picturesque, seeing how Sausalito used to be a fisherman's village up until some twenty years earlier. Then came the economic boom and the riches' invasion. They were slowly going back to normal.
Like every morning, Margareth Wright walked into the luxurious entrance hall of Jason Wittman's residence. Wittman was a famous pathologist of the university of San Francisco, California, esteemed professor, dean of the Department of Pathology of the university's study centre. Some of his most important contributions to the scientific community include some intuitions on the road to develop a vaccine against HIV. He was one of the co-founders of Biotech FourStreet Laboratories Inc. and, according to Science magazine, he ranked third among the most brilliant US researchers of the last two decades.
No-one in town could say they knew him well: a reserved character, he had only recently moved into his enormous villa in Bulkley Ave., right across the port. He was married to Francine Deloitte, a doctor from Chicago, of French origins, who still lived and worked in Illinois. She only went to California for the holidays, theirs was a typical long-distance marriage with no children. She was 39, a beautiful, refined cardiologist; he, 49, was a tad overweight and constantly glued to the microscope. All their friends wondered how he had managed to woo her – money, the whispers said, but the truth was that he was never that rich. Theirs was truly a marriage of love, intellectual love, blossomed in the university halls as he was a junior lecturer and she a student who had come to California for her postgraduate work. They had met never to leave each other again.
Margareth Wright had started working for mister Wittman one year earlier, when he moved there from downtown San Francisco. She was the housekeeper: she dusted, cooked and washed, the usual routine. On that day, as she arrived, she noticed something strange: the professor's car, a gray Lexus RX450-h, was parked in the villa's tree-lined driveway. And by then, it should have already been on Route 101, with the doctor on the driver's seat, on his way to the lab. Margareth imagined that Wittman might have felt ill and stayed home. As the woman walked through the entrance door, she noticed that the living room's lights were still on despite the sunlight coming from outside. The housekeeper gently closed the door

behind her, taking care not to make any noise as she handled the golden knob. She put the keys on the walnut Louis XVI style fall-front desk and, following her suspicions, she looked around before starting with her work proper.
The white wooden house was a typical Victorian building, two stories plus turret: from the the entrance hall, light wooden stairs led to the upper floor, with three bedroom and two bathrooms; on the left, a spacious kitchen with a marble peninsula and, next to the brass sinks, the door to the porch. On the right, the main hall with its wide white windows offered a good look on Sausalito's small harbor.
The interior design showed attention to every small detail: light tones, a damask couch and vintage pieces of furniture matched refined items with a modern design. It was one of the most beautiful houses of the area, not just from an architectural and structural standpoint, but also thanks to the taste that went into choosing its furniture and paintings, the latter coming exclusively from early twentieth century France.
Miss Wright walked into the kitchen to drop her linen jacket on the counter and then moved toward the living room, calling mister Wittman out loud. No replies. She then opened the door to the closet to fetch her rubber gloves, broom, bucket and detergents. Carrying along all her supplies, she crossed the white arch that separated the entrance from the living room. As she went through the motions of calling for her employer one more time, her voice even louder, she saw a naked foot sticking out from beyond the beige sofa. “Oh my Goooooddd”. Instinctively, she rushed to the body, throwing the bucket and everything in it to the ground. As she reached the corpse's feet, however, her instinct was to cover her eyes with her hands.
The scene was horrifying. Wittman was lying on the ground naked, his skin livid, his eyes empty. On his forehead, blood-red letters read: “SHAME ON YOU, WORM”. His tongue stuck out of his mouth slightly, showing a probable asphyxiation.
The corpse's position had been set up on purpose, the killer's intent clearly being that of creating a morbid sight. The body lay on the parquetry in the middle of a round clock face drawn in blood. His hands and feet were tied, while shoulders and hips had probably been dislocated when Wittman was still alive, his torture aimed at creating the perfect set for the killer's vision. The man lay in an unnatural position, almost like a mirrored 'L', with his

legs used as the makeshift clock's minute hand and his arms as the hour hand, pointing at seven o'clock. On his chest, a wide post-mortem wound may have been inflicted by his murderer to draw enough blood to complete his writing as well as that morbid setup.
On the white wall, orange paint traced the shape of a hand; the handprint was the victim's.
Police was quick to arrive, called by the housekeeper as soon as she caught her breath. Then again, Bulkley Ave. and the Sausalito Police Station in Johnson Street were barely six minutes apart by car. For the cops, the issue was not so much arriving to the villa, but getting inside according to procedure. The local agents weren't accustomed to such brutal criminal acts and ended up contaminating the crime scene by accident. They walked all over it with their shoes, didn't stop nosey neighbors from trespassing into the garden and moved poor Wittman's body after the coroner's first report, which stated that the cause of death was choking with a nylon wire.
As San Francisco's CSI unit was eventually called on the scene, most of the biological traces they could have used had been erased or rendered unusable.
Among the investigation team's direst mistakes was their failure to consider the orange hand on the wall as evidence. They thought that, as it belonged to the owner of that place, it had to be related to 'artistic' renovations of some sort and not part of the crime scene. The can of paint was right beside the victim, but the investigators misinterpreted its relevance. Lastly, no fingerprints were found beside those of the villa's regulars.
The investigation was carried out by San Francisco's homicide squad, but the agents couldn't riddle it out. As the murder took place, the victim's wife was, of course, in Chicago. Due to the time zone lag between the coasts, she was only notified of her husband's tragic fate on the following day. As the shock set in, she had a nervous breakdown that led her to almost a month of hospitalization in a psychiatric clinic. The only lead was a note, an orange piece of paper held by the victim's right hand, which said, in broken English: “You chose waiting even if you was sure of the consequences. The god money corrupted you, your soul you lost it. So your time has stop forever: WORM.”

Questionings were carried out at Jason Wittman's workplace, but nothing of interest came up. He was an esteemed researcher, respected by his colleagues and by his associates at Biotech FourStreet Laboratories Inc.. The company had been founded in 1991 thanks to the professor himself along with two other young pathologists. One, from Denver, died of cancer in 1997; the other, an Italian man who had moved to California at the end of the Eighties to pursue a scientific career, was attending a medical conference in Rome as his partner was being killed in his home. Matteo Bolzoni, that was his name, told the investigators as he flew back to San Francisco that he was deeply saddened by the death of his good friend Jas and that he would dedicate to his memory the HIV vaccine they would eventually discover. His statement soon ended up on all the international newspapers and scientific publications.
At the end of the Nineties, FourStreet had turned from a mere lab to a leading center in the fight against HIV. Born as a branch of the University of San Francisco and working side by side with it, it could count on help from international pharmaceutical companies, the U.S. Department of Health and European ones as well. The top brains in the world had converged there, under the Golden Gate Bridge, to fight against the HIV virus, but up to that point, their progress had been minimal. Just like the investigation into Wittman's killer.

The investigators were running in circles and the pressure kept piling up: politicians, press and public opinion wanted answers, but they could only find more questions. They tried to poke around the academic community, but the victim was a talented, beloved university professor. No enemies, nothing suspicious going on. His only transgression appeared to be a mad love for golf. Everyone described him as being deeply in love with his wife, who appeared to reciprocate, albeit from a distance. No-one could imagine who could have killed him in such a cruel way, nor why.
The investigative blackout seemed to come to an end at the beginning of September, when the FBI digital database of unsolved cases showed that a Biotech FourStreet Laboratories Inc. had been murdered two days earlier in San José by a homosexual suspect. The two cases were initially assumed to be connected, but the murders were too isolated and no-one wanted to imply that Jason Wittman may have been homosexual or

somehow involved in a menage a trois between men. Political pressure immediately made them drop that line of investigation, to avoid a stain on the eminent pathologist's name.

V

"His life wasn't easy.
He managed to get back on his feet
when anyone else would have
shot themselves or thrown themselves under a train."

The merciless screen kept on flashing red, while the alarm clock marked '4:00' in green numbers on the display. On a Safari tab, my online bank account's page was a bloodbath. I would have been terrified of not making it to the end of the month had it not been for Jenny's check, which I had cashed in on Friday afternoon.

My home was a mess. Dirty clothes were all over the place, while pizza boxes dominated the kitchen: *I like Italian pizza!*, they said. And truth be told, my face was a mess too: the mirror reflected a pale man with glassy eyes. As I always say, Jack Daniel's isn't the best antidote to depression.

I should have done the same thing I did years ago, when I played rugby. I broke my knee's ligaments in a University League match in Montréal and, rather than abandoning the sport I've always loved, I chose to subject myself to almost ten months of strict rehab. It was my fourth year of university and I could've spared myself the effort, as I knew, deep down, that sport wouldn't have been part of my life for much longer still. Yet I didn't want to give up, even after being tackled by the League's biggest prop: Jason Marshall. He was a real first-class player, and it's no coincidence that he ended up playing professionally in Great Britain.

As soon as I saw him coming, I felt a light *crack*. My brain blared before I could even understand what was happening. It was my knee, bursting into excruciating pain that felt like an arrow pierced into my flesh. But as soon as I got out of the hospital, I wanted to go back to playing. I couldn't stop myself, despite being far from a young hope for the Canadian national team. I locked myself in the gym and went back to the fray just in time for the last match of the season. No-one had believed in my recovery.

Results? None. My sports career was over. I only played for a few minutes before realizing that there was nothing left for me to do. And yet, those months helped me see that even in our darkest moments, we cannot give up. We must shrug the sand and mud off our back and get back on our feet. Rugby can be hard, it can be a little unorthodox at time, but it's a school of life, it expands your mind and shows you how to give others the look of someone who never gives up. A match is always fought to the death, just like life itself. But at the end of the match, all animosity and tension get washed away in the shower.
I couldn't keep on napping on my couch. My life started anew. The next game, moving on. Jenny had been clear, I had to be in her office at 9 o'clock. And I certainly couldn't be late for my first official job meeting.
As I went to bed, I kept on thinking about that meeting, with the same question echoing in my head: “Who is the businessman?” I was dead set on making her spill the beans, she would have to tell me straight away. After all, my cutting questions almost always got me the upper hand against tight-lipped opponents.

7:00, the alarm clock went off like a bomb. It was, finally, Monday, September 12th, the day of my rebirth. After checking my bank account from my iPhone, to make sure that Jenny's check had indeed gone through, I pushed the blankets away and got out of bed.
Shower, shaving, clothes. I took care of it all with impressive coldness and detachment. I was feeling alienated, as always early in the morning. I grabbed my shoulder bag, closed the door behind me and coldly descended the apartment building's stairs. I athletically hopped on my Vespa, which I had left conveniently parked just out of the front door.
Milan had woken up already, showing a face I had rarely had the chance to see from up close. I was used to working until dawn and sleeping late, so the hours between 6:30 and 11 in the morning were a novelty to me.
The road was long, I had to basically cross the entire city. The cold breeze prickled my face and the feeling wasn't pretty. I trudged through and eventually made it to my destination, after all the vibrations from the cobbles and tram tracks. Under my body was a 50cc engine that wasn't meant for this kind of business.

I wouldn't have thought that September could be so chilly, early in the morning on a motorcycle. But this day was the moment of my waking up from a life on the edge: the scooter trip was part of the set and I was the main character.

“I'm Joe Brigati, I have an appointment with Jennifer Blasquez. Thank you.”
The intercom's electronic voice crackled: “Please, come in.”
I passed the bar that marked the border of the private parking area and dropped 'my ride' beside Jenny's black Porsche.
The hall was crossed by a lukewarm ray of sun coming in from the glass at the entrance. The place was neatly looked after: it hosted about ten studies throughout five stories, with a shared entrance and telephone operator. After a quick check to my watch, a small cry of joy passed through my lips: 8:50, perfect. I had never been that punctual in my entire life.
“Welcome.” The voice coming from behind me sounded familiar. “Hi Joe, how are you?”
Jenny appeared from a door behind the phone operator, who, for the record, was also very cute. Jenny walked like a boss, with a faint smile on her face and sunlight kissed her skin, making her look even more angelic. Her refined clothes painted her as a wealthy businesswoman: light blue suit and four-inch heels, along with a white shirt with just the right amount of open buttons.
“I didn't think you'd come. You've made up your mind, then.”
“Well, before committing to writing the book, I would like to have another talk.”
The idea was to create a bit of suspense before accepting the job. A little act, as I'd already cashed the check. But she didn't pay attention to any of that. “Please follow me, let's go to my office. Do you want something to drink? Coffee?”
“No, thanks. I'm fine.”
I wanted to look as professional as I could manage, which is why I refused her offer. I wouldn't have minded a cup of coffee, really, if only to drink something warm after my chilly ride there. But when I wanted to play

upstanding journalist, I had to stand up to the primordial lure of a coffee-and-Marlboro combo.

The office was very elegant, dominated by a crystal desk. Its white walls made the bookcase on the right stand out: the antique's dark wooden tint gave the place something extra and made the room feel tranquil, welcoming.

Jenny made herself comfortable on the beige leather couch and said: “If you're here, it means you want to write this book.”

“It's not a done deal yet.”

She cocked her head slightly and smiled, freezing me with her sweet gaze. “You can stop pretending.”

“I'm not pretending. Before I make my choice, I need to know who I'm going to write about. Don't you think it's only fair?”

“Of course, I imagine you'll have thought about this for the entire weekend. But no first and last names. It would be too easy.”

That talk felt pointless, but Jennifer knew where she wanted to lead it to. She had the reins firmly in her hands and was steering me toward her goal. All of a sudden, she had a fit of pique.

“Pito... fuck, Joe, do you or do you not wanna write? You've gotta tell me, I can call someone else.”

I smiled. She was the one who craved to know what I was thinking now. I mentally cheered – the wind was turning. Then she froze, offered me a mocking smile and whispered: “On second thought, don't bother. I see you've already cashed your check.”

Her voice was as sharp as a blade, thriving on what she saw on the PC monitor in front of her eyes. I had just managed to look like a complete fucking asshole.

“Fine, let's start working then. Let me fetch my notebook”, I said in an attempt to save face.

I brandished all my journalistic investigative talent and started things off with my first toughie: “Let's start from your relationship. How'd it start?”, I asked with a little sneer.

She sighed and shook her head. “No, I'm the one who starts to tell you something about him. I want you to get to know him in the right way, I lead this game, not you.”

'Him', no two ways around it: the main character, mister X to me. I was entirely at Jennifer's mercy. Perfect, thanks Andrea: what a shit friend. What an impasse he'd led me into.

"His life has been troubled, one could say he's a self-made man. But I don't mean it like the usual businessman narrative of pulling oneself up by one's bootstraps. I mean for real."
Jenny shot a look at a picture on her desk. I tried to peek at it too, but from my uncomfortable position, I couldn't see that far. My chair was much shorter than hers and with the desk in the way, getting to see the frame would have required my neck to do a 360°. Noticing my attempt, Jennifer grabbed the picture and swiftly locked it inside a drawer.
"Calm down, Joe, all in due time... You'll get to know him little by little.
But why all this secrecy? I was starting to grow irritated. "Hey, I'm a journalist after all... You can't dampen my curiosity!"
She didn't answer, dead set on her goal. She started talking again as if that interruption had never happened. In the meanwhile, I looked around for more details, anything that could show me the features of our protagonist. Nothing. Or, rather, maybe something on the rack to my left. Opposite the antique bookshelf, on a crystal shelf, I saw a portrait of Jenny with a man. They smiled, hugging each other, and looked very happy. I clumsily tried to get up from my chair, with many mental thanks to contemporary designers for their creative and unpractical ideas about seats.
While my narrator's voice kept telling me about her relationship with the biography's main character and about the personality thereof, I nonchalantly got close to the picture.
The plan was to let Jenny think that I needed to stretch my legs. And when I had come a mere inches from the picture, the bummer: the couple was posing with a cake that said '*Feliz papi!*'. Fantastic. That was her dad. I looked around some more, netting no results. There were no other details or pictures.
"Hey, Joe... you listening to me?"
"Sure Jenny, of course..."
All I could do was go back to listening to her tale.

“From his childhood, he has overcome any obstacle in his path. He managed to get back on his feet when anyone else would have shot themselves or thrown themselves under a train.”
Her gaze turned dark – it was obvious that something wasn't okay.
“Life wasn't generous to him, in the beginning. But he fought and fought to come up on top. All he has now, he has gained with with his own hands and the sweat of his brow. He grew up alone, both as a businessman and as a man.

Curiosity killed the cat, as they say, but journalists are well on their way too, when a story bites. If we can't understand parts of what we are going to recount, we push and push in search of useful info. And that was what I was feeling: an extreme need for answers.
I tried to analyze and decrypt the first concepts of that absurd puzzle, to no avail.
“How did you fall in love with him?”
I couldn't be more straightforward.
She lowered her gaze and answered, in a softer voice: “I wouldn't know... there are many reasons...”
Her eyes glistened again after that moment of sadness. “He's got grit. I fell in love with that. We met at a party, I had just walked the catwalk. That's where it all begun... He found me a home, this job, and together we shared unforgettable moments...”
It must be true that girls love bad boys with a heart of gold.
Jenny spoke again: “He's a great man, truly. And he is very generous. But lately, he has changed... he is gloomy and reserved. A few months ago, he would have been here with you himself for this interview. Now he doesn't want to remember the past, he says... I know him well, that's why I took his place here.
“You'll forgive me, but I really can't understand why we should write a book about his life, then. If he doesn't want to remember...”
Her answer was curt and irate. I had awakened a bear from its slumber. “I'm telling you again, Joe: I don't care for what you think. All you have to do is write.”
As straightforward as she possibly could. Still, I wasn't convinced. I didn't want to be offensive, of course, but anyone in my place would have asked

the same. My drive to know the reasons behind this book couldn't leave me alone. I had bad thoughts brewing in my head, swept away by the memory of the freshly cashed money. Lots of money, possibly too much money, as I was starting to fear.

Something was up, it had to be.

Our conversation, at any rate, resumed.

“I'd like to see you in his stead, Joe, enduring even a fraction of what he went through. At age six, would you have liked to walk five miles and a half to go to school? Or, rather, five and a half to go there and another five and a half to get back?”

My face turned dark. “Of course I wouldn't. You have to understand, I'm not questioning his worth as a man. I'm only trying to do my job, but with all this secrecy, I cannot do it well.”

Her voice slowly ground to a halt and she stared at me with rage.

I had once again crossed a line, so I folded. “Keep on talking, Jenny, forgive me... please tell me about his beginnings...”

She squinted and stared at the desk. Seemingly getting into character, as if she were in a trance, she told me about his childhood.

Time passed quickly, word after word, concept after concept. His life, his beginnings, his difficult family. I slowly came to terms with the simple fact that she was right: there was plenty of material to work with and that man's life really had been hard. He was a good man, with big, brass balls. The one thing I couldn't fathom was how he had managed to reach such professional heights. Some passages didn't add up, they felt too contrived to be real. Besides, the world of pharmaceutical companies was selective and cliquey, especially for someone without a degree.

And yet, out of nowhere, he opened a pharma company. Impossible, or at the very least weird.

1PM was upon us and the interview didn't show hints of being anywhere near its end. Both our stomachs were growling.

Usually, when that happens, any interest I may be showing is faked, at least when I am facing someone who is spinning an uninteresting tale. But in that case, it would have been hard for me not to be interested. On the contrary – when Jenny's secretary walked in, I could have killed her. She interrupted our talk at a crucial moment.

"Forgive me, miss, there's a man waiting for you. He says he knows you and that it's urgent."
I piped up: "It's all right, Jenny, we can continue another day. I have enough material to get started. One last question..."
I couldn't even finish my sentence. A tall, brawny man with a buzz cut came into the room, wearing a dark suit and tie along with a white earpiece.
He looked at me, but didn't greet me, as if he either didn't see me or didn't want to see me.
"Joe, I can't talk anymore, I'm sorry. I'll let you know about the design project."
She waved at me and rushed out of her office, with that bull in tow. And I stood there like a chump, staring at the empty room. I didn't understand: design project? What could that mean? Her expression was very weird, almost scared.
"I'm sorry, you should leave the office", Jenny's secretary reminded me, visibly annoyed.
"Sorry, I'm leaving."

So I went back to my Vespa, turned the engine on and lit myself a cigarette. My so-called "Thinky Marlboro", aka the one that should help me out in the moment of need. But as I threw it away, all I had gathered was more confusion. Some details didn't add up and others plainly didn't make sense: in that design studio, why did she look nothing like an assistant? By the looks of it, she was the boss. Certainly not a model working two jobs between one runway and the following. And that final goodbye, with that brute in tow, her embarrassed, maybe even scared attitude... it made me shudder. It reminded me of when I had tried to ask her the name of the book's protagonist.
"Look, how can I describe someone's life, charming and interesting though it may be, if you don't tell me his name?"
"I appreciate your efforts... but I'm going to tell you later."
"But I took the job, doesn't that account for anything?"
"I can't tell you now. You'll only learn his name at the end of your book."
Nosiness aside, it was crucial data to me. How could I write a biography without the main character's first and last name? Impossible. And she kept

on postponing. First she said that she'd tell me once I took the job, then only after the manuscript was complete.
“Jenny, this is not a joke. I can't write a biography without that kind of reference. What do I call him?”, I insisted.
“Pick one. Your own would do just fine: Joe Brigati.”
“What?!? My...? Sure, now you're telling me he's called just like me...”
She looked at me and said: “That's likely.”
I couldn't believe my ears. I tried to go back to having an earnest talk.
“Seriously. Please... do you want me to pull back now that I'm starting to learn how this works?”
Her eyes shot up with hatred and fear: “I don't think you've quite understood, Joe: you can't back out now. You know too much already: the game is on!”
Her deep stare couldn't be more eloquent. And it scared me. A lot.

VI

"We don't always manage
to be accurate when we describe someone.
This wasn't one of those times,
even without a name."

You can imagine my ride back home. I crossed Milan like an arrow. Unlike that morning, the air was hot. And my helmet was starting to feel too tight, with sweat slowly trickling down my forehead, drops falling as softly as feathers on the water. And my brain kept on twisting and turning. Had it been possible, it would have rolled out of my skull to rush home on its own instead of staying holed up in that smelly cage.
I had spent half the day in her office, in Jenny's office, to listen to the deeds of a man I did not know. An animated morning, one could say.
Those had been peculiar hours. We mostly talked about his childhood in general, not much more. A good day's work for any ghostwriter, at least up to the point where she hastily made her exit. Questions kept on bouncing in my head like a series of pinballs gone haywire. I didn't want to run into trouble for that book, even though I had to see it through.
My cogitations were brought to a halt by the background growling of my stomach. It was 4.30 PM and I still hadn't eaten a thing since the previous day. I could fucking kill for a kebab, so I turned onto Viale Forlanini avenue and parked on the first available driveway, illegally like the good adoptive Milanese I was. After all, I had a Vespa.

"Hi Karim!"
The joint's entrance was smelly, long and narrow. Beside the window were two empty stools, while leftover food was on display in the glass shelf.
"I'm ready for your magic kebab!"
"Ohi, Joe... it's been too long! Where'd you end up? You can't forget your friends like this!", said the owner from behind the counter, with a funny tinge of irony.

They all somehow manage to look the same, every döner kebab joint is identical to the next. Same furniture, same lacking food presentation, same lacking cleanliness. Their owners, too, are carbon copies of each other: thirty to thirty-five years old, dark skin, shaved hair and a goatee or a bit of a beard. And all very likeable, possibly too likeable, acting all buddy-buddy with everyone.

"Go for it Karim, give it your best... Meat, tomato, salad, onions, don't you scrimp on onions, fries and good spurt of hot sauce."
"A what, Jo? Sport?" Well, the man came from Algeria, not Milan, he couldn't be familiar with the whole dictionary.
I tried to explain myself better, gesturing with my hand: "Go Karim, don't worry: just toss it in... toss it all in, everything you have on the counter.
I was looking at him with a certain defiance and he took pride in it.
I grabbed my bag, payed and went straight back home, holding my breath to avoid the nausea caused by the smell of the meat on the spit. You can't imagine how tasty a doner kebab is – its only setback is the smell one has to endure while buying it.
I was all fired up and ready to get to work this time! No more napping on the couch!
As I got home, I dropped my bag and jacket on the table by the entrance. All I brought with me were the kebab in its foil wrap, my notebook and a beer out of my half-empty fridge.
A few moments before the best bite, the phone's shrill ringing echoed in the flat. The display said: "Andrea office".
I picked up.
"What do you want?"
"Hey, Joe, what's up? I heard from Jenny, you made an impression! You did manage to pass as a professional. How cool is that?"
His irony could be devastating at times. "Thanks Andrea, much obliged... now what do you want?"
"There's an issue."
"Don't tell me. And what might you mean by 'issue'?"
"Chill, now. Jenny asked me to tell you that she wants the first and second chapter by tomorrow."

"What did you just say?"
"Tomorrow, 4.30 PM, in her office. You really didn't know about that, Joe? Good thing I called you or you would have lost the job right off the bat and you'd have to give the money back. You know, Jenny is quite fastidious when it comes to this sort of things. If you don't do what she tells you to, you're out. A little like her boyfriend... But what would you do without me?"
His laughter soon turned into the classic, unpleasant sound of a disconnected call. He hung up on me, running from trouble like a hare.
Once again, without a word, Andrea had screwed me up. He was always good at that kind of games. On the flip side, I was planning on writing all night anyway. Might as well have a clear deadline. Sure, it had been months since the last time I typed away at the keyboard for something longer than an article. All I had to do was finish my lunch-dinner, Karim's 'magic kebab', and then get to work. The atmosphere had to be worthy of a noir writer, with the lights soft and the windows closed shut, even though summer was still at its peak.
I couldn't let the cars outside distract me. Their constant roaring could be an issue and, as beautiful as Milan can be, it's too noisy for a writer's creative phase. It felt like being a football player about to score a penalty kick and having a *lepatata* – Tswana for 'vuvuzela' – being blown in your ear.
I didn't want to take any risks: I closed the windows and wolfed down my food. I sipped the beer and, once it was all over, I went to the kitchen to throw away all the remains. In the corner of my eye I saw the huge plastic bottle of Coca Cola Zero on the kitchen table: it had to be mine! My only companion in the following ten hours, along with the red and white pack of cigarettes.
I looked at the watch and plugged the computer in, struggling to find the plug: I hadn't done any household chores in a while. The display said 17:46, short before the start of Milan's beloved happy hour.
We don't always manage to be accurate when we describe someone. This wasn't one of those times, even without a name. I could picture the first phases of his life clearly in my mind and I probably wouldn't need to reread my notes or listen to the recorded interview on my iPhone.

But, I wondered, how could a child overcome certain wiles of fate? Opposing it so strongly, to the point of managing to become a successful, rich businessman? Early on, I'd thought that it had to be all a figment of Jennifer's imagination, but as the minutes went by, I realized that she was a hundred percent serious. She wasn't making any of it up, he really did overcome all those traps, or most of them. To think that he had seen his beginnings in a small town of the Italian South that didn't exactly offer exciting perspectives.

It was the end of the Sixties, in the middle of the Italian economic boom. Yet in Ciuriddia (Floridia, a Sicilian village in the province of Siracusa, a far shot from the American Florida), the nation that was discovering the Fiat 500 and the weekend getaways on a Vespa GT felt far, far away.

It was still a rural land, its communities tied together by the Italian South's typical values of family and respect. The town, elevation 364 feet, was quaint and picturesque, but offered next to no opportunities for the local youth.

Do you know those neorealist movies where the film's frames almost seem scorched? It's a clever trick employed by the director to convey to the viewers the feeling of the sun burning the characters' skin. That's the idea I wanted to convey to my readers.

I wanted them to picture a boy, with his short pants and white shirt, living with his family in the deep, blazing hot Sicilian South. I wanted them to see him loiter around on his bike, making deliveries for the local grocery store when he was only ten years old. And that hadn't even been his first job. He was born when his parents were very young and sometimes life forces us to roll up our sleeves and look forward. And that's what he did, right from his childhood. He was the oldest of three brothers and the job crisis that had struck Sicily in those years had slowly turned his father violent.

His childhood was not, in short, all sunshine and rainbows. On the contrary. From the very beginning, he figured out that his life would be full of bumps, just like the road he walked every day to go to school, dusty and potholed, surrounded by fields. But it was his life and he wouldn't back down.

And he would make it alone, because our protagonist was always a loner, from his birth to the moment he met Jenny. His solitary attitude was his choice and part of his personality, but also due to how his life panned out. He didn't mind school. He attended it like all kids his age do, looking at the world with eyes wide open, observing all that happened around him, but unwilling to study. Or maybe he would have wanted to, but his family's situation didn't allow him to.
The afternoons left him little time to spend with his nose in a book, as he had to help his parents earn some extra. In the evenings, he stole wooden fruit crates from the town's shops and brought them to the prostitutes on the streets, who used them to fuel their bonfires – more comfortable and less pricey than an electric sign like in Amsterdam's red lights district. He knew them all, all the girls and ladies who worked the streets. He didn't judge them: to him, they were simply clients who paid good money for that kind delivery service. Those were hard times, with his parents often fighting over their economic situation and other relationship problems – among which ranked his father's heavy drinking.
As I tried to stick to the schedule Jenny had imposed on me without any prior notice, I made my first narrative choices. I would describe his life in first person, skipping some chronological steps but highlighting his M.O. and his way of thinking. I would focus on the important circumstances that would make him grow or change, both as a person and as a businessman.
I was finally ready to start writing. As a precaution, I decided to turn off my phone and avoid pointlessly wasting my time. Then I glanced at the clock.
"Fuck, it's 6:40 already. I need to get down to work!", I cried.
I booted up my Mac and created a new Pages file.

VII

"Had I known
what the future had in store for me,
I wouldn't have cursed
all the misfortunes in my life."

The red Marlboro slowly burned away, my mouth half-open, letting it drop on the right. It was my fifteenth cigarette throughout the night, plus the swigs of Coca Cola that had left the bottle almost empty. I cracked my knuckles, like a boxer does before putting on his gloves. I had just completed the first two chapters, in a hard but gratifying full immersion. I was happy with the result, I felt that it matched the character. All I had to do was reread and proofread them. I closed my eyes and rubbed them before opening them again to look at the screen. I scrolled back to the beginning of the first chapter, the cursor blinking at the top of the file.

***

The window was dirty with the dust of the road, which had set down on the glass in a translucent coat.
I watched the garden's grass sway beyond that barrier and I felt small, very small. And I was. But from the moment I was born, I have been forced to brace myself and grow up quickly, so as not to stay behind when the world rushed ahead of me. Some more hugs would have been nice, though. I could always do with a little comfort.
I could not figure out what I would become as an adult; I was young and naive, but my brain kept on obsessing on it. I looked forward, I thought about the future: I grew up too quick. I had been working for my small town's grocery store for a year already, earning some money to make ends meet.

My father had just lost his job and drank to forget. I never knew how it happened, my mother never fully explained it to me. They were never really in love.

But the things that my brother Gabriele told me years later, as grown-ups, those were just out of malice. He said that it was my fault that our parents had been forced to marry and live together: had I not been born, they would have led their life elsewhere, each of them for themselves.

They fought every day, there was no peace left at home. As time went by, I learned to understand certain couple dynamics. Family came first, family was sacred, but some of the things that happened to me, I'll never forget them. I'm never going to marry.

At any rate, it was up to me to take care of everyone, to start earning something, which was why Calogero's shop looked like a good place for me.

I loaded the crates on the bike and soared away, faster than light, toward all the clients. An efficient delivery service, thanks to the beautiful bike that I had dreamt of for so long and that I could finally use.

I have never owned a bike, but being allowed to use that one for work was enough to make me smile. I carried everything: milk, bread, vegetables, Marseille soap. Anything that could be good and useful in a home. All they had to do was ask.

That afternoon was weird. Even from home I could feel that something was acting up. Only a few people were in town and the heat was becoming unbearable.

I didn't care, all that mattered to me was riding my bike. Still, in hindsight I should have understood that that silence could only be a prelude to something very bad.

Yet I decided to go out anyway, soon after lunch. School was finally over, summer had started and I could commit myself to my job. My first order of business was reaching Calogero in his shop. I took the bike, which they sometimes let me use even when I wasn't working, and rushed toward the town. I forgot to add: I lived in the outskirts, if that's what one could call our little house in the middle of the fields. It was a farmhouse, far from where Floridia's real gentlemen lived, but it was my house and no-one could take it away from me. Or so I thought.

"When are you going to go to Don Raffaele?"
The question came from my boss, my first real principal.
"Right now, sir, if you'll give me the list I can load up a crate and go."
My job was simple: Calogero gave me a list, written in pencil, with the products the clients ordered, and I prepared the deliveries. There was no need for an address: I knew everyone in town and everyone knew me. But for Don Raffaele, the job was different. Custom tailored, in a way. And he was the only client with no account balance. Calogero sold on credit to everyone, but at the end of the month, everyone had to pay.
But not Don Raffaele. He didn't pay. Or rather, he paid in his own way, with his protection. He was the real boss, more so than the mayor.
He was a good person, at least with me. It was clear that he cared for my wellbeing, in his own way. He had thick gray mustaches and always wore a hat – no, not a mafia flat cap. It was a straw hat, like a panama.
I loved to go to Don Raffaele, his delivery was always my favorite. I usually got tips from various people in town, but with him it was different. Every week, I got from him more than I was paid for the whole month.
Had it not been for him, I may have never had the chance to become the man I am. Without that money, I would have never been able to get a ticket to Milan when my mother decided to send me away.
I prepared the crate for Don Raffaé, as everyone called him. I had to be very careful about getting everything he had asked for or I could forget about my tip.
Every time I went to his home, I had to pass a sentry post. I didn't understand, back then, why they had to check my purse and pockets every time, even though they knew me well. That afternoon was an exception and the fact made me happy: "Figure that, maybe now I'm one of them, a big deal?", I thought to myself as I crossed the driveway of his villa, right outside town.
"Good morning Mimmo, I'm bringing a delivery to Don Raffaele."
I waved at him as I braked. On the porch, I saw Don Raffaé sitting on a wicker rocking chair.
He was staring at the grass and didn't look very happy. Which was weird, because he usually broke into a smile when he saw me. I think I reminded him of his nephew, who had died a few years earlier in a weird accident on a hunting trip.

Everyone knew it was a revenge kill in a clan war, but at poor Mariolino's funeral, with the whole town in mourning, not a single word was uttered. The blame was shifted on the unsafe firearms of the time and even the priest, in his sermon, raged against that brutal, cynical sport that murdered innocent animals and now even the town's youth.
"Come here, boy, come closer." Don Raffaele looked gloomy, he greeted me with a wave and pointed at a chair in front of him.
"You see, dear, when life turns its back on you, you've gotta be honest with yourself. You've gotta understand when it's time to fight back and when, on the other hand, all you can do is raise your hands to the sky and ask the Virgin Mary to give you a hug."
I couldn't understand at first. I would only be able to connect everything later.
"I think it's for the best that you don't come here anymore. Consider yourself free from the delivery job to my house. It's not your fault, this is not about you. You have always done a good job and have no reason to be sad, understood?"
I nodded weakly, then lowered my gaze.
Don Raffaele placed his hand on my head. "Remember this always. In life, everything we do, it comes back. And true men don't go back on their choices and actions, even when faced with extreme solutions."
At that point, he took a big banknote out of his vest's breast pocket.
"Here, this is for you. It's my last tip to you, but I want you to remember me for this too... and this small present..."
His hand reached lower, toward his pants' pocket. From it he took a pocket watch which dated back to the turn of the century, made of silver, with inlay work at the bottom. A name's initials, or a coat of arms. I couldn't see it very well, nor could I understand what was happening.
"This is yours. Don't you ever give it away, you understand? It'll be a reminder that'll allow you to understand that men keep their promises. Those who don't are nothing more than straws in the wind... Now go, leave your groceries here and go. Don't turn around as you walk out, promise me!"
I nodded, unconvinced. "Good boy, you really are a good boy." I thanked him for the huge tip and for the watch. I tried to refuse, out of courtesy, but Don Raffaé's face turned dark as I had barely started to move my hand

back toward him. God forbid anyone should contradict him, so I pocketed the present. I dashed back to my bike and pedaled away, tearing up a little. Weird. Never in my life had I cried without a reason. That was my first time.
As I got back to the entrance, right beside the gate, I saw two people in a car headed toward the porch. Our paths crossed and I stared at their eyes as I would never stare again in my life. Afterwards, I only heard a few sounds: a hard braking, fast steps on the gravel and one clear shot. Like from a rifle, or a large calibre gun.
I stopped my bike on the driveway and turned my head: in the distance, I saw the wicker rocking chair toppled on the ground, with Don Raffaele lying on his stomach. It looked as if he were sleeping, but clearly that was not the case.
The two characters were back on their car, quickly coming my way, and I decided to flee the scene. I didn't say a thing to my mother, or I would have never heard the end of it. But Calogero knew what had happened and knew that I had witnessed it. He knew I was there on the day Don Raffaé died in a terrible accident – he too, as fate would have it, got hit by a stray blow as he was polishing his hunting rifle. So said the police, even though everyone knew. The rule of silence, omertà, took over and no-one ever asked me about that day, not even my boss.
The town slowly forgot about Don Raffaele, 'loved' in life as much as he ended up poor and forgotten in death. Only his closest relatives set foot in the church at his funeral. People didn't say it out loud, but they were afraid: nobody knew who would take his place. And attending the funeral could be read as standing up for the old guard. Never wise, around these parts.

Life slowly went on. Home was always a noisy mess and I kept on doing deliveries. I pedaled all over the town on my bike, at least until it got stolen right in front of the parish priest's house.
Great: you go to church to deliver some bread and come back out to find yourself without your tool of the trade. A true mockery. What kind of divine protection was that? Incredible.
I didn't have the guts to look at Calogero and tell him that his beloved bike was gone like a straw in the wind, as Don Raffaé would have it.

"Signore", I blurted out.
"My bike got stolen, I don't know how it happened. I left it propped on the rectory's wall, just the time it takes to get upstairs and leave the package to Father Ettore."
I was humiliated, but not resigned. My boss frowned and stared at me, with a side order of slamming his fists against the counter.
The candies jumped in their jars. "You better, boy", Calogero said. "You better find it again soon. If you don't turn up tomorrow sitting on that bike, I'll be forced to give you the boot."
No way: that, I could not accept. It was the first injustice life slapped me with and it would not be the last.
I sprinted back home, I had to use my money, whatever part of Don Raffaele's tips I had managed to save. I gave mother most of my earnings but there was a plank in my room, exactly between the wall and my bed, that I used as a safe. I left my money there, as well as the watch.
It was my hiding place.

I was out of breath as I got home, and sweatier than ever before. I slammed the front door open and froze in shock. My father was standing in the kitchen, with my mother sitting in front of him, her legs slightly stretched, her dress' left shoulder strap broken. She was terrified, her face turned toward the window and her hand shielding her left cheek.
I can't remember what he was telling her, but it wasn't anything kind, for sure. He was drunk, which was hardly news, but hitting mother was too much.
I launched myself at him, trying to claw at his face. Mother tried to stop me, but I looked possessed by the devil. I kept hitting him until I heard him cry: "Stop!! Stop!! You little bastard, if it weren't for you, I'd be far away from here now. You got me trapped!"
For an eleven year old boy, that was a terrible blow. I wavered and he threw me on the ground.
Of course, a man like him could have beaten me to death, but drinking dulled his strength as well as his wits. I got off lucky, but I knew all too well that I wouldn't be that lucky come next time.
At any rate, I grabbed my money and ran away from that hell.
All I could think of was getting my bike back.

The road was long and, as I walked, I kept on thinking about dad: he was a real dick. How can you hit such a fragile woman? And also: why did she still want him home? I couldn't understand. What I did understand was that my mother didn't fall down the stairs as often as she said: her bruises came from his big, greasy hands.
I tried to take my mind off all that, but my thoughts immediately drifted to my stolen bike. In that bleak day, life really felt unfair. I couldn't find a way out, every thought leading me to despair deeprt into a long tunnel with no end in sight. Sometimes, crying is the only solution, the only consolation that can ease the pain. I did not cry on that day: on that long walk toward Alfonso's "The Bike Home" shop, I understood that in the end, problems can be solved even by ourselves.
Inside the shop I saw a bike that looked exactly like mine propped beside the window. Or, rather, it was my bike. I was sure of it, it even had the groceries rack.
"What do you want, kid?", Alfonso said as he saw me come in. He was a spindly man in his forties, with a short beard, and his physique showed a past as a professional cyclist.
Or rather a professional supporting rider, of course, in a whole other league from immortal champions like Fausto Coppi and Gino Bartali, this was your run-of-the-mill suburban cyclist, accustomed to cobbles and dust.
"I'm here to take back the bike you stole from me!" I don't know how I happened to blurt out that sentence, but it wasn't my brightest moment.
The former professional's face stiffened. "Beg your pardon, what'd you say? No-one here stole anything. If you want that bike, you can buy it. Understood?"
'No, not at all', I thought to myself.
"That's my bike. Now, either you give it back to me or I'm calling the police."
His face got even darker. He rolled up his overalls' sleeves, in a clear threat, and stared at me:
"Boy! I'll be the one calling the Carabinieri if you don't cut it out."
Fine, my bluff hadn't worked. I found myself forced to buy it – the only courtesy I got from Alfonso was letting me buy it by installments, the first

ones of my life. So I managed to avoid throwing all of Don Raffaele's money to the wind.

And life went back to normal. Calogero fave me a triumphal hug as he welcomed me back, or rather greeted the bike first, with tears in his eyes, and then yours truly. But he never let me use it again after work. Yet another unwarranted injustice. I was starting to get accustomed to it, but bitter pills are always tough to swallow.

At home, mother grew ever more tense, while father didn't miss a chance to taunt me in public. I barely even noticed anymore. I was still under the suspicion that he beat her, but he had widened up and did it far from my eyes. And she kept on protecting him. Let's be honest, I was really scared. Dad hid a gun at home, an old Beretta. I tried to explain to mother that sooner or later he would lose control and cause a tragedy, but she always turned a deaf ear. And I didn't know how to protect her. Until that fateful Wednesday in 1972, late in July.

Time had quenched some resentments on both sides. That day, I came back home at the usual hour, satisfied with the small sum I had earned in tips. I wanted to share that happiness with mom. I opened the door and saw her on the floor. My blood froze in my veins: I thought of Don Raffaele by his porch, his wicker chair toppled by the side.

As luck would have it, she was still alive, although her face was all swollen, almost to the point of making her unrecognizable. She feebly tried to cover for him: "I fell, it's not his fault." Of course she knew full well that I wouldn't believe that for a moment. I wanted to go fetch her a wet rag, but she grabbed my arm, trying to keep me close to her.

I shook myself free and dashed to their bedroom, where in the night stand to the right, under the drawer, lay the Beretta. I grabbed it and bolted to the courtyard, shouting: "Where the fuck are you, bastard. Come here, I'm gonna kill you..."

I was almost twelve.

I went round the corner and there he was. In the courtyard, fixing the car, calm, like a good husband. Wearing only his undershirt, he gave me a bewildered stare. He wouldn't have thought me capable of going that far. "What are you doing?" His eyes seemed ready to fall out of their sockets. "Drop that gun, don't be stupid."

"You promised you'd let her alone, and yet you almost killed her. You're not my father anymore, go away!!"
From his initial bewilderment, dad switched to hilarity: he smiled at me, he almost seemed amused by the situation.
"You don't have the guts to shoot your father, now mom will come and you know what'll happen? You'll be in trouble. You have ten seconds to drop that weapon before I decide to hurt you. And when I lay my hands on you, I swear to God, there's gonna be trouble."
I honestly don't know what went through my brain in those moments. I can't remember. I felt a huge rage inside, an overwhelming pressure that pushed my finger against that trigger.

Did I shoot?
What was that deafening noise?
I couldn't understand what was happening, all I knew was that my legs were feeling weird. I felt a light tremor at the end, a mix of fear and anxiety that was slowly growing.
"Put down that weapon, put it down immediately!", the voice was sharp and dry.
It reminded me of someone, but I couldn't understand who that could be. It wasn't exactly familiar, but I may have heard it in the past already.
"Fine, I'll put it down...", was the last thing I uttered before passing out. The tension was overwhelming, too much for a boy my age.
I opened my eyes in my home's living room, or rather what passed for a living room. Today, its decor would be called minimalist. Back then it was called poor. A few pieces of furniture and a couch.
And on that couch I found myself, on the dark green velvet that dad loved so much. Back when he still had his job, he always slouched on it when he came home and wore out the lining to the point that it got a rip, with frayed yellow wool sticking out. In front of me, staring at me, was Massimo Calcese, corporal of the carabinieri station in Floridia.
'So that's who that was', I told myself as I came back to my senses. It was his voice.
"Where am I?", I whispered. Pointless question, I knew it all too well, but I wanted to play dumb until I could figure out what had really happened.

"In your home. You tried to kill your father. Good thing I arrived in time and stopped you. What the fuck did you think you were doing, eh? Have you gone mad?"

It could look that way to a stranger, sure, but I had my reasons. And he had to realize that my behavior was just a direct consequence of his violence against mom.

"Did I kill him?"

Massimo adjusted his hat – with its silver flame, symbol of his corp – and smiled: "What, with an unloaded gun?? No, you didn't kill him. You didn't even wound him."

Damn. But my disappointment was short-lived – as I observed his expression, I rather started feeling like a real idiot. What was that? Unloaded?

"You're lucky that your father", he said, "keeps his magazine away from the weapon. Or you would be in real trouble."

So what was that booming noise? Who pulled the trigger? I asked my question as I tried to raise my head from the couch's arm rest: "And who shot, then?"

"I did. Seeing how you didn't react when I ordered you to drop your weapon, I fired a shot in the air. And you dropped to the ground like a sack of potatoes. What did you think you were doing? Boy, try to come up with a believable reason to avoid juvie."

I didn't want to cry, but I would have wanted to. So I held my breath, trying not to look helpless, and words started coming out like a flood. "Corporal, you see..."

Massimo understood my anxiety. He stopped me and put a hand on my forehead. It had been a while since the last time I had felt such a gentle, loving gesture on my skin. "Call me Massimo and don't worry..."

He softened up, having seen how I was still shaken by emotions and anxiety. So I told him everything, starting from one year earlier, when I saw mom being beaten, and how my life was slowly turning into a hell.

My eyes were misty and I was hoping with all my heart that the uniformed boy, barely older than thirty, could help me solve it all.

"I'm going to investigate this, okay? In the meanwhile, you have to swear that you're never gonna do anything like this again."

It was sheer luck that on that day, the corporal had gone to check on a previous offender who lived less than a mile away from us. He saved my life.
The unloaded gun would have been just the pretext for dad to beat me to death. I felt a huge relief come over me in those moments: the carabinieri would come, arrest him and drag him away. Forever. They would make him stop beating mom and she would finally understand that it's better to live without him.
In my heart and mind, emotions were all jumbled up: I felt that the end of that agony was coming near.
'Justice? So it really exists', I thought, clenching my fists. More of a muscular spasm, a throwback to my earliest childhood: I was looking for a tranquil shore in that sea of anxiety.
Well, after that day, I did not trust institutions anymore. Investigations turned up to be a few questions, nothing more.
Yet another bitter pill to swallow.
As expected, my mother did not press charges and dad ended up as the victim of that farce.
Mom's swollen face didn't raise any suspicions, as if it weren't there. Those five minutes of folly in my home's courtyard forever destroyed my hopes of finding a solution to all that wanton violence. Justice? Bullshit, if you'll forgive the term: much better to take the law into one's own hands and act alone than wait for the police and their investigations.
You can only imagine what life awaited me at home in the following days. I couldn't look my mother in the eyes. She had chosen to look the other way and ignore such an extreme gesture aimed only at defending her. She had chosen him and turned her back on her son.
She was dead to me. I had only ice left in my heart. She understood, knew that she had disappointed me, but didn't want to admit it and pretended to lead a normal life when our relationship had nothing normal left anymore.
Time slowly passed. From that day, my father never spoke to me again.
Delivering groceries was nothing but a futile routine and, deep down, I started to feel the need to turn over a new leaf. I wanted to flee, grow up elsewhere. Sicily had nothing left to offer, I wanted to make a new life for myself even though I was only twelve.

Some nights, you try to look at the stars and reflect, on your past and your near future, but all you can see is the endless darkness surrounding you. That is how I felt.
Every night I opened my window and looked at the sky, limpid and dreary. I looked at those stars I never saw again in my life. And I cried, alone.
I still remember so vividly the day mother decided to send me away from home. We were all sitting around our rectangular table for dinner – cheese, bread and sausage, our meager meal. With a harsh expression, she stared at me and said: "I think it is time to find you a new accommodation. Up North."
My blood froze. I was happy to leave all that squalor, but the sudden change made my anxieties flare up.
"There is no work for you here, you can't go on delivering groceries on that bike forever. You'll go live with your uncle in Bergamo."
My heart stopped. It was obvious that I was being sent away with the goal of sending money back to sustain the family. And I never even asked myself: why me?
Deep down, I wanted to go. Some part of me knew that the choice of sending me away was my father's idea. But I didn't care much, it was the right thing to do, even I could see it. I had to get out. I felt strangled by that deadlocked situation and every day I had to live like that was an agony for everyone. From that moment, my life in Floridia ended.
"You'll have to get ready, it's a long ride. Don't turn back when the car starts moving or you'll make me cry." My mother's only kind words to me. But where was Bergamo? And the famed North?
I had always heard the tales: all those who go there, if and when they come back, end up being praised like war heroes. Welcomed with great ceremony, mostly thanks to the tales that get spread in town: "Do you know that guy? He went to Milan and made a fortune there... Have you seen that other guy? He arrived yesterday on an Alfa Romeo and parked it in the town square, you can see he works in Turin and he made millions there..." All like that.
Maybe the starve themselves up North, but when they come home, they tell tall tales of money and fortune. They feel on top of the world, even when they work in an assembly line for a nondescript company.

I, at any rate, was sure that by getting away from there I would have more chances. I was ready to work day and night, but I wanted to become someone at all costs. I had to make it: nobody could deny me this opportunity after all I had been through.
So I would go live with uncle Ernesto. My father's brother had left Floridia a few years earlier in search of fortune. In Lombardy, he had found a job as a construction worker first in the city of Brescia, then in Bergamo.
The day of my departure eventually came. I had a few cardboard bags with me, and 'cardboard' was practically an euphemism. I sat on the back of Ernesto's Alfa Romeo – he had come back to his hometown to collect me and visit his relatives. I rolled down the window and saw my mother crying.
Everyone was with her except for my father: that bastard had preferred to spend his time elsewhere and forfeit my goodbye. That was his payback.

***

"Hey? Hello?"
I couldn't understand what was happening. And, most importantly, who the fuck was on the line. I took a phone call once I was done proofreading my chapters, my iPhone back on. Anonymous caller.
On the other end I could hear a distant voice I could not recognize. "Hello?"
"I'm Joe. Who's there?"
They hung up the phone before I could even finish that sentence.
"Whatever, they must've misdialed."
I lit myself another cigarette, thinking back to my writing: 'It doesn't look half bad to me. It's linear.'
I gave another look at the notes I had taken during my meeting with Jenny and compared them with the first chapters. It was better to double-check it all before delivering it to the client.
Editing had to follow two different, yet parallel tracks: writing falsehoods wasn't allowed, no wild flights of fantasy, but on the other hand, the reader had to be hooked. The words had to flow well and without mistakes.

This was the most nerve-racking part: editing may reveal a horrible prose, which is a common occurrence when one is out of practice. But more embarrassing still is rereading one's efforts and seeing how those hard-earned pages turn out to be so few. You think you have all the time in the world and in the end you're forced to rush through everything like a madman to make it to the deadline.
I remembered how, as a rookie crime writer, I got a contract with a small publishing house – the first step toward celebrity, they said. After getting a couple books out, a big multinational publisher offered me to write two novels that would be part of their line of crime fiction from emerging writers. It's thanks to them that I got to meet Andrea. Back then, I didn't much care for writing books: I was a journalist for the *Gazzetta della Martesana* and that was just a way to make ends meet. One that paid handsomely, at that. But I much preferred to scamper around on my Vespa, on the hunt for real news, to making up murders. I went round and round, paying no mind to the fact that there were texts and, most importantly, deadlines waiting for me at home. One month, two months, three months without a single keystroke. Up to two weeks from the deadline.
Panic. I don't know how I did it, yet in the end I managed to write both novels' drafts in time. I didn't sleep, my fingers speeding like bullets on the keyboard at night. My only company were coffee, Coca Cola and caffeine pills. The end result wasn't half bad, but of course nothing comparable to what I would have sent in if I had used my time wisely and erased all typos.
The bureaucracy behind every book is all rather strict. All writers must jump through their editor's and proofreader's hoops, with all their analyzing and scrutinizing as if they were coroners performing an autopsy. Those two crime novels of mine, however, were really embarrassing. It was obvious that there was talent behind them, but that their writer – that is to say, me – had written them in a rush and, even more importantly, without an ounce of creative inspiration. The publisher decided not to renew my contract. Engrossed as I was by my day job, I basically took a breath of relief. I didn't understand that it was a personal failure.

This time was different. I had time and it was the last chance of my life.

I got up and went to the kitchen in hopes of finding something left to munch on. It was 3.45AM and I wasn't sleepy. The risk of leaving my stomach in shambles, however, made me opt for a pause.
Self-harm can be a phase in one's life, but not a constant. I had to focus on the book, not on how to destroy myself, I couldn't afford it. I only poured myself a sip of coffee from the glass pot. The mug evoked my old sports glories: 'Toronto University: 2003 Rugby Cup Senior'.
The air in the living room was putrid. The lingering cigarette smoke evoked a charming noir atmosphere, but it also made the place unbreathable, even for a chain smoker like me.
I made it to the terrace, or rather to the miniature balcony that gave onto the street. Outside, I lit up a cig and left the balcony door open behind me to breathe some fresh air into the apartment.
The city was deserted, with no chattering nor other noises on the horizon. It felt like a live postcard picture, unreal, given how during the day those streets were crowded with frenzied passerbies and noisy, polluting cars. With a little help from the imagination, even the air could feel clean.
I looked down and stared at the cars parked by my apartment building, under a row of trees. Something caught my attention.
“What the fuck is that man doing in the bushes?”
I first imagined a drug dealer, or a drunkard taking a piss, but then I noticed that he was staring at me.
As soon as he realized I had spotted him, he scuttled into a black car with darkened widows. It was a long wheelbase Mercedes, not unlike a limousine. Neither a pusher nor a hobo, then.
He turned on the xenon lights, lowered the window on the passenger's side and leaned out to check on me. I stared again, he stiffened and raised the window up again.
The car skidded away just like in the movies. I didn't give it too much thought, even though, truth be told, finding a ripped man with a buzz cut, suit & tie combo lurking near my home at four in the morning left me a little puzzled.
He looked like Jenny's escort, the one who had come to collect her in her office at the end of our interview.
Was I being paranoid? Maybe.

Yet it felt like he really was looking for me. In all of Milan, at dawn, I was the only one who felt watched.

VIII

"Some nights, you try to look at the stars
and reflect on your past
and your near future...
but all you can see
is the endless darkness
surrounding you."

12:30. The alarm clock urged me on, my eyes resisted. The lingering warmth of my bed sheets was amazing. Don't wake up, Joe.
But I had to, this time I had to, no matter how marvelous that feeling was. Jenny was waitng for me in her office to review my drafts and I couldn't loaf about.
I made myself a quick American-style breakfast: bacon, eggs and beans. It had been a while since the last time I had cooked for myself and I could feel it in my soul, that I was getting better, that this job was dragging me out of this tunnel of dejectedness.
Shower, clothes. I wanted to look pretty this time, so I went for something elegant: blue blazer, white shirt, jeans.
I hopped on my Vespa and roared back on the holey streets toward the Bicocca district. Again: motorbiking in Milan is hard and dangerous, but sliding through gridlocks like a slalom has its incomparable charm.
I arrived a little earlier this time too, 4:21 PM. I went to the red bricks building and rang so they would let me get into the parking lot, beyond the red and white striped bar.
"Good afternoon, my name is Joe Brigati. I have an appointment with Jennifer Blasquez."
The answerphone crackled with the secretary's voice, who curtly said: "She is not here, I am afraid. Can you come back another day?"
What? I tried to keep the talk going, I saw no reason to be left outside like a beggar.

"At any rate, I'll need a phone number to make a new appointment. Would you kindly let me in?"
"If you don't have her number already, call her here at the office. Again, I'm telling you that you cannot get inside without permission. I'm sorry, goodbye."
Amazing. Humiliated like that by a secretary on the answerphone.
I decided to call Andrea: the outrage was unbearable and I had to find out if I could have possibly misunderstood either the time or the date of the meeting. I did so after parking my motorbike on the other side of the road, to keep a low profile.
"Hey, Andrea?"
He groaned in reply.
"I'm at Jenny's place, but she's not here. And most importantly, they're not letting me inside."
"Joe, what can I tell you? She must have forgotten. Here, this is her number: 3... 4... 8..."
He spelled out all the numbers, then said: "Try to call her and make another appointment. Don't take it personally, come on..."
It wasn't that. The thing is, that setback was throwing me back into my anguish, voiding all my recent psychological progress.
I was frustrated and worried, last but not least because ever since meeting with Jenny, I had started to feel shadowed. Or was it just the biography that was making me see things, influenced by the main character meeting with a mafia boss and then having him killed in front of his eyes?
What was I supposed to think? Logically, anything out of the ordinary, no matter how small, could look bad, very bad.
But I couldn't tell any of that to Andrea. It would have been a breach of the writer-client privilege. So I dropped the topic.
"Okay. Sorry Andre'... I'm sorry I bothered you... thanks."
I was about to hang up when I saw the parking lot open. A car came out: a brand new Mercedes, black. Then a second one advanced slowly behind it, finally a third. They all had darkened windows, but they weren't dark enough that I couldn't spot, sitting on the second car's back seat, a woman with her hair tied up. Was it Jenny? Maybe. But I couldn't be sure. That procession of cars, however, whetted my journalistic appetite. I decided to follow them, without, to be honest, any real reason. As soon as that idea

struck me, adrenaline started pumping in my veins, it was a deep call I could not refuse. A crime journalist's unconditional response.
I hopped on and gave pursuit. Everything seemed to be normal, they weren't getting away. I tailed them at a safe distance.
We turned on Corso Sempione avenue, then right, then left. Then something started vibrating in my pocket, I felt it on my thigh. It was Jenny, calling me on the phone. I was about to take the call, but a sudden flash of doubt made me desist. Maybe she knew I was tailing her.
Was she trying to make me slow down? Astute, but I was smarter.
So I decided to ignore the call.
A hiss behind my shoulders startled me, but I didn't have time to react. A violent blow unbalanced me and threw me on the ground. Sparks surrounded me and a metallic screech deafened me soon afterwards, as I rolled on the asphalt like a sausage on a barbecue. In a few seconds, I found my chin brutally pushed against the ground.
"What the fuck... is..."
I tried to move, but everything hurt too much.
I looked up and found a person with a mocking smile amid a small crowd. '*Memento audere semper*', read the letters on his leather jacket. I was sure of it. I read the Latin, but I could not focus on his face. My eyes blurred from the impact. I could hear voices, but I could not make sense of them. I realized I had been run over, a car must have mercilessly hit me while I was turning.
Yet I couldn't remember driving carelessly. I had even used my turn signal. That car had appeared out of nowhere and that hiss could have been a sharp acceleration. No honking, no steering, no braking. It had just moved into my side of the road as if I weren't even there.
Pain came over me, I couldn't find a single part of my body that wasn't bruised and my strengths were slowly dripping away. It was like a tackle, but a hundred times stronger than on a rugby field. I felt hazy and couldn't get up. Did they want to kill me? As usual, my first thought was a conspiracy, and I hoped it wouldn't be the last jolt of my professional bias. I could feel blood's bitter taste in my mouth and I suddenly felt like sleeping.

I was living one of the scenes I had seen play out so many times in all my years of crime journalism. Except I was the protagonist, lying in the middle of my asphalt stage. Then came the darkness.

I came to my senses. Something had rattled me and the pain made me jolt awake. I could hear a distant siren, sounds. No, it was me lying in the ambulance and a bump in the road had sadly brought me back to reality. Beside me, a very pretty nurse and a huge man in an orange uniform. The stretcher carrier, I deduced.
"What happened to me?"
Her expression seemed puzzled, but gentle. "It was a hit and run. We don't even know your name. But you don't have to worry, it looks like you broke a rib or two, nothing more."
"My name is Joe... my documents are inside my bag. The shoulder bag, with a computer inside."
"What bag?"
A shiver shook me to the point of my toes.
"What do you mean, what bag? You aren't saying that..."
And then my strengths gave up and I fell into darkness again.

The noise of medical machinery was deafening. *Beep... Beep...* It buzzed in my head like a wasp on a flower. I was in a hospital room, the writing on the bed sheets said *Niguarda Ca' Granda*, a hospital in the northern outskirts of Milan. I tried to move, but it wasn't the smart thing to do: even hooked to an IV with painkillers and saline solution, I could feel pain in every part of my body.
"Welcome back among us, mister Brigati."
It came from a male voice I was not familiar with. I turned toward it and had a glimpse of someone wearing a light, elegant suit. I had never seen that face before. My neck hurt big time and the grimace on my face didn't hide it. "Stay where you are. I'll move."
"Who are you?"
"Max Flecter, from the Canadian embassy in Milan. I have come here to give you the necessary support."
I gave him a puzzled look before imagining that they may have found my bag, with my documents and Jenny's chapters.

“So you've found my shoulder bag...”
“Mister Brigati, you have to remain calm. Once the hospital sent out a statement through the hospital police, we immediately recognized you in our databases. You've been through a lot, but you can be assured that the investigation is already underway...”
“Hey, hey... what investigation?”
I was informed that my bag had regrettably been lost, or rather, it had probably been stolen during the accident. With no documents on me and given how I wasn't listed in the Italian police databases, the hospital had called all the embassies in Milan looking for info on my identity. No-one had answered except, of course, for the Canadians, after almost a day. “We know you were the victim in a hit and run... The policemen would like to ask you some questions. They are standing outside the room now. Do you feel up to it?”
“Okay, let them come in.”
They didn't look very reassuring. Two agents in a blue uniform walked toward me, followed by a third figure. It was the chief of the Squadra Mobile police unit, Mirko Gaudenzi.
“Oi, Gaudenzi... what's up?”, I said with a cough. I felt weak.
“I'm fine. You... not so fine, it seems, eh, Brigati? Always in trouble! Where'd you end up? I didn't see you around anymore...”
I didn't know what to reply. Pain and painkillers blurred my imagination, so I went straight for the truth: I was fed up with spouting bullshit to save face.
“I quit. I write books now, and I think that's the reason why they tried to kill me...”
He looked puzzled. “Kill you? You're still seeing conspiracies everywhere, aren't you! No, that's not what this is about. You had more alcohol in your blood than is allowed, Joe, you were driving under the influence! That's why you thought they were out to kill you.”
“Impossible! I didn't drink this morning, let alone this afternoon... and they ran me over, it has to mean something to you cops...”
Gaudenzi nodded. “Of course it does, which is why we're here. Hit and run ain't legal, the car ran away.”
“Were there cameras? A detached bumper? He must have left a trace...”

"No, Brigati. All we have is some car paint we scraped off the fairing of your Vespa. So we wanted to ask you a couple of questions."
The inspector stopped again, shaking his head, this time showing displeasure.
"As you didn't pass the alcohol test, your testimony won't have legal standing... as you know. But it's a start for us, a way for us to understand something of the situation and move our investigation along."
I understood immediately. They had managed to discredit me, to frame me as a drunk driver. But who could have done something like that? And most importantly, why?
"Anyway, do you remember anything about the accident? The color of the car, any small detail that could lead us to its driver..."
"Honestly, no. But I am sure that they ran me over on purpose. I think I upset someone dangerous..."
I tried to sit up, to find some focus, but I only managed to go half way up. I fixed the pillow behind my shoulders. "I had an appointment with my client today, but when I got there, she wasn't there... then I think I saw her leave the building in a car. I was tailing her when they tried to kill me."
Gaudenzi stared right at me, he looked puzzled. He instinctively raised his hand, signaling me to stop: "Slow down, Brigati, one thing at a time. What are you talking about? What kind of client?"
"I am writing a book for her, a biography. My client, Jennifer Blasquez, disappeared. We were supposed to meet in her office today, but she wasn't there."
"And couldn't she have forgotten about your appointment?"
Sure, but it was hard for me to believe.
"True, but the past few days have been weird. I have a feeling that I am being shadowed, more or less since I started working for her. Once I found out she wasn't there for our appointment, before the accident, I saw three suspicious black cars come out of Jenny's office. I started tailing them because I think I saw Jenny herself sitting in one of them."
"Why'd you do that? It was none of your business...", the inspector stared at me.
"Journalist's instinct, there was something fishy. And I wanted to talk to her, ask her why she hadn't turned up... Go figure, she even called me on

the phone to try and throw me off... and then I was run over. Does this look unconnected to you, eh?"
Gaudenzi finally showed some interest. "Okay, let's say this all happened. But who could have it in for you and this Jenny? Maybe she just had some business to take care of outside her office, or she didn't want to see you, Joe."
Honestly, I don't know how the following words came out of my mouth. Who knows what leaps of logic my brain followed, it must have been the painkillers' fault.
"For the main character in my book, Jenny's boyfriend. He's in the pharmaceutical business... I'm sure he is behind all this."
"Okay... and what's he called? Let's go ask him some questions, so we'll clear our doubts."
I paled. I couldn't see myself, but in that moment, my face probably turned as pale as chalk, giving me a stupefied look. I lowered my gaze. "I don't know... she didn't want to tell me... but Jenny is a model, you can look her up on the internet... she exists!"
The stares from all the people in the room pierced into my flesh. It hurt, their irony for what I had just said. The two policemen smiled. Max Flecter had to get away with a hand on his forehead. Gaudenzi, however, knew me a little and knew I hadn't gone crazy. He was still serious and attentive. I know, those agents thought me mad. But I wasn't. In a stupor, yes, but I hadn't lost my marbles yet. Then I was struck by an idea: the bag could prove my theory!
"Look for my bag, it disappeared after the accident. It contained the first two chapters of the book and my notes on that man's life."
The inspector, almost moved to compassion by my situation, turned toward me and smiled.
"Alcohol and the accident did a number on you, Brigati. Get some rest, we'll let you know if we find anything."
"Look for Jennifer Blasquez, she's the one who commissioned my book! Please! She's Argentinian..."
I felt like dying.

It's horrible to be treated like that, when you are seen as nothing more than a stupid who can spout nothing but bullshit, and yet you know that you

are right, that you are telling 'the truth and nothing but the truth'. It's like being in a glass case and shouting. People look at you from the outside and smile because you look funny. “Look at that guy, how he flails around, how weird his face gets... Wonder what he's saying?”
That is how I felt. Humiliated by a lack of credibility.

Three days went by after that visit. Max Flecter didn't show his face. In light of my clinical improvement, the embassy decided it best to leave me alone. They would mail me my new ID directly at home and I didn't need anything else. I also asked them, since my condition wasn't that severe, not to notify my relatives in Canada. My parents never learned about the accident.
I ended up with two cracked ribs, some bruising on my back and two scratches on my chin. They kicked me out after four days of hospitalization and I went back home alone, hailing a cab. I didn't know where they had brought my beloved Vespa and I had no way of contacting inspector Gaudenzi as his phone number was written in my Moleskine, which of course was inside my stolen bag.
So I decided, when I was just a couple blocks away from home, to go to the police station instead. I wanted to talk to him directly, last but not least because that drunk driving business still drove me up a wall. I couldn't understand how it could have happened and who would have wanted to frame me that way.
I told the taxi driver that my destination had changed and he turned around, toward Fatebenefratelli street.

“Hello, I'm looking for chief inspector Gaudenzi. Where can I find him?”
The cop stationed at the entrance gave me a weird look, possibly due to the bruises and scratches on my face. I was still wearing the same torn, bloodied blazer and jeans I wore as I got run over. And no shirt, that one got shredded in the ER. I looked like a killer who had just committed a murder.
“Please wait here...” He made an internal phone call. “He's coming.”
The cop stared at me while I paced up and down the waiting room, never letting me get out of sight.
“Hey, Brigati... what are you doing here?”

“Straight out of the hospital, I wanted to know if there were news of any kind... And most importantly, where is my Vespa?”
“No news. Your motorbike is at the city tow pound, impounded as we still need to get all the evidence we can on the rogue car. They're taking samples of the paint from the fairing. But even if you could get it back...”
His face turned dark as he took his cellphone out of his jacket's pocket. I immediately understood that my beloved partner in crime had to be in shambles. “It's a miracle you came out of it alive, jumping out of the vehicle before the car ran you over was a skillful move. It literally ran over the Vespa, trampling it in a terrible crash.”
Yet I couldn't remember a single thing. “Do you see, then? I wasn't drunk! How could my reflexes have been so sharp?”
“I'll get a patrol car to drive you home, come here...”
The inspector probably pitied me. Out of the station, the white and blue police car awaited me as if I were a newly appointed President.
Gaudenzi opened the rear door for me, smiled and told me, with a hint of melancholy: “Investigations will continue in the following days, but if we can't find the car, and since the injuries you sustained are light, we'll have to close the file. Try to get back to work soon, far from those weird thoughts... no-one wants you dead!”
I arrived home and went to bed. I was still weak.

IX

"Charon was more wiser,
when he carried he knew
of who were the souls.
You instead played ignorant.
But you are just like them".

Monterey, a lovely town in California, 320 miles from Los Angeles and 120 from San Francisco. With a population of 30 thousands, its fame is due to its wooden buildings, in the typical colonial American style. There is not much to see: the town centre is picturesque, but hardly bigger than a football field. Everything else is modern and unattractive: your average crisis-stricken suburbs. Yet Monterey hosts more than four million tourists each year, drawn to the local natural reserve and to the Bay Acquarium, one of the biggest in the United States.
Every summer, young and old people alike flock together between Prescott Ave. and Cannery Row, hoarding souvenirs and keepsake photos. They gaze at the Pacific Ocean from the pier, look at the seagulls fly over the seaweed-encrusted beach. Big, black seaweeds, giving a gloomy outlook to the whole scenario.
Tourists religiously queue to visit the acquarium, which up until 1984 was a sardine-canning plant. In Monterey, the harbor and the sea have always sustained the economy before tourism changed the heart and soul of its inhabitants.

5:35 AM, August 26th, 2012. Jeffrey Cunningham was a young architect from Seattle lodging with his fiancée, Presley Scott, at the Intercontinental The Clement Monterey Hotel. One of the most beautiful hotels in town, in the historic heart of Monterey, a short walk from the sea and from renowned restaurant Bubba Gump. Like every morning, Jeffrey went out of his room early for a jog. It was his passion and he wouldn't go without it even on holiday. He waved at the hotel concierge and crossed the hall to the revolving door. As soon as he stepped outside, he started the timer on his watch and switched on his heart rate monitor, and off he went toward the sea. The wind was strong, as is to be expected by the Ocean. Be it summer or winter, day or night, those piers withstood gusts that could reach 75 mph.

The briny smell of the sea was inebriating, seagulls feasted on the beach where the tide had left small fishes trapped on the rocks with nowhere left to flee. Jef-Run, as his friends liked to call him, started his morning run by sprinting like a panther along the promenade. Dawn was starting to light up the waves of the Pacific. His iPod's music, coming from his armband holder, beat on his eardrums. Everything was perfect: no-one on the horizon, the town was still sleeping.

Then the runner had to stop, unable to discern what he thought he had seen. As he was running on the pier, he had noticed a swarm of birds gathering on the cliffs, but he was too far away to see what was attracting them. Now, a light blue rain slicker was floating with the undertow, right in front of him. Abandoned. Getting close to the railing, he saw that down below, along with the dead fishes, was a man. White, in his thirties, athletic. His gaze was blank, his body half naked. His right arm appeared to have been amputated.

Jeffrey instinctively reached for the cellphone in his right pocket to call for help. But his form-fitting jogging pants had no pockets. There was no time to lose.

He sprinted down the wooden stairs, rotten with sea salt, in an attempt to give aid to the man, who could still be alive. But as he reached the last step, he heard a noise behind him. He turned around, expecting a cat, or a seagull. Instead, in the shadows under the pier was a man. The figure leapt out and grabbed him by the throat, tearing off his earbuds and trowing him on the ground. The pair fought on the black beach, Jeffrey trying to grab his assailant's neck in defense, but to no avail, he only managed to brush against him. He felt overpowered. He wasn't lacking in strength, but his opponent was a fury and he was being kept on the ground by the man's right forearm, unable to break away from that hold. Then he felt a pang in his right side, his energies slowly drained away and he finally felt serene. The peace that came over him was even better than the feeling of a morning jog.

His hands, weighed down by an invisible force, brushed the gravel on the beach. His eyes instinctively searched for the murderer's face, but the latter covered them with the palm of his hand so he wouldn't be seen. Or to avoid the sight of death taking him away.

The view was really unusual, it was a pity that no-one was there to witness it and that most of the evidence got carried away by the wind, the water and the seagulls. Two corpses were found on the beach by a passer-by around 7:30 AM. One had an amputated arm, which he was not found. The other had a wound to his right side, probably made by a hacksaw, which almost crossed him whole.
Both men were strangers to John T. Pillik, chief of the Monterey Police Department. Then Presley Scott, looking for her fiancé, ran into the scene of the crime around 8:30. She had been roaming the small harbor for minutes, imagining that her boyfriend must have had an accident which had prevented him to come back to their room on his own legs. It had already happened once in Seattle, she had found him lying on a bench near home, with a swollen dislocated ankle.
Then, from atop the pier, she saw all those police cars and then his body, and she gave out a scream before passing out. An appalling sight. The police assisted her and grimly noted the particulars of at least one of the corpses. The girl did not recognize the other one. She didn't know who he was and stated over and over the he couldn't possibly have any ties with 'her Jef'. They were only there on holiday, she didn't know anyone, they were meant to leave on the following day to go to Hollywood and visit the studios. She was questioned once again a few days later, just to be sure, but her version of the facts did not change. She said, again, that she had never seen that man.
San Francisco's forensic team came over for the usual survey, bringing along a coroner who could fetch the corpses and carry out the autopsies.
The CSI people didn't have a lot of work in front of them this time. Evidence was scarce, just a number 19 hastily drawn on the gravel with a pointy object. Under the stairs leading down the pier, they found an open can of orange paint. Besides, close to the corpses, they found two different items of clothing, a light blue rain slicker and a torn white shirt, probably itself a victim of the scuffle. On its back was the fresh print of an orange

hand. The fingerprints matched the amputated arm of the deceased man. His identity was not discovered, but the missing arm was found amid the cliffs, half-eaten by seagulls, some three hundred feet away. It was first seen by a fisherman who was taking his habitual spot on the rocks.
In his hand they found an orange card with a message written in red pen. The language was so broken that it may have looked like a joke in bad taste. "Charon was more wiser, when he carried he knew of who were the souls. You instead played ignorant. But you are just like them: a BASTARD." A clear threat, but its receiver remained a John Doe, unidentified.
San Francisco's homicide squad stayed in Monterey for about three weeks, working side by side with the local department. Mostly for Jeffrey's sake, as nobody denounced the other corpse's disappearance.
The trail was feeble. When they tried to compare them with other murders that had taken place in the area, the items found on the crime scene had no match in the database. The note, the paint and the clothes were locked up in a box and they went back to looking for more clues.
The hacksaw's rust found in the stomach of one of the two corpses during the autopsy and the 8.5 size shoe prints on the gravel didn't lead to answers.
The murder weapon in the second killing was never found, probably thrown in the sea right after the fight. And the item's chemical composition was too common, it could have been bought in any hardware store. Ditto his shoes, sneakers in a common size.
John Doe, on the other hand, was strangled by a nylon wire, then his arm was violently amputated, hence the amount of blood on the shoreline. Cunnigan's face – his eyelids, to be precise – provided the murderer's fingerprints, but they didn't turn up in any database: again, a dead end. Lastly, the DNA found under those poor sods' fingers was in a state of decay due to the weather conditions and couldn't be used.
The detectives questioned the few witnesses, to no avail. All of them had seen the corpses on the beach, but not a trace of the culprit, no-one had met nor noticed anyone suspicious around the area.
Monterey's mayor pressured California's governor to close the case. Nothing significant had come up, so he didn't want policemen and detectives front and center in his little town: visitors were decreasing and

tour operators were starting to skip the acquarium stop. With one of the victims being a young tourist himself, knowing that the police were running in circles wasn't exactly good publicity.
So the police along with the mayor's office issued a press release, which got picked up by the main local and national news stations. It stated that the investigation had been permanently called off. The tourist had been assaulted by a stranger, possibly due to a mugging gone bad as poor Jeffrey Cunnigan's ears were lacerated. The killer had tried to steal his iPod and the situation escalated. Jeff was hailed a hero, trying to defend himself up to his death.
At any rate, the local administration would start patrolling the beach day and night to grant visitors an adequate level of security.
They also stressed that it was an isolated case, with the unidentified corpse probably being the killer himself. A hobo passing by, mentally ill as he had amputated his own arm after killing the tourist and then had killed himself. The media, of course, were not aware that John Doe's arm had been found far away from the corpse and that his death predated that of the Seattle architect. It was impossible for him to be Jef's killer, it was a double murder.
Two weeks later, thanks to a note from Long Beach, they found out that the ship Boavista, flying a Panamanian flag, was missing its second-in-command, a 35-years-old man from Ohio with a criminal record. He was born in Port Clinton, on Lake Erie, and those same waters had witnessed the start of his sailing career. He then boarded a cruise ship, but a few months later they threw him out as the video surveillance system, then a pioneering piece of technology, had shown him stealing from the passengers' cabins. Once out of jail, he dedicated himself to cargo ships, rising ranks from deck hand to, eventually, second-in-command.
The container ship should have sailed on September 14th toward Shanghai, but Mike Curley hadn't turned up early, as he always did before a long journey. So his mates had called the authorities. The harbormaster notified the metro police department, the missing persons bureau quickly cross-checked his data with the unidentified corpses found in California in the past days and John Doe turned out to be Mike Curley.

His colleagues were luckily en route to China and the poor second-in-command didn't have any family: no-one showed up at the funeral. No-one notified the press and everything quickly returned to normal.
The Cunnigan family had found answers, albeit false ones. The media soon found other topics to obsess about, while nobody cared for Mike Curley's reputation. In Monterey, tourism once again flourished, to the mayor's content. And the economy – that one, at least – was safe.
The two murders were filed away as unsolved crimes.

X

"I couldn't just shrug it off.
She had been gone for days
and I kept on wondering
who the shadow man could be
who tailed me from up close."

It had been days since I had last managed to contact her. Jenny seemed to have disappeared, one appointment, then the black-out and the accident only made everything more complicated.
I had lost my documents, the computer with the novel's file, and my Vespa was totaled. I bought another Mac, used this time, and a cellphone, keeping my old number via SIM transfer.
As for my job, I wanted to keep on writing – after all, there may have been no connection between it and that disaster, like inspector Gaudenzi had told me.
So, after I got her number back from Andrea, I started to bombard Jenny with phone calls. Nothing. At first, the phone kept ringing, uninterrupted. Then the number got deactivated.
I wanted to go to her office, but before that, I called Andrea again, to avoid him a gaffe.
"What the fuck is this? I can't work like that!"
From the other end of the phone came Andrea's reply, in a raspy voice.
"Listen, Joe, let's be real: why the fuck do you care? Just keep on writing, no hurry, especially after that blow you took. I've already told you not to ask yourself any questions... It may be a drag, but take the job as it comes..."
It all felt so damn simple to him.
"Fine, Andrea, but who the hell is gonna tell me that my work's okay?"
He laughed. "Chill, they paid you already... you don't have to give a shit..."
"That's not how I work. And besides, where am I supposed to get the story I need to write into the book?"

"Oh, Joe! Take that stick outta your ass, it's all right... What you know, you write, what you don't know, you invent... no?"
"Enough!"
When I do something, I want to do it properly, to the best of my abilities, not following Andrea's half-assed philosophy. I calmed myself.
"Look, if you talk to her, tell her I need to see her. There's also weird stuff happening and I'd like to know if it's all connected to the book."
"Weird? What's that?" Andrea's raspy voice was gone in an instant, his voice back to its usual vivid tone.
"I'm saying that I've been having a funny feeling in the past few weeks. I'm experiencing things that aren't your average daily routine... I think I am being followed, tailed... Then the accident, you know..."
Actually, I felt hunted, but I didn't want to look like a scaredy cat, so I minimized.
"Whatever, don't worry Andrea... odd stuff happened and that's it, I wanted to hear your opinion."
For his part, he seemed lost: "Joe, are you for real? You sound like you've gone crazy... listen, I only asked you to write a book, not to start wearing a tin hat. And let me assure you that Jenny ain't no CIA agent. So chill and go back to work and she'll turn up eventually."

Milan was frantic and I was scared. I knew, I was sure of the cause of my anxiety. It wasn't Jenny's silence so much as that brawny, well-dressed man with a buzz cut I kept on seeing everywhere I went. I was under the constant, horrible impression of having eyes trained on my head, staring at me from a distance.
Not even my journalistic career had ever made me so embarrassed of walking down the streets. It wasn't fear, it was just that I didn't want to realize that someone was tailing me. Like an ostrich tries to avoid danger by sticking its head in the sand, I stayed holed up at home.
I was sure that man was there for me, yet at the same time I didn't want to believe it and feared that possibility. So I only ventured out of my home for the barest necessities.
"He's not tailing you, calm down", I told myself over and over again under the shower.

I decided to go out, that psychological issue needed to be solved. I went to buy something to eat, the sensible thing to do at 1:30 PM, when housewives are busy in the kitchen and bachelors at work. That's the kind of time I prefer to go to the discount store, it's better when there's not much of a crowd.

I walked into the store. I hadn't bought any food in two weeks.

I was loitering around the fruit aisles when I saw him. The same man. Always sharply dressed, looking at nothing in particular, as if I were invisible. Clearly an act.

I was sure he was following me, even though he was pushing his cart like any regular customer. It only contained a few items, as if he had grabbed a handful of products from the closest aisle to appear less suspicious.

A shiver went up my back.

I tried to lose him as I made my way to the checkout, but he didn't lose a beat. I could see him calmly following me, as if he were there minding his own business, buying groceries in his wife's stead. As I walked around a corner, I noticed that he had disappeared behind the detergents.

"Where the fuck did he vanish to?"

"Beg your pardon?" The cashier gave me a very perplexed look.

"Sir, do you want to pay or not?"

"Yes, I'm sorry. Here's my cash card... Did you happen to see a tall man, in his thirties, with a buzz cut, get out of here? He is wearing a black suit and white shirt... He was behind me."

The look she gave me was telling. "No sir... it's thirty-four Euros and sixty-seven cents, do you have a rewards card?"

I felt like an idiot.

Then I saw a janitor pushing a cart, his cart! The items inside were the same, I was sure of it. Details were always my forte.

"Hey, boy... hey!! Whose cart is that?!?"

I sprang toward him, struggling to cross the checkout line in reverse. My bags bounced against the other clients' carts. I tried to wade through them like Moses through the Red Sea. Everyone was staring at me, people thought I was crazy.

I launched myself against the cart, staring right at the janitor: "*Whose is it?* Where'd you find it?"

"I don't know, sir... it was abandoned in one of the aisles, the detergents' I think. Someone must have left it there and walked away."
I knew it: mine weren't delusions. He was following me and when I spotted him he escaped. But what did that man want from me?
My legs were shaking.
Being tailed didn't happen every day. In my life I had always lived on the edge, without a care. Then again, when you follow a journalistic lead, when you're onto news, your eyes are always set on the goal: that's all that matters. You don't ask yourself about the risks and you don't fear the truth. This time was different: I was the prey. As I went home, I tried to think if I could have done something wrong in the past, if I could have accidentally stepped on someone's toes. Back in my flat, I downed a generous serving of Jack Daniel's right from the bottle.

I paced around my home without knowing what to do. The living room was exceptionally bright. It was 5:30 PM and I felt I was going crazy. The events at the convenience store were still playing back in my mind, I couldn't focus, it was like an obsession that had taken hold of me.
I got up from the table, put down my empty glass and went to look out of the window. Just because. I didn't open the blinds, limiting myself to staring out of the fissures.
I jumped. "There he is!" The man was still there, among the bushes, near the cars parked in the street under my flat. Just like a few days earlier.
I didn't stop to think. I had to stop him and know what he was after, I couldn't let him go away.
Pumped, I threw myself down the building's stairs: adrenaline coursed in my veins as if I were about to play in the RBS 6 Nations. Even the pain from the accident had subsided.
I had an advantage: he hadn't seen me as I observed him from behind the blinds. He couldn't know. I could use this and catch him by surprise, to finally ask him what he wanted from me. I didn't care about the danger.
Step after step passed under my Adidas and I couldn't think of anything else: I had to talk to him. I was proud of being right, of not having dreamt it up. My journalistic intuition had won once again: the mystery man really was tailing me. No doubts about it.

I opened the front door and accidentally ran into mrs Tina Canfarelli on the doorstep. She came in, I went out.
“Fuck, I'm sorry... you alright?”
She was a nice, sweet old lady who lived on the third floor. I must have talked to her four times, tops, in all the years I spent in Milan. But I couldn't ignore her after throwing her on the ground, I was just lucky she wasn't hurt. I could have killed her or broken her leg.
Her oranges were all over the sidewalk.
I hurriedly picked them up, after I picked up mrs Tina herself like one would grab a child from a stroller. I had to be quick, I feared I would lose my man, alarm him with all this ruckus, and I couldn't spend too much time picking up my neighbor's groceries.
“Forgive me – may I help you? This fell out of your jacket.”
The voice was warm, like a radio host's. I raised my eyes and saw him there, standing in front of me with a smile. He handed me a white envelope without stamps nor writings. I grabbed it without a word.
I was very embarrassed, almost shocked, and could barely manage a: “...sorry?”
He replied gently, smiling.
“It's nothing, you're welcome.”
I couldn't believe it, my stalker was right in front of me, talking to me and giving me a letter. Absurd as it may seem, all the adrenaline I had built up in my body as I ran down the stairs turned into shock.
I could hear mrs Canfarelli ranting, while my man hurried off along the street just like that, as if nothing had happened.
“Hey, you...”
Mrs Tina's face said it all. She looked at me as if I had gone mad. She couldn't understand what was going on, just like I couldn't understand what that man wanted from me.
“Hey, slow down a minute, what do you want? Where are you going? Stop!” I ran after him, he walked faster and then pulled close to a Mercedes that had been slowly driving by the sidewalk.
I tried to make my way across the parked cars to cut them off, but didn't make it in time. The man was already sneaking inside the vehicle. The car took off and disappeared in the traffic.

Seeing that black car get away felt like being slowly choked by a nylon wire. I would have to be on constant vigilance, someone wanted to send me a clear message. But what for? I opened the envelope: it contained a USB drive. Nothing else.
"Everything alright?"
The sudden pressure of a hand on my shoulder made me jump. And my heart raced, but it was just mrs Tina.
"Yes, madam... it's okay."
"Could you explain what is happening? You came out of our building like a madman and then ran after your friend, but why?"
I couldn't understand: "Beg your pardon, what friend?"
"That man! Your friend, I'm telling you..."
I was pretty sure that mrs Tina didn't suffer from memory loss or other senile diseases. Had I heard that right?
"I'm sorry to contradict you, but... that's not exactly a friend of mine, on the contrary..."
She frowned. "Oh, how odd... Yet he told me yesterday that he was just that... I had my doubts, you know? When he started to ask all those questions, I got suspicious..."
"What questions? What did he ask?" I was heating up and I grabbed her by the arms. I never knew how much the others could know about me. I had lived in that building ever since coming to Milan from Canada, but I never stopped to have a chat with the neighbors. Aside from the occasional greeting, my mind had always been far away from that kind of chitchat. Yet those nice ladies, porter included, knew everything. It took just a few words for the truth to come out: mrs Tina had 'sung'. She had told the mystery man everything about my life, past and present.
"But what did he focus on? It's of paramount importance that you tell me!"
"Your job, he wanted to know if you are still working for the paper, if you're still writing crime pieces."
I tried to get the talk back on the track of what that man wanted from me, the most important thing. But at the end of my chat with that nice neighbor, I didn't have any more useful info. The only truth? Someone was at my heels. But who?

I barely had the time to help the old lady get back to her apartment, with all her oranges and the rest of her groceries safely inside their bags, before making yet another terrible discovery.
"Hey, what the fuck has happened here?"
Someone had broken into my home. And, judging from the mess, rummaged through my things. I could spot the differences, even though I always lived in a mess. So by rushing down to the man in the street I had played their game, they had lured me out to get inside my flat and ransack it. It was a diversion, and more than one person was involved. My bad, with my brilliant idea of rushing downstairs to catch that man. Had I minded my own business and shut myself inside, none of this would have happened. And besides, one should never get outside without turning the key in the lock. But I was in a hurry.
I looked around, hoping to figure out whether they really had stolen something and whether someone was still in there. Everything seemed to check out, nothing was missing and I was alone. As I sat down at the living room table, my Mac still running, I tried to take a deep breath and connect all the pieces of that impossible afternoon.
From the convenience store to the face-to-face meeting with that weird character on the sidewalk, all topped by the break-in. Every little detail could be useful. Was this whole shebang connected to the book I was writing? I kept thinking back to all the crime stories I had poked into during my career, in search of possible ties. Nothing. I could only focus on one thing: Jenny had been gone for days and I kept thinking about the identity of the shadow man who was tailing me from up close.
I put my hand in my pocket and realized: "I have the USB drive!"
I inserted it into the computer's port.

XI

"This descends from the words
of our great founding father
Benjamin Rush. He foresaw
the risks, but no-one
wanted to listen to him."

I turned my computer on and double-checked that the drive was correctly inserted, so as not to damage the files. I felt impatience rise as the apple logo appeared on screen, then the blue screen, with a background of photos from a trip to New York's Little Italy, my forever desktop.
Used as it may have been, the Mac booted up fast. I opened the 16 GB drive and found a folder named 'Orange Hands'. I opened it, finding a video inside.
The video player filled the screen as soon as I clicked on the icon, offering me the image of a hand on a white background. It looked like a bloodied handprint, except the blood was orange. The image also featured some words in English: OH-MTLF 'Orange Hands – Medical Treatment Liberalization Front'.
The following screen was more vivid.
It showed the close-up of a man in his forties, well built, with large shoulders and wearing a white shirt with the orange hand drawn on his chest. He spoke English, but didn't sound like a native speaker. He presented himself as one of the movement's leaders, but throughout the video, he never revealed his name or nickname. He hid behind a balaclava and the audio was filtered through a voice changer.
He spoke: "Our front is lethal, we won't take prisoners. We will not spare the life of those who sacrifice human health to the idols of money and power."
Then the man was silent and the video faded to black. Pictures of African children, gaunt and sick with AIDS – shown by the boils on their bodies

appeared on the screen, accompanied by heart wrenching screams of suffering.
Then young, maimed Kosovo soldiers, stranded in a military field hospital without medicines, desperately crying. I recognized the logo of the UNO K-FOR peacekeeping force.
“These are but examples of what they will do to us: unscrupulous people who want to enslave us through fake drugs and crush us with viruses. They are already testing these techniques on the weakest populations, they want to wipe out our children like those poor African kids destroyed by AIDS...”
What was he talking about? It felt like something out of a Muslim terrorism video, like those people who manage to convey to their viewers all their hatred for the Western nations before blowing themselves up. But these weren't terrorists. I had never heard of the Orange Hands front.
“We cannot allow any more abuses. We will attack our enemies without clamor, from the shadows, and prove that all this isn't fantasy.”
More shocking images of sick people suffering horrible pains followed.
“For years, our group investigated the pharmaceutical lobbies. We gathered data, names and foreign bank accounts that are used to grease the cogs of international policies. Now we are are going public. And we will do it our own way.”
After a moment's pause he spoke again, in a calmer voice: “Our founding father, Benjamin Rush, was right. He saw the risks two hundred years ago, yet no-one listened. Now we are paying the consequences. The system is wrong; in the past century, we allowed huge financial capitals to fagocitate the entire American healthcare system and then to expand like a virus.”
The video showed a succession of bankers, university professors, businessmen, politicians, scientists. People young and old, alive and dead, some famous, others less so.
“How did they do it? First by controlling education in universities. 'Effective philanthropy', they call it, but it's the start of a dictatorship, of mere physical, economical and mental slavery for us common men and women. Now they control the international pharmaceutical market, they choose what we can need, when we have to fall ill... how and whether to be treated...”
The background music went up a notch.

"Remember what dear Hans Ruesch said: the pharmaceutical industry is as powerful as the weapons industry. But war comes an end, sooner or later, and illnesses do not, as long as someone keeps them alive."

I paused the video and checked the 'Orange Hands' folder. I was starting to get tired of those pointless, slightly unsettling rants. I loved conspiracies, but this was too much. Inside the folder was a multitude of neatly organized files, plausibly the result many people's efforts and years of work. One folder was named 'Statute'. I opened it, in search of more info on what I had just seen and learned in the video.
I opened a .pdf file that looked painstakingly compiled.
Perfect line spacing, justified text, it looked like a notary deed.
But it didn't show any seals nor signatures.
I went on to read it with the utmost attention, if a little skeptical.

'CAPITULUS MAXIMUS'
'Orange Hands Brotherhood of Science'

"Should we fail to contemplate in our Constitution the concept of freedom in the medical care, a time shall come when medicine will turn into a covert dictatorship, with no way for the people to understand that change. A time shall come when the attempt to limit the art of therapy to a single class of people will be the Bastille of the medical science."

Benjamin Rush (January 4, 1746 – April 19, 1813) Signer of the Declaration of Independence on July 4th, 1776.

I scanned through the pages, trying to focus on the most important paragraphs. I was starting to get worried. This had all the markings of a lodge, a secret association created by common people against 'the strong, occult powers of the financial and economic world', specifically aimed at the international pharmaceutical circles. Everyone could become part of it and add documents, files and information, for the sake of the common good. And what could that be? The circulation of knowledge, of the proof that lobbies were perverted and corrupt.
They wanted to topple Pandora's box once and for all.

The source documents were generated autonomously and continuously, propagating ever further, like a chain or the internet. The system was based on anonymity, while its goal was to come out of the physical and moral slavery dictated by the pharmaco-economical market that influenced us, that told us that we were ill just to cure us with inadequate or straight-up fake drugs. It didn't look like a joke: it all looked very real and very distressing.

[...] In order to win this battle and once again reclaim for ourselves the rights to a healthy life, we need a huge popular movement that will sustain the freedom in the medical care, the global diffusion of natural treatments and of those that, however artificial, are based on real scientific results that are not contaminated by vile money [...]

[...] For these reasons, the Orange Hands front is born. Because orange is the color of freedom, our hands joined together can form a chain to block out this horror and return us our freedom to live healthy lives. Orange like the color of the Netherlands, the fist liberal nation to recognize health as a primary and essential right. [...]

[...] Our true enemies are medicine's hidden dictators. They are many and they are well integrated everywhere. They take on many faces. It matters not whether they wear the clothes of 'university magnates' or of 'researchers', whether they blend into the 'academic lobbies' or work for 'pharmaceutical multinational companies'. They are the ones who 'matter' and they 'govern' official medicine, they are the ones we must fight against [...]

[...] On the liberal, open minds such as ours falls the task to react to this rising tide of antiscientific intolerance. Regrettably, in the two hundred and twenty years since our founding father's prophetic words, the man who gave us the tools to rise up – Benjamin Rush, physician, educator and writer – this healthcare dictatorship has taken hold [...]

[...] Together, we must free ourselves from the shackles of the pharmaceutical multinationals that control us. They are occult operators

who crush our psyches, making us slaves to useless, paradoxical drugs. They are the ones who, with their money, feed the malpractices in the international healthcare system and keep us ill. They are the ones who ruthlessly carry out terrifying tests, unleashing lab-created viruses on the weakest parts of the world's population, those who cannot raise their voices to let the entire world know [...]

[...] Health is a primary necessity and we cannot forget it. It must be protected from such monsters, engendered by modern society. We can win them with our wits: that, they cannot take away from us [...]

I read through some more files and found references to the 'effective philanthropy' mentioned by the man in the video. It was a huge folder, with more than 4GB of material, covering the history of the Brindeber Foundation, almost one hundred years old, with branches in more than 50 countries worldwide.

I had heard praises about it, reading and watching what the media wanted us to know, through well-aimed and well-paid news reports. Its creation, dated 1916, was the result of a strong wish of famed oil tycoon and philanthropist Franklin J. Brindeber, patriarch of his family, one of the most influential American dynasties along with the Rockefellers and the Kennedys. It was one of the richest families in the world, along with the European Rothschild, of Judaeo-German roots.

The Foundation's goal was to support non-profit research in many fields, including, case in point, scientific medical research. It had several ongoing funding programmes on a pro bono basis; among them, one of the most famous was aimed at overcoming the scourge of AIDS. That is what they had led me to believe up until that day.

Time flew as I started to pay attention to the files I was reading. The folder contained stolen, strictly confidential documents: bank statements from shell companies used to illegally support politicians all across the world. In turn these would put in a word with the control boards that greenlight the sale of new drugs after a careful evaluation of their collateral effects on patients.

There were also names, businessmen who handled various activities in the field, on the Foundation's payroll in order to fudge or sway the market.

And there was an endless list of scientists and researchers, all indexed along with pictures of their respective families up to the third degree of kinship.
"But who might have an interest in shining a light on all this? What's the point?" After all, they were just doctors, chemists and biologists.
I understood the reason why soon afterwards, finding ties between thousands of pharmaceutical multinational companies which were, in theory, competitors. That is what they wanted everyone to believe, rigging the system and exploiting those same people as guinea pigs for their profits. Indeed, the biologists themselves were the Foundation's test subjects, allowing them to get the highest market earnings. A true cure-all for the philanthropists' wallets. By directly or indirectly controlling most international companies and their scientists, they in turn controlled the prices, handled demands and increased or decreased the patients' expectations. Absolute masters of the healthcare world, they decided which products had to sell more and which ones less, which active ingredient to launch, which company was supposed to discover which vaccine in their labs. They could have handled pandemics if they wanted, or make an entire nation kneel with lethal viruses by creating powerful bacteriological weapons on demand.
An impressive pyramid system controlled by Brindeber themselves and created through several, well-compensated frontmen. The latter pretended to own shares of pharmaceutical corporations, but only did so on paper.
About two hundred of the most famous international companies were clearly owned by the Foundation proper, as the documents I was reading demonstrated with clarity and transparency, step by step, person by person. One thousand, three hundred and ninety-seven more were also supposed to belong to them. But Orange Hands' network of information was still being updated. Those suppositions lacked clear data. The orange front was expanding like wildfire, swallowing everything and everyone, starting from the States and arriving in Europe. Those four gigabytes exposed the largest and most influential illegal financial institution in the world. Thanks to those files, the entire dark cosmos of the scientific and medical world could be unmasked. The chart contained one hundred and twenty-seven thousands contacts, listed in great detail:

NAME, SURNAME, DATE OF BIRTH, ROLE, EDUCATION, BANK ACCOUNT AND PLACE OF RESIDENCE.

Corrupted individuals were marked in yellow, the dead were red. Black meant most influential.
There were also chapters on finance and politics, two folders worth 6 GB each. I leafed through the latter, leaving the former for later.
Most of it was suppositions, however unsettling. Some examples? 50% of George H. W. Bush's administration was made of top pharmaceutical executives. Coincidence? Probably. On top of that, his Secretary of Defense, Donald Rumsfeld, had been CEO of several multinationals. In what field? Pharmaceutical, of course. Surely another coincidence. What was certain was that the Brindeber Foundation, through the big groups it controlled, had always, legally sponsored all the presidential campaigns of the various candidates to the White House. All of them, therefore managing to keep any potential winner on a leash.

I was breathless. I went back to the video, now paying more attention. I found the masked man again, whom I originally considered nothing more than a mythomaniac.
Play.
He started moving and talking again under the balaclava that concealed him: "It's time to act, no mercy. We need to keep up our data retrieval, with even more energy and results. We need to unmask all the rotten underside of our current world."
His voice turned stronger and harsher: "We will also start to unravel from the inside this illness that is killing our society. We will eradicate it. Forever. We are the vaccine, because the world's health is no joke."
Many brand logos appeared on screen, all known pharmaceutical multinational companies belonging to the same 'family'. "Now a warning. Abraham Lincoln says that they 'can fool all the people some of the time, and some of the people all the time, but they cannot fool all the people all the time'."
The video was coming to an end. Its conclusion was theatrical, possibly a little too melodramatic for my tastes. The logo of the orange hand on white

background came up, accompanied by a disguised voice, slowed down and with an unsettling tone. My computer's bass echoed in my brain.
“You will not crush us, our blood has changed its color.”
A moment's pause, then: “It is orange now, like the pills you forced on us. This will be the color of our freedom, of our violent, underground revolution!”

XII

"The image was appalling:
the body of a man
in his forties without his feet,
sawed away at his ankles."

What were those documents for? Why collect them? Who was behind all that?
The questions whirled in my mind.
Most importantly: how did this lodge work? How could one member of the organization trust the other? I went back to the statute in hopes of finding something there. As I read on, I shivered. Everything was based on indirect terror inflicted on the group's members.

[...] Anonimity is a valuable asset, more than health and wellness. More than life. Anonimity must be protected at the cost of one's life. Remember: everyone can become part of our organization. But those who come in cannot walk out. Remember: there is always someone watching. Infamy is the incurable evil [...]

[...] Our DNA, upon which everything is based and everything will thrive, is as follows: "VALEO SI VALES", my well-being depends on your well-being. Each member can only introduce a single acolyte and it will be up to them to monitor their behavior. The 'introduced' who disgraced their mentor shall be eliminated like a virus. And the 'introductor' shall fix the damage caused by the person they ineptly inserted in our body [...]

[...] The order to eradicate a member shall come from above, from they who gave you life in the Front. Only they who introduced you may tell you what to do. Only they are your reference. You cannot defy their will. Remember [...]

I was deep in thoughts. I couldn't believe it, it was a journalistic scoop of incredible reach. It would get to international politicians, entrepreneurs, lab researchers and scientists. How many heads could roll, how vast the economic interests in play! And everything was in my hands, but why me? I could feel the cold sweat on my forehead. Up until then, I had covered murders, not international conspiracies.
I was about to close the folder and light myself a Marlboro when I heard someone knocking at my door. The scare made me jump on my chair. I decided not to open the door. The knocking continued, insistently. I looked at the clock: 7.30 PM.
"Who the fuck is it now?"
A shout came from outside, followed by two rings at the doorbell. "Police... Joe Brigati, open the door. We know you are home!"
"Police?" I closed my laptop, hiding the USB drive under the couch's pillows. I had no idea of the reasons behind their arrival but allowing them to find those documents would have spelled my end.

I ran toward the entrance, heart beating faster and faster until I opened the door, breathless. I swallowed a little bit of saliva that wouldn't go down. Anxiety gripped me. I looked beyond the door.
Inspector Mirko Gaudenzi was standing outside, proud of his coat and of his threatening look, aided by his baldness. Beside him were two uniformed agents.
"Good evening, Brigati. Would you kindly follow us?"
Bye formalities, he couldn't have been more eloquent. He looked particularly tense, as if he were trying to avoid telling something bad. I, on the other hand, feared that the reason behind his visit were the files. Silence.
My heart stopped at once. In my brain, electric discharges froze my muscles. Were they really there for me? But how could they have found out that I was in possession of those documents? I couldn't be sure of anything anymore.
"What's up? Did you find the guy who ran me over?"
I tried to dissimulate.
"Maybe, but you'll have to follow us. We need your help to identify him."

So I wasn't under arrest. I replied with some irony, but really, it was a breath of relief.
“I thought you wanted to arrest me!”
“Why, you got anything to confess?”
The inspector's gaze was particularly serious and gloomy.
“No, of course... let me once again state that I don't remember a thing about the accident.”
“Don't worry. But you still have to follow us. It's just a formality.”

The squad was right in front of the building's front door. The custodian, at the end of her shift, stared at the scene as if Christmas had come early, enjoying the sight of my arrest. At least, that's what she thought, I am sure. The blue flashing lights cut through the evening light. The agents opened the back door and let me inside by gently pushing my head, which was a treatment usually reserved for criminals. At least they'd spared me the handcuffs.
“Fuck, the drive!”
I had forgotten it under the pillows, I had to hide it better. They had already broken into my flat once, I couldn't allow it again, not with that material.
“What drive?”
The inspector turned weirdly curious.
“Nothing... I was just thinking out loud, I forgot to shut down my Mac with my work notes inside.”
“Don't worry, you'll be home soon...” But he didn't sound so convinced.

Mirko Gaudenzi was your average old-style cop, except in a young man's body. He couldn't be more than forty years old, even though the hair loss and the wrinkles on his face made him look older. The rest of him, however, didn't look half bad: tall, with broad shoulders and icy blue eyes. He was married to a beautiful woman, a kick-ass judge, which granted him a sort of 'immunity' on the job. He was one of his unit's *untouchables*, fastidious to a fault during investigations though a little lacking in inventive. I had met him during a drug bust where he cooperated with Genova's police department as well as with the DIA, the Anti-Mafia Investigation Department. He was brilliant there, blocking a group of Colombian drug traffickers who were smuggling heroin and cocaine in

Milan through Genova's harbor. I wrote a good piece on that story: as I mentioned, it made my journalistic fortune.

The car flew through Milan's centre, sirens blaring. I could see Via Turati street and the headquarters of Milan's eponymous soccer team pass by the window.

But we weren't going to the precinct. I knew that route all too well, I must have driven my Vespa to and fro a million times in all my years as a journalist.

“Were are we going? Via Fatebenefratelli isn't this way, is it?”, I promptly asked.

“No, you're right. We're not going to the precinct, we are heading toward the place where we found the car that hit you.”

“And where is that?”

“You'll see, Brigati... don't worry.”

He always acted like that and it always drove me up a wall. Every time he had to say my surname, the inspector stressed the lack of a letter. And indeed, he was right. My father's name was Brigatti, with a double 't'. But as he emigrated to Canada, his new documents lacked a letter, omitted by distraction.

My father never lifted a finger to change it, as he thought it sounded more Italo-Canadian, but I attempted to file a complaint once I came of age. It never went anywhere, though: the red tape was long and messy, so I eventually dropped it. Besides, I couldn't have a different surname from my father.

We arrived in a lot under Milan's eastern bypass – under its 'C' ramp specifically, the one that goes from the nearby town of Agrate to the city centre through Via Rombon street.

Law enforcement was all there: forensics, regular cops and two traffic corps squads. There was even an ambulance. Traffic was jammed both ways. In the small parking lot, wedged under the bypass' pillars, only trash on the ground and two old abandoned tires.

Our car slowed down for the roadblock, with Gaudenzi lowering the window and signaling an agent to let us through.

“I have the witness...”

What? Had I not been clear enough? I had no memories of the accident, how many times would I need to repeat it? I decided not to point it out, so as to avoid friction with the inspector.
We approached a construction site, close to the bypass' bridge and to a small stream. Right outside the police tape we could see the side of the funeral coach.
"Inspector, what happened here?" I was tense.
He didn't reply. As I got out, I looked at a big car nearby. It was a black SUV, a Cadillac Escalade to be precise. The area was floodlit by powerful lamps powered by portable generators.
The car's hood was crushed, half-hidden by the bushes on the stream's shore The driver's door was open. On the side of the car I saw a handprint in orange paint. A shiver ran through my back: 'Orange Hands'! They were there? What about Gaudenzi, did he know everything? I opted to shut up for the time being.
"Were you not a journalist, I wouldn't have led you here on the scene of the crime. What you are going to see is horrifying. We found a mutilated corpse inside the vehicle that hit you a few days ago."
My salivation slowed down again.
"Are you sure this is the right car?"
"The paint found on your Vespa is a perfect match. Besides..."
The inspector paused, I pressed him on.
"Is he the one who tried to kill me?" My finger swiftly pointed at the corpse.
"We can consider it a very likely theory, even though something's off. Just like your blood test, with the high level of alcohol. We really think they were tampered with in the lab. But why?"
I knew it, they ran me over on purpose and then tried to frame me as a drunkard: motherfuckers! Someone wanted me dead. But what for? And most importantly, who did?
I still hadn't been handed over the sensitive documents. Up to a few hours earlier, I wasn't even aware of 'Orange Hands'. How could I have already been on their hit list? Alternatively, why try to kill me and then hand me over all that material? I couldn't understand what was happening.
"We have precious few info. The driver was killed. They made a mess of him, mutilating him as he was still alive. We'll have to wait for the DNA

tests to find out his identity, if he is in our database already. No ID yet. No documents, the car was a long-term rent paid for by a foreign company: Biotech FourStreet Laboratories Inc., in San Francisco."

Gaudenzi stopped talking and looked down, pushing a hand in his trench coat's pocket. He fished out a plastic bag containing several pictures and gave it to me.

"On top of that... As I told you, we are sure that you were a target. This was found on the passenger's seat, look at it..." The photo showed me, with an X on my head, in a shot taken from the distance while I was going home. I had been tailed and captured on film.

I wanted to cry.

I was in a huge mess, without even trying: they had framed me.

"Brigati, you have to tell us everything you know. We must understand who holds a grudge against you and how you are involved in this homicide."

"Involved? I'm a victim!"

I was about to finish my sentence when an agent arrived and asked the inspector to follow him. He motioned me to stay there and went behind a bush with his underling. I was alone. I looked around, close to a couple of agents busy with their surveys.

I couldn't resist: I had to see the dead man's face. I walked up to the Escalade's door and looked inside. I froze and then was shaken by a spasm of vomit.

The image was appalling: the body of a man in his fifties without feet, which had been excised with a hacksaw from the ankles. His jeans, too, had been ripped up, in a brutal, fastidious job considering the blood that had ended up on the windows and dashboard.

The seatbelt was still fastened. The victim must have been driving, or the killer must have tied him up to keep him still. Amputation is a painful form of torture and victims tend to struggle.

He had no hands left either, cut at the wrist. No teeth, taken out one by one. Possibly so that the victim wouldn't be recognized quickly. With no fingerprints and no dental records, DNA was the last remaining option, and it wasn't a quick one. The murderer would have all the time to flee.

Inside the Escalade was a bloodbath. The car mats had turned red, dripping with drying, dense, dark blood. It looked like he had been killed there and then abandoned.
“Who could do something like that? It's horrible.”
I had seen my share of graphic imagery during my career, but that was terrifying. I dared not imagine the victim's suffering.
I looked at the rest of the body and noticed that his blood-stained brown leather jacket had a crest close to his heart, which read: '*Memento audere semper*'.
“Hey, wait a second... It's the one I saw after being hit, as I lay on the ground... but that man was on the street and they told me that the car ran away immediately after the impact, without stopping. How could it be?”
Gaudenzi was standing behind me. “Brigati, what do you mean?”

The interrogation room was cold. Very different from the ones on TV. As we went to the precinct, the agents asked me to go inside and release my statement, explain to Gaudenzi what had happened to me in those past days and try to find ties to the murder.
I was informed of the retrieval of the body's missing pieces, by the stream next to the car. Which was why the inspector had been called to supervise and left me beside the Cadillac. Hands and feet had been put in a bag and charred, after a careful flaying of the fingertips. The teeth, on the other hand, were nowhere to be found.
No doubts about it: that was the work of a killer, a capable and ferocious one at that. But I knew even less about him than the agents in front of me.
The inspector was there, along with an assistant of his tasked with recording the meeting and a third man, wearing a blue suit and tie, his white shirt wrinkled and unbuttoned. He looked like someone who had just arrived from far away and the way he kept his eyes wide open made him look very tired. He hadn't introduced himself, so I didn't know who he was.
“Well then, Brigati. Let's start from the accident, shall we? What do you remember?”, Gaudenzi said, firm yet gentle.
“As I already told you at the hospital, I was following those cars when I heard a noise behind me. The last image I remember is the writing on the

jacket. Jennifer had just called me on the phone and I may have been a little absent-minded, but I remember the writing well, as I lay down..."
The stranger intervened: "Have you tried to reach her?"
"Do you mean Jenny?"
"Yes."
"After the accident?"
"Exactly."
"Many times, but now her number doesn't even exist anymore."
"We 'll try to contact her ourselves, write the woman's particulars and phone number on the piece of paper. But why are you convinced that she is involved in all this?"
"Because her... Hey, wait a moment: beg your pardon but who are you?"
I didn't like his attitude and he hadn't even introduced himself. The files I had read terrified me, I was seeing the world through different eyes. I was sure that that man wasn't there to find out who the body in the car was, but for me, to find out what my ties to the case were and what I had uncovered up to that point. Gaudenzi smiled, than gave me a proud stare. He appreciated my rebellion and it was obvious that he couldn't stand that weird individual either. But judging from the latter's behavior in the interrogation room, he had to be a big shot.
"That's nothing you should concern yourself with. Just answer the question." He slammed his hand on the iron table.
"No, fuck that... I'm a witness, no, a victim! I am here to share info and I should be protected, not put through the wringer. I am also here as a journalist, you know? I'm not saying another thing, fuck you. If you insist, I want my lawyer."
The man reacted by promptly grabbing my shirt's lapel. I had walked out of my flat like a hobo: frayed jeans, wrinkly Ramones shirt and Adidas shoes. He lifted me and shouted to my face.
"Listen, Brigati, you don't know who we are up against: it's dangerous people, there's a bunch of massive interests behind this deal. Speak, motherfucker! Who wants to kill you?"
I froze on the spot. The USB drive at home came to mind.
I replied to his violence by untwisting my arm and freeing myself.
"Hey, fuckhead! What do you think you're doing, eh? You tryin' to scare me? You feel all cool because you're behind the barricade, don't you? I'm

done, I've got nothing to say. And if you really, really want the truth, I know less than you do. This is the only truth!"
I slammed the door behind me – they couldn't detain me. My personality was changing, I had never reacted that way. And I had never felt so proud of myself. Adrenaline coursed in my veins like gasoline in a car's engine.
Gaudenzi ran after me and reached me in the corridor, grabbing my right arm.
"I'm sorry, Joe. I wanted you to know that I didn't want it to end like this..."
It was the first time the inspector had ever talked to me in such confidence.

XIII

"From the last time
we had met,
she was devastated: pale and without makeup.
But always well-dressed, of course."

Gaudenzi didn't want to let me go, he vigorously opposed my decision to go home. I was the target of an assassination attempt, he said, and he had to take some necessary – and mandatory – precautions to safeguard my well-being. At least until his investigations would turn up the person pulling the strings. Or prove that no-one else wanted to hurt me and that, consequently, I was out of danger.
I tried to persuade him, night had fallen already by then and I didn't want to lose anymore time. Besides, my killer had died a few hours earlier. Why worry? My real intent was to hurry home and find a better hiding place for the USB drive which I had left for an entire evening under the couch's pillows. My home had already been broken into once, I couldn't risk those precious documents.
The inspector asked me if I wanted to conclude my witness statement on the following day, with just him and not the other man. I refused: I had nothing to add. That whole business was still fishy, I wanted to get a clearer understanding of it myself before spilling the beans.
In the end, he let me go, making me promise that I would call him in case of emergency. He gave me his calling card and had a police car drive me back to my apartment. The same car, he said, would stay parked right outside the building until dawn.
We got to my front door and I approached the agents.
"Thanks for the ride. You wanna come upstairs and have a drink?"
Least I could do to show my gratitude.
"No, thank you. We'll stay down here if you think it's necessary."
I seized the opportunity as I saw it: "No, thank you, as far as I'm concerned, you can go. I don't feel in danger. Unless you have orders..."

The cop at the wheel replied: “It was a touch of courtesy from the chief inspector. He asked us to stay here in case you needed us, but it's not part of our orders, per se.”
“You can go, then.”
“Are you sure about this? It wouldn't cost us anything, we're on patrol anyway.”
It was better not to have them around. I had to be free to go outside in case I wanted to go hide the files related to 'Orange Hands' somewhere else.
“Yes, I'm sure. You go do your job, don't worry...”
“Fine, then... as you wish. Have a nice evening, Brigati.”
I closed the door, waving at them both. The police car quickly steered away while I looked for the keys in my pocket.

The crisp air of the evening made me crave tobacco, so I lit myself a Marlboro as I approached the building.
It was an old-style entrance, with a tall, double-shutter wooden door, into which a smaller door had been carved to be used as pedestrian entrance.
When I smoke, alone and outside my house, I like to observe the world around me. To see the leaves rustled by the wind or the cars wantonly parked on the sidewalk. Even though at that hour of the night, surrounded by silence, they all seemed to follow a strict order of their own.
It was very dark. The avenue's thick trees covered the street lamps, as the municipality had forgone the routine September pruning. I yawned and glanced at the time: 1 AM. I couldn't wait to drop on my bed.
I balanced the cigarette between my thumb and middle finger and flicked it up in a tall parable. Following its glowing trail, I saw it land on the asphalt and give out a burst of little sparks, which soon got lost in the night. I turned around to open the door.
A hand blocked my shoulder.
I hadn't heard anything come up behind me.
I turned around, fearing the worst: adrenaline coursed in my veins. Right when I'd turned down the police's protection.
Luckily, it was Jenny, alone and with a gloomy expression.
From the last time we had met, she was devastated: pale and without makeup. Always well-dressed, of course, with a form-fitting, patterned

beige dress. She was wearing flats, which made her look shorter than usual.
Her hair was tied up in a dark, elegant ponytail. Her pale skin made her flushed cheeks stand out, along with, as I noticed for the first time, a beauty mark to the right of her upper lip. A coquettish touch to her femininity. Then again, it was the first time I looked at her from up close. Her eyes were dark and red-streaked, it was obvious that she had just cried.
“Hey, Jenny... Where'd you vanish off to? I feared you...”
“Hi Joe, please follow me. I have to talk to you and I don't have much time.”
She grabbed my right hand, jerking me away. I tried to break free.
“Wait a second, you disappear from the face of the earth and then drop here and ask me to follow you without an explanation? How's that for fair?”
Her eyes said enough. She was terrified.
“I know, Joe, trust me. If I didn't have a good reason to be here, I wouldn't be here. I know I have things to explain to you and that is why I need you to come with me to a safe place.”
“But then... You are up to date with...”
“Yes, Joe. And it wasn't supposed to pan out that way. I'm sorry, but let's not talk about it outside.”
“So you're the one behind all this?”
“Follow me and you'll understand.”
I couldn't refuse. The thought of the USB drive worried me, but I had to go with her.
We got inside her car, her black Porsche Cayman parked close by. The engine's deep roar had a sinister echo in the avenue's nocturnal silence. We rode off.
“I am sorry, Joe. I apologize, with all my heart.”
Her voice wavered. “You were only supposed to write that godforsaken biography, that was all. It wasn't supposed to go like that, fuck it... I wasn't...”
I stared at her, curious. She gave me a worried look and went back to focusing on the street.
“Jenny, what the hell is happening?”
She opened the glove compartment and handed me a gun:

"Keep it. It may come in useful."
I made a face.
"What?!? Are you fucking mad? I'm not touching that weapon, what if they get my fingerprints on it... I don't even know where it comes from, maybe they used it for a robbery or what have you..."
"It's mine, trust me. I have a carry license."
"Jenny, let me say it again: no!"
"As you wish, but do know that we're in a hell of a mess."
"If I knew about it, I could make my choice accordingly... don't you think?"
My words got a smile out of her. Some trace of serenity on her face as dark as the night. Which only made her look all the more ethereal and angelic.
"Where are we headed?"
"My place. I need to give you some documents and I cannot wait anymore."
"What kind of documents?"
"About the biography."
And that was the end of that conversation.
In the silence of the night, Milan went by my eyes, lit up by its cast iron street lamps. The deserted historic centre was as beautiful as a charming middle-aged lady. Its monuments were like jewels, highlighting its delicate features.
Jenny wasn't in a speaking mood and I decided not to press the matter. I gathered that she didn't know anything about the 'Orange Hands' files in my possession or she would have mentioned them. But then, what mess was she talking about?
It was two in the morning when we came to an underground parking lot in the heart of Milan, close to Via Montenapoleone street. The car park's exit stairs led us to the corner of Via Adalberto Catena street and Corso Matteotti avenue. Her flat was right on the street corner, above a men's fashion store where the streets' colonnades meet.
Jenny lived in the middle of the city centre, in a beautiful building dated beginning of the 20th century: luxurious to say the least.
We walked inside the entrance door and up four pink marble steps with a red carpet, making our way to the elevator.

“Paolo got this for me”, Jenny told me as she pushed the second floor button. The elevator was an old, noisy thing, all wood and glass. Outside the cabin, the wrought-iron meshes slowly went past us, a stark contrast with the marbly whiteness of the surrounding stairs.
“What, the elevator?”
She smiled. I pressed on.
“Paolo who?”
“You'll understand soon enough.”
The landing was spacious, hosting three wooden doors with their typical brass doorbells. The walls were an elegant pale pink.
She opened the middle door and went inside, with me in tow. The apartment was tasteful, adorned with elegant stucco ceilings, dark parquet flooring, pastel-colored walls and assorted vintage furniture.
A mirror set in a gold frame dominated one of the living room's walls; under it were the Milord-style sofa and two armchairs in the same vein.
A shiny steel modern kitchen could be seen nearby, while on the left a door led to the bedrooms. On the opposite side of the room, a carved stone fireplace and a 56" TV screen. Magnificent.
She sat on the white sofa, leaning on its purple pillows. I followed her, careful not to trip on the Persian rug. A laptop was running on a crystal table. She lowered her gaze and, falling prey to discouragement, brought her hands to her face, to cover her eyes.
I patted her left shoulder in an attempt to cheer her up. She stared at me and broke into tears.
“Paolo broke up with me. He says I would risk my life if I stayed by his side... I must not talk to him anymore, but I can't...”
“Jenny, please, explain yourself: who are you talking about?”
“The main character in your book: Paolo Iorio.”
I finally had a name and surname, but that certainly wasn't the way I would have liked to find out.
“It's just that it's all my fault that we're up to our necks in shit...”
I couldn't parse her last sentence. I tried to make a deeper connection and an idea sparked in my mind.
“Jenny, don't tell me this is about 'Orange Hands'...”
She looked up, petrified. Even the tears that were flowing from here eyes seemed to stop at once.

“And how comes you know about that?”
“I can deduce it, Jenny, I'm still a journalist after all...”
She stared at me in terror, this last assertion of mine had knocked her out.
“Maybe it's time for me to start explaining myself, starting from the beginning this time...”
My hunch was right.
But many pieces of that complex, sprawling puzzle were still missing.
Jenny imagined that it would be a long night, ora rather, morning, as the hour was already close to dawn. She walked up to a corner cupboard, still early twentieth century, all floreal inlays. I think it was Florentine craftsmanship – antiques are not my forte, but those pale wooden lilies were unmistakable.
She opened a bottle of Ballantine's 30 years old, poured two fingers of that marvelous blended scotch whisky in two glasses and offered me one of them with a fierce gaze. She was certain that I would not pull back, especially not after that day. A day which, by the way, still had not come to an end.
It was still missing its linchpin, the event that had led to the disasters of those days and to Jennifer's devastating anguish.

XIV

"My father's name was
Francisco Blasquez. He was a chemist.
Mostly involved in crop protection products.
Our country bases a big chunk
of its economy on agriculture."

Her words came out in a flood, she couldn't stop: she had to talk, she wanted to tell me what was happening and how she was involved.
I could see from the very first day we met that something was wrong in her soul. She felt guilty for her past, one could see it clearly by carefully observing her sad, beautiful yet lifeless eyes. She was torn in the very depths of her heart, which was a reason why I felt close to her. I was coming out of a difficult time in my life, struggling with depression, while she may have just come out of one. Or so I thought, even though now someone, or something, had reopened old, healed-over wounds.
Jenny started to talk and her face contorted into a suffering grimace. Possibly due to the whisky slowly dripping into her esophagus.
"My father's name was Francisco Blasquez. He was a chemist. Mostly involved in crop protection products. Our country bases a big chunk of its economy on agriculture. Back then, before the golpe in 1976, cultivating the land was the most valuable asset. My father thought that adding chemistry to agriculture would be a good place to start... It caused his ruin."
"What do you mean?"
"He came from a rich family, his father traded agri-food goods with Spain. He could do anything. But he fixated on one thing: he wanted to become famous, to invent a compound that could change the fate of humankind... for the better, obviously."
Jenny paused. She picked a paper handkerchief from an engraved silver box in the middle of the small table. She tried to talk again, with effort, as she delicately wiped the tears from her eyes.

“He had barely finished his studies, this was at the end of the Fifties. He was working for a chemical company in Buenos Aires when he was contacted by Major Pedro Eugenio Aramburu's loyalists. His university thesis was focused on the analysis of a chemical compound that bonded dichlorophenoxyacetic acid with trichlorophenoxyacetic acid. These herbicides were already being developed for agricultural use in the Forties, but his new way of synthesizing them doubled their effectiveness.”

“A great stroke of intuition.”

“True, his studies made a splash. But then the government decided to use his discoveries for war, I don't know the details.”

Her voice cracked in her throat, as if someone were trying to strangle her.

“He didn't want that. He opposed that plan with all his strength and even risked getting killed over it. Everything crashed down in 1962, when president Frondizi was accused of giving in to Peronist pressures. In those days, the army deposed the government and elected President of the Senate José Marìa Guido.”

“What happened then?”

“His father, my grandfather, forced him to flee by getting him a one-way ticket to the USA. It was yet another drastic action for his son's sake, after having already freed him twice from the military prison where he had been tortured for days on end. They wanted to understand how to recreate that chemical process at all costs, but he held onto his secrets even as he risked his death.”

She walked to a walnut cupboard by the apartment's entrance. She opened the first drawer and picked up a photo album to show it to me.

“That's them, in their last picture taken together. He is my grandfather, whom I never met. And this is my father before he fled.” She pointed at the figures, an air of sadness over her. Francisco was a handsome man. He was tall and dark and had an intense look, unmistakable even though the photo was in black and white.

“Your grandfather?”

“He lost everything. His company, his house, his son, whom he obviously never saw again. He died a few months after having all his assets expropriated, they found him stabbed to death in a park in Buenos Aires. I think the military killed him. My grandmother, on the other hand, died

in childbirth, as she brought into the world Francischito, as they called him back then."
She paused for a moment. "My father escaped along with his fiancée, they crossed the Chilean border by car and then got on a plane to the States. She sadly died shortly afterwards, having fallen ill during the harsh journey that led them to San Francisco hidden among corn containers. My father, alone and desperate, worked as a kitchen hand until the American government granted him citizenship as a political refugee. His name was well-known, so he soon found a good place at a chemical company with a focus on agriculture: MonteForte Company."
Jenny paled as she uttered that name. She had to stop and take a deep breath.
"It looked like the beginning of a happy life, of his rebirth. He talked to his bosses about his research in Argentina and they convinced him to put it all into practice in their labs. He managed to earn a lot of money very quickly, and in less then two years he already bought a villa in Kansas City, Missouri, where MonteForte was located."
Jenny was opening up, it was possibly the first time she talked about her past with someone and, most importantly, in that way. She leafed through the photo albums, showing me serene places from her childhood along with the sources of the demons of her past.
"I lived in Kansas City for the first seventeen years of my life, then moved to Buenos Aires until I came of age. My father died and I went to live with uncle Jorge, the only still-living member of my father's family. But I didn't feel free, I suffered for it. Everything reminded me of my past, of my origins. I needed to turn over a new leaf and find myself. So I took advantage of a fashion model casting to leave for Milan. I took up modeling to pay for my studies: Law at the Cattolica university."
"Law? What about design?"
"Joe, that's all a façade, that studio was a front for other activities..."
My face dropped. I suspected it, but I also feared that I would come to learn of worrying information that up to that moment had been hidden from me.
"What happened to your father?"

"The weight of his past took its toll on him. It killed him slowly from the inside, a terrifying agony in front of my eyes... I was powerless, I saw him suffer and then one day..."
Jennifer broke into tears. I tried to hug her, but she refused, wriggling away from the embrace: she only wanted to talk and to explain herself. I looked at her in the eyes and she smiled, a forced expression meant only to reassure me.
"I'll manage, I'll manage... don't worry, I'm strong... as I was saying, one day we found him in the garage, dead. I was only 16 at the time. He died of a heart attack, I think, you say *crepacuore* here in Italy, *heartbreak*, don't you?"
"I think so..."
"My mother found him, she screamed and I rushed over: he was lying on his belly. The doctors said his heart gave up. In those days he was more worried than usual, he feared for his life."
"What was the reason behind all this anguish?"
Jenny showed me a picture of her mother: Gabriella Pedro Blasquez. She had met her father in the Eighties, she was a young researcher of Spanish origins – Spanish father, Colombian mother – born and raised in New York, where she still had some distant relatives.
She had always wanted to be a lab researcher and it was between phials and microscopes, in Missouri, that she found Francisco's love. They married early. Their relationship was deep, possibly more intellectual than physical. There were almost twenty-five years between them, but they didn't feel them. She left her job as soon as she was pregnant with Jennifer: their only daughter, whom her husband had so desired.
Then, one day, Gabriella was diagnosed with lung cancer. "My father was certain that it was a result of her job at MonteForte, he felt terribly guilty... He was the one who hired her, he was the one she had her first interview with..."
"That's when your dad's slow decline began, right?"
"Right... *El rematar*! The finishing blow! He had suffered for years. For my grandfather, who died for his sake. But mostly, he felt the crushing weight of MonteForte Company's actions in the Sixties, in Vietnam... that was the hardest blow to his soul. He felt the weight of billions of victims:

instead of saving the world with his intuitions, he had compromised its habitat and the health of its inhabitants."

It was a terrible tale. And she told it with an icy phlegm: her words bounced like lightning in my mind.

After hiring Francisco Blasquez in Kansas City, MonteForte Company tricked him into giving up his discoveries. They swore that those pesticides would never be used for military ends and he believed them, in a time where a handshake was worth more than a contract. But signing the transfer of his rights to the multinational company was all they needed to take him out. He should have seen it coming, but his candid soul had led him to trust them anyway.

Along with him, they developed the synthesis of dichlorophenoxyacetic acid (2,4-D) and of trichlorophenoxyacetic acid (2,4,5-T). It wasn't their common synthesis, nor the one he had discovered in Argentina a few years earlier, but rather a solution with thrice the power. Why? To increase its effectiveness. According Blasquez's bosses, all that work was aimed at speeding up their effect, nothing more.

"He was led on by the dream of helping American agriculture, but the company's real plans were very different..."

Military plans, specifically, which ignored Francisco's own requests. His voice was powerless by then. Once the creator and executor of that damned project, he was not its censor anymore.

"He couldn't understand why the army would be so interested in it, in Argentina first, then in the States."

It was pointless to wonder. Maybe better not to know it altogether.

"It was the birth of the Vietnam war's dreaded AGENT ORANGE. He was the one who created it, in those very laboratories in Missouri. Can you imagine the burden he carried?"

She uttered that name with such vehemence that I felt an odd sensation on my skin: not the usual shivers, rather a glacial cold. As if all the blood in my body had frozen over, while in those few seconds, my mind had already pictured a possible involvement of 'Orange Hands' in that whole mess.

Morning had come, but exhaustion had washed away with the darkness.

"What was it for? Why do you mention victims?"

"The officially stated military use was that the defoliant would remove the leaves from the trees and thus eliminate the Viet Congs' cover. Other herbicides were used by the US Army during the same period, in varying quantities, all with the same goal. They were color-coded, mostly to easily tell them apart. They were all safe for the population, except for Agent Orange..."
"Why?"
And here came the question that no-one, in their entire life, would want to answer to.
"Are you sure you want to know, Joe? This is all classified, not even the army's top brass know what I am about to tell you."
I was already neck-deep in that rotten bog. I nodded. I wanted to know the truth and I couldn't stop anymore.
"The product itself is a colorless liquid, it takes its name from the stripes painted on the barrels it was stocked in. They had to keep it separate from the others, but not due to its use. Do you know the real reason why? It was deadly and they knew it right off the bat. But the government always denied everything."
"How can you be so sure?"
She stared at me and smiled. "Care to explain why 2,4-D and 2,4,5-T are still used to this day as effective herbicides? Those are not harmful to people, trust me..."
"What is, then?"
"My father told me shortly before he died. He needed to open up to someone, he was very scared and carried a heavy burden on his conscience... He thought they wanted to kill him because he knew. Many groups of veterans and sick people were starting to sue the manufacturers as well as the American government. He was an important witness. I am certain that he was killed, but I will never be able to prove it..."
"Okay, but what did he tell you before he died?"
"My father was threatened, they forced him to mix into the synthesis some highly toxic dioxins. It was the army's idea so they could more hastily exterminate the fighting populations of communist Vietnam. Afterwards, as the side effects manifested themselves, they claimed that the government didn't know about it, that they couldn't know... they blamed

the chemical and its producers. But they knew everything, it was their plan, the rest is bullshit..."
She was furious. She would have killed with her own bare hands the true responsible for her father's death, her father who had been murdered twice, morally first, then physically, by the same nation that had saved him from Argentinian persecution.
"This is why I decided to leave the States and go back to South America after his death. I could have flown to New York, to my mother's relatives, but I was disgusted by the USA. I wanted to flee: I was scared!"
Jenny got up and pushed aside an elegant and heavy ash wood folding desk, revealing a built-in wall safe. She opened it by punching four numbers on its panel and took a pile of yellow folders from it.
"As he told me the whole story, he left me the reports from MonteForte's internal investigations. Look... It's all there!
Documents compiled through years of research as well as top secret material that her father kept in his safe before he died. All stolen from the offices of the company he used to work for and from Missouri's military archives, thanks to compliant executives of the American government.
"As he gave me these papers, I found out that my father had been one of the founders of the 'Orange Hands' group, which you mentioned earlier... They are a secret, non-violent organization, which strives to stop the dirty political and economic interests that are making the international scientific and medical community rot from the inside."
"I wouldn't exactly call the non-violent..." I smiled.
I could still see that dismembered corpse abandoned in the dark SUV.
"What do you mean by that, Joe?"
She looked at the time and froze.
"Fuck, we've got to move. All this has nothing to do with your job."
I nodded, but I had to explain that last bit to her, at least.
"Fine, but wait! Jenny, they killed a man today. And right by the body, they found the symbol of an orange hand... I don't think it's accidental, especially considering that the victim tried to run me over a few days ago, while I was tailing you..."
"Tailing whom?"
"You, in front of your office. You went outside with two black Mercedes as your security detail, remember?"

She made a face and shook her head.
“Look, that wasn't me... I was in San Francisco, pointlessly trying to talk to Paolo. That was the reason behind my disappearance. I also disabled my phone and bought a new SIM card to avoid being traced.”
Jenny spoke again.
“And anyway, I really don't think the homicide can be attributed to 'Orange Hands'. True, death is contemplated in exceptional cases, but they have to be truly exceptional. Until now, in all these years spent underground, nothing of the sort has ever happened...”
But then, who did I tail?

XV

*"Knowledge is our creed,
the purest, most scientific
knowledge possible. This is
the organization's real goal."*

7:10 in the morning. We had spent the last remnants of the night talking about her father. That whole international affair was overwhelmingly dramatic. Jennifer was exhausted and so was I. We decided to put an end to our conversation for the time being and go back to it on the following day, or at least after a good sleep.

"I should probably go back home, Jenny, we're both tired... But I want to ask you one thing. Who is Orange Hands' founder? You mentioned your father and other people, but..."

She interrupted me, neglecting my question.

"I need to talk to you about Paolo and the Front first..."

"Okay. Fine."

Her gaze was blank. Eventually, she decided to help me out and add some more details.

"One of its fundamental principles is anonymity. Each member is sure that they won't be ratted out, because members do not know each other. Each member only confers with the person who introduced them to the group. The 'introductor' trust the capability of the 'introduced' and vice versa. It's a closed pyramidal structure."

I knew about that already, but I didn't want to show my hand. I let her talk.

"Each geographical area is handled by a 'Chapter': European, North American, South American, Asian, Oceanian, African. Those who lead these areas can only interact with their respective 'introduced' members, who therefore act as 'Vice Chapter'. They, in turn, command a 'Capo', for *capo decina*, head of ten. Each State is a *decina*, Joe, just look at these papers and you'll understand..."

She showed me diagrams that explained the whole thing, but her tale was detailed already, her structural analysis clear.
“Each 'Vice Capo' commands a 'Linchpin', who in turn chooses the first of the ten 'Elected' who will then proceed to great the national work detail.”
Jenny stopped to double-check that she hadn't forgotten any step of that complex chain.
“Telling you all this is a huge risk for me, but it is necessary if you are to understand what is going on.”
“It's an underground world”, I said.
“*Correcto*, Joe... a veritable spider's web, whose members are all above suspicion, joined together to defend the human race's essential rights. Such as health.”
That sounded a little sinister. “What do you mean?”
“Our society is based on economic power. People who possess this power can destroy or subjugate you. Our creed, on the other hand, is knowledge, the purest, most scientific knowledge possible. This is 'Orange Hands'' real goal: to collect as much information as possible, about everyone and everything. Information is our only weapon that can allow us to fight from the inside the cancer that is killing our society, to save us from this indirect dictatorship that *is* slowly killing us, just like it slowly killed my father.”
I was flabbergasted. The end goal was noble, but it didn't all add up, while other details were downright distressing.
“But who is collecting all this information?”
“I have already told you too much, Joe. I can't tell you who stands above the 'First Chapter'.”
“But Jenny, aren't you worried? This thing is too dangerous, it can destroy our world! Spying on people, violating their privacy...2
“Why, do you really think they don't do the same with us? Thanks to social networks, they know everything about everyone! And they're never going to stop... And we even give them the chance to keep digging deeper into our lives by adding more and more data to our online profiles...”
I flinched. I didn't want to listen to another word.
I had always hated all the various social media platforms, because they all end up preventing you from minding your own business. Those revelations certainly weren't changing my mind.

"What about that scandal a while ago, about the Vatican's documents? Vatican-leaks is your doing, then, I understand..."
"Don't press it, Joe. I am risking too much already. Believe what you will, but don't ask me a thing."
"What's gonna happen now?"
"Up until now, the organization focused on spreading its web and collecting information, creating an enormous database from nothing and protecting it with an uncrackable encryption system. Then... then the inevitable will happen. Knowledge will reign supreme, for everyone's greater good. The true revolution hasn't begun yet, Joe..."
Her eyes shone. Her father's death must have shaken her to the point of blinding her to the terrible risks of such a subterranean lodge.
"What are you talking about?"
"I do not know. Nobody knows, as I told you, secrecy is the basis of this huge common project. And even if I knew, I couldn't tell you..."
"I'm sorry Jenny, but what is your role in all of this?"
"I am a First Elected."
"Your 'introductor'? Your father, I suppose?"
"I took his place. He joined the organization as he lost faith in the institutions. The same that were supposed to protect him. He thought that the United States were a free country, but he was wrong... He thought that money could save him from pain, but he was wrong..."
I stopped her: "Wait, wasn't he one of the organization's founders?"
"He was one of the first to join... 'Orange Hands' was created by members of the scientific community and then quickly spread to all other sectors. At any rate, my 'introductor' assigned me a task a while ago: I was to investigate the agricultural companies owned by MonteForte in Argentina. That task, which required a year of work, brought me to Italy..."
This latest development piqued my curiosity and I had to ask:
"How does it work, when you have to travel? Do you change contact?"
"Same as always. Let me remind you that the only person you can talk to is your 'introductor'. Your contact doesn't change, even if you are thousands of miles away from home. And they, in turn, get their orders from above, so..."
"And if they die?"

"You take their place, and obviously answer to their superior, the godfather of your deceased 'introductor'. And then you pick someone else that will take your old position, your new 'introduced'."
Jenny went back to her tale, almost annoyed by my questions. But I was still a journalist, after all.
"Nowadays, MonteForte is a multinational company focusing on agricultural biotechnology, but in 1923 it bought a British pharmaceutical firm, FourStreet Chemical Ltd in Birmingham, where it started producing vanillin and then aspirin. In the Thirties, it expanded and became a leader in the production of generic drugs in Europe."
"What about now? Does it still exist?"
"Of course! It grew ever more powerful as time went by, even though it closed down its British plant. Even without its production, in its sector it is still one of the ten most important companies worldwide. Doesn't it sound weird to you, Joe?"
Actually, yes. I nodded without a word.
"That's what I imagined. Me too. Let's say that it prefers the shadows to the limelight and that it indirectly controls, on MonteForte's behalf, the shares of a swarm of SMEs worldwide, both pharmaceutical companies and research labs. One of these is Iorio Farmaceutici in Bresso."
Now everything was falling into place. I swiftly added: "And you fell in love with Paolo, the owner..."
"That wasn't supposed to happen, I volunteered to be hired by that design studio he owns. They design the packaging of the products the company puts on the market: blister packs, boxes and more. And the inevitable happened, we fell in love... I found a real, hard man in him, but also someone who was as good as my father... He isn't part of all that shit we're facing now..."
The puzzle looked complete. But what did I have to do with all of that, why trap me? My life had been uprooted by a narcissistic entrepreneur. His vanity almost cost me my life.
"What about me?"
"You, Joe, you were only meant to write his biography. Andrea knew me as a hostess, I called him to find me a writer, like Paolo asked... and so I came to you. That's all..."
"But why?"

"It was his idea..."
I knew it. My usual bad luck. I gave an annoyed smile, as if I wanted to thank him.
"I thought it was just a whim at first, but then I understood that to him, narrating his life was a defensive measure... They want to kill him, which is why he pushed me away."
"You don't think that...", I tried my luck again. The corpse in the SUV showed how the orange lodge wasn't really that unaccustomed to violence.
"No, Joe... that's impossible. He doesn't know I'm part of 'Orange Hands', he isn't even aware of the name, nor of the organization. It's not us who are trying to kill him, I am sure of this."
"Why a biography, then?"
"Telling his life as a way of saving himself... Showing that he is a good person, and leaving a message fo posterity even if anything were to happen to him."
"Meaning?"
"Don't you worry. You'll understand everything by reading his notes: here they are."
Jenny turned toward the black laptop on the crystal table, pulled it closer and fiddled with the keyboard. She eventually unmounted an USB drive and gave it to me.
"So you won't have to bombard me with phone calls anymore, there are also audio files...", she said, finally smiling. It was like walking in the middle of a desert and seeing a peaceful oasis from afar. I was shocked and shaken.
"I'll leave you the keys to my car: I'm not gonna need it for a while anyway. I'll be leaving for Argentina tomorrow, hiding at my uncle's place as a precaution. It's better that I disappear for a while. I want you to hold onto these documents for me, my father's files need to remain here in Italy, protected. You are a stranger to me..."
That last sentence stung, I was hoping I would be more than that to her. But I understood Jennifer's intent. She feared she would be followed and she couldn't afford to be caught by airport security carrying these files in her bag. And leaving them in an empty house wasn't an option either, no matter how well-hidden the safe could be.

I tried to refuse anyway, but I couldn't. She gave me a bag with her father's secret documents and the USB drive with the notes on Paolo Iorio's life, by now decidedly ancillary to everything else. She gave me everything in front of her apartment's entrance door, with a melancholic smile.
“Have a safe journey then... take care...”
“I know how to take care of myself, Joe, but you... watch your back... I'll keep in touch, don't worry...”
We hugged. Even though I would have wanted something more. I took the stairs down to stretch my legs and happily noticed how lively and sparkling the city was at that hour, just like fresh morning air. Cars, buses and people were starting to cross Milan in all directions, busy with school, work, shopping.
Everything was as normal.
And no-one could imagine what was about to happen.

In the following pages: the organization's vertical and international scheme.

'Orange Hands Science Confraternity'
Vertical structure

European *(or African, Asian etc…)* Chapter
|
Vice Chapter
Capo Decina
|
Decina *(Italy or other Country)*
Vice Decina
Linchpin
|
First Elected
|
Second Elected
|
Third Elected
|
Fourth Elected
|
Fifth Elected
|
Sixth Elected
|
Seventh Elected
|
Eighth Elected
|
Ninth Elected
|
Tenth Elected

'Orange Hands Science Confraternity'
International structure

African Chapter

Vice Chapter
Capo Decina
Decina (Country)

-

European Chapter

Vice Chapter
Capo Decina
Decina (Country)

North American Chapter

Vice Chapter
Capo Decina
Decina (Country)

South American Chapter

Vice Chapter
Capo Decina
Decina (Country)

Oceanian Chapter

Vice Chapter
Capo Decina
Decina (country)

Asian Chapter

Vice Chapter
Capo Decina
Decina (country)

XVI

"It is possible that I had already seen
victims during the war,
but that I erroneously thought them suffering
from spina bifida
or something like that."

Driving a Porsche Cayman was a real joy. Accustomed as I was to the seat of my Vespa, the sporty pace of a custom-built car was a whole other experience. Pure pleasure. I once had the chance to try a Ferrari, some time earlier, with a friend of mine and his girlfriend. The car was great, too bad its owner – who had lent it to us for the occasion – was a real imbecile. Your typical man without a weight, more interested in appearances than in anything with substance. Those were the days when I hung out with the glossy world of Milan's VIPs. Bad times. For that reason, I always preferred the fresh air offered by a motorbike to a car's cabin. I didn't want to be one of them. Okay, it was also because of money.

Milan is beautiful early in the morning, even though it is also chaotic. I was starting to love it and also to get myself accustomed to those clerk-like hours, though in this case I hadn't even slept. I could have maybe done without all those youngsters struggling to catch their trams and buses. Youths with an uncertain future, running in frenzied swarms and invading the streets with no respect for road safety.

I was dead tired, all I wanted was to drop on my bed and stop thinking, I wanted to turn off my brain. That avalanche of news had short-circuited me. I felt beaten and whipped like a strawberry in a barman's mixer, ready to be served in a frozen caipirinha as a red puree.

I parked Jenny's car away from home and thus avoided leaving an easy trail for anyone who might have tried to tail her or me. Truth be told,

there was no suspicious car behind me. I checked, systematically, every minute I checked the rear mirror. I had turned paranoid.
With all the documents I had on me, I'd better be careful.
I turned the key inside my front door, opened it and threw myself on the bed with my clothes still on.
Finally, peace.

2:30 PM, the phone on my nightstand started to dance by my left ear. Its vibrating ringtone made it move on the crystal surface as if it were convulsing. Even my iPhone was awake, so I decided to follow suit, opening my eyes and going back to my regular vital functions.
A quick and, most importantly, frozen shower woke me up completely. It was followed by a cup of black coffee, scrambled eggs and bacon. I had to get my energies back, my plan was to study Paolo Iorio's files and go back to mashing my laptop's keys. My promise to Jenny, that I would go back to writing her beloved's biography, was too important: to me, my word is paramount, even though Francisco's documents, her father's, intrigued me more. I couldn't get them out of my mind. I hesitated, should I look at them or not? Who would have even known? So I prepared my work station in the living room: Mac running, files at hand and second cup of scorching hot coffee in front of me. Cigarettes, of course, weren't lacking either, by the keyboard along with the white ceramic ashtray. I got the USB drive back from under the couch's pillows, put it on the table and started going through Paolo's folders. But my head was throbbing, I was tired to the bone, and I really didn't feel like working.
Besides, looking at the computer screen burned my eyes, already strained by scarce, restless sleep. I turned everything off and thought about the documents. I gave in.
I jumped up and went back to my bedroom. I opened the leather bag I had abandoned earlier in the morning and went through Francisco Blasquez's documents. I opened the zip and stuck my nose inside. The bag contained many stacked yellow folders, a little ruined by the passing of time. They were mostly confidential US Government

documents, and who knows how they had been smuggled. There was also a top secret folder. Truly an interesting discovery.
So I ended up losing myself in a parallel world.
After a few minutes spent reading those files, I could feel the weight that Jenny's father had carried in his heart. All the files in my possession were never divulged, but they depicted an alternate truth to the one the media fed us throughout the last decades of the twentieth century. The topic? The Vietnam War. Terrible news, massacres, always covered up through crass lies. With these documents, I could have ridiculed and brought to their knees the entire American military and political system. In one fell swoop. I could have brought to light the suffering of thousands of Vietnamese children who were born and raised without a future.
I could see why Jennifer was scared, the risk was enormous: strolling about with these documents in her purse would have alerted the entire US intelligence. This, on the assumption that they were not, in fact, already after her and most of all after the papers.
All I could be sure of was that Agent Orange had destroyed part of Vietnam and of its civilians. How that went down, however, was not clear. Sure, rumors abounded, the same rumors that sometimes resurfaced to shake the apparent calm that covered that black page in American history.
The accusations? That no-one ever tried to stop that silent genocide. Word had it that in order to win, the Americans used bacteriological weapons banned by the international treaties. And did so by camouflaging them as herbicides. Besides, once it became clear that they would lose the war, they increased the doses out of sheer revenge. All this was hidden from the public eye by banal excuses: “We didn't know Agent Orange was poisonous, sorry”. At least this was the official post-war comment.
A hard sell for those almost five millions of men and women who had fallen gravely ill because they were 'purportedly present during the spraying of approximately 2,6 million gallons of herbicide'. Purportedly – and with vague numbers – because the American government never released those data. It was all supposition, data

gathered by journalists on the field and by the Vietnamese government asking for a refund for the material, non-material and environmental damage sustained.
I had the proof in my hands. As I leafed through those documents, I realized the burden I had accepted. I would dot the i's and cross the t's of a piece of history that had been silenced by painting stars-and-striped angel faces on devils' bodies.
I could tell the gallons of sprayed products, there were pictures of the stored barrels and, most importantly, a map of all the routes of the airplanes and helicopters of the US Army. No patch of land was spared. We're talking 4,027,540.69 gallons.
Those highly toxic dioxins were responsible for an array of illnesses and birth defects in the Vietnamese population. Agent Orange, as Francisco synthetized it in his lab, unfortunately presented carcinogenic properties that proved to be most harmful to women. It was teratogenic, which meant that it could cause monstrous mutations in fetuses. Among the most common were harelip, cardiac and ambulatory defects, crippled limbs, gigantism. Truly a disaster.
It was a miracle that Jenny was born a healthy child, considering how her father had worked with the product for years and that even her mother, years later, had worked on a less powerful synthesis of the same chemical.
That happened because even though the product was withdrawn from the market in 1971 – with the end of the war in Vietnam – MonteForte Company kept on working on it, in secret, under request from the American government as a possible evolved bacteriological weapon. Lab safety luckily helped on that front.
I was speechless. As I anxiously turned those pages I noticed another folder, with a rusty paper clip attaching a picture to a soldier's file.
He was a pleasant looking lad, 6.4" according to his file, blond, his eyes probably light. The black and white picture didn't do him justice.
Attached was the transcript of an interview held by the American military secret service. It was the first in a very long list of interrogations featuring that very soldier: officer Benjamin Schroder, head of logistics for Agent Orange, then twenty-six years old.

MILITARY INTELLIGENCE U.S. ARMY
Classified interrogation, denomination:

'AGENT ORANGE – SIDE EFFECTS'

This document is classified and shall be kept in the National Military archives until further notice.

INTERROGATION TRANSCRIPT – February 21st, 1972

Military Secret Service Agent: Identify yourself.
Questioned: My name is Benjamin Schroder, captain of the US Army, decorated for valor.
A: What was your role in Vietnam?
I: I was responsible for the logistics and storage of highly toxic materials and bacteriological weapons in Saigon.
A: Was Agent Orange one of these materials?
I: Absolutely, yes. As well as other substances, such as napalm and...
A: Do not digress. Just answer the question.
I: Yes, sir. Yes, Agent Orange was one of them.
A: What information was relayed to you about that product?
I: It was to be handled and stored with great care. The chemical can kill, cause illnesses and deformities. It is an incredibly powerful poison that was not to leak from its barrels.
A: What was the procedure?
I: The barrels were delivered to us via ship and cargo planes. They were handled during night time, for security reasons, until they came to our logistic center located by Saigon's airport. There, they were unloaded in restricted sectors, with a fork lift arranging them horizontally and stacking them one upon the other.
A: What happened then?
I: When they needed to be loaded onto the planes and helicopters for the spraying, the barrels were delivered to the respective units. They

were loaded on the vehicles without being opened and connected to the spraying system.
A: Do you know how these systems worked?
I: Yes, sir.
A: Explain it to me.
I: Yes, sir. They were basically suction pipes that were connected to the barrels' receptacle. Through a pumping system, the chemical was carried to the diffusors, which were situated under the helicopters or in the aircrafts' wings.
A: Back to the storing system, then, were your underlings aware of the danger of their task?
I: Absolutely.
A: Where are they now? Did you keep in contact with some of them as you came back from Vietnam?
I: I did, with some of them. But almost all of them are dead.
A: What is your state of health?
I: I suffer from lung cancer. I believe I still have 2-3 months to live.
A: Were you in good health before leaving for the war?
I: Yes, sir.
A: Do you believe that contact with the chemical was the cause of your illness?
I: I do believe so.
A: You believe?
I: I am sure of it, sir.
A: Did some of your fellow soldiers father deformed children?
I: Three, to be precise. All of them assigned to storage and then killed by cancer. Their children are hospitalized in institutions for the gravely ill.
A: Did you talk about it while you were in Vietnam? About the consequences of that chemical compound, I mean.
I: No, we did not. It was forbidden by the Military Police. Those few who did talk about it ended up in military prison or sent to the front lines. They never came back.

Digging further into the file, I noticed an added document which was classified as 'Dangerous file/person'. It was another interview, but most of the names and several lines were covered by a thick black ink. The subject was an army photo-reporter, but his name and role had been omitted.

[...] The soldiers' morale was low. They talked about how the government had shown the same care for the Vietnamese and for their own military, who died because of Agent Orange or went back home to conceive deformed children. [...]

So US soldiers were apparently accidental victims of the compound's spraying.

[...] We should have figured. There were rumors about the mix's lethal effect in 1970 already. One of Saigon's antigovernment's newspapers also published pictures. Back then, the government had already covered it all up by insisting that the symptoms were a consequence of STDs caught from prostitutes. I tried to investigate on the ground, but I found myself barred from entering all orphanages. It seemed that the news were spreading that the American press had to be kept at length – military press especially. On top of that, my superiors wrote me up. Looking into this had been my decision, a choice which certainly didn't fill the commander-in-chief of the US Army's informative system with joy. But I was a journalist first and foremost, and only then a soldier.
In short, I didn't manage to access the children's hospital in Saigon until my return to Vietnam, after the end of the war. [...]

The soldier must have been interrogated after his visit to the war zones as a civilian, a few years after the end of the conflict: the date was erased.
But the worst was yet to come.

[...] I went back to Vietnam a few years later, in order to look for the truth. I worked for an international paper, tXXXXX (omitted), I wasn't in the army anymore. I finally understood. I saw many devastating scenes. The worst one had to be the child who was born without a brain, but the number of deformed young children or dead fetuses was immeasurable. In that time I finally realized that-gained familiarity with the effects of Agent Orange I realized that it was possible that I had already seen its victims during the war, but that I erroneously thought them suffering from spina bifida or something like that. [...]

The interview went on.

[...] Sadly, I, too, developed intestine cancer, one of the possible side effects of Agent Orange according to the government-compiled list that was never shared with the media. I was heavily exposed to the chemical, especially as I flew over the damaged zones on a helicopter. I inhaled quite a lot of that filth. Saigon itself was hit by Agent Orange, as many steel barrels that once contained the herbicide were reused for storing fuel. Agent Orange gets much more reactive when heated. That thing got mixed up with gasoline and puffed out of exhaust pipes, killing trees. We joked about that at the time, because we didn't understand the causes. Only later did we find out about the barrels' origin. Should I get tested now, my blood would still carry it, in high quantities. [..]

It didn't sound like the journalist was being questioned so much as releasing an interview to the military secret service after he quit the army. I was shaken and I wanted to stop. But professional ethics – not

to mention the curiosity that had taken hold of my body – forced me to continue.
I remembered the folder marked 'top secret' and decided to open it.
Inside, all I found were two papers and some hand-written notes. I couldn't figure out whether they belonged to Jenny's father or to some secret agent they were stolen from, in which case they wouldn't belong to the military but rather to the CIA.
The first paper looked like an official document. Scrap that, it was an official document. The Vietnamese State requested compensation, in a somewhat faulty English. I read the date: it was probably shortly before Francisco Blasquez's death. I made my calculations using Jenny's age as a basis.
The President of the Socialist Republic officially asked for compensation and reparation for the victims of that silent massacre, possibly even crueler than the atomic bomb as it didn't just kill the 'living' but also condemned the unborn babies and took their parents away from them with the tumors. I read it.

Our Country does not ask for money in exchange for what Imperialism and human savagery did to us, but we do need it to build places to treat and assist our people. Should you accept our request, every single dollar shall be devolved to hospitals, sanatoriums and compensation for the victims. We trust in the intelligence and generosity of the Obama administration. Should you reject it, we are ready to take the story to all supranational courts and press charges for your war crimes.

The document was signed Nguy□n Minh Tri□t, President of the Socialist Republic of Vietnam.
The other document, being the official response of the American government, was nothing short of embarrassing.

'There sussist no real motives, other than specious accusations, to attribute the use of such a substance to the conduct of the United States beyond reasonable doubt.'

Except the contents of that leather bag proved the very opposite.
I closed the folder and put it back with the others, zipped the bag close and pushed it under the queen bed.
All that was left was for me to close my eyes and rest a while. Those last two days had been something else, I don't think I ever ran into such an amount of classified, nefarious information in my entire journalistic career.
I thought back to the corpse in the car and to Orange Hands. I thought back to Jenny and to her tale.
Lastly, I thought about myself and what would be best for me at that point. Ignoring everything, writing Iorio's biography as if nothing had happened and fuck all that? Or publishing at least a fragment of what I had in my hands, bringing it to light? But Jenny would be crushed by the consequences and I couldn't bring myself to get her into trouble. Were I to talk about either the secret organization or the documents on Agent Orange, she would end up being involved.
I suddenly remembered the attempted murder on my person and Mirko Gaudenzi's words, with the inspector suggesting that I go back to doing the job I was getting paid for and ignore the rest.
I went to the living room to fetch my Mac. I took out Paolo's USB, slipped it into my pocket and went to smoke on the balcony. A breath of fresh air would put some order into the thoughts that were storming through my head.

Picture: Spraying of the chemical compound and storage areas, from classified army files.

Picture: Examples of side effects on Vietnamese children. 150.000 of them showed birth defects.

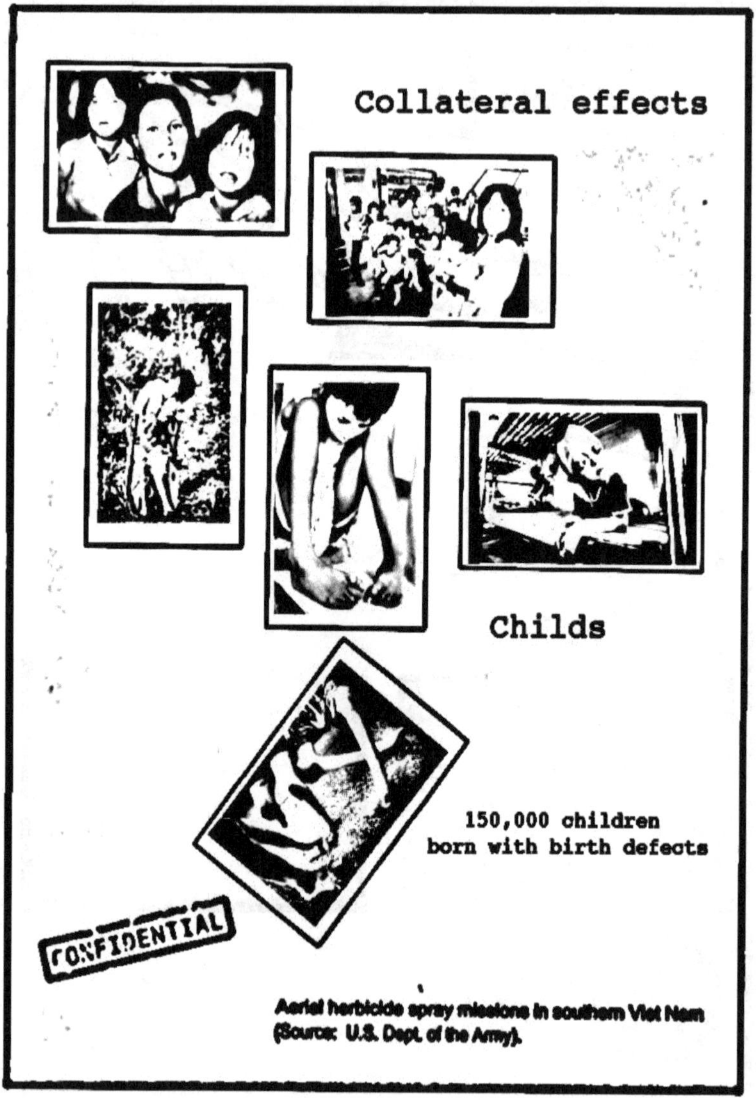

Picture: Map of Vietnam showing the areas where military corps sprayed Agent Orange.

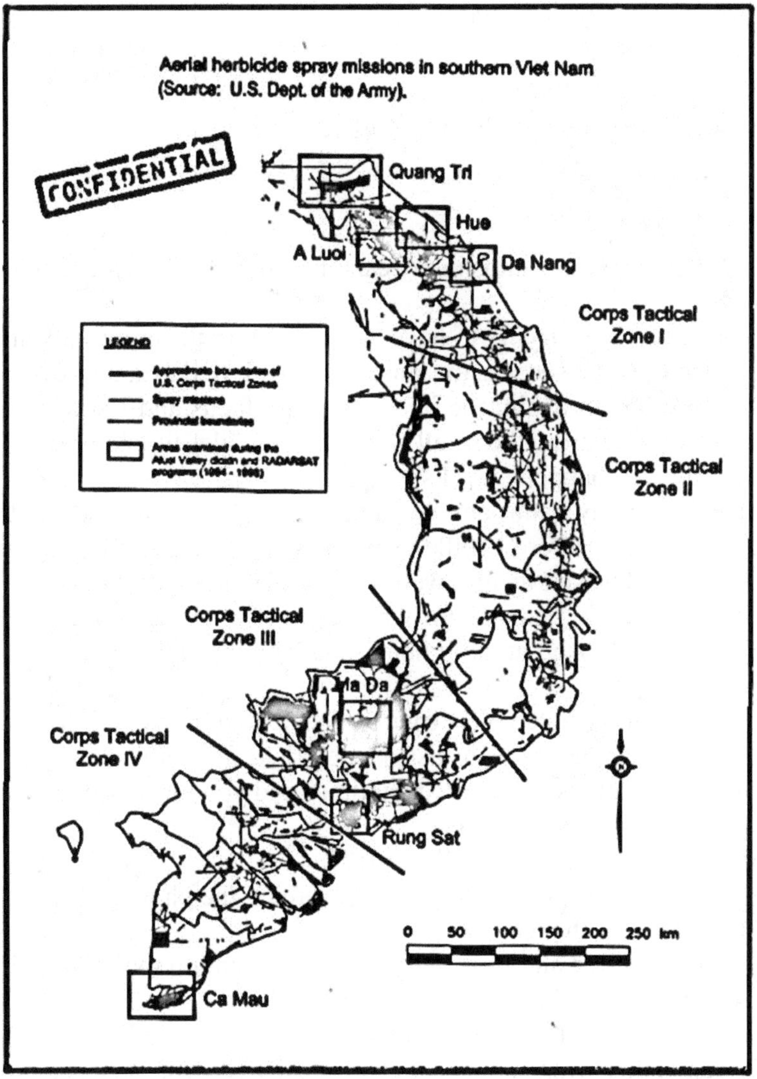

XVII

"I squeeze my eyelids, the image
gets into focus
and I see blood gush out...
drop after drop falling on the floor."

It felt like I had mosquitos in my ears. I was cold, my hands tingled. I felt horrible.
I opened my eyes, trying to have a clear look at the environment around me, but all I could see was the sink. Possibly. I tried to squeeze my eyelids and opened them again: the image got into focus and I saw blood gush out... drop after drop, the small white ceramic tiles turned red.
"What the hell happened?", I shouted.
I was lying in my bathroom, unconscious. Well, unconscious up to a few seconds earlier. Before I could even get up, I felt a sharp pain in the back of my head. I wasn't feeling well. I lay down on the tiles once again, like a lizard on a rock. I passed out again, I don't know for how long, until my phone rang. I looked at the iPhone screen by my right hand, which read: 'Unknown caller'.
I replied with a feeble voice, trying to get a hold of myself: "Hello?"
"Joe, what happened? You disappeared, I heard a noise and then I lost signal... Are you okay? I called ten times and you never replied."
No, actually, nothing was fine.
"Gaudenzi? Why are you calling me?"
"Are you kidding me? I told you: we were on the phone... You called me first. You sound shaken."
More like puzzled and fuzzy-headed, not to mention the sharp pain in the back of my head which had left me breathless.
"I don't understand, I am lying in my bathroom with a head wound and I can't remember what happened... Did I really call you, Inspector?"
"Yes, about an hour ago. And I told you, call me by name, no need for formalities..."

"Sorry..."
"Can you confirm that you are in your home?"
"Yes, I fell in my bathroom. At least I think I did... Or maybe not... Now that I think about it, I think I was assaulted. I remember now! I was on the phone with you, but I can't remember what we were talking about. I heard a noise inside, I was on the balcony, and I went inside..."
"That's what you told me... But who were they? Can't you remember?"
"I don't know, I don't know. It's a blank, I can't even remember why I'm in the bathroom, truth be told!"
"Can you get up?"
"Yes... yes."
"Do you want me to send an ambulance over there?"
"Don't worry, I can handle this... Just give me a minute."
"Stay where you are, I'm coming with a patrol car."
I hung up immediately. All those questions were making my head burn. I had to try and get up.
The last thing I could remember was that I had spoken to Gaudenzi on the phone for a couple of minutes, as I was smoking on the balcony. I had found his business card in my jeans' pocket and for some reason I had felt like calling him.
Then I remembered: I wanted to know whether there were any news on the corpse found inside the Escalade. Actually, I also wanted to tell him something about the orange print found on the black car, just to point him toward the right track. I had decided that I would not talk about the documents nor about the events of the previous two days, but I felt compelled to tell him at least something, especially with how he was bending over backward to help me. He deserved that. Then that noise from inside the apartment had caught my attention. Someone must have broken in by popping the lock, maybe thinking that they would find the house empty. It can't have been much later than 15:30, I was smoking on the balcony. From the window, I saw a shadow move inside the living room and... nothing. From that moment, total blackout.
What could have happened? Good question. No-one would be able to help me. I was the only one who could reobtain that knowledge, by digging deep inside my battered memory, shaken by the blow to the head.

I tried to get up, I was feeling better. I held onto the sink with my arms and noticed the ledge from which the blood was dripping. It was almost chipped, I must have hit it with my head. A heavy blow, considering the damage.
I placed a hand on my neck and felt an excruciating pain – I could feel a deep wound. I looked at the mirror: "Shit..." My Doors shirt was all blood-stained, even ripped up. I slowly fetched bandages and a disinfectant from the bathroom's medicine cabinet and patched myself up.
I kept on going back to the Latin sentence '*Memento Audere Semper*', the one that was printed on the leather jacket of the victim they had found in the outskirts.
But why? I also remembered a logo with a hand... Whatever, I couldn't make any more efforts.
I could hear sirens blaring in the distance. Maybe it was Gaudenzi with his patrol car, as he promised.
I started to look around, searching for possible damages and signs of forced entry. Holding my head tight in my arms, I could feel the bandage start to drip with blood. It flowed beyond the back of my head, drifting toward my neck, while my wound throbbed. It was the disinfectant's effect.
I had to his the USB drive before the Inspector came in. The Orange Hands drive, but where was it? I tried to remember, to no avail. I rushed from one room to the following, finding everything in disarray. I picked up the living room table, which had been violently thrown to the ground. Everything was gone: the laptop, for the second time, and the secret organization's documents. I was sure of it.
"Fuck, they got me good! This is what they wanted..."
I ran to my room, threw myself under the bed and... "At least, the bag is still here..."
I heard hushed steps beside me, someone grabbed me by the ankles and pulled me away from that position.
"What the hell are you doing, Joe? It's one thing to be scared, but..."
It was the inspector, with his two agents in tow, a standard fixture by now. They had found the entrance door open and had come inside.
"Nothing, Mirko, it's just that..."

His face was pale. I was sure that he believed I'd been so scared that I hid there.
“We invited ourselves in, not that it makes much of a difference...”
His expression turned proud of his own joke. I could have honestly done without that, but that was Gaudenzi for you. As capable an investigator as he was disastrous when it came to humor.
“What happened, Joe? Within a few days, first they try to run you over, now they break into your home... weird coincidences, don't you agree?”
I couldn't lie anymore. I explained it all to him, as appropriately as I could. I began from what little I could remember of the break-in, before I passed out on my bathroom's floor, but mostly, I told him about the stolen files and about the stranger who had given them to me a few days earlier.
Gaudenzi asked me a thousand questions about the origin and content of those documents. I decided to bluff and simply told him that I had only skimmed through that huge amount of folders, that all I could tell him was that there was a secret lodge by the name of Orange Hands, whose symbol was the same hand that was found on the door of the black SUV. To tell the truth, it didn't look like a coincidence to me.
“Fine, but what's the link? I mean, I can't find a tie between these documents and your life, Joe... Are they connected to the biography you are writing?”
“Absolutely not, Mirko. I can't give you an answer, if I could I wouldn't have called you. I wanted to hand them to you, these documents, but they broke into my house and... You know, they stole them.”
His expression had changed. From the satisfaction for a third-rate cabaret joke to disbelief in front of a complicated situation to decrypt.
“We were on the phone and you told me that you had something on your hands, but in all honesty, I couldn't understand what you were talking about. The signal came and went, then the conversation was interrupted. I could hear a static in the background, I think you were bugged, Joe. As soon as they heard that you wanted to give me the documents, they hurried to your home...”
The inspector picked up the phone and dialed the headquarters' private line. He ordered a pre-emptive check on my mobile number, immediately, without waiting for the judge's warrant. All he needed was to see if I had

been wiretapped, if someone else had tapped into my phone during my conversation with Gaudenzi.
“We'll get results soon... But Joe, you really can't imagine why they gave you those documents?”
“I really don't know... They must have mistaken me for someone else. And how could they have known that I was about to hand them over to you? I didn't mention that on the phone...”
“Whoever they are, they rushed in to intervene. Professionals don't make this kind of a mess if they can avoid it. Besides, we're in the middle of the afternoon, the hour is too risky for this kind of business.”
I turned my head toward the mess that was my living room. I sat on the overturned sofa and ran a hand through my hair.
Pain came back like a stab to the back of my head: I had forgotten about the wound. I looked around and smiled. Gaudenzi was right: it looked like my personal belongings were all still there, except for the documents. It wasn't burglary for the sake of burglary.
“They were caught by surprise, they didn't think you were talking to a cop and, in order to avoid any issues, they swooped in on your apartment and looked for the files.”
“What about me? Didn't they know I was home?”
“They knew, but you were collateral damage. Actually, you were lucky they didn't kill you. You must have fought back...”
I stared at my torn-up Doors t-shirt and felt like crying. I was attached to that thing, it was a present from Mary Jefferson, my first girlfriend. I had never ruined it, not even under the effect of drugs or alcohol. Then came a flash: it felt like my mind had opened up, lighting up the darkness.
“Wait, wait a moment... I remember now! I came back inside, still talking to you, and I saw this man in front of me. Leather jacket, black pants. He was rummaging through the things on living room's table. He looked straight at me as he moved some sheets of paper from over the USB drive. He didn't seem in the least worried by my presence. So I tried to shout in order to scare him, but someone grabbed my shoulders from behind...”
So that was why I had felt that weird sensation of fear when Gaudenzi pulled me from under the bed. I had subconsciously connected it to that physical aggression.
“There were two of them, then?”

"Yes. One was looking through my things, the other pushed me to the ground. He tried to hit me with kicks and punches... on my hands and knees, I quickly retreated to the corridor. I got back up and went to the bathroom to pick up my scissors; they must have pushed be against the sink then and that's it... I died, or rather passed out. From that moment, you know how the story goes..."
"And with you out of commission, they had plenty of time to turn your apartment upside down, find the documents and analyze your laptop."
"Exactly. They probably weren't expecting to find the USB drive on the table. But why did they take the computer away, too?"
"Easy, Joe, because any document could have been recreated by the department's IT experts. Every file you open on your screen, even if the source has disappeared – like our USB drive – can be recreated by analyzing the hard disk. It was better for them to wipe everything. That is the reason why I believe these people were professionals."
I put my hands in my pockets as I talked to Gaudenzi. I had remembered about the other drive, the one with Paolo Iorio's documents, and it was still there, it hadn't disappeared. Luckily, real luckily, I had slipped it in my pockets short before the assault.
"Joe, are you sure this has nothing to do with that Jenny you talked so much about?"
I jumped. I couldn't fall into the inspector's trap, I wanted to protect her, considering the bag full of key documents that was hidden under my bed.
"It can't be, I saw her recently, she was away for work, which is why she didn't pick up my calls."
"It makes you think, though..."
His face turned dark. He had something in mind, I stared at him and got him to talk, fearing that he may have tied some detail back to Jenny.
"What are you thinking about?"
The inspector pulled out a small white business card from his pocket.

MAS Security Top Quality

Milano - Bruxelles - Dubai - New York - San Francisco

“Look! You mentioned a leather jacket and black pants, right?”
“That I did, why?” I looked at the card in his hand.
It was the slogan I couldn't get out of my head after the assault.
“We found this in the victim's jacket, it's a security company based in Milan, with branches abroad. The head office is in Italy, even the owner is Italian: Norberto Riesp, born in Veneto but living here in town. He is currently in Bruxelles, we'll question him as soon as he comes back. We don't have enough evidence to request him to fly back.”
“But they're vigilantes! What does this mean?”
“Not quite. They mainly provide surveillance services for malls. But...”
I remembered that the murdered man was also wearing that jacket, with a similar logo embroidered in gold. He was wearing the uniform of the MAS Security Top Quality company.
“Hey, but the man in the SUV...”
“Indeed. We found out who he was, Joe. He was a former member of the Folgore Parachute Brigade, recently employed as a security guard for a mall in Busnago: Marco Prola.”
“Is he the one who tried to kill me?”
“Apparently not. His badge shows that he left work after the accident. But he doesn't have any relatives or friends who can confirm this alibi. His colleagues and the mall's visitors haven't told us anything relevant either. Nobody saw him, the cameras don't show him coming in or out. Which is why we asked his boss to come back to Italy, without him, no-one in the

company can release a statement and we don't have enough on our hands to get a warrant."
"What do you think?"
"That they are too secretive and that their offices only show two computers and a secretary. That's too small for their purported yearly turnover of more than twenty million Euros. On top of that, headquarters made it clear enough that I should be careful with this murder investigation."
"So what?"
"At any rate, I think Prola was the one who tried to run you over... But I still don't have the evidence to back that claim. And I also think that the MAS company is only a front, but again, no evidence."
"Knowing you, you've got to have something on your plate. What makes you say that?"
"My informers confirmed a hunch: this company only hires former soldiers with no family ties. They pay them handsomely and send them all around the world acting as security guards for privates or companies. As a cover, they use traditional surveillance systems, such as the ones you can find in malls."
"Do you mean..."
"Yes, Joe: they are a sort of private secret service. They accompany wealthy managers in their business trips, even in high conflict war zones. They watch over the economic interests of the world's international giants, even in dangerous, remote areas. They do the dirty work for anyone who's wealthy enough to pay them. People who can't allow mistakes in their dealings."
"But what do they want from me?"
"Obviously, someone was interested in recovering those files. It's for the best that you didn't get to read them, Joe, at least you won't end up in trouble!"
Yeah, if only.
At least I had found out why I was being followed and who wanted me dead. I would have to be very careful from that moment onwards and flee as soon as possible.
"And who's behind that?"
"I don't know. But we're gonna ask Riesp."

"Do you think he's gonna talk? Maybe he's not involved..."
"Now you listen. The boss is a former Folgore who turned to the private sector after leaving the army. He comes from the violent world of Padua's extreme right wing. It only took him eight years to create an empire from nothing, it's too fast for a company with that kind of connections worldwide considering he had no startup capital to speak of. Word has it that he founded MAS S.r.l. with just ten thousand Euros. Yet now they have no spending restrictions when it comes to men and equipment, employing more than six hundred people scattered among their offices in New York, Dubai, San Francisco, Bruxelles and Milan. Curious, isn't it?"
"Now that you mention it..."
"If he tries not to talk, we're gonna make him. Even though I still fail to understand how you ended up in the middle of this madness..."
I knew. But I couldn't talk, at least not at the moment. I just shook my head. And he kept on monologuing.
"I am convinced that Marco Prola is the one who tried to kill you, and that someone used his badge to give him an alibi. But then something went haywire..."
Everything did, especially for me. I didn't care about the others, honestly.
"Well, I'm going back to the precinct. I need to get a clearer view of the other matter, the one you talked about... the orange hand..."
"Fine, you know where to find me if you need me..."
"Don't worry, my men will be gone as soon as they're done with their survey. I'm going to leave a mandatory patrol under your house this time, understood? And get your front door fixed."
"Okay, thank you."
"I almost forgot: go get that wound checked!"
As he walked out of my apartment, despite his slow pace, Gaudenzi seemed determined.
I, on the other hand, was confused. The dangers of the situation scared me. It felt like fire-walking, I absolutely needed to think of an escape plan to get out of that murky business. But how?
My only way out was to frame the people who were hunting me. But who were they, where would I find them? And most importantly, supposing I could find them, how could I face them? I was alone.

After a thorough consideration, as I waited for the locksmith to come fix my door, I made my decision: I would play it cool and pretend nothing had happened. If the documents were what they really wanted, now that they had them in their possession, I could wash my hands of all that and go on with my writing. It wasn't my problem anymore.
Up until some other sign of danger for myself turned up, I would simply play the good Italian-Canadian citizen: silent and content with his life.
In case of danger, I would flee.
Or something like that.

XVIII

"My sixth sense wasn't wrong,
I was correct:
FourStreet PromoPharma Ltd.
The name isn't new to me.
It's the same English company
Jenny mentioned."

The wound was still throbbing. I eventually put a big band-aid on it, which was hidden by my thick hair.

It was the only quick solution to my predicament, certainly faster than getting to the E.R.: that way lay at least four hours of Italian red tape to wade through. Italian hospitals are a far shot from the ones in Canada, everything is much slower and more complicated.

At any rate, I could finally understand what dirty clothes might feel like when thrown inside a washing machine. The intensity of the last few days had left its toll on me. After the assault, I told myself I wouldn't get involved in any more trouble. I was fond of my hide. I couldn't stay idle, I had to keep myself busy somehow, but by doing what?

Writing. I would have to finish Iorio's biography to the best of my possibility, and quick, so as to be done with any personal involvement. I would hand it over to Jenny, or directly to Paolo, the main character, wave goodbye and go back to Canada. I certainly could not, and did not want to, work in Italy anymore, and in Milan specifically. I didn't feel safe out in the streets, it would be better to disappear for a while. This situation showed me that I was professionally compromised. No national paper would hire me as a journalist: to colleagues, all I had was connections, to my bosses I was a hothead and to cops a pain in the neck. Goodbye crime department, my reputation would precede me at any Italian newspaper. My career as a biographer, on the other hand and considering the situation, was over before it could even begin. Having risked my life for my first book, what could ever happen with the following one? As I said, the best

thing I could do was probably to go back home and put an end to all this. Help my father with the family business and finish my studies. Stop.
"What the fuck am I supposed to do?" The voice of conscience was tearing at me from the inside. I started to cry like a child lost at sea, alone in the middle of the night. I cried, overcome by the waves, my saddest, darkest thoughts. The uncertainty of my goals didn't allow me to rest.
"I must finish the book, I must finish and..." But from the farthest recesses of my heart came a battle cry. A feeble voice that I could not ignore. It's just who I am, I can't come to terms with my stubborn personality. Even when I am insecure, even when I am scared. Every time I get an idea in my head, even the most harebrained ones, I have to put it into practice.
This time was different. I had to do it, not just because of my honor and of the documents in my possession: Jenny's father had died in the pursuit of truth and I could not flee from my ethical obligations as a journalist. I had to finish Iorio's book. But I also had an obligation to make public that other issue, the secret documents detailing the effects of Agent Orange, I had to do it for those children and their mothers. Justice once and for all. Jenny never asked me to, but I felt that it was necessary. Yes, but how? I started to think.
I had to put the pieces of the puzzle together: Paolo and his company, FourStreet, Orange Hand, Jennifer's father and Vietnam. On top of that, I needed to find out who wanted me dead and why. But where to start from? The answer was simple: from the info I had on me. Iorio and his life.
During my first months as a journalist in Italy, I had learned a simple truth from my senior colleagues: every story, every article must be based on verified information and in order to be certain of that, one must start by elaborating what one already has in their hand. Even though it may appear scarce at first. By applying this philosophy to my situation, the method I was to use became clear: in order to find useful hints, I would have to understand Paolo's involvement in this madness. Was he a victim of the system, a simple pawn or a perpetrator?
Before checking the files Jennifer had given me, then, I decided to pay a visit to Iorio Farmaceutici, *Iorio Pharmaceuticals*, in the nearby town of Bresso. It was the only tie I had. I thought it very odd that a young man without a degree would be able to open such an important company in

such a short time. Something smelled and a little investigation could only help sort out my thoughts.
Dangerous? Absolutely not. Had anyone noticed me asking questions around, I could have always said that I was gathering material for the book. I needed to talk to people who had known him well during those years. It was a perfect cover and it would also end up being useful to get a better feeling of Paolo's personality in order to write his biography in a first person point of view.
So I decided to go outside. Later on, I would stop by the Apple Store to buy another Mac and be able to reprise my writing.
I looked up the company's address on the internet. Without a computer, all I had was my iPhone. Iorio Farmaceutici S.r.l was not listed on Google. All the search turned up was an official page titled 'Iorio P. Farmaceutici S.r.l' which said 'Website under construction'. Nothing else, no useful info on boards or unofficial pages.
At least an address existed.
Jenny's car was parked two blocks from my home; I reached it doing my best not to be tailed. There was no such thing as too much caution, considering the situation. I headed toward that place which, up until that moment, I had never visited. It was a pleasant day and now that I had a Porsche, albeit a borrowed one, I didn't mind the trip.

Bresso was gloomy.
It's not an ugly town, mind you, and the mayors who followed one another on the first citizen's chair did their level best to embellish it, especially in its central streets. All that does not, however, change its nature as a pseudo metropolitan suburb masquerading as an independent town, set in the south of the lower Brianza. Definitely not the kind of place one wants to live in. It's part of the so-called Grande Milano, Greater Milan, bordering on the towns of Sesto San Giovanni, Cinisello Balsamo, Cusano Milanino and Cormano.
The residential area, on the other hand, gives onto Milan's North Park, the only green lung of the area, which also hosts a small airport.
I left the car parked in a provincial industrial area with no personality. I could have been anywhere in Lombardy if it hadn't been for the 'Bresso – Industrial Zone' sign by the town's entrance, off the A4 highway.

It was a soulless place.
In front of me stood a massive glass palace, four or five stories tall. Its design was far from refined, it looked like a thousand identical transparent cubical buildings. A drab, impersonal prefabricated building.
I got closer to the house number and saw a sign taped to the doorbell: 'Iorio P. Farmaceutici S.r.l.'. Fantastic, I had arrived to my destination.
I rang.
No reply.
I rang again, more insistently.
Nothing.
"What happened to them?"
Could they really leave the place abandoned during the week? Weird.
"I'll have you know that the company is not located here anymore. They moved."
The voice came from behind my back. Very high pitch.
I snapped around to face it, even though that feminine tone didn't feel particularly dangerous.
"Beg your pardon?"
"You're here for Iorio, right?" In front of me stood a small lady in her sixties, round glasses, bob cut dyed black. She looked like the caricature of a woman: a statue from a Neapolitan nativity scene, so small and frail that I felt like a giant from atop my six feet of height.
"How do you know that?"
"Well, you did ring their bell, didn't you?"
"Yes, right. I mean, how do you know they moved?"
"I was their cleaning lady. All that's left in this building is a financial consulting firm that has nothing to do with them. The two floors Iorio used to occupy are empty now."
"Do you know where they relocated to?"
"Abroad, I think. They laid off thirty workers and then the owner hit the road about a month ago. Disappeared, he did."
"Thirty workers? Aren't those numbers a little low for a pharmaceutical company?"
"What, Iorio S.r.l?" The tiny woman let out a big laugh, then sobered up.
"No way... they were consultants for pharmaceutical products, not producers..."

"With that name, I thought..."
"What name?"
"The company's name, I mean... with 'pharmaceuticals' right in the title, along with the founder's name and surname..."
"No, no, everyone falls for that. Invoices actually made out to 'Iorio Promo Farmaceutici S.r.l.'."
"Are you sure?"
"Absolutely, I saw them in the boss' office."
"Why were their offices so big, then?"
"Ah, I wouldn't know anything about that. Maybe they didn't want to be cramped... But why do you care, if I may ask?"
"I am a journalist and I am investigating this company... would you happen to know anyone who used to work here?"
"So they can expose what happened?"
"Sorry, what?"
"How they closed up shop in a hurry. Two years of work and then they gave everyone the boot... with no real reason. The clients' payments were in order. Crisis schmisis, that's what they all say and then poor folks like us are the one who end up flat on their butts. Mister Iorio used to drive one of those big pricey cars, he sure wasn't in dire straits... People like him, they always land on their feet."
"Yes, that's what I am here for... to bring justice."
Lying was the only option that would give me a lead.
"That's what I want to hear, justice is what the people who were left without a job need..."
"You can help me, then? Do you know them?"
"Who?"
"The people who used to work here at Iorio..."
"Sure, Marco... Marco Ghezzi, he's my nephew. You can find him at the Bar Centrale coffee bar... he's a barman! He was lucky he found this job, after his degree and losing his job, he makes coffee and serves drinks. Poor guy, but one has to make a living somehow, right? To think that his parents took out a lot of loans to pay for his studies."
"I can imagine..."
I quickly bade goodbye to the lady, thanking her for her help and her courtesy, and, without letting her see me, I tore off the sign taped to the

doorbell. I wanted to see what was written underneath. My sixth sense wasn't wrong, I was correct: FourStreet PromoPharma Ltd. The name wan't new to me. It was the same English company Jenny had mentioned. What did it mean? As far as I remembered, Iorio P. Farmaceutici S.r.l. was the one who had been bought by them, not the other way round.

I had to find the Bar Centrale. 'Central bar', that seemed descriptive enough, yet the bar was located in Piazza dell'Immacolata, a square which was not set in the town center proper, but rather on the ground floor of a three-stories building dating back to the beginning of the Twentieth century, its walls a shade of amaranth, located one block away from the town hall. A far shot from Canada's vast expanses, here in Italy everything is pressed together, fastidiously slipped in its place without room for mistakes. Except for that one time, where the 'central' coffee bar wasn't, per se, part of the town's center.
I entered the place, in search of my barman.
"Coffee, please. I am looking for Marco Ghezzi."
A boy perked up from behind the counter. Short black hair, dark eyes, bright expression, can't have been older than thirty.
"Who's looking for him?"
I knew that had to be him: "I am!"
"'I' who? Look, I don't know you, so..."
"Can I drop the formalities? I'm a journalist, I'm investigating for an article about Iorio."
"That bastard deserves some noise... Who are you writing it for?"
Good question. I couldn't tell him that I was on the payroll of the 'bastard' himself in order to write his biography. I kept on lying.
"Repubblica...", almost true.
"Fine, I'm Marco. Who sent you here?"
"Your aunt... I met her outside the offices."
"I don't have aunts..."
"Well, she was a stick-thin lady..."
"Ah, Vanda... she's an old family friend..."
"My bad, she talked about nephews and parents, I assumed she was your aunt. Lovely person, at any rate!"

“Yeah, I've known her ever since I was born. So, what do you want to know?”
“Everything you know... Tell me how you started working for Iorio and what you did for the company... If things were going fine or if you could smell something fishy going on...”
The boy spilled the beans, and gladly so, all too willing to teach a lesson to his former employer. Being given the boot after he had taken out a 40-years mortgage and proposed to his fiancée had ruined him.
Luckily, living in a small town such as Bresso meant that everyone knew and helped each other, so he had been able to find a job there at the bar. With his university degree, he was way overqualified, but his situation was hardly unique in Italy.
Anyway, the info he offered on Paolo Iorio and his company were particularly juicy.
“So you maintain that it was a shell company?”
“It had to be, they hired me without batting an eyelash. Straight away, which is weird for a recent graduate. And my degree is in marketing, what's it got to do with pharmaceuticals?”
“Well, it doesn't mean... Weren't you supposed to be a promoter, helping them gain clients through presents and assorted complimentary items? That's a job for the marketing department after all...”
“Yes, yes... that's what they all say, but look, it's a serious job... But that's where it gets weird!”
“What do you mean?”
His face turned into a mix of puzzled and amused worthy of an ancient Greek theater mask.
“We didn't have specific products to add to our portfolio, nor productivity goals. All they were ever fastidious about was this one thing: we had to fill out with extreme care the dossiers of the doctors we visited, marking their main personal and professional characteristics. Some sort of detailed global x-ray, if you will...”
“To what end?”
“Nobody knew.”
“General practitioners?”
“No, even esteemed professionals.”
“And Iorio?”

“They selected some of them, from our dossiers, he and his right-hand man Carmine Balzaretti, and they contacted them. From that moment onwards, no-one had to have anything to do with those doctors anymore. Or we were out.”

My mind wandered. I thought about the storage.

“But, if you can answer me this, why were your offices so big?”

“They belonged to FourStreet, the British company who bought Iorio. They needed the space to store the products. We couldn't enter those rooms, that was forbidden too.”

“For how long were you located there?”

“Two years...”

“And the people who already worked there, what did they say? I mean, how did they handle the change of ownership?”

Marco laughed.

“How'd I know! No-one there ever stayed for more than twenty-four months, there was always fresh air at Iorio, and fresh people... All that, until thirty days ago, when we were given the slip and that was it...”

“The people who left before the fusion, where did they go?”

“Gossip has it that they were mostly absorbed by other divisions, the chemical sector especially. Many of them were transferred to MonteForte Company, its Italian branch I mean. Lucky guys...”

“I beg to differ...”

“Fuck that, it's a steady job at a multinational corporation, the dream: paycheck for life, it's like a government job...”

He could not, of course, understand my reaction.

“Yes, sorry, you're right. When would you say was the beginning of the end?”

“Lately, the boss was tense. Then ever since his partner died in a road accident, he became unmanageable... Let's say it all started approximately two months ago, ever since those odd people came to the office...”

“Partner? I thought he was the only owner...”

“Balzaretti, you mean? No-one could ever figure out whether he was a co-owner or not. He was the one who handled my job interview. A good contract, reimbursement of expenses, a company car... A dream! Then...”

“Then?”

“Lately, they argued a lot. Until the accident. A sad affair, fuck, he slammed against a wall as he was coming home from work. He fell asleep at the wheel, it seems.”
“Maybe he killed himself due to debts?”
“Mmmm... I don't think so. Until Iorio told us that they were moving everything to Great Britain, to the headquarters, work seemed to be going fine. As you know, medicines are always in, the crisis didn't hit that sector.”
“And how did he motivate the relocation?”
“He didn't. He told us and that's it, just a few words while his lawyer was there. Then he flew, leaving us with his lawyer and up to our neck in shit.”
“What's his name?”
“Don't worry, he's dead too. Heart attack. Which means our lawsuit is going nowhere, we don't know who it is that we're supposed to sue. And weeds are already growing in Iorio's house... it's empty.”
“Motherfucker, he can't be gone in a puff of smoke like this! What about the authorities?”
“Trust me, nothing's moving... Judges and trade unions? They follow their own interests, not ours. They have recently started negotiations with FourStreet and say that the redundancy procedures are all in order. We went to the courthouse to protest, but no results so far.”
“Was the company always here in Bresso?”
“No. Both the offices and the storehouse used to belong to the British firm. But no-one had ever used them.”
“And Iorio Farmaceutici?”
“I think they were located in Brescia, but it could be bullshit...”
I decided to get some fresh air.
That story was beginning to stink. But first, I needed to ask one last question.
“Out of curiosity, who were the weird people who came and went from your office?”
“I don't know, folks in suits and ties, driving big, black cars... But the biggest bitch was this one woman, I never knew her name... She always arrived escorted by three cars: she came in, shouted at Paolo and went out. She came three times and after those visits they gave us all the boot.”
“So the outsourcing is her fault?”

"I think so..."
"What was she like?"
"She wasn't older than fifty, dark hair tied up... thin as a stick..."
That description reminded me of the car I had followed outside Jenny's marketing office. I thought I was following her, but the profile I had seen through the car's darkened windows must have belonged to that woman.
"When does the article come out, then?"
The boy shook my arm. I energically broke free, suddenly awoken from my thoughts.
"Oi, I'm sorry, uhm... Soon, I think, as soon as I'm done investigating. Thank you for your help!"
"You're welcome, now go kick that motherfucker's ass!"
I nodded. I tried to pay for my coffee, but he refused.
"My treat, don't worry."
I thanked him and rushed outside, I absolutely needed to breathe. I reached the Porsche back in the parking lot, opened it with my remote, sat on the comfortable leather seats, closed my eyes and let myself go. Peace.

XIX

"There is a man on the ground.
I hurry as I cross the road,
avoiding the few passing cars.
I come closer and jump:
there is a body lying down and I know him."

By then, I was in too deep and I couldn't fold.

The puzzle, meanwhile, was slowly coming together. As I turned the key inside the Porsche's dashboard, my mind began to consider what my following move would be.

"Now, Joe? What's the second clue?", I asked myself out loud in the car's cabin.

Thinking out loud usually helped me find the concentration I needed to find a solution to garbled messes.

There was no doubt that the most intriguing tidbit I had collected was the description of the mysterious woman in town with those two cars as her escort. Maybe she was the owner and Paolo only a front, that would explain a lot.

I could not, of course, be sure that she was the same person I had followed on my Vespa a few days earlier, believing her to be Jenny. The following step in my personal investigation would be to find out. But I had to be careful, all those accidental deaths could be anything but: the partner's car accident, the lawyer's heart attack and Iorio being AWOL didn't leave a lot to the imagination. Maybe I should get my tin hat out: I see conspiracies everywhere and I may be even paranoid. But this time, who wouldn't?

"I need to find more deets on that woman."

Yes, but how?

"Come on Joe, think... Hey, wait. Where'd I see her last time?"

I decided to go to Jenny's office, maybe her colleagues would share some relevant info.

I passed the airport and turned to Viale Fulvio Testi avenue, following the road toward the Bicocca district. It would be fun to see if the kind lady on the intercom – the one who had already turned me down once – would oppose me again. In that case, I was ready to break down the parking lot's bar. I was on the hunt for answers and no-one would stand in my way.
I parked the Porsche on the street's corner, so as to avoid being seen, and walked to the entrance gate.
I rang.
Nothing.
Deja-vu. I didn't lose my spirits and rang again, more insistently.
“Who is it?”
Finally, a female voice.
“This is Joe Brigati, I have an appointment with miss Blasquez. May I come in?”
“Beg your pardon, with whom?”
I was dumbfounded, only able to babble a few words in reply.
“Blasquez... Marketing...”
“Ah! I'm sorry, you see, the company that person worked for, they're closed now. They moved elsewhere, they're not here anymore...”
A glacial shiver ran through my back.
“Can't you tell me where?”
The gate was opened remotely. I got inside.
I once again went through the glass sliding door that had marked the beginning of this murky tale. Another operator came to greet me, much prettier than her predecessor.
“Are you the person who was looking for the marketing company?”
“Yes, would you know where...”
She interrupted me.
“No, look, I'm new, I've only worked here for five days. I think they either closed or moved outside Milan... They came to take away the furniture yesterday...”
“And the operator who was here before you?”
It was the only line of questioning, at that point, that could lead to infor about the mysterious woman.
“She changed jobs.”
“Can you tell me where?”

"I wouldn't know – actually, I shouldn't be talking about it at all... they expressly told me that I was not supposed to say anything. That if anyone came asking about a marketing company, I should pretend not to know anything."
The girl heard steps echoing from the corridor adjacent to the entrance hall. She gently pushed me outside, in the parking lot, and followed me showing worry and interest at the same time.
She brought me up to the corner of the building, so we wouldn't be seen, and leaned closer as if she wanted to kiss me.
I don't understand why I always seem to find available women in the wrong circumstances.
"You know, when I saw you on the intercom's camera, you looked like an okay guy, so I decided to let you in."
"Why? What's with my face, sorry?"
"The owner said not to open the door to distinguished suit-and-tie types asking for that company... but you're different..."
I looked at her straight in the eyes and winked.
"I could be a cop, don't you think?"
"Nah, you don't have the face for that. Besides, they were already here this morning."
I didn't know whether to feel flattered or offended.
My thoughts were interrupted by a huge hand. I felt it grip my right shoulder from behind and squeeze it, as if to break it. I couldn't understand who it was, I couldn't look. The girl fled, terrified, rushing back to the red bricks building as if she had seen the Loch Ness monster behind my back.
I turned around, worried about that violent pull that had almost made me fall down.
"Joe, Joe... listen... you have to stop being a naughty boy..."
I was facing a hulk of a man, though he didn't look ripped. On the contrary, he was a big, overweight man who wore his extra weight well. All things considered, with all the meat he carried around, he looked harmonious, as if he were floating.
Thin glasses, round face.
Never seen him before in my life.
I would have placed his accent as coming from the Veneto region but, as a Canadian, Italian dialects are not my forte.

“We know what you do and where you go, yet you never stopped being a bother. When will you ever learn, eh?”
“Hey, hold up, who are you? And most importantly, how do you know me? Let me gooo...”
Wiggling away was always a talent of mine. No police tape, no guards could stop me from reaching the evidence of a crime I was reporting. This time, though, it was proving to be impossible: his hands felt like claws.
“You don't need to care about who I am, just what I can do to you. You are in a private area, without authorization, and you are very much persona non grata.”
It felt like flying, he swung me around at an incredible speed. I couldn't fight it.
I ended up beyond the bar and barely acknowledging it.
“Listen, you have no idea. You don't know anyone, and most importantly, you have to be careful. If you insist...”
“What?”
“Nothing. After all, you are already compromised.”
“Are you by chance threatening me?”
“No, far from it.”
His expression was sarcastic.
Looking at him, he looked like a nice fellow. Happy-go-lucky, my grandfather would've called him. His eyes didn't look evil, his face even had a sweet frame. Even his gargantuan looks were courteous. Yet his words implied something else entirely when it came to my person.
“Cheers! And do say hello to your friend Andrea for me.”
What did he have to do with anything? I was confused. The man fixed his black suit and went back toward the building's entrance as if nothing had happened. I called him, asking for an explanation of that last sentence of his, but he didn't reply.
I went back to the car, checking – with good reason now – that I wasn't being followed.
I was compromised, what did that mean?
I got into the car and slid the key in the ignition, which was on the left side of the wheel. Porsche cars are weird: all the other manufacturers place it on the other side. It's a pedigree thing. But it's hard to remember it. So for

the second time in just a few hours, I got it wrong, but I was shaken and hardly focused.
I decided to abandon my investigation for the time being and head toward central Piazza San Babila square, facing the city's rush hour. Another day had gone by and I had barely noticed. I hadn't eaten, either – then again, any rumbling in my stomach was frozen by the sight of that man's icy blue pupils.
I wanted to have a talk with Andrea, that sentence was too fine a bait for me not to take it, I wanted to ask him who that giant was and to warn him. He was in danger, I didn't know what could happen to him but he would have to understand.
Evening traffic is nerve-racking, which is why I hate cars. I missed my beloved Vespa.
I slowly drifted through Viale Zara avenue, though the traffic jam in that avenue was nothing compared to what awaited me as I turned from Viale Brianza to Corso Buenos Aires. After some forty minutes of madness, I finally came through to the restricted traffic zone that marks Milan's so-called fashion quadrangle and with it my destination, Piazza San Babila square.
As usual, parking was a myth, but, as I was in a hurry, I followed Andrea's own example and parked on a crosswalk.
I put my hazards on and got out of the car. As soon as I closed the door behind me, I heard a weird hiss, followed by a dull thump behind my back. I pictured a rear-ending, but the noise was unusual in the middle of the city, it was faint, I only heard it because I was in a restricted traffic zone. People were shouting, probably women.
I closed the door and turned around, trying to focus on the pedestrians and find any hint as to what had transpired and where. I stared at several faces before noticing a knot of people gathering on the other side of the street, not far from the colonnades.
There was a man on the ground.
I hurried across the street, avoiding the few passing cars. I got closer.
I shuddered, then felt a sharp pain, as if I had just been hit in my stomach. I knew that body. It looked familiar, but I couldn't understand why. That white coat reminded me of...
"Oh my God! Andrea..."

I tried to push through the crowd and get closer.
I shoved two men away to sneak among the crowd, it was the only way to move forward.
Those sad witnesses were wondering what had just happened. They couldn't understand, but sadly, I did.
I kneeled down on his body, checking for vitals.
Pressing a finger to his neck, I had to acknowledge that the impact had been fatal: there was no pulse.
I got up, wiping his blood from my hands by brushing them on my thighs and smearing my jeans. My heart was pumping fast, not so much due to seeing a corpse, I'd seen plenty in my time, but to the risk of being next in line.
“Fuck that man...” I thought back to the brute and his cryptic greeting.
My shock was, of course, also due to the loss of someone I knew, someone I cared for. But, in all honesty, that was the least of my worries at the moment. When one's blood gets shot up with adrenaline, compassion and sadness take a back seat – they usually crash later, all at once.
His spotless coat was turning red.
His fall from the second floor had torn his his forehead apart, pressing it against Milan's gray asphalt. He lay down on his belly, the palms of his hands facing up.
Something was wrong. As I said, corpses weren't new to me. Suicides, too. And all of them, as they fell, always gave in to their survival instincts and had the time to try to shield themselves from the impact with their arms. Andrea didn't do that. Why? I turned around and watched the crowd, which was getting bigger as time went by.
“Did anyone see where he jumped from?”
“Up there, from up there”, shouted a distinguished old lady with light hair, pointing at a window on the second floor. I knew that place, it was his office. That was the balcony he used to send me to when I wanted to have a smoke, ever since the smoking ban in public places had come into effect.
I had to understand if someone was with him before he jumped.
I ran toward the entrance. I got inside, ignoring the porter's astonished stare.
I rushed upstairs, quick on my legs, without feeling fatigue. Inside his office, everything seemed normal, just a work day like any other.

Nobody had noticed the tragedy.
The door was open, as always, to invite clients inside.
“Andrea, Andrea...”
His assistant stared at me, not realizing what had happened – my breath was short, my pupils dilated due to the strain.
She was puzzled, so was I. Then I shouted:
“He jumped, he juuumped!!”
The girl snapped on her feet and ran toward his office, saw the open window leading to the balcony and burst into tears.
“Was he alone? Was he alone?” I grabbed her arms and shook her.
She shouted: “I don't know, I didn't notice anything, I swear... Nothing!!”
I tried to calm down, patting her on the shoulder to reassure her.
“Ilaria, it's important that you tell me, you have to tell me who Andrea was with before he jumped.”
She tried to give me a detailed answer between sighs.
“A man came in, asked for him. I had never seen him before. A few minutes later he left with a smile on his lips. Had he not waved me goodbye, I might not even have noticed that he was leaving so soon.”
“How long ago did he leave?”
“I don't know, ten minutes... maybe five.”
“Please describe him, try to focus!”
“He had dark hair, young... fit, tan...”
“Any accents?”
“From the South, maybe. Or no, wait... Joe, I don't know, I think he sounded Roman. How could this happen?”
I didn't have time to waste, so I didn't answer.
The girl couldn't help me, she was too shaken. I let her out of the room as I stayed inside to examine Andrea's desk in search of clues.
Could he really have committed suicide without leaving a note? Even though I didn't think it was suicide at all, I decided to check all the same, just to be sure. After a few seconds of rummaging through his things, I saw a piece of paper by the phone.
“I can't believe it!”
It was a fucking setup.
It was a note for his girlfriend.

Dear Monica,

It is with sadness in my heart that I have decided to end it once and for all.
Debts give me no respite, there are no solutions within the Law. I Dislike the very idea of leaving you, but I am left with no other choice. Without me, at least, you will be able to lead a happy life. I did everything in my power to avoid this.
I tried to sell the office, but with the real estate crisis, I couldn't find a buyer in time to save me.
I love you deeply, madly, and if There is one thing I'll never get tired of repeating, it's this.
Remind Joe that chemistry is important, in love. He can't give up in his search for a soulmate, I know that he will be able to find the right woman that way. And I know that by reading these lines, he will know who I am talking about. I care for his happiness, it was love at first sight and she reciprocates too. He can't give up, tell him to say, I Owe it to Andrea!
Then again, it's all a matter of sparks, it's a Jig, he's the king of the night, even if he is a tad paranoid. He can't fail to understand this.
Back to us, Monica, even thought there must be tears in Your eyes and your face will be wet because of me, don't be sad.
Enough talk, let me bury my Axe. All I want to tell you for the last time is that I adore you and that you were so beautiful yesterday, like a dame at a Tourney of old.
I love you,

Andrea

PS: if you Feel like handling this, tell your daddy that the 19th century wrought-iron bathtub I Won at an auction for our house in the countryside, the one he liked so much, is his now. He can keep it as a memento of me.

“Hey, wait. He talks about me in his note? What's that mean?”
That looked weird, definitely hiding something. We weren't that close.

Besides, that note was unintelligible, some parts didn't mean anything and it suffered from a bad case of random capitalization. As a journalist, it wasn't something I wouldn't notice, accustomed as I was to reading and rereading everything I wrote. I often spotted typos even on the cans of beans I got at the store. And Andrea poked fun at me for this, he said I was paranoid.
"The fuck was he on today? And what does chemistry have to do with love, was he suggesting I should use Viagra? Was he cracking jokes right before he died?"
I could hear an ambulance arrive and the police soon afterwards. Their sirens zeroed in on what I was growing more and more convinced was the scene of a murder.
"Think, Joe, think carefully: what do all these mistakes mean? They aren't random... Paranoid... what could he mean?"
Then the flash of inspiration, the SPARK. As Andrea hosted his socialite parties, he was used to cracking anagrams for fun. The apex of his events was always the moment the cake came, decked out with those sparkly candles they use in discos, the ones they bring along with the bottles of champagne. And then he bored his guests with his stupid wordplay and I never forgave him for that. I always mocked him for it.
And he used to reply: "You're always the same old paranoid motherfucker, Joe! Go find your typos in your articles... I'm the king of the night! Remember it well..."
He was telling me to read between the lines, to anagram the nonsensical parts marked by the capital letters in order to find out the truth.
"Fuck, Andrea... what were you thinking? There was a chance in a million I would figure out your note... The spark, of course the spark!"
Lucky me, logical analysis (not the kind they teach in school) was my forte.
I reread the letter, using the capital letters as my starting point to crack the code. I picked a piece of paper and started to doodle letter after letter, arranging them, weaving them in so many different ways.
"Law... Dislike... There... Owe... Jig... I don't understand, Andrea, what were you trying to tell me? And what's this about an axe?"

I obsessively stared at the letter. It was talking about Jenny, he wanted me to find her. And most importantly, he wanted me to solve the anagram sprinkled in the text.
But how? Minutes went by, I feared that the police would barge in and prevent me from finding a solution to all those questions. Then, possibly thanks to the adrenaline in my veins, I found the key.

Law Dislike   I was killed

There Owe Jig Your   Joe you were right

Axe Tourney   You are next

Feel Won   Flee now

The answer to all my questions.
Suicide my ass. I was deep inside this mess and I was risking my life.
And no-one could help me.

XX

"The taxi ran fast,
while the city put on her elegant
curvy black evening dress.
My mind wandered,
searching for answers."

I got inside the car, trying to get away from the crowd. Anyone could notice me and point the cops toward me, revealing that I had been the first person to assist Andrea after he jumped.
I didn't want the police to stop and question me.
I couldn't lose time getting mixed up in pointless investigations. I was so close to Jenny's apartment and I could still hold onto the vague hope that I would find her before she left for Argentina. I didn't know the date and time of her flight, but all things considered, it was worth a shot. I needed to find her and warn her, maybe Andrea knew everything and thought she would be in danger too. With a U-turn, I launched my car on Corso Matteotti avenue.
As I stared at the glove compartment, I remembered the gun, the one Jennifer wanted me to have at all costs. I brought it with me, just in case. If they wanted to kill me, I'd better go prepared. I had never shot a single bullet in my life, but there's a first time for everything. I left the car in the underground parking by her house, where Jenny herself had left it when I first got there. It was handy and, most importantly, safe from prying eyes. The Porsche was swallowed by the ramp.
I climbed the gray steps to the car park with a short breath and then rushed toward the colonnades and the clothes shop by the building's entrance. I went inside, under the unconcerned look of passer-bies who paid no attention to the blood stains on my jeans.
We truly live in a dulled society, I could've ben a killer and no-one would have lifted a finger to call the cops on me. On second thought, all the better, in this specific case.

I rushed on the marble stairs and tried to remember the floor of Jennifer's apartment. During my return home the other night I was too distracted by my thoughts and, mostly, by alcohol to take notice.
There it was, found it: I rang the bell.
No reply, yet I could hear faint noises coming from inside.
Steps. Those were steps. As if someone were trying to drag themselves to the entrance.
The door opened.
Jenny offered me a feeble smile, but she was very pale.
"Joe, what are you doing here? I told you..."
"Jenny, you have to listen to me... We are in danger. Andrea died just a few minutes ago!"
I bolted the door as I talked to her. She hauled herself toward the couch and dropped on the pillows.
"What's happening?", I worriedly asked.
"I didn't tell you everything... I'm on dialysis, due to all the chemical experiments my mother came in contact with at the beginning of her pregnancy, before taking a maternity leave."
"Okay, but what's happening to you?"
"I am eagerly awaiting a kidney transplant, but the waiting list is long... I went to the hospital today for the usual transfusion, so I wouldn't run into trouble during the long flight to Argentina tonight, but..."
She looked worn out and didn't seem to have grasped what I had told her a few seconds earlier.
"Jenny, okay, that's too bad but... did you understand that Andrea, they killed him?"
"Yes, sure..."
She didn't look worried, then her expression changed.
I stared at her face as tears started falling from her eyes. Tears of blood.
It dripped out of her orbits like in a horror movie, slowly at first, then picking up pace. Lastly, a red rivulet came out of the right corner of her mouth.
"Jenny, hey..."
She passed out before I could finish the sentence. I slapped her face, but she didn't react. I shook her vigorously.
"Jenny, fuck... Jenny!!"

Luckily she came to again, looked me in the eyes and opened her fleshy lips slightly. She struggled to get closer to my ear and whispered: "Joe... find Paolo, please. Tell him he is in danger. He's in San Francisco, you'll find everything in my PC... Promise me you'll finish wr..." She passed out again, coughing twice, and her blood splattered on the white fabric of the Milord-style sofa.
"Hang tight, Jenny... I'm gonna call an ambulance... hold on."
I looked around the living room in search of a phone.
A wireless one lay by the corner cupboard she kept the booze in, the one with the pale lilies. I dialed 118, the emergency number.
"Quick, come here soon... My girlfriend felt ill. She bleeds from her mouth and she passed out..."
Honestly, I don't know why I called her 'my girlfriend'. I blurted it out spontaneously in those moments of panic. As they say, the heart is true in the most adverse conditions.
On the other end of the phone, they tried to calm me down, asking me what symptoms she had shown before passing out, what the address was, the floor and any details about the girl's health that could prove crucial.
I delicately rested her hair on a purple pillow.
"I can't be found here... It's too dangerous... What would I tell the paramedics? That I'm not the boyfriend? I need to go..."
I gave one last look at Jenny's suffering face and her body lying on the sofa. I hoped the ambulance would come soon and that she would understand why I was running away. She was alone and helpless, unfortunately. I would have liked to hold her hand on her way to the hospital, but I couldn't.
I saw the black laptop on the table and took it, then quickly went down the building's stairs, leaving the apartment's door half-open. I faked indifference as I passed by the porter's desk, but luckily it was as empty as it had been on my way in.
I reached the car in the underground parking. As I stood in the lift, near the second underground floor, a thought struck me: "No, I cannot take her car. They could trace me back to it."
Paranoia? No, I was truly terrified. They could see me from the garage's CCTV footage already, but as things stood before, I would have been able to come up with any trivial excuse such as 'she lent me her car for work'.

But taking her car when she was within an inch of her life or already dead, no, that was too dangerous. I walked out of the garage and, as night started to descend upon Milan, I heard the ambulance's siren, followed by the sight of its blinking blue light. Two orange-clad boys darted out of the vehicle and went inside the building with bags and stretcher. Luckily, they had been very quick, maybe the ambulance was the same that had hopelessly attempted to give aid to Andrea a few blocks away.
I walked toward Via Montenapoleone street with a crushing anxiety. What was I supposed to do at that point? How could I get to the end of that tunnel? I could only hope that Jenny, at least, would be safe. That was my wish.
But what would happen to me?
I had to find some form of transport to get home without being noticed. I walked in the middle of the city center with a switched-off look behind my eyes, a computer under my arm and someone else's gun in my pocket. The longer I remained in a crowd, the more vulnerable I was.
I flipped through my iPhone's screen until I got to the taxi app.

The car ran fast, while the city put on her elegant curvy black evening dress. Milan's lights were reflected on the faces of the succession of busy passer-bies parading under my empty eyes.
My mind wandered, searching for answers.
"Mister, your phone is ringing."
I looked at the taxi's rearview mirror and found the driver's puzzled eyes staring back.
"Yes, you're right... You're right, I was lost in thought for a minute", I answered.
"Joe Brigati, this is inspector Gaudenzi. May I talk to you for a minute?"
I kept my reply vague, it wasn't time to spill the beans yet. Here was hoping that Gaudenzi wasn't about to bring any more bad news.
"Go on, talk at leisure. I hope it's not trouble."
"Well, let's say it's not, even though... Anyway, I wanted to tell you that the agent who questioned you last time – remember him? – checked that marketing company you mentioned. It doesn't exist. Are you sure that's the right address?"

“I don't know? I think so. But who was that man? He didn't look like a simple agent, with how he ragged on me...”
“True that. Let's say he is a little further up than I am...”
“How little?”
“I cannot say... Getting off the subject, there is bad news as well.”
I feared for Jenny, holding my breath.
“I need to ask you a few questions about your friend Andrea Marchi.”
At least it wasn't about Jennifer's health.
“What questions?”
“They saw you in his office today, after his suicide. What were you doing there?”
“Nothing special. I was there for work when tragedy struck... But I didn't see anything special.”
“Always knee-deep in trouble, huh? Were you aware of his debts?”
“That seems to be the case... And honestly, no. He was more of a work acquaintance than a friend.”
“I find it hard to believe, with how he spoke about you at length in his suicide note...”
“Really? How weird, what did he have to say?”
I hoped he would buy my lie, I was never that great as an actor.
“The note mentions a woman...”
“It could be a dear friend of his, whom he introduced to me. We are going out together and he would have very much liked to see us start a relationship...”
“Mmmmh... That fits. You're right, Joe, he mentions love at first sight. Well, that's all from me. I'll let you know if you can be of more help.”
“Do you really think it was suicide?”
“Why shouldn't we, Joe?”
“No, just... wondering.”
“Everything fits, from his books, which were deeply in the red, to the note. Besides, people close to him reported that in the past two days he had become paranoid, maintaining that someone was following him... a typical case of pre-suicidal stress.”
“Fair, that fits. Gonna hang up, I've just arrived.”
“Fine, goodbye.”

The taxi stopped and I could see my house's front door from the window. I handed a fifty Euro note to the driver to pay or the ride.
“Keep the change and remember, you never saw me, okay?”
I'd always dreamt of saying that, just like in a spy movie.
“Fine, change is only two Euros anyway... and go get yourself cleaned up, you've got red paint everywhere, heck I was worried you'd stain my seats...”
I looked at the taximeter: €48,05.
“Well, that's for the best... I hate coins.”
I grabbed the PC from the other seat and closed the taxi door with my shoulder.
I noticed a man walking to my left on the sidewalk. He stared at me and hid behind a parked car. It looked like he was tying his shoe.
I pretended not to take notice and put my hands in my pockets searching for the keys. I briefly touched the gun I kept hidden under my shirt to check that it was there and ready to use.
“Hey, Brigati...”
That voice was far from new to me. Regrettably.
“I wanted to offer you my condolences in person. The ones for your dear friend Andrea... I'm so sorry! I hope you got to say goodbye to him like I asked you to...”
I looked right and, against the light of the street lamp and opposite the hidden man, I saw a bulky silhouette. It was the giant from the marketing office and he was smiling at me. Meanwhile the other person, who was hiding among the cars, ambushed me and blocked my arms.
“Poor Joe, what are you doing on the streets at this hour, all alone and covered with blood? When night falls you have to go back home like Cinderella. They're going to arrest you tomorrow early in the morning... might as well enjoy your last night of freedom, no?”
I burst out laughing, I didn't want to let them believe that I was terrified.
“Arrest me? What the fuck are you saying? And what do you want from me?”
I tried to wiggle out of his hold and once again failed to do so.
“Of course, poor Jennifer Blasquez... Killed because she didn't reciprocate your love and you couldn't accept that you were being shoved aside in

favor of that small-time businessman... Pal, you're gonna get fifteen years if you're lucky..."
"What did you do to her?"
"You're the yellow-bellied coward here... the piece of shit who couldn't stand to kill her while staring at her in the eyes. So you decided to follow her at the dialysis centre and secretly injected her with a lethal dosis of heparin... You familiar with it?"
"In passing... what of it?"
"Well, just so you know what you did today, it's a natural anticoagulant. The dose you shot into her blood while you pretended to be a nurse would kill a healthy person, let alone one like her..."
I put on a defiant face.
"What do you mean?"
He laughed and continued his morbid tale, spouting precise medical terminology with a falsetto voice to make it all even more ironic.
A truly irritating way of getting a rise out of me.
"For people on dialysis, the effect is quicker. There's a mild failure at first, but the best part is when the heparine gets to the kidneys, all at once: it's called thrombocytopenia, which basically means those poor, sick organs of hers go boom and collapse forever... Meanwhile, blood flows through the whole body and the capillaries ooze platelets due to the high blood pressure... and finally... Booooom!! There goes the stroke that'll spell her end... Poor girl, she was so beautiful, such a pity... And you know what the best part is? The symptoms are hard to read, they come too late and you can't realize how dire the situation is until the body collapses. But then it's too late to save the patient..."
I would have liked to smash his face. But at least I knew I had gone to see Jenny in time to save her, or so I hoped. And he couldn't know that.
"A smart way to kill someone, perfect even! Kudos..."
So I tried to play along, mocking him and adopting his same attitude.
"And I would've managed all this alone? I must be a real genius... Too bad you're lacking evidence, don't you think? I was in Bresso today, there are witnesses who can confirm it..."
"Oh, I really don't think so. The investigators are going to find a syringe with your fingerprints in the department's trash. Remember that glass of whiskey you had at Jennifer's place? We copied your prints when she

wasn't home, right when she was going to the hospital where you'd kill her. She still hadn't done the dishes, lucky us she wasn't the world's best housewife. You know, all it takes is a little bit of transparent tape and black powder... and voila!"
Okay, fatty here was smart. And smug, too, he was gloating as he recounted how clever he had been in framing me.
But the witnesses were on my side. And they would prove the contrary.
"Right... I almost forgot. You were in Bresso today, weren't you? Do you know that the lawsuit initiated by Iorio Farmaceutici's former employees suddenly came to an end? A trade union agreement was reached... and good old Marco Ghezzi found a job like he always wanted, at MonteForte Company, as head of the marketing department: his dream position!"
He laughed.
"What did I tell you? You played with fire. And you compromised yourself forever... Had you minded your own goddamn business, now you wouldn't be facing your last night out of jail..."
"I can always tell everything to the police and blow you all to hell!"
"Sure, go on... Who's gonna believe you? Not even your dear friend the inspector. Your blood tests after the hit and run were faked, they found out about that, didn't they? But no-one can deny that you like to drink... And that you were obsessed by that poor girl."
He grabbed my face and pressed his fingers against my cheeks, then impersonated me, still in that falsetto voice.
"Don't you remember? 'You have to find Jenny'... 'Jenny disappeared'... 'Where's Jenny'. Isn't this you? How many times did you repeat all this to the cops? You're depressed, unemployed... human trash! Come on, you're not believable: you even told them that she works for an agency that doesn't exist! You're pathetic..."
The man wrestled the computer away from me. He smiled and whispered:
"Do you have cellars in here? Open the door, we need to have a word in private... I think that a fitting end to this tale would be for them to find you hanged, having taken your own life out of desperation...
"The keys are in my pocket..."
I jerked away from the brute at my back, freeing my right hand and pretending to look for my keys.
He loosened his grip.

I held my breath and drew my gun, quickly sidestepping onto the street so I could have them both at gunpoint. My move caught my opponents by surprise: they weren't expecting a hidden weapon.

“Well now, my dear boys. What's it gonna be?”

The big guy looked at me and smiled.

“Looks like your suicide will have to wait. What do you wanna do, kill us?” He almost looked amused.

“Mind you, if you shoot – if you have the guts to shoot, that is – all you'll ever manage will be to dig yourself even deeper. On top of being a murderer for love, you'll be a madman who shoots at random passer-bies in front of his house... another fifteen years maybe?”

“So you're fleeing... who's the shitstain now?”

“I have no intention of being killed by you, Joe dear... What does it matter, you're still compromised. This little chat of ours won't be anything more than a fantasy of yours to the police, something your wild imagination cooked up so you could avoid indictment...”

He turned around and dropped the black computer.

“Whoops... silly me. Was it new? You wouldn't have been able to use it in jail anyway...”

The two men got away, heading toward the end of the road with a leisurely stroll. They got inside a car, a Cadillac Escalade that looked similar to the one that had tried to run me over a few days earlier. They passed by my front door again, lowering their window and waving at me.

“Beware, prison is a bad environment, you never know who you're gonna share a cell with...”

I could only observe them as they drove away, still clinging to my gun and looking like a boxer who had just been beaten to a pulp by Mike Tyson. Not physically this time, but morally.

Deep down, I felt down for the count: ko.

XXI

*"The private security company
works for the most revolutionary faction
of Orange Hands. As soon as they knew
that the love story with Paolo Iorio
was real, they tried to kill her."*

I couldn't put the pieces together.
No, not the investigation. To be honest, that puzzle had gained a life of its own even without my input. The situation was plummeting without a chute.
I meant the PC, given how duct tape wasn't sticking to its black plastic. As I always say, Macs with their aluminium cases are the best. I know, I'm paranoid.
I was damning myself to find a passable solution, as that imbecile had broken my only contact with Jenny and her world. I was sure that her files would give me the info I needed to find Paolo Iorio in San Francisco.
Without those, I would never be able to talk to him.
I used to be pretty good with electronic DIY. I remember the days when I disassembled and quickly reassembled my father's radios in order to study their components. Those were good times, free from worries and responsibilities. The tween years are the best, then you grow up too soon and end up in a world full of pitfalls and hardships.
"What the hell do I do now?"
I couldn't leave the PC like that, it was unusable.
I quickly went through my iPhone's contacts, looking for the phone number of the IT guy we used to call when I worked for *Repubblica*. Maybe he could help, even though I feared that the hour was already too late.
"Hello? Fabrizio?"
"Yes, who is this?"
"It's Joe, Joe Brigati... Remember me?"

"Ah, hello... It's been a while... Why are you calling me at eleven PM? Did anything happen at the newspaper?"
Evidently, nobody told him that I had left the job. I took advantage of that fact.
"Actually no, I'm calling for an urgent business. I need to get a piece done by tomorrow morning and my laptop took a dive... I'm panicking, it's not working..."
"I can hop by the newspaper if you want, you're lucky I'm outside, I was going home just now..."
"No, actually, I'm in my flat. How much would an on-site intervention cost me now? I am so sorry to bother you, but I really need to get those data back."
"Well, seventy Euros is my standard fare. But I can't guarantee I'll be able to patch it back immediately. It depends on the kind of damage... But we can give it a try."
He might as well have asked for one thousand Euros, I would've accepted anyway. I told him the address and hung up.
I quickly packed a bag as I waited for him, with just the bare necessities and the USB drive with Paolo's files.
I erased every trace of my presence, slipping all possible personal effects inside the bag: passport, assorted pictures, address book, documents, battery chargers and the hard disk with all the articles I've written in my life. I treasure them dearly.
They had to think that I'd disappeared.
I had to take along with me Jennifer's top secret documents too, hot though they were. I couldn't leave them home, no matter how well hidden. Too dangerous.
I was back in my living room as I started getting second thoughts.
My conscience's voice grew clearer: "Hey, Joe... What the hell do you think you're doing? Have you gone mad?" I should have gone to Gaudenzi, probably, to explain everything to him. Rushing to the States wasn't the smartest idea.
"What if he doesn't believe you? You would lose your only chance to prove your innocence." The voice of the devil on my shoulder – tempting and a tad distrustful of cops – was right. I had to seize the moment, *carpe diem* as the Latins said. Most importantly, I had to come up with a plan.

I sat on the couch and focused.
Who would pay, in the end? MAS? Gaudenzi would take in Norberto Riesp for questioning, but I highly doubted that the company's boss would spill the beans.
I still didn't understand why they were trying to kill me. As I thought back to Jenny's talks, I could only find one possible explanation: the private security company worked for the most revolutionary faction of Orange Hands. As soon as they knew that the love story with Paolo Iorio was real, they tried to kill her, frame me for it as I had been let in on classified secrets, and take out Andrea too, our only go-between.
Were they about to launch the global revolution Jennifer mentioned, then? Or was this all an isolated act meant to take care of possible 'collateral damage' sustained by the organization? Good question. All I had figured out was the real architect behind my frame-up.
My plan? Simple.
I would have to find Paolo, warn him that Orange Hands people wanted to kill him and, with him safe by my side, go to the police so he would tell them everything and clear my name. Besides, forcing the investigators to carry out more thorough checks on MAS would lead them to find out that both Iorio and I were innocent.
The documents from Jenny's computer would do the rest, they would take the lid off the secret world of the orange hand and stop their purported global revolution.
Of course, my hope was that Jennifer would wake up from her coma, then her testimony would be the final nail in their coffin. Even though she would risk an indictment as well, I would find a way to keep her out of trouble, that was the least of my worries.
The doorbell rang. I looked through the spy-hole and saw a man I did not recognize. Feeling a jolt of fear, I grabbed the gun and tucked it in my pants. You never know.
"Brigati, this is Frank Pascale, Interpol. Open, please. Inspector Gaudenzi sent me."
My brain froze: were they here for me already?
"We know you're home. I just need to ask you some questions."

I looked through the spy-hole again and saw that he was presenting a badge, complete with picture. Unless those documents were fake, he really was a cop.
I opened the door. I had no other choice.

His face was pale. Black hair, receding hairline, overweight and with a scruff, it was obvious that he hadn't slept much. Or maybe he had been woken up specifically to come talk to me.
His suit wasn't tailor-made, it was rumpled and unworthy of an Interpol agent. Gray tones, white shirt, burgundy tie.
He looked at me standing in the middle of what was left of my living room; after the attack, I still hadn't cleaned up. He didn't seem to care, sitting on the couch and taking care to lift the hem of his suit so it wouldn't be ruined. Too bad the rest of his clothes looked straight out of a spin dryer.
He took out a notebook.
"I will only need a few minutes of your time. You see, for weeks we have been trying to make sense of a series of murders. And you appear to be in possession of relevant information..."
"Murders?"
"Apparently. The car that attempted to run you over had an orange handprint on its side. The same symbol has come up in other cases as well..."
"Where?"
"United States. Let me just tell you that it was hard to put the pieces together. The people involved all come from different social backgrounds, they had nothing to do with each other and only a few of them had ever met. Go figure, in some cases, the handprint wasn't even catalogued as evidence. Yet..."
I couldn't understand the meaning behind that chat, but as long as he wasn't there to arrest me, I wasn't complaining.
"Yet?"
"As I was saying, yet we managed to scrap together a working theory or two. We are currently looking into this trail in Milan looking for a

breakthrough. My superiors got the info from the Milan police department and sent me here to ask some questions."
"What do you think the hand means?"
"Brigati, I'm supposed to ask the questions..."
His listless, gloomy face brightened up a little. I smiled.
"Fine, sorry... But I wouldn't know how to be of help."
"Actually, Inspector Gaudenzi told me that as you identified the corpse in the car, you mentioned that a woman might have been involved... That same woman appears to have been admitted to the general hospital a few hours ago, in dire conditions. A crime of passion or yet another unsolved case tied to the orange hand?"
He showed me a picture – it was Jenny.
That talk about a crime of passion made my blood freeze in my veins.
"Brigati, do you know her?"
I gave him a fearful look.
"Yes, it's her... Jennifer Blasquez. Is she dead?"
"Actually, no, but she's in a coma and I don't think she has much left to live. They are looking for her boyfriend, one Paolo Iorio. We believe that he was the one who attempted to poison her and then, as the guilt set in, called an ambulance before he fled. But, again, the investigation is ongoing and we don't know a lot yet..."
I had accidentally thrown everyone off my scent.
"The only hitch would seem to be that he is supposed to be in San Francisco. Iorio purportedly flew back to Italy a few days ago only to return to the States immediately. It could be an error at the customs in Malpensa airport, though, we need to ask our colleagues in Denver to double-check, as that's where most European flights headed for the West Coast stop. Brigati, have you seen Iorio lately?"
"No, actually I've never met him."
"And miss Blasquez?"
"Yesterday."
"Did she look healthy?"
"Fit as a fiddle, as far as I could tell."
"Mmh... So how could this fella kill her if he'd left the country already?"

“Could you please stop talking about her as if she were dead? It bothers me...”
“Ah, right... Professional bias. I beg your pardon.”
I tried to get a better understanding of Jenny's situation.
“Agent, if you don't mind, why do you think it was attempted murder?”
“At the ER they found high traces of heparin in her blood. Considering that no-one would inject themselves with such a high dosage, we think it was administered to her. Besides, her fiance disappeared, so doing the math...”
“Makes sense. What does the orange hand have to do with it?”
“They are two different things, but considering that the symbol was on the car they used to run you over... I was pointed in your direction. That's all, I only wanted to understand if Miss Blasquez's untimely end and the orange hand could be connected.”
“And I'm the one who's supposed to tell you?”
“If you believe so, yes...”
Honestly, I didn't trust him. He looked like a deadbeat New York detective, hardly enthusiastic about his work. And how could such a type be actually working for Interpol?
“I don't think so. In those days I was worried for Jenny's disappearance, but the truth was that she had flown to her fiance in San Francisco. And I didn't know about it. Which is why I mentioned her during the questioning...”
“And do you have any clue as to AISE's presence during said questioning?”
“The what?”
“AISE, the External Intelligence and Security Agency.”
“No, I mean, what do you mean?”
The agent realized his faux pas and stepped back.
“Never mind, I must have read the transcripts wrong... Nothing, nothing, I'd say...”
So that was the man who hadn't even introduced himself before chewing me out in front of a dumbfounded Gaudenzi. That was the reason behind Mirko's silence: the Italian secret services were involved.

The story was getting more and more convoluted.
The astute investigator drowned me in pointless questions for minutes, questions to which I answered as curtly as I could, looking for any chance to get him out of my flat as soon as possible.
“Listen, while we're at it... I'm leaving for Canada tomorrow, I want to visit my parents. Do you think that leaving the country would be an issue for me?”
“Oh, not at all... Canadian, eh? I'm Italian-American, I've been here since 2007 and I don't plan on going back, considering that my wife is from Pozzuoli.”
I didn't care. At least I understood what that weird cop was doing in Italy, though. All I cared for was that I would be allowed to travel abroad. Had anyone asked, I would've mentioned that my flight had been greenlit by Interpol.
To wrap it all up, I asked my last question: “What do you think of the hand, then? I fear I wasn't able to properly aid your investigation. I am sorry, but I don't know anything...”
Oh how I loved to act all worried.
“Ah, nothing... You and Ms. Blasquez were our only lead. But since neither of you can disclose any useful information, we can only conclude that they were isolated crimes... We hope to be able to find this Iorio fellow soon, so we'll discuss the matter of the attempted murder of his girlfriend...”
“And that other affair?”
“I'd say that the hand on the door of the car that hit you can't be connected to the American cases... Even though I can't imagine how it ended there. But that's what I already told my bosses: it was pointless to pursue this line of investigation. It was obvious, the murders were too different and, most importantly, they took place thousands of miles apart from each other... But they never believe me...”
Oh gee, I wonder why! The cop trotted toward the entrance door and waved me goodbye as he went out. He looked pleased.
I closed the door with a grin. Lucky me, they hadn't sent their best and brightest to question me. Maybe he was the only one they could reach at that hour of the night.

XXII

"A hidden world.
The deepest side
of cyberspace, a dark free zone
where documents can be hidden."

I looked at the hour: almost one in the morning.
Fabrizio had been poking around Jennifer's computer for twenty minutes – he'd arrived just as the man from Interpol had left and got to work with the usual courtesy.
"No, Joe, I wouldn't know what to tell you... It's working now, but all the connections to the deep web are lost. You can only access what you already downloaded, nothing more... I'm sorry."
I made a face at him: "The deep what?"
"What... The deep web, Joe you've got a shortcut on your desktop, how can you not know about it?"
"Ah, I'd forgotten about it! I think my girlfriend created it... Could you tell me what it is that we're talking about?"
"I thought it was a journalists' thing, a way for you guys to exchange confidential info! Sorry... Well, how can I explain it in simple words..."
Fabrizio then embarked in an exhaustive description of the web's underbelly, things I had no idea even existed. He accidentally explained to me what system Orange Hands used to upload the classified info that the lodge's members collected all around the world.
That was how they cultivated the massive database where one day or another everyone would end up, neatly catalogued.
Jenny, of course, had access to it.
"Let's say it's a hidden world. It is considered the deepest side of cyberspace, a dark free zone where encrypted documents can be hidden. It's an endless expanse of information, created by people who exploit anonymity for their shady businesses."
"Meaning?"

"Browsing the regular internet gives us access to approximately two billion documents – the deep web hosts about 550 billion of them. And it keeps expanding. It's located underneath the world wide web, its contents are not indexed by search engines nor can they be accessed through URLs like, say, Google. Long story short, they're impossible to reach directly."
"So how do you reach them?"
"Do keep in mind that the system installed on your computer is different, it looks encrypted at source, I've never seen anything like it... It allows you to upload data, but not to read what other online users are uploading. It's a modified deep web that uses the same framework."
"Okay, but how does it work normally?"
"The data servers are everywhere and they are unreachable. It's not exactly easy to access them, the easiest and safest way is to modify the Firefox browser through an extension that allows it to latch onto the Tor network. This system is called Tor Browser..."
Sounded like a bunch of technobabble to me. Could it be, that I had never heard anything about this? I was out of the loop, as they say.
"Tor? Like the Marvel superhero?"
"That's right, Joe, but without the 'h'... It stands for "The Onion Router", it's just a tiny program that creates a web of users that distribute and encrypt connections between the senders and receivers, so that tracing the identity of the users becomes near impossible."
"You never get caught, basically."
"Almost never. But this systems you've got installed on your PC, this one isn't only encrypted, it can also simultaneously redirect your position in 30 different nations... Unbelievable! Who the hell installed this thing? It's a work of genius: you're surely not gonna get caught with this baby..."
"So, like, Wikileaks..."
"Uses the same system to find their news and distribute it. But the one you have looks a lot safer, more powerful and secret..."
I was bewildered, incapable of saying anything after all those news.
"Fabrizio, please promise you're not going to say anything to..."
"Don't mention it, I didn't even think something like this were feasible, if I were to tell my colleagues about it they wouldn't believe me!"
I paid him and accompanied him to the door. He had been really useful: by repairing Jenny's computer, he allowed me to access her private

documents, to find out what information she had collected on Iorio P. Farmaceutici Srl and uploaded on the encrypted web server before she entered a relationship with the owner. Too bad that the laptop's fall forbade me from browsing the deep web in more detail, to find out more about Orange Hands and about the person pulling the strings behind it all.
But for my more urgent needs, i.e. Paolo's address in the States and the evidence that would clear my name, the downloaded data was enough. I could leave for San Francisco without a second thought.

I had a bad feeling as I closed the front door.
I couldn't know whether I would be able to come back home at the end of this story. Yet I couldn't stop. I had to save my reputation at all costs, I didn't want to be branded a murderer. I could imagine how amused my former colleagues at Repubblica would be as soon as the news got out.
They would surely laugh at me, or even better, they would indulge in comments such as “We knew he wasn't all right in his head”.
The same trite commentary that is all over the place in the interviews broadcast on television, when after a heinous murder, the news show the killer's neighbors and their fake exclusive gossip on the man. Even though before the tragedy, all they knew of him was a brief hello in the elevator.
It was almost dawn.
The taxi quickly drove me to Malpensa airport.
Last time I went there, I was coming back from Canada after the Christmas holidays: almost one year earlier.
I got inside, eager to get my ticket: a flight to San Francisco, with stop in Denver. I paid with my credit card directly to the airline's booth, goodbye money, and good for me I'd been paid in advance for the book or my finances wouldn't have allowed me this solution to begin with. Meaning? A sure-fire conviction and no way of getting away and putting my plan in motion.
The double weight of the shoulder strap and the suitcase were bothering me – I've always hated dragging a luggage and having another thing hang from my shoulder. I checked both items as hold baggage, keeping just the PC to myself. I had to work during the flight.
I passed the security checks with my heart in my throat, I feared that my picture would've already been broadcast by the police.

I did not, however, experience any hindrance, not even when handing over my passport.
I waited until my flight's departure. I usually had to wait for ages, but on that day, luck was on my side: take-off would be in one hour, at 6.30AM. Could it be an omen of more good luck to come? I hoped so.
Time seemed to have ground to a halt.
I listened to some music, but I was too shaken.
They eventually called for my flight. I looked around, in search of prying eyes, trying to figure out whether anyone was following me or checking on me. I gave myself the green light.
I was, finally, on the plane. All that was left to do was to work, while the Boeing did its thing and brought me safely to San Francisco.
The last remaining variable was the stop in Denver.
I would have to get off the plane and back on a different one, thankfully skipping the whole red tape with passports. But I could be intercepted in case of an international arrest warrant. I didn't care.
All I wanted to do, after having fastened my belt and safely lodged the computer inside the seat pocket, was to get some shut-eye. It could only do me good.
I woke up, startled.
I'd hoped I could sleep a while, considering that I hadn't had a chance to rest in the past twenty-four hours, but my body wouldn't have any of that. I didn't sleep for longer than an hour.
I booted up the computer and inserted Paolo's USB drive. Ultimately, I wondered what point there could be in continuing to pen that man's biography. But Jenny had asked me to continue, almost on her deathbed, and I always keep a promise. I'd also already been paid and I didn't feel like dropping everything without a reason.
I thought back to her words, that telling his life was a way of saving him. I wondered what she meant by that.
I opened a new Word file and the program's interface felt like a slap, accustomed as I was to Pages. But I would have to get used to it.
Thanks to my good memory, I easily rewrote the first two chapters, which had been lost in the accident. The flight was calm and I wasn't feeling sleepy anymore.

I browsed through the USB drive and found a folder: "Life reflections – Paolo Iorio". I opened it and read his notes, transforming them in new chapters of the biography. There were some audio files as well.

***

Emptiness, distress and, first and foremost, the worry that I would not be able to put an end to all the existential doubts that had filled my head for months. Those were the thoughts that tore at me from the inside as I drove toward Bergamo. My journey of hope, filled with expectations.
Uncle Ernesto was our paragon: he'd left with a luggage full of hopes, leaving for a time his wife Adele in Floridia, and came back less than one year later satisfied with his success. In a few months, he had found a home, a job and a future, and he could comfortably bring his wife along with him as he came back from the summer holidays. But Ernesto couldn't have imagined that his return would pan out like this: he couldn't have imagined that he would have to drag me along, but that's life sometimes. Unpredictable. Maybe he considered me a nuisance, a burden for a young couple who only wanted to make a new life for themselves in a town miles away from their old home. Of course they never said me anything of the sort, but I wouldn't live with them for long and I understood that from my first minutes in their car already.
They treated me well and considered me a son, but I didn't want to weigh on them. Adele was pregnant and their family rightfully needed space. Besides, I wanted my own independence: I fully intended to go live on my own as soon as I could.
Beyond the windows of uncle Ernesto's Alfa Romeo, a line of trees skirted the highway. The more miles we put behind us, the more the landscape changed: everything turned darker, gloomier. Sicily's sun was behind us and I noticed that the spaces were smaller – less grass, less green, more and more buildings and constructions. I could almost feel all that concrete crushing me, but it didn't matter as long as I could build the future I wanted for myself. I was ready to turn over a new leaf regardless of the kind of landscape that would greet me. My first day in Bergamo was peculiar, I felt like a fish out of water. People all around me were always in distress, running to and fro, always busy, always in a hurry. There were

so many cars, at least compared to what I had seen in Sicily up to that moment. My room was truly beautiful: I had a pale wooden bed of my own and a cupboard in the same tones. It was vaguely reminiscent of those mountain cabins. I felt like a little lord, I couldn't have asked for anything better. Of course none of it was designer furniture, but I had everything I could ever need. It wasn't actually my room, but rather the one that would eventually belong to my unborn cousin. I set camp there for the moment, in the three-room apartment uncle Ernesto had rented to be able to live comfortably with his family.

The flat was close to the town's centre, part of a newly built three-story building.

It looked like a lovely setup for a pleasant, gratifying adventure, but that was not in the cards. On the contrary, the first problems arose just a few days after my arrival in the North.

My parents had been clear from the outset: their sustenance was all on me. They were already waiting for my first earnings, I needed a job and I absolutely needed to get moving. School was a thing of the past, my only goal was to try and maintain the family I had left in Sicily. Luckily, Ernesto had managed to befriend some colleagues during his first months in the North and through their word of mouth he learned which companies were looking for a young assistant, resourceful but lacking experience. That was, all in all, my biggest flaw: I was young, possibly too young, and most importantly inexperienced. I hadn't studied and all my work experience amounted to 'grocery clerk'. I was truly starting from scratch.

No factory hired me and I could only stand by and wait for two weeks. The more time passed, the more I felt restless. I always had something to eat, my uncle and aunt never left me wanting, but it felt like living in limbo, with the sneaking awareness that deep down, both my uncle both his wife Adele were starting to worry that they would have to care for me until I came of age. Ditched by my parents first, and now close to becoming a burden on my new family.

The tunnel grew longer and longer, the end wasn't in sight even there in the North. Darkness kept ruling over my life, leaving me feeling ever more alone and and swept up by life. It was in those hard days that I understood how much strength and grit I had inside me. It was the first signal of my

eventual survival: Paolo would overcome every difficulty. Paolo would not succumb to discouragement, he would make a living for himself.
The realization that I could make it, under any circumstances, flickered into my mind in those days. What gave me all that positive energy? Hunger biting at you, survival instinct and rage pushing you from the very depths of your heart. This has always been the fuel that has made me go on, day after day. And it always will.

XXIII

"Losers walk among the fools,
winners with the intelligent ones.
It may be a strong stance,
but I'm honest: this is what I believe."

The flight luckily didn't hit any air pockets and only three hours were left until our stop in Denver. I kept on reading Iorio's notes, trying to turn them into a lively narration on that white Word page.
Truth be told, I wasn't very focused.
Sitting beside me, a tall man with a beard oozed garlic, which didn't help my writing. Sadly, the constrained spaces of airplanes often lend themselves to unfortunate short-term cohabitation. And in those cases, all that's left to do is ignore one's nose's protests and pretend that nothing's wrong.
It did, however, made it hard for me to find the required linguistic variety and a pressing narrative rhythm. My mind was elsewhere.
As I reflected upon my writing, I came to an easy conclusion: Iorio's life was hard. He grew up alone, overcoming the copious snares of existence. A man to respect, even more so considering that he even moved up, albeit in ways I hadn't yet discovered.
I took a little break and browsed Jenny's files in search of pictures, so I could have some references once I landed. How would I be able to find Paolo, otherwise?
I had to pinpoint the places he used to hang out at during his previous travels to San Francisco.
I found a folder named 'US holidays', opened it and was glad to find out that the businessman had a home in town, at least judging by the photos' backgrounds.
I didn't know whether he owned the place or just rented it, but it didn't matter.

What a stroke of luck! I had to celebrate and promptly ordered a fresh beer from the flight attendant. Finally, good news.
He and Jennifer appeared, smiling, in some digital snapshots taken under a white porch outside a beige building in Art Nouveau style on the city hills, the city's famous up-and-down hills that feature in every film that was ever set there.
Zooming in, I barely made out the name of the street, or so I hoped: 'Masonic Avenue'.
"I'll look it up on Google Maps as soon as I get an internet connection."
I had a starting point. The dark red of the opposite façade could also be of help in determining the house's position. With a little luck, I would be able to locate it. And I could only hope that Iorio hadn't moved since taking that picture.
At any rate, I felt more relaxed, having overcome the first hurdle of this trip.
I could go on with my writing, trying to find the appropriate and necessary focus.

***

How all those sensations and those stirrings were born inside me, I cannot know. The spark came from chance and luck: just when everything seemed lost, I was called. It felt bigger than being called to play for the national soccer team: "I've found a job for Paolo. It's not much, but still better than staying at home", my uncle said one evening as we were dining. My persisting unemployment had made the mood at home tense for the previous three days. "You'll have to be ready at five tomorrow, they'll come fetch you. You're going to be a construction worker in Cologno al Serio, the place ain't far."
I couldn't sleep well that night, I was shaken. I feared that I would end up in a world of adults – a construction site felt like a place populated by pissed-off behemoths, embittered by their harsh lives. And I was only a tiny, frail twelve years old ready to be thrown into the fray. But I knew that I couldn't back out. It was during that long, frantic night that my harsh personality began to take shape. I wouldn't bow down to anything, even though, truth be told, that would be easier said than done. My eyes only

closed at 3.30 in the morning, about one hour earlier than my appointed departure for the construction site. My first real job was about to start, a far shot from bike deliveries in Floridia.

The morning was chilly. Brine covered the few plants in the park outside the three-story building. Beyond the glass and aluminium front door, the pick-up was waiting for me, with four people already inside. Their faces were hardly visible beyond the windows, fogged by the heat inside the cabin.

"Hop on, push these three idiots aside and get a seat." The driver was from Bergamo, his name was Ettore Cavagna. He drove in the morning and worked at the site for the rest of the day. He got the additional job due to living right beside the building company's warehouse. At the beginning of the shift, he drove to all the employees' homes nearby and collected everyone to go to work. That drive allowed me to glean a few more info on the job I was about to be enrolled in. First off, I found out that I had been 'summoned' thanks to the help of a friend of my uncle's, whom everyone called 'il Siculo', the Sicilian, and whose real name was Filippo Misumeci. He had also come from Sicily a few years earlier and he lived in the building next to ours.

"Boy, you have no idea of what's gonna be awaiting you once you step inside the construction site's gates" were the first words I heard from our Sicilian neighbor as soon as I got in the pick-up van.

"I've been working there for a few years and I've never toiled so hard: it literally breaks your back. But if you're smart and want to learn, it's always a honest job that can make you grow and put some bread on your table."

That was a start, wasn't it?

I was tasked with following the foreman like a shadow and helping him during the most delicate parts of the day. Organization, handling of materials, preparation of components for bricklayers and solderers. At every step the chief, Giacomo Rota, explained to me what was going on in that part of the site of how. I couldn't ask for anything better, I learned and walked, walked and learned. A few days later, though, this idyll ended.

My life became a bona fide hell. I woke up a five in the morning, I was dropped on a pick-up and ended up in a construction site. I worked like a

madman, up and down the scaffolding, until 5 PM, then I went back home. The actual time when I made it home was always a mystery: it could be 6, if the workplace was near Bergamo, or I could arrive as late as 8, if it was really far.
I worked a whole seventeen construction sites in my life before finding a better job. Water, snow, rain and hail didn't scare me, let alone the scorching sun in June and July, not too far removed from the heat of Sicily. It was similar because it seared your skin, even though the sunburns here were often more intense.
Not even the sad lunch could make me lose heart and consider forfeiting my fight. It was a simple prosciutto sandwich, which I ate sitting on the foundations of a building that, in a few years, would possibly become an office, or possibly the home of some wealthy entrepreneur. Even though my colleagues were at the pub. I had to spare my money and couldn't allow that kind of expenses.
That was my goal: the more days passed, the more motivated I felt. I had to give some meaning to my life, find a better job and start trying to earn a little more. I couldn't end up being a construction worker all my life. With my full respect to construction workers who keep their job for life, I really couldn't see myself as part of that world for long.
So I decided to enroll to school, night school to be precise. When I came back from the site, I ate a quick dinner and went to study what little I needed to cover the basics: Italian grammar, maths and something more. Basically anything I would need to make a breakthrough and be hired to work in a factory, one day – a day I hoped would come as soon as possible.
That would be my life for two years in a row. I didn't even stop in August, when the construction company was closed and everyone was on holiday. Ernesto and Adele were back in Floridia to spend time with their relatives, I stayed in Bergamo to work. I absolutely refused to go back to Sicily. I wanted to go live on my own and I would have to pay one year of rent in advance, which was why I needed the money. I could always find some small job, especially when the construction company was closed for twenty days of holiday. As a consequence, my back and arms hurt like hell even during the purported holidays. But in those days I felt a breeze blow across my heart: working alone was amazing. It gave you all the responsibilities and you were the master of your own self. I would never

forget that feeling, which I first experienced on that second summer in Bergamo. It stayed with me for my entire life.
Risk and trust in one's talents are a constant. It's like feeling a light murmur when your heart beats out of the joy that comes with results and feeling it flutter unnaturally as it ponders the mysteries that are awaiting in every upcoming day.
Meanwhile, summer was almost over and I was getting ready for another round of school. Off we went again. I wasn't what you'd call a genius, but I wasn't lacking in good will, either. I am sure that with more time to study, I may have gotten myself a degree. I like reading, but in those days, my energies were devoted to the skills that would prove useful in getting a job: I needed to learn as much as I could on the workplace in order to move up. I was good with my hands, smart enough to bridge the gap with my adult colleagues, and I was getting physically stronger after all my daily efforts. I was growing, not only in my head and personality, but in my body as well: my physique was getting closer and closer to that of the other workers.

Being hungry really sucks. And I don't mean the peckish feeling you get when your nose picks up the inviting smell from the kitchen at home or at the restaurant you've just walked in. I mean being hungry for success, wanting to accomplish something big in your life. Feeling appeased and satisfied of your lifestyle and of what you have accomplished, being available and necessary to others. Latent form of narcissism it may be, but narcissism was always a fundamental part of my personality. Even though up to that point, I hadn't had much luck when it came to family and had been forced to give to them more than I had gotten in return, I still felt the urge to do something important for my loved ones. Being at the center of attention made me strong, invincible.
For that reason, as time went by, the people I kept by my side always had to remain 'under control': both the ones I loved and the ones working with me. I had an obsessive need to keep a close eye on everything. You can't be certain of your professional and personal successes if you don't centralize your power and don't make yourself indispensable to the people around you. Else you'll always remain in the background, and they will, sooner or later, crush you and kill you. This postulate has always led my

life, along with another concept: losers walk among the fools, winners with the intelligent ones. It may be a strong stance, but I'm honest: this is what I believe.
These beliefs allowed me to leave the construction site and find a job in a company near Bergamo, in Palazzolo. It was a small firm, whose elderly owner had begun his career as a chemist and then branched out to parapharmaceuticals.
Finally, my first results, a new job. I would become a chemical expert thanks to my evening school studies and I would soon get the chance to rent a small apartment above my uncles'. I was self-sufficient by the age of 17 already, a record considering where I had started from. Once in a while, I could still feel that famous 'flutter' in my heart.
Following my superiors' ideas, be it the company's manager or the owner above him, was inconceivable to me if what they asked me to do was wrong. And I never restrained my opinions: when I had something to say, I said it. This characteristic of mine was favored by the owner and by some colleagues, who considered me a trusted, frank, straightforward person. Loyal, even. But my superiors' envy, who feared for their job and their image, lurked behind every corner. Those were the days where I understood what it meant to be hated, to be considered as an enemy to be purged.
"Hey, Paolo! Fuck, pay attention!" It was my supervisor. A mediocre person, characterized by a huge drive to get ahead. He was very close to being too old for a promotion and had to prove himself and show off at any opportunity.
The company was abuzz with talks of how a big American multinational company would take over our small, family-run business. With that upcoming stars-and-striped invasion, there would be promotions as well as layoffs.
Of course, those were nothing but dubious leaks. "We need to increase the production of these blister packs, the Americans are accustomed to much higher numbers than ours. Understood? Now get your ass in gear..."
I replied in kind.
He tugged at my suit, as a display of superiority aimed at the colleagues who were watching us.
I went for the jugular and gave him a savage beating.

Thinking back upon it, I don't know what happened to me. It was a primordial instinct from deep down.
We had to be separated by our colleagues, with no small struggle.
I don't know why they didn't fire me. For all intents and purposes, I had assaulted one of my superiors, breaking his nose and disfiguring his face with solvent. I was young and inexperienced, but my action was absolutely deplorable.
Maybe my childish face made me look like a victim myself. I wouldn't know. I was pardoned and even got a transfer. Indeed: from production, I was sent to the commercial department, so I would avoid getting in trouble with colleagues. Goodbye machinery, I would go take care of the company's clients.
I realized that these developments would cause no small amount of trouble to yours truly. In the production department, nobody even looked me in the eye. I was a pariah.
The traitor, the sellout. A weird rumor started circulating: that I had managed to be promoted – instead of fired – by talking shit about my colleagues. As bad luck would have it, the leaks turned out to be true and the Americans took over. The new board of directors laid off some employees to make ends meet and this purge was seen as a consequence of my 'betrayal'.
On the other hand, you can imagine the sort of reception I got at commercial. My new bosses immediately antagonized me, especially the trusted man sent by the new American owners who was to act as a supervisor.

The US company who had bought us was called MonteForte Company. As I had never heard of them before, I gathered that they were active in the chemical sector, nothing more.
Through a British branch of theirs, FourStreet Chemical Ltd., the company was gaining a hold on the Italian pharmaceutical market.
The man they designated to lead us was an inflexible drill sergeant from Birmingham. Beside him, as my boss in the commercial department, his goon, a young, overambitious young man from Milan who had just gotten his university degree.

Said young man considered himself one step above a hillbilly like me, doubly so since I came from the South – I was the fake consultant, the boorish Sicilian peasant.
Actually, he was all smoke and mirrors. He was thirty years old and more than ready to use me as a doormat. So we started faking some sort of interest toward each other, but it was far from the truth, on the contrary: as I said, the tension was thick as mud.
On top of that, everyone in the office looked at me with suspicion in their eyes: they believed that I had been transferred there in order to spy on them, a rumor that grew and grew regardless of my actions.
I even bought myself a couple of suits and two shirts so I could better measure up to my coordinator. No ties, though: I can't stand them, they make me look insecure. But the clothes were hardly quality, not to mention that my bearing and my calloused hands were clear signals that I didn't really belong there.
I held up two, three, then four months. I couldn't afford to be fired, so I bit my tongue. I knew that the young man beside me was much more respectable in the eyes of our superiors. "But one day I'll get my breakthrough", I used to tell myself. It was the only thought I could hold onto.
In those days, many and dramatic changes occurred. As we imagined, the Americans changed the production cycle, focusing on less quality and more quantity. The new management also spiced up the commercial side of things: we needed to fill the orders box with more contracts.
Our small reality was turning into a real pharmaceutical company. They moved the plant in an industrial area outside Palazzolo, tripling its size. They also built a state-of-the-art chemical lab and a small area where they would breed the animals they needed to carry out brutal tests.
From one hundred employees, our big family expanded to about one hundred and fifty, and of course the local media and institutions couldn't stop praising the new management for the opportunities they were offering to the whole area.
New, ambitious salespeople were also hired. Our new goal was to contact a growing number of doctors, even specialists, and chemists, in order to promote the Group's 'Life' product line.

We were to advertise the candid face of international pharmaceutics, its public face, the one we see every day on TV. There, the ads show happy families in need of a cure, getting invariably, inevitably cured by the latest astonishing product. But the pharmaceutical world is anything but candid. Behind that positive image were people completely enslaved by money and gains: us. All we needed were new orders, regardless of any other concern, even at the cost of selling drugs which would be useless or, as some rumors insinuated, which were untested. So I was tuned out and given the cold shoulder, as I did not like that new way of doing our job. It felt dirty to me. And I almost risked to be given the boot due to faltering productivity.
Truth be told, I still had a long way to go before I could say I understood how the world turned. What I could say for certain was that I was starting to feel a frenzy, an urge to grow up.
I wanted to prove to myself, and to the people around me and to anyone who ever tried to hamstring me or to shadow my talents, that they were wrong. But how?
It was surely the 'flutter' in my heart gaining traction. And I was becoming a rabid dog, hungry, reacting to every negative external prodding.
Some nights I dreamed of my future with my eyes wide open, without sleeping. It often happens when you are tired, very tired, that you are too exhausted to fall asleep. And in those moments, you imagine a radiant future, full of satisfactions.
You imagine a full biopic about yourself, and flopping isn't an option. Defeat is not part of your mind's vocabulary.
Then, your bed's warmth lulls you and makes you feel less scared, less alone as you think of the days to come, days when you will sometimes have to come to compromises which you will regret for the rest of your life.
I had to create something of my own, for myself. It didn't matter what: I wanted to go self-employed.
But I couldn't gather enough courage.
The opportunity came thanks to someone who appeared to be very kind, but was in truth corrupted like the others.
Marta Beretta, from atop her experience, threw me the bait I had been waiting for so long and I took it, hook line and sinker. She said: "Go freelance, open your own company". She was a lady in her fifties with a very distinguished, professional look. She used to take care of accounting

for the old company and was staying with the Americans so she could reach retirement.
She always complimented me, saying I was a good boy, and smart. But it was all fake.
Back then, with my wage, I barely managed to make ends meet and send some money back to my family so they could get by as well, given that my father never managed to find a stable occupation again.
I couldn't shoulder any further costs. I was in a constant loop, feeling that I had reached the moment to spread my wings and fly, but unable to figure out how. Until one day, as I said, my life's occasion presented itself.

In some points of one's existence, the most sudden of changes are the ones that make your character. Others break it and distort it forever.
Marta had indirectly learned from her boss that they were looking for a bold young man from commercial who would be willing to open an activity that would run parallel to Palazzolo's pharmaceutical industry, always within the field of promoting medicinal products.
They were interested in moving products that were being tested internally, or that had just been launched. But they didn't want to use their current employees to that end.
Marta was the one who brought forward the idea to me and, at the same time, suggested my name to the 'sergeant' from Birmingham. And he agreed to meet me. On that day I understood that the step I was about to make had no way back.
I should have imagined that the affair wouldn't be legal.
Or rather, as far as the law was concerned, it was fine, but it was on the brink of the human, moral precipice, to tell the truth.
I yielded entirely a few weeks later, when the entire board of directors of FourStreet Chemical Ltd. and of FourStreet Italia S.r.L. gathered for the occasion and gave me the good news.
Everyone believed in me. Finally, they had noticed me, from high atop their walnut desks. They told me I would have to resign and open my own activity, and they would take care of the rest: they would find employees, give me the money I needed to set things up and anything I needed or wanted.

Of course, I didn't think about it twice: I accepted on the spot and got many smiles and pats on the back in return.
The job was simple, too.
It consisted in convincing doctors to select patients and test the side effects of new pharmaceuticals on them. These people would thus become unwitting guinea pigs, unaware of the risks they were facing. But the doctor would get a nice, legal consulting contract out of it – in exchange for compiling the modules detailing the side effects – and the patients got the drugs for free once they signed a discharge against the company. Everyone was happy and I earned money, lots of money, I'd say.
Another task consisted in pushing the use of harmless drugs that would have no effects on patients. Covert placebos. They were needed to increase turnover and sales volume, all aimed at 'maintaining' university professors and their researches. And those same professors were the ones who suggested which new drugs would be launched on the market: the business started from them.
Cozying up to the doctors required an array of gifts: books, holidays disguised as conferences, envelopes filled with banknotes for the more reticent ones.
We were pushing this thing to the limit, but it was the true 'circle of health' and no-one could get out.
I hesitated before signing my new company's instrument of incorporation, knowing what risks I was going to face. But success has always been a bad companion in certain situations, and then again, evil is everywhere. A cancer that can hide even in the pharmaceutical market, by definition candid and padded, meant to help the weak, those who need our support and solidarity.
I accepted, not without qualms. It was the only way of saving some money in case I eventually wanted to make it on my own.
Adrenaline was pumping, my anger toward those who never believed in me had turned into a need for payback. I wanted to see the faces of all the people who had turned their backs on me, look at them one by one and make them understand how wrong they were.
I wanted to look them in the eye, once I'd become a top manager, and whisper in their ears: "See? You can make me fall all you want... But I get back up, and when I go back to running, I'm even more intense and

determined. No-one can stop me, I always move forward. And the people who turn their backs on me get torn to shreds. They'll pray not to cross my path again."
That was my goal and it was within my reach.

***

A blonde flight attendant brought me back in line as she asked me, with a smile, to please put my seat back in the upright position. I would also have to turn off my laptop and prepare for landing. Standard procedure: fasten seatbelts, turn off electronics, close the tray in front of my seat. I was so immersed in Paolo's tale that I had missed all the captain's announcements.
From atop her stilettos, the girl was right: Denver sprawled under us, I could see its skyline from the window. I was definitely too wrapped up in Iorio's story. As I read his notes and transcribed his biography, the tale became ever clearer and more transparent to my eyes, and I could begin to understand why telling the story of his life would be so important. It would make a powerful statement against the system and the puzzle was coming together in front of my eyes, magically and effortlessly.
Through the book, Paolo wanted to explain all the evils perpetrated by himself and by FourStreet Chemical Ltd, but most importantly by MonteForte Company, the occult mastermind behind it all. But why? It was counterproductive, he would risk ending up in jail.
I felt my heartbeat rise. Was there a reason they put me in that situation?
"Yes, Joe... he's spilling the beans. But why? What does he hope to obtain from all this? Now I'm starting to understand who might want me dead..."
"Beg your pardon?"
Beside me, the man who oozed garlic was giving me a horrified look.
"Nothing, sorry..."
Every time I talked out loud to myself, I did so in English.
In Italy, there weren't many people who knew the language well enough to pick up on the slang and it was easy for my thoughts to remain

confidential. Only the younger generations could decipher it, maybe after a holiday abroad, but most people I had come in contact with possessed a mastery of the language that could only be defined as 'Italian style': a meager handful of words, just enough to get by.
The passenger was still staring at me, sitting still. He had understood my musings.
“Okay, okay... It's a joke.” I smiled at him.
I turned toward the window with nonchalance, trying to diffuse his worries. I had forgotten that on an intercontinental flight, almost everyone could speak some form of English. The mirth was short-lived, though, as anxiety overtook me. I would need to get down this plane and on the following one. I fervidly hoped that I wouldn't be stopped by the police and arrested as a murderer in front of all those tourists who were travelling on my same route.

XXIV

"I felt close to the end
of this sad tale.
Even though I wasn't so sure anymore
that Iorio would want
to come to the police with me."

What could I do? I was sweating like a pig.
It wasn't due to the heat, though. The climate was pleasant, with the airport's conditioning.
It was anxiety. The corridor to my new gate slowly scrolled under my feet, seemingly endless.
I had left the plane like the rest of the passengers, but I wasn't a simple tourist, eagerly awaiting his upcoming holiday. I kept staring at the far end of the corridor, looking for any policemen who might be waiting for me.
I hoped I wouldn't find any, but I couldn't be sure. Meanwhile, my heart beat fast, jolting and jumping in my chest.
Denver International Airport is huge. Most of the flights bound for the entire American continent stop there. With its 34,000 acres, it is the largest airport in the United States and the third largest worldwide. Moving from one terminal to the next even takes boarding a special train.
As you can imagine, the possibility of getting lost was high and security was even higher, and if I had an international arrest warrant for homicide on me, I wouldn't have it easy.
The artificial light of the passengers' waiting area blinded me for a moment. I had arrived.
At the exit, I anxiously checked to my right, then to my left: nothing suspicious.
I was safe.
I quickly headed toward the new boarding area: starting from number 12, I had to reach 31.

I spent ten minutes strolling through international fashion brand stores – I didn't want to risk being spotted.
Once I finally made it to my gate, I sat down and waited for my turn.
No-one else was there.
No other passengers had shown up yet, with two more hours until boarding.
I opened Jenny's laptop and, through the airport's wi-fi connection, I searched for more info on FourStreet Chemical Ltd...
I wanted to find out where their San Francisco branch was located, if they even had one there. I might have needed to pay it a visit in case contacting Paolo proved to be difficult, especially if the house on the hills didn't turn out to be his.
Besides, I wanted to get a good look at them and their activities. After the things I had written in the biography, my nose smelled even more troubles.
And I was getting to the end of my rope.
Googling the name of the company along with San Francisco's geographical area made me jump: among the first results, an article from the *Chronicle* talked about a murder in Sausalito, with the victim being a famous researcher, Jason Wittman, pathologist at the University of San Francisco, CA. Dean of the Department of Pathology of the university's study centre, he was one of the co-founders of Biotech FourStreet Laboratories Inc..
With every passing hour, the pieces of the puzzles were coming together. But every detail painted a more unsettling picture. This researcher's murder couldn't be due to chance.
"Oi, Joe... Aren't you going overboard with this? The States are a dangerous country, robberies gone tragically wrong are commonplace", I mused out loud.
Sure, all the data pointed at anything but a casual death.
As I browsed through the man's bio, I found out that some of his most important contributions to medicine included intuitions on the nature of the possible vaccine that would defeat AIDS. He really looked like a big deal on the international scientific scene.
The details of his murder were picturesque to say the least. Hands and feet tied, dislocated shoulders and hips. The body had been placed on the floor face down, naked, in a position that vaguely hinted at Leonardo da Vinci's

Vitruvian Man. Stuff like this could only happen in the States. The journalist also mentioned '7 o'clock', with the man's limbs making up the hands of a clock drawn on the floor.

"Who could ever do something like that? A deviant! Or that's what they wanted people to believe, in an attempt to steer off the investigation?"

I looked for more news related to that death, as I was beginning to harbor the suspicion that it was Orange Hands' fault.

Mine might as well have been a journalist's intuition, but anyone would have thought the same. I couldn't believe that such a well-respected researcher – on FourStreet's payroll, to boot – could have died of unrelated causes and then be positioned according to that choreography. A red herring? Or a message to someone? But what message, and most importantly, to whom? I couldn't find any answers.

I kept searching.

Soon afterwards, I found an update of that same article mentioning further progress in the investigation: the authorities had discovered an unusual symbol on the scene of the crime. An orange hand traced in paint. I knew it, they were behind it all.

The clue had initially been overlooked, but then, thanks to the FBI databases, it could be connected to another murder that had taken place not far from there, in San José. The second victim, Mark Bongher, was also an employee of Biotech FourStreet Laboratories Inc.

I was, however, surprised to read that the two murders were eventually declared to be unconnected. Bongher was gay, married in an attempt to hide his true sexuality. Wittman, on the other hand, was assuredly straight. So the investigators came to the conclusion that the famous pathologist was killed during a robbery gone bad. Everything was filed away despite the symbol's presence on both crime scenes.

"Fuck, it's impossible! This isn't random, how could they wash their hands of it all?"

It was patently a case of cover-up. They had quickly put an end to that story, but the truth was, Orange Hands had killed them both.

The information I had acquired in those days, on top of my own experiences, wouldn't let me believe anything else.

As I went through the events that had turned my life upside down in the two weeks leading up to that moment, I thought that it wasn't all that unlikely that the truth would be even more complex.
The loudspeakers crackled my flight's boarding. I turned off the computer and looked around, breathing an air of relief. No cops. I orderly followed the queue like a schoolboy.
I thought about everything I had uncovered and, shaking my head, told myself over and over: "Fuck, Joe, you're in big trouble!"
Yet strangely, I felt more relieved than anything: talking to the police with Paolo with all that mass of information would certainly clear my name, not to mention help vanquish an international conspiracy.
Of course, a question followed suit: after all I had written, could I be sure that Iorio would want to come with me to the police? My mind drifted back into darkness. I was scared, scared that I would not be able to prove my innocence.
During the flight, at any rate, I would keep on writing. With very detailed notes on my book's protagonist at my disposal, and lacking an internet connection that would allow me to continue my searches on the two murders, I would carry on with my first-person narration. Paolo Iorio's life and thoughts would soon be turned into the biography that I had promised to complete.

***

I was finally feeling good about myself. Money was starting to flow and I was beginning to be free to enjoy life.
Up to that moment, making a profit had been my only goal, squirreling away as much as possible so I would be able to achieve something great. I covered expenses and lived to work, that was my life. Family came first, a family with which I hadn't had any contact for a long time, but that I still maintained. They had been, after all, my main drive to move North.
On the workplace, I had experienced many setbacks, but nothing had been able to stifle my fighting spirit. Do you know why? Because I wasn't scared to get my hands dirty. And I knew all too well that in order to become a successful businessman, the quintessential self-made man, one couldn't be scared of sacrifices nor of hard work.

I knew I would make it, and I did.
A few years after I started it, my pharma promotion company was sailing smooth: we were quickly expanding, gaining more and more shares on the Italian market. Other pharmaceutical companies asked us to add them to our portfolio – which was of course impossible, as we had a symbiotic relationship with FourStreet Chemical Ltd. and could not agree to represent any third parties.
Those were the years when the pharmaceutical world was starting to stir: up until then, companies didn't really compete with one another, they didn't fight through aggressive pricing, they were content to share their slices of the market pie equally.
As I came along, everything changed. It's not that I was important, personally, I was nothing but means to an end. Regardless, the scenario drastically changed. It was the late Eighties, the time when the true war between multinational companies began, a ruthless fight where every move was allowed, every move was fair, and the role I played was crucial to the Group: I was their black soul.
The system was simple: my company had about a dozen clients, all of them middle-sized pharmaceutical companies. Each of them had a different owner, who was in truth nothing more than a front man for MonteForte Company. They, in turn, handled the operation through their British channels so they would not be traceable.
It all worked like a set of matryoshka dolls: one company nested within the other, with a single big boss ruling from above, governing the market, crushing the opposition. We were supposed to work for a plurality of companies, but deep down, the occult client-owner was just one. It was a circle, head and tail coming together.
Once in a while, to throw some dust in the supervisory authorities' eyes, the pharmaceutical companies fused, through fraudulent mergers, in order to steer the market and shake the international stock market. Those actions, too, ended up as profits for MonteForte Company.
What that couldn't accomplish, bribing politicians could. There was a full-fledged fratricidal struggle to win over contracts, and yes, those bribes were clearly signed off as contracts.

I took care of everything, handling the Italian ties of the Brindeber Foundation through proper, legal agreements for the dissemination of scientific knowledge.
Senators and MPs took part in the non-profit conventions organized by my company, indirectly promoting the pharmaceutical firms I had exclusive contracts with, and received ample reimbursement for their 'expenses' from the sponsoring Foundation. This put the politicians on our payroll, but none of them ever received money from the single companies indirectly owned by FourStreet and therefore, in turn, by MonteForte. That would have been illegal.
Reimbursement of expenses from a non-profit Foundation, on the other hand, wasn't. Every law has a loophole.
We also handled one-time donations to political parties come elections time.
In the shadiest cases, we handed out bona fide monthly bribes to specific politicians. Every month I left for Rome and toured the government buildings, both the Senate and the Chamber of Deputies: I met certain assistants and handed them the money they would deliver to their respective senators and MPs.
The objective was to ensure that once certain amendments would need to be voted, the result would be favorable to our needs.
Pharmaceutical marketing, on the other hand, was still an unexplored frontier. So I, along with my occult British bosses, to whom I was to deliver a weekly report on the developments of our project, decided to open a new company. They would handle design and packaging, all the visual aspects of marketing, and they would be able to launder the money that we would then need to invest in bribes.
It was a major bet, and in that case, too, one that I won. Both activities were turning a profit: the former made lot of dirty money, the latter was a little more transparent and kept on growing.
I slowly won over the heads of MonteForte Company. The British board of directors kept on talking about this ambitious young man, Paolo Iorio, and so it was that they decided to meet me.
I was summoned to their headquarters in Kansas City, Missouri, and flying to the States proved to be the first real journey of my life.

From the outside, they looked like one big family: a humongous chemical company, headed by good, simple people. Its real face was the devil's den. I spoke to the bosses, or to those who looked like them. I had taken English classes for some time before leaving, specifically for the occasion. I was hoping to avoid gaffes and bad impressions, though they ended up being inescapable: during our meeting, I only understood very little of what they told me and spoke only a few words myself.
At any rate, it mattered little. I had become their 'strong arm', the man who would handle their dirty deeds. I didn't feel morally repugnant, because I tried to hide my depravities behind a flimsy shield: money. All I cared for was money, and in all honesty, I didn't care how I earned it.
Our promotional activity was gaining steam, so, in order to avoid trouble, we enforced a strict employees turnover after two years. That way, they didn't ask questions, didn't get the chance to learn enough about their bosses and, most importantly, didn't have time to create dangerous ties between them. The system was perfect: everyone was transferred to other companies in our great family, receiving promotions and raises every twenty-four months. They left happy and didn't question it too much.
We chose our staff among the newly graduated, young people who, by definition, still don't have high expectations, who are willing and immature. In order to avoid losing their first stable job, blinded by a wage and by benefits, such as a company car and high bonuses, like few of their peer could hope to achieve, they all turned meek and tame.
I was over the moon in those days.
My affluence had peaked and it didn't take me long to understand how the world of business worked in those years marked by the economic boom.
All it took was knowing the right people and having the right ideas, refraining from asking questions and everything would go just fine.
I started looking for a new house to buy and got myself a nice sports car – I really had become a yuppie. I needed the car to leisurely reach my 'clients' and send out the right image. I even started hanging out with some beautiful models, something my former lifestyle had imperatively banned.
I was a young man who was starting to ride on the wave of success and who, little by little, kept forgetting the pungent taste of the sweat of his brow.

And that proved to be my ruin, that relentless attempt to forget my past as a poor man. I dove head first in a whirlwind of parties and feasts with my clients, all under the motto of 'sex, drugs and rock 'n' roll'. We had everything: cocaine and alcohol, women and money. And even though I spent a lot, within a few years, my bank account showed a pretty hefty total.

I felt like a king.

"The fuck are you doing?"

There was white powder on the table and it didn't take a genius to figure out what it was. My eyes were red, I hadn't answered my phone in days. They didn't accept any delays or useless wastes of time, so they sent Balzaretti to check on me.

Carmine, that was his first name, was yet another one of FourStreets' shadow men. He started out as an unloader at the pharmaceuticals warehouse in Bresso, then rose to the status of trusted bodyguard of the British company's head of HR, Natalia Birkman. She was a good-looking woman of about forty-five, with long hair, always travelling across Europe to pull the string of the big Family. She was the one who handled everything on behalf of MonteForte Company. Rumor had it that Balzaretti was her stallion, that is to say her lover.

It was by no chance that he had been hired directly by the British company. He was also the only trustworthy member of the small crowd of bodyguards who always followed Natalia around: ten of them total, employees of an Italian security firm with branches abroad.

Whenever they moved, they put together a procession worthy of a head of state, with three cars in a line. She was paranoid about security and always wanted to have two men patrolling outside the black cars she travelled in. Never far behind and completely anonymous, they had eyes on the situation and were ready to intervene from the outside in case of danger. A strategy worthy of the military.

In those days, on the other hand, I was trying to hide my shame for what I had become: I alternated between days where I was filled by a subservient spirit and days when coke made me nervous and cantankerous.

My conscience was slowly mounting a revolt. It was hard to live with it, it struggled and didn't give me rest.
"Come on, Paolo, get out of that office. Follow me, we're going to Birkman's...", Carmine said.
"I told you to knock when you come in! Get it? I'm the boss here..." was all I could manage to say.
I was pitiful, my stare a mix of anger, fear and disappointment at having been found out.
"Knock? Fuck you, Paolo, I go wherever I want, do you get it? And you're sniffing coke, are you out of your mind? Do you want to screw up your life so bad? You're a fucking junkie, how can you not think of the consequences?"
He grabbed me by my shirt's collar, pushed me over, threw me to the ground and hit me hard on my chest. I ended up with two broken ribs and a broken cheekbone. I was furious, but I couldn't find it in myself to react. But this time, I'd been the shithead. I had been offered the occasion to become somebody, to create something important, and I was throwing it to the wind. And that meant everything to me: I couldn't be a winner if the first thing I did as soon as life gave me the chance to enjoy it was to chase after fleeting pleasures, compromising my business and relationships, instead of playing along.

I done fucked up, for real: I'd thrown a shitload of money down the drain, some of it I'd earned, some taken from the company.
FourStreet's money, not mine.
My method was obvious enough, I'd pretended to raise the politicians' bribes. Those parties had fucked with my head, the poker games and all the rest. A wicked life. As the days went by, in order to avoid facing my conscience, I dove deeper and deeper in self-destruction.
Anyone could see that something was wrong with me and on that morning, they came to get me.
They wanted to dig deep, understand what trouble I had been getting into and what I was doing that was so important that I wouldn't answer to my bosses. The effect was terrifying: I was sentenced to death. Their verdict was obvious: I knew too much and I wouldn't be of any use in that state.

I asked for some more time, I explained my situation but I wasn't offered any alternatives: dirty laundry can't be aired in public after all, and I was primed to be banished, sacrificed for the greater good of the family.
For months, I had heard a voice inside me, telling me to disappear forever, but I had never had the guts to follow through. Now, after all that, I decided that I would do it, in the true sense of the word.
But just as the worst inexorably comes along when everything seems to be going for the best, likewise when you hit rock bottom and are about to drown, life lifts you up again and you make it to shore.

Carmine Balzaretti respected me and wanted to help me. I honestly don't know why, probably because we were very similar and he had picked up on that. We both came from the streets, from poverty.
He asked Natalia to appoint him as deputy manager of Iorio Promo Farmaceutici S.r.l., so he would keep an eye on me and put me back on track. I don't know how he managed to convince her, considering her reputation as a ruthless woman. But he made it.
The rumormongers whispered that all it took to make her yield was a night of passion. I, at any rate, didn't believe the rumor that they were lovers.
It was the beginning of my rebirth.
Not an ethical, but a physical one. Slowly, with effort, I got clean from cocaine, but as is often the case, any gain obtained with the help of bad people bears along a hefty cost.
I was on a short leash, they didn't trust me anymore. In order to keep me under pressure, they gave me dirtier and dirtier jobs. I was compromised anyway, without a way out.
Meanwhile, my company was moved from Milan's city center to the nearby town of Bresso, by the warehouse belonging to FourStreet PromoPharma Ltd. That was the company they used to sort out and disguise the peddling of the products that were still in their testing phase, the ones that were handed out for free to human test subjects by the crooked doctors we had picked out and bribed. These then notified the producing companies of the side effects they observed during the course of the treatments.
The phials were all marked as free samples for the doctors; they were the goods produced by the front companies I was assigned to.

PromoPharma was created specifically by FourStreet so that they could keep close ties with the companies it controlled from above but that, at the same time, the dealings couldn't be traced back to them. It was then PromoPharma who distributed all the samples from their affiliates.
It didn't produce anything, but de facto assumed the command of the production chain, aided by their other distributing firm: PharmaLogistics, who engaged in the distribution of the drugs on the consumer market.
By then, the only peaceful haven I had left was the marketing and design agency in Milan's Bicocca district. I could be myself there, even though Birkman insisted on appointing someone to handle business in my stead, a coordinator. That way, their little plots wouldn't be ruined and, most importantly, they would keep me under control. It didn't have to be someone from their inner circle, the agency's activity was legitimate, nothing dirty going on. So they followed the same principle we had always used to find new blood: young, keen people, ready to follow orders without asking too many questions.
At that point in time, my life was blessed by a ray of sunshine, my first true love: Jennifer.
I had met her at a fashion show some time earlier, she was an Argentinian model who knew how to carry herself. We had a chance to know each other better during the backstage party and so it happened that we dated for a few months before I decided to put forward her name as the agency's coordinator.
Natalia didn't like it, as she believed that a sentimental relationship between the two of us would end up ruining everything. Once again, Balzaretti was the one who came to my aid, managing to change her mind. Jenny then started leading the marketing agency, with extraordinary competence, and even though her resumée showed a background in law rather than communication, appointing her was the best professional choice I made in that time.
Meanwhile, she abandoned modeling forever.
My life was heading toward a dangerous split. On one hand, I was experiencing the most wonderful love story I could have ever wished for. I finally had a real woman by my side, the first honest person I could share my days with. The time spent with her was happy, whether we were on holiday or going through our daily lives.

On the other hand, I was digging my grave ever deeper as a slave to the system.
The Brindeber Foundation increased donations for the fight agains HIV, a topic so dear to the masses and so mediatically relevant. Several Hollywood actors and actresses were hired as testimonials to endorse this war.
On the papers, rivers of ink; on the main networks, thousands of hours of programming celebrated and spread that decision.
Last but not least, politicians glorified Brindeber's non-profit work. Millions of dollar were spent to hold conventions for the world's best scientific researchers, while they made a show of donating funds to laboratories all over the world for their work against this social virus.
Consequently, FourStreet entered the fray. They hired the world's leading expert and took over his Biotech Laboratories Inc. in San Francisco, which from that day onward became Biotech FourStreet Laboratories Inc. That was the company that the Foundation – and therefore MonteForte Company – had chosen to defeat AIDS. At any price.
And this was the cradle they had chosen for the creation of the ultimate vaccine for humanity. A model of efficiency tied to the local university, which in the past had already received subsidies from several international pharmaceutical companies and even from the US Department of Health.
I got sent on assignments in California so often that I decided to get a home in a lovely neighborhood on the hills. My goal was to keep an eye on the work of pathologist Jason Wittman, forgetting all about Iorio P. Farmaceutici S.r.l.: Carmine would take care of the latter. With a fake transaction, FourStreet carried out the acquisition of my company and they would soon make Jenny's marketing agency disappear as well. They weren't strategically relevant anymore. Natalia Birkman would move them to Great Britain to handle them internally. Then, within a few months, she would create a new firm from scraps on the Italian territory. Business as usual.
By exploiting the lingering Italian crisis, she would find no trouble in eliminating any possible complication. She would lay off the remaining employees, who, of course, would end up blaming yours truly: the titular Paolo Iorio. To add insult to injury.

As for my new assignment, I would be at Wittman's mercy; should I fail to produce results, I would be eliminated and so would Jenny.
According to them, she knew too much. Despite my repeated claims and vows, they didn't believe that I never mentioned FourStreet's clandestine activities to her.
Which meant I was a disaster as a man as well: I had involuntarily condemned to death the only woman in my life. I would have given my life to save hers, but those weren't the rules of this game.
Balzaretti was the one who told me all this, as well as implying that he wouldn't be able to help me this time. On the contrary, he was worried for his own safety.
"Paolo, I don't know what to do this time, I'd risk my life too if I tried to cover your ass... I think there's interests bigger than us at play now. Natalia is worried too, she's under enormous pressure from upstairs."
Wittman's lab activities, however, didn't look like they were set on giving positive results in the long run. There were tests they ran on animal subjects, whom they deliberately infected with HIV and then exposed to the vaccine they called WIT02. The subjects developed an impressive capacity for recovery from the alterations in the immune system caused by the virus and which generally persisted even after a successful HAART therapy.
Everything seemed to turn out for the best, as the most immuno-compromised test subjects were the ones who appeared to gain the most benefits from the treatment. But the effect was short-lived. As soon as it expired, the infection progressed at an increased pace, as if it were benefiting from WIT02 itself.
All the test subjects died earlier than they would have from HIV alone. It was the right path, the pathologist insisted, but not the definitive one.
Testing proceeded on a tight schedule and explored results on different species in order to examine the treatment's effects on different metabolisms: mice first, then dogs – illegal though that was – finally chimps.
The British top brass were starting to lose their patience, they wanted to pressure the researcher and applying that pressure was all on me. I was the one who had to threaten him, I was the one who had to make him

understand that his beloved wife in Chicago could fall victim to a tragic accident if he didn't cough up a vaccine soon.
It wasn't enough that I had handsomely bribed doctors and politicians for years, it wasn't enough that I had exploited unwitting human subjects. Now they wanted me to threaten and possibly kill people who were victims of the system. I couldn't stand it anymore, I was crushed by all that anguish.
The point of no return, however, was yet to come. Animal testing wasn't producing results, so one day, I was told that the management had implemented a different system and that I would have to take care of it myself.
I will never forget that trip to San Francisco. The pressure crushed me, I had no way out. I felt lost.
At the airport I was collected, as usual, by one of the pathologist's colleagues and business partner: Matteo Bolzoni, a fellow Italian. He was the one who acted as an interpreter during my visits to the lab, to compensate for my bad English.
We immediately headed to the office, where we would meet another scientific researcher: Mark Bongher. He was the one who told me what I would have to do. I would have to find human subjects. It was the only way to verify whether WIT02's effects were so ineffective on men, women and children.
We know that such experiments are usually carried out by pharmaceutical companies on volunteers, only after being greenlit by the relevant national health authority and scientific ethical committee. These authorities only authorize treatment when they believe that the risk for the patient is limited, that is, that everything can be clinically kept under control and that there aren't any risks for the involved subjects.
In Europe, for example, the applicable law is the Convention for the protection of Human Rights and Dignity of the Human Being with regard to the Application of Biology and Medicine. In the States, it's handled by the Food and Drug Administration, a child agency of the Department of Health.
This situation, however, hardly applied, and no bribe could be enough to act as an incentive for experimentation. Tests up to that point confirmed

that the procedure could cause the patient's death faster than the illness itself.
The risk was too high and no scientist or politician would ever authorize such experiments. Yet there was too much money riding on them, that lab was the fulcrum of too many interests to just drop everything. It was like condemning innocent people to death, everyone knew it. And they had picked me to be their executioner.

XXV

"It's a sight that exhilarates
the heart as well as the mind,
the red hues of the metal
unflinchingly sweep away
every woeful thought."

San Francisco is one of the most beautiful cities in the world.
Its architectural charm is unrivalled, with its fusion between European tradition and history and American modern canon for tall skyscrapers made of glass and steel. It is characterized by colorful slopes, thanks to California's flowers, and scented by the Ocean's briny smells, carried by the strong wind that grips the coast.
From the sea to the hills, every corner of the city is fascinating. For one, the winding Lombard Street as seen from atop Coit Tower.
There, by the *art déco* tower atop Telegraph Hill in Pioneer Park, Christopher Columbus' statue oversees one of the area's most picturesque vistas. The bright little dots in the distance that liven up this colorful postcard are the Victorian buildings in the Haight-Ashbury neighborhood, where San Francisco's ambitious, wealthy youth reside.
It is here that the quirkiest businessmen love to take refuge, taking their leave from their struggles in the city's economic hub. They leave the Financial District behind, with its tall, oddly-shaped buildings such as the Transamerica Pyramid. The Bay under them jealously keeps Alcatraz's horrible secrets as well as housing the friendly sea lions at Pier 39, right next to Fisherman's Wharf and not far from folkloristic Chinatown.
I had already been there a few years earlier, along with a friend from the University of Toronto – a hypocrite, who later turned his back on me without a reason. It's really true that in life, one always has to be prepared for everything. Memories of those days came back to my mind.
The taxi drove me to the city center; luckily, I hadn't found any cops waiting for me at arrivals, either. I had managed not to run into trouble for

the entire flight and now that I was blending in that crowded, multicultural place so far away from Italy, the would never find me. I would have to carry on with my plan and prove my innocence before they found me. I had made up my mind not to turn on the phone, so that I wouldn't immediately be traceable via GPS.
The airport was slowly disappearing behind my back. Its mirrored windows reflected the sunlight and blinded the cars on the junction that connected it to Route 101, a federal highway that runs from North to South, through Washington, Oregon and California, from near Seattle to Los Angeles, and cuts through San Francisco skirting around its Bay.
The yellow of the car melted away in the suburbs' abominable traffic, and we struggled to make it to the literary, cultural beating heart of the city: North Beach. I already knew where I would get a room: the small Da Vinci hotel, owned by an Italian-American couple with Neapolitan origins and located in San Francisco's Little Italy, right next to the Financial District. In the Fifties, beat culture was born right next to it, in the popular City Lights Bookstore owned by poet Lawrence Ferlinghetti. Even today, one can breathe a blues/jazz atmosphere by strolling through the strip clubs that dot the area. By the bookstore, crossing Jack Kerouac Alley, Café Vesuvio is another lively historic landmark from those years, and the excellent Italian restaurant Monnalisa is located nearby.
My tiny two-star hotel was right around the corner from those fairytale places. The atmosphere was homey and everyone spoke Italian: I felt at home.
Before checking in, though, I wanted to eat a *real* hamburger in one of the joints nearby. It was superb, with double cheese and chili – I really needed it.
I went back to the hotel and greeted the owners, giving a fake name. My excuse was simple, I got mugged waiting for the taxi and they stole my wallet, complete with passport and plane tickets. On the following day, I told them, I would go to the Italian embassy where they would issue me a new passport and that would confirm my ID: Enzo Rossi, a tourist fresh from Milan. Thanks to my proficiency of the language, passing myself off as Italian was easy and they bought my lie, greeting me with pats on the back and a round of the traditional song *Funiculì Funiculà* as a welcome. My good boy charms struck again.

I went to my room and threw my bags on the ground. I was exhausted, my brain was blanking out. All the info in Paolo's biography had been destabilizing and the jet lag had done the rest. My body was giving up.
I opened the window and breathed in relief.
I was standing on the fourth floor, but thanks to the hills that crowned the Bay, even from my small balcony on Columbus Ave. I could see the magical Golden Gate Bridge at sunset. It dominated the city landscape as its uncontested protagonist. That sight exhilarated my heart and mind, the red hues of the metal unflinchingly sweeping away every woeful thought. At least for some hours. I managed to catch some solid sleep, charging my phone just in case.
I got inside the linen with a sigh and dropped down like a sack of potatoes.
Peace.

It took me a while to realize what that odd noise was. It was 9 in the morning.
Something was buzzing in the distance. I lazily opened my right eye and saw my phone vibrating among the bed lamp's cord on the wood-like night stand, its screen lit up. The room's furniture was in poor taste and even poorer quality. I had forgotten that by plugging in the iPhone, it would automatically turn on as soon as it charged.
"Fuck, they found me!"
The call came from Italy, but I wasn't familiar with the number. I picked it up, what else could I do. It was better to get it over with than to stew in my doubts, asking myself who was looking for me.
"Hello?"
My drowsy, sleepy voice sounded pained.

"Joe, where did you disappear to?"
It was Inspector Gaudenzi, probably calling from his office at the precinct.
"Hey, Mirko, sorry, it's just that..."
"Sorry my ass, what did you do? I have an arrest warrant on my desk... I shouldn't even be calling you, but..."

"What?"
My voice didn't sound too worried.
"You didn't even flinch, I imagine you were waiting for this, weren't you?"
"Yes, even though I wasn't planning on hearing about it from you."
"Joe, we found your DNA on the syringe which was used to try to kill Jennifer Blasquez. I hope you have a good explanation for this and it's better that you come here immediately, to the precinct, to talk about it, or you're in serious trouble and I'm going to have to arrest you for real..."
"I'm not home, I can't come right now... How is she?"
"Better, but she still hasn't woken up from her coma... But what's happening, where are you?"
"Listen, Mirko, it's a long story. I can't talk now, but I promise that before long, I will let you know everything and turn myself in. I have to prove my innocence first, the situation is too complicated..."
"Joe, you do realize that I have to pass this onto Interpol, don't you? I can't lie... They're gonna issue a red notice, which is far worse than the piece of paper I'm holding in my hands right now... Especially if you turn yourself in!"
"I know, but I can't tell you more... I was framed, it was the MAS Security guys. They killed Andrea, tried to take out Jennifer and finally tried to pin the blame on me. It's a conspiracy, but now I have evidence... all I need is the last piece of this puzzle and then everything will be over. I swear, all I need is a little time, at least twenty-four hours..."
"Do you realize what you're asking for?"
His voice suddenly turned pained and feeble.
"I do. And I want you to bring in the owner of MAS for questioning. You have to find an employee of theirs, tall and buff, wearing glasses... He was the one who got me in trouble and he even threatened me the other night on my doorstep... Once you find him, bring him in and grill him."
A long silence followed. About ten seconds, possibly, but to me they felt like hours.

"Hey, that's weird, that sounds like... You're talking about Norberto Riesp! The owner... Actually, we've just finished questioning him. Among other things, he says he doesn't know you..."
His voice gained a metallic edge, like a robot's.
"Look, Mirko, he's the one who got me in trouble, he's lying. He got my fingerprints from a glass in Jenny's flat and put them on the syringe so he could take me down... Please, run some tests... You'll see that it's the truth, please find that glass!"
The call cut off.
I really was compromised this time.
I paced around the room, my hands in my hair. I had to flee, they had probably already localized me via satellite, all they needed was a fax to the competent authorities and I'd be fucked.
I showered as quickly as I could and changed my clothes, then turned off my phone, though it was probably too late for that.
I had to abandon the room, it wasn't safe anymore, the police would crash the place at any moment. But I couldn't drag my suitcase around town either, so I grabbed the bare necessities, stuffed them in my shoulder bag and pretended to get out of the hotel to go to the embassy. Jennifer's documents about Vietnam had to remain in the room – a necessary risk, they were too bulky and wouldn't fit in my bag. I had to leave them in the case.
I hailed a cab and asked for Masonic Ave., pretending to be a tourist.
What followed was a short tour of the area, with the driver stubbornly detailing all the architectural hotspots we passed through and me pretending to care. Truth was, I was trying to find Paolo's infamous home, while he was pretending to be a former tourist guide to string out the trip and get some more dollars out of it. Sure, a Pakistani San Francisco driver who could hardly find a street without his GPS. Very likely.
I opted to be dropped two blocks from Masonic Avenue, so that even if he got taken in for questioning, the taxi driver wouldn't be able to tell them where I was headed.
I would have gained at least an hour over my pursuers.

The neighborhood was a lovely, picturesque thing, with its sloping road that gave the impression of a mountain trail, endlessly extending into the horizon. My breath was getting shorter and as I looked at my watch, I realized it was almost noon. The sun was high over my head and it burned. In this part of the world, September's sunlight wasn't a feeble remnant of summer: in the evening, the Ocean's chilly wind blew through the streets, but the days still saw warm temperatures.
I walked through the street, looking for that art nouveau façade with its dark red hues. I found three of them in total. Unfortunately, it appeared to be one of the most popular shades around and the wooden architecture was basically the same for every building. Only one of them, though, had a nice-looking beinge house sitting in front of it, with a quaint white porch.
I held my breath.
I rang the bell, which was only marked by the house's street number, no names, neither companies' nor people's.
No reply.
I tried again.
Again, nothing. No-one seemed to be home.

I walked up to a window to try and look inside, but peeking didn't reveal anything of interest: elegant furniture, not unlike the items that could be found in Jennifer's flat in Milan. But it was hard to spot anything clearly through a dirty window, and with the sun's reflection to boot. At any rate, all my evidence seemed to be encouraging: "I'm in the right place, I can feel it!"
There were too many coincidences. The puzzle seemed almost solved: all I had to do was wait.
I spotted a bakery on the street's corner, ordered a cup of coffee and sat down at a table by the window.
I turned on the laptop to look at the picture some more and remove all lingering doubt. A quick screening of the area, compared to the background of Jenny hugging Paolo on the computer's screen, comforted me enough to make me smile. I was sure that that had to be Iorio's home.

The final showdown was close.
From the shop's window, I scanned the area to check if any shady-looking individuals were hanging around. All clear. So all that was left was to wait for the owner of the place: he would have to come back sooner or later.
It was a matter of sheer luck but, up to that moment, luck had seemed to favor me. Since the day the man from MAS framed me, everything was, finally, turning in my favor. I was climbing back up. I could only hope that my upward trend wouldn't be reversed right at the crucial moment. I looked outside, full of hope.

4:30 PM. Not a soul on the horizon. The bakery's owner was side-eyeing me, so I ordered a slice of cheesecake. I wasn't hungry, but it was the only way to take her distrustful eyes off me. A client like me, hanging out in her shop for more than five hours with just a cup of coffee in front of him, would have aroused anyone's suspicions.
As I was about to take the first bite, a black Lincoln parked by the house's entrance. A man in a dark suit got out, passed the porch's steps and rang.
His looks were familiar, and as I thought back to the horrible last few days I realized that he was the buff, shaven person whom I kept on seeing wherever I went. The same person who had given me Orange Hands' files on my doorstep in Milan.
I jumped up, abandoning my bag and laptop on the bakery's table.
With a cry, I asked the owner to look after my stuff, as I absolutely had to stop that man and that left me no time to close the computer and stuff it inside the bag.
My eyes full of hatred, I threw myself on the road, looking for answers, running like a madman. He didn't notice me. I was fast, but silent. The man was slowly walking back to his car the way he came. Big mistake. He saw me as he looked up at the end of the driveway: I was panting, he was confused, lost in his thoughts.
After a moment of hesitation, he probably read my facial expression and ran toward the car, trying to escape. I lunged at him, like in the movies, and landed on his back. We both fell down, with me on top.

He tried to fight back with all his strength, but my hold was strong, and with my knees on his back, he couldn't escape.
I would have to thank my mother, who used to force me to take judo lessons when I was a kid. Then, when I turned fourteen, I finally switched over to rugby, and the mix of those two sports greatly helped me on that day, between a flying tackle and the art of holding the opponent on the ground. Too bad we had asphalt under us instead of grass or a tatami.
"Hey... Hey! Stop."
I gave my order in both Italian and English.
"Lasciami, lasciami!!", he replied in Italian, *'let me go, let me go!!'*. So that's where he came from. His voice was warm, a little shaky, maybe, after his efforts to break free.
"Why were you trying to flee, huh?"
"You were coming after me with bloodshot eyes, what was I supposed to do?"
"Who are you?"
He tried to get a good look at me, with some effort considering that his face was pressed on the asphalt.
"My name is Matteo."
"And what do you want from me?"
"I'm looking for Paolo Iorio..."
"Same. What's your motive?"
"I work for him, I'm his assistant..."
"And where is he now?"
"I don't know. I had to come fetch him at his house, but he must have gone out on his own. And he's not answering his phone."
"If I let you go, will you promise that you won't flee and that you'll answer some more questions?"
"I swear, I swear!"
I kept a firm hold on his arm, but let him get back up. My jaw dropped as I realized how tall and how beefy he was: I smiled, proud of having tackled the most massive prop of my entire life.
His face was scratched and scared, his suit dirty.

He tried to dust himself off with his free hand, but I didn't allow him to: he had to answer my questions first.
“Why were you stalking me in Milan?”
The man's eyes lit up as they connected my face to his memories.
“So it's you!”
“So?”
“Listen, I'm the assistant to doctor Iorio. I take care of his health, of his safety and I drive him around. He told me to check on you because...”
“Because?”
“He thought you were his girlfriend's lover... That's all! I had to keep an eye on you and report your moves to him. See who you were seeing. That's it.”
“And the USB drive?”
“He told me to give it to you at a good moment. I thought it was a threatening video or something like that, something my boss cooked up. Some way to persuade you to stop seeing miss Blasquez. I don't know what was on it, I have no idea, I swear!”
So Paolo knew about Orange Hands and that Jenny was a plant.
“He wanted me to find out about everything, but why?”
“Beg your pardon?” The man gave me a puzzled look.
“Nothing, nothing...”
As I racked my brains about all those questions, I patted his jacket to check if he was armed. The other gun, Jennifer's, was still in Italy and I would need to protect myself. I couldn't bring any weapons on the flight to the States and while fetching a weapon here was easier than in other countries, it would be safer for me not to buy anything. I would have to show my documents to get a gun, and that would be too dangerous.
“I'm gonna take this, okay?”
I nimbly pulled his gun out of its holster. He reacted.
“Hey, listen... I have a license to carry and I don't want any trouble here... You can't take it! You assaulted me and I didn't use it, specifically because I don't want to stir up trouble outside the Italian border! Now leave me alone, fuck!”

He pulled away and I understood that truth be told, the reason I had managed to tackle and hold him down up to that moment wasn't a combination of my skills, but sheer luck: up to that moment, he hadn't really fought back. He wasn't lacking strength and he shook himself loose in a few moves.
“So you work for MAS Security?”
“No, absolutely not... I'm Iorio's private employee, a freelancer, I've been working for him for a few months. I'm not affiliated with any company... It's the very reason he hired me!”
He didn't seem to be lying and the news were great: that meant I could trust him. I gave him his weapon back. I also tried to dust off his suit, to try and make amends for my earlier belligerency.
“Fine, I'm sorry for all this mess. But I need to talk to your boss immediately, it's a matter of life and death.”
“I told you, I don't know where he is.”
“Are you sure?”
“I swear. He's been behaving oddly lately, sometimes he disappears, then he pops back up. He's been going off on his own for weeks and then he comes back home as if nothing ever happened... I can't know everything about him! I'm growing tired of this behavior... He told me to come here, that it was urgent, that I would absolutely need to follow the orders he would give me here... But he isn't home... Enough! I don't like being shown up!”
“Is he going to come home?”
“I think so, try and wait for him... I don't know what to tell you...”
“May I ask you for his phone number?”
“Whatever you want. Again, I don't want trouble... I have a family and frankly, I'm considering dropping this job: these conditions are no good! With all these mysteries...”
I decided to comfort him.
“I promise, I'm gonna let you go and everything's gonna turn out fine in the end.”
He gave me a perplexed look, as if to say: 'This job ain't changing my life, buddy, do you know how many Iorio’s are out there waiting to hire me? I have no intention of taking risks!”

So much for a fearless bodyguard.
Then he dictated the phone number.
"Italian prefix... then 3... 4... 9..."
Once we were done, I waved him goodbye, once again extending my apologies to him. He looked at me as if I were a raving madman, jumped on his car and steered away.
So I went back to my coffee and my cheesecake. As I went in, I immediately noticed the owner's horrified stare.
She was looking at me. She had seen everything from afar.
I didn't know what to tell her, so I made up a lie on the spot: I told her that I was a cop and that she shouldn't mind what had just transpired. I was on a stakeout and I would remain in her shop for a long while more. She asked for my badge, but I nonchalantly sat back, pretending that I hadn't heard her. My best badass impression completed the picture.
I ordered another coffee, I needed something warm – mine had turned cold by then – and woke up the computer. As I waited, I would read and listen to Iorio's notes again, turning them into a lively narration in the biography I was typing up right during those weird, weird days.

XXVI

"In this very place, a storage room
had been turned into a lab.
The human test subjects were
washed, dressed again,
visited. Then the
doctors' work began."

Executioner. What a nasty word.
Yet it was a good descriptor for my new job from that day onwards, at least until the vaccine could reach a stable form, ready to be introduced on the international market.
I was a slave to my work, dominated by my bosses, but most importantly, I was responsible for other people's deaths.
I tried to speak out at first, to make the others come to reason, talking to anyone from the top brass to the least important link in FourStreet's occult piramidal chain.
Nothing, no reasoning scratched their conviction. The interests at play, as Balzaretti put it, were too big to stop that assassination machine. And I was nothing more than a gear: necessary to bring the project to fruition, but disposable. I could be eliminated and replaced in the blink of an eye. They would easily find somebody else who would be willing to dirty their hands with innocents' blood without asking questions.
But what was I supposed to do? Even for that question, the great family had found a plausible answer.
It was an easy task to boot, truth be told: all I had to do was talk to one person, the broker of human test subjects, and set up a transport system with him. We would need to be quick, efficient and silent. In some respects, it was like arranging simple logistics. Except instead of goods, these were people. My conscience was already kicking and screaming.
For three long nights, I couldn't sleep. My eyes were wide open, staring at the ceiling.

Then, with the help of the alcohol that I kept drinking so I could forget and steel myself, I made contact with this man.
I called him at a landline number I wasn't familiar with, probably a phone booth. When he picked up, I could hear, in the distance, the creaking of cranes and the seagulls' unique call. It could have been by the docks.
His voice was calm and piercing. In a faltering Italian, he talked of our cargo with the assuredness of someone who is handling your average wares.
He told me to meet him at Pier 39, a place full of tourists busy with their shopping and with watching the sea lions on the shore. It was absurd that the highest privacy and guarantee that we wouldn't be recognized would be obtained by meeting in a place full of people.
It was a contradiction.
He would show up with a green baseball cap, Oakland Athletics. And he would carry a rolled-up paper under his arm, standing in the middle of the Pier, between an ice cream shop and a place that sold maritime-themed souvenirs.
I showed up on time, at 7 PM.
As soon as I saw him, my blood froze in my veins: he was a young man, good-looking, possibly some ten years younger than I would later find out that he was thirty-five, with a lean, muscular physique.
His name was Mike Curley, a big boy from Ohio, funny and sociable at that. He was the second-in-command of the Boavista, a Panamanian container ship docked at Long Beach, six hours from San Francisco. He handled long routes to China. He would be my contact.
Why did he do all this? He liked to live life, he liked beautiful women especially, and his standards were much too high for his meager sailor's wage, officer though he may be.
He explained to me that stowaways often boarded the ship in Shanghai. After finding many of them, he decided to turn it around and make that setback into a profitable activity. So he began to 'give a future' to those poor Chinese stowaways who were following the American dream.
As he explained it, he looked like a bona fide benefactor. He maintained that if he hadn't done anything himself, for a price, they would've turned up anyway, sneaking inside the ship in hopes of making it to the States. And in order to stay hidden, they would have picked who knows what sort

of dangerous hiding spot on the ship, possibly risking their lives as they got crushed by the engine's gears.
With his system, on the other hand, the safety of their travel was guaranteed: they would spend it inside a container, with enough food and water to survive. And he would get some cash out of it, which didn't hurt. Of course, should some port authority get nosy, they would play dumb. He had enlisted the help of three fellow sailors, who helped him move the 'cargo' safely and anonymously, without being caught. An easy gig.
This time, though, the situation was different. I tried to explain it to him during our meeting, but he stopped me in my tracks, saying: "Hey, I don't wanna know anything, alright? The less I know, the better... I'll only tell 'em that once they disembark, they have a job already waiting for them in America. Stop."
Sure, he'd give a job to those people: a job that would lead them to certain death.
He laughed, he laughed so hard as we drank a beer at Boudin, right next to Pier 39. We then decided to continue our talk as we strolled through the shops in Jefferson Street. He always had that irritating, mocking grin on his lips.
He was trying to convince me that it was the right thing to do. 'Mors tua vita mea', said the knights of old when they battled in tournaments: your death is my life. "Listen, I really make good money out of this and I have no intention of backing off. I'm doing this for a while and then good-bye work, forever... It's how life goes: those people can choose, all we do is offer them an alternative to their life in China. If shit happens once they're off the ship, that's life! Not our problem."
He stared at me right in the eyes as he said that, holding out his right hand as if to seal that death pact.
"Deal, my boy? Trust a man from Ohio... we're the real deal!"
He gave me a hard handshake, as if to show his virility. Actually, he was nothing but a faded image of what a real 'man' should be.
I will never forget that handshake.
We set up another meeting, in Chinatown this time. In order to prepare for the arrival of our 'goods', we would have to find an interpreter who would explain to the subjects what they would have to do once they arrived in

San Francisco. With a caveat: they would never learn that the tests were deadly.
Those people would then be persuaded to donate their blood and would then get a transfusion with infected bags. Unaware of their death sentence.
Afterwards, right at the end of the virus' incubation period, they would be injected with the vaccine, presented to them as an experimental alternative for the treatment of a nonlethal Asian flu.
They would be constantly monitored by the researchers of Biotech FourStreet Laboratories, their every physiological reaction catalogued.
Their compensation would be a hundred dollars each and the much sought-after Green Card, granting them permanent resident status, by virtue of having been willing to aid the health of American citizens. A fat bag of lies, as nothing of the sort would ever happen.
Mike would also be on the lookout for girls who'd already contracted HIV. In the red lights districts he used to hang out at in Shanghai, he wouldn't have trouble convincing some prostitute. Even better if they were pregnant: the researchers would be able to monitor the fetus' reaction to the therapy.

The target goal was to collect the widest possible range of data, offering an adequate array of responses to the biological reaction to the vaccine. The research involved men, women and children, young people and old, healthy and infected. The more varied the test subjects, the more data on how to complete the vaccine the researchers would get: this was FourStreet's theory.
Mike knew a boy in Chinatown who in turn knew someone who could be our interpreter and translator. That person would need to make the test subjects fill out certain questionnaires and then translate them into English, data which would be useful to gauge the clandestine immigrants' health before subjecting them to the tests.
Two days after our encounter at Pier 39, we met in the city's Chinatown. We talked with a person who accepted that translation job. Everything was going as planned.
The night of the first shipment was horrible. Nightmares, only a few hours of sleep. I woke up at 3 in the morning in order to reach the port of Long Beach, with the ship coming in at 10. In order not to raise any suspicions,

we preferred to carry out the operation under the sun, as if we were unloading any regular international cargo.

As they docked, the first cargo that touched ground was the one with the sacrificial immigrants: nineteen total, twelve of whom men, the rest women and children. Basically two full family units: mother, father, children, grandparents and uncles. They had been all instructed not to talk during the unloading phase, so that no noise would attract attention. The custom duty officers had been conveniently paid off so they would look away and arrive once the unloading was well underway.

The lorry travelled on the Interstate Five for about seven hours, through Oakland first, then to San Francisco. The route was linear and we didn't run into any police. The HGV ended its sad ride in the lot of a depot in the middle of forgotten Cargo Bay, a sparsely populated industrial site by the sea.

As the new cargo ships revolutionized freight transport in the late Eighties, the port of San Francisco lost a big slice of its relevance, as it wasn't equipped to handle that sort of cargo. So it happened that many warehouses were considered obsolete and abandoned forever. Only recently has a rivitalization process started that will turn them into offices, malls and exhibition premises.

Cargo Way, on the other hand, was far from those projects and allowed for the highest degree of anonimity.

And there, a warehouse had been turned into a dorm. The human subjects were washed, dressed and examined before the doctors' work could begin. Four workstations were quickly built and just as quickly dismantled after the procedure.

The machinery was owned by FourStreet, had the cops run some checks they wouldn't have been able to track its origins. Better safe than sorry.

The guardians of this present-day lager were the men of an Italian security company which had a branch in San Francisco. All of them former soldiers, with the order of setting fire to the warehouse in case of a bust by the San Francisco Police Department.

That's right: at the first sign of danger, they would burn everything, thus erasing all possible evidence. They would then be able to easily cover up the entire business: it would all be the story of a bunch of poor clandestine immigrants, hidden in an abandoned warehouse, who had found their untimely end in a fire.

The days went by and the tests didn't achieve the expected results. Not even all that fire-power and that amount of law-breaking had managed to nudge the research toward some kind of result. The vaccine wasn't getting any stabler and, just like the animals, all the human tests died quickly. Children first, then the elderly. And lastly, the younger ones: women and men.

'Cleaning up' was carried out by two haul trucks and even then I had to keep an eye on the job the security men were handling. They loaded the bodies among the gravel, on two articulated lorries they had procured for the occasion, and then carried them to mile 26 of the San Felipe Road, in San Josè, almost a two hours drive on Route 101.

In that town, so full of people but so empty at the same time, where everyone works and works and doesn't care about anything else, no-one would ever discover our mass grave. No connections, no risk for the Family.

Meanwhile, I had gone back to cocaine, but there was no drug nor alcoholic drink that could soothe the anguish in my guts. The faces of those nineteen people annihilated me, killing me from the inside.

I was ordered to proceed with a second shipment, that macabre ritual seemed to have no end.

And in that moment, I took the most important decision of my life: no more. I had dug my own grave, led by the breeze blowing in my heart. I wanted to become someone, I wanted to be a businessman. I wanted to help my family, to make one of my own, to become a cornerstone, essential to the people around me, authoritative yet friendly at the same time, the same figure I could never have beside me. My father was a loser. And the truth was that I had become even worse than him. On top of being a complete failure of a human being, I had also become a murderer. And like a murderer I would burn in Hell.

This was what led me to cut all ties with Jenny: that pure soul couldn't hook up with a man like me, she had already suffered enough in life.

The guilt was overwhelming, I couldn't find any adequate solutions that could put an end to that sad tale and allow me to forget it forever.

I analyzed all possible ways out before the second shipment came in.

Talk to the police? With all the ties Birkman and her bosses had, the case would be shot down and buried in a heartbeat. And I would get killed in prison.
No, I would go out with honor. I would say 'enough' to FourStreet and to that game of massacres, like a real man.
I would tell them these simple words: "I can't do this anymore, I'm out, motherfuckers". And I would accept the sad fate that had already been written for me: death. But sadly, as had already happened in my pathetic existence, I could not find the courage to go through with it.

XXVII

"I had fallen into
FourStreet's hands, like
the protagonist of my autobiography.
I had given myself in,
sparing them any particular effort."

Rather than a businessman's autobiography, the text I was penning was shaping up to be a long testament, or rather a long indirect confession. Turning Iorio's audio recordings and digital notes was becoming increasingly difficult from a moral standpoint. Transforming all that material in a tale that would be pleasant to read wasn't easy. Coming into contact with that kind of information kept me from serenely focusing on the lexical and syntactic aspects of writing without asking myself questions about the text's contents. It was a statement from an unwilling murderer of clandestine immigrants, himself a victim of a sick pharmaceutical and scientific world. But that was his life, sadly, and my only task was to recount it. I would turn into words that path of human and professional growth, with its hardships and gratifications, I would show the man before and during his mad rush against suffering, the slow decline of a broken personality, destroyed by guilt. His alienation, sought, desired and found in the frantic idolization of money and of life's fleeting pleasures.

Once you are past the point of no return, death seems like the only way out.

My protagonist's end goal was to cleanse his conscience, to tell all the good and the evil he had done throughout his life. Jenny was wrong, this book would never save his life. It would, however, forever free him from an unbearable weight, a burden that his heart could not stand to endure.

The latest MP3 files and written notes weren't exhaustive. It appeared that Iorio had kept on shuttling human test subjects, unable to put an end to his involvement in that bloodshed. His words were broad and elusive, as if the last page of that crazy existence had not yet been written. The only thing he was clear about was the reason why he had broken up with Jennifer – it was his last attempt to save her, useless as it may have turned out to be.

As I was looking for a way to finish my tale, I realized that I was holding in my hands one of the biggest scoops of the past two decades.

In the modern journalistic world, never had something so huge and so evil been exposed. My career would flare up, not to mention the incredible weight of the files about Agent Orange. All I would have to do was find a newspaper or magazine that would print my story – or rather, find the most prestigious one and pick up the phone.

A far shot from the end of the line I had envisioned just a few days earlier. I was restless, excited and worried at the same time, an incredible mix of emotions that made my body jolt on the chair of that little bar in San Francisco.

I would have to find as much hard evidence as possible amidst that sea of blood. My potential reportage would have to expose everything with plenty of detail, to prove my thesis beyond all reasonable doubt, or no publisher would have the guts to go along with it.

There were too many people involved, most of them very powerful and vengeful.

The simple act of writing is free, but the consequences of what you put on print can be very heavy indeed.

First things first, though: I would have to talk to Paolo and convince him to testify in his favor. It wouldn't be easy, it could even prove to be impossible considering his deviant personality. But it would be the only way for me to prove that I had been framed and thrown in the middle of that violent, shady mess against my will.

I would have to tie that bloodbath to MAS Security, prove that they had been the ones to attempt on Jennifer's life and frame me because I knew too much – indirectly involved by the biography, I had come into contact with sensitive information that would put both the security firm and their British employers at risk.

The same could be said for Andrea, unwittingly involved, an expendable pawn in that perverted puzzle. He would have been able to prove my innocence, were he still alive. He could have stated that I had never had a

story with Jennifer and that it was therefore impossible for me to have killed her as a scorned lover.
With Iorio's help, I would also have to explain that Orange Hands – thanks to years of Jenny's underground researches – were killing all of FourStreet's scientific members as an act of retribution for the grim traffic of human subjects from China, which Iorio had headed.
There was a lot to untangle, but I would have to get to the bottom of it, it was a matter of life and death: mine, specifically.
As for Jennifer and Paolo's legal status, that could wait until the investigation was over.
If I thought about it, she wasn't risking much: despite having violated the privacy of several international companies, she had never divulged strategic business information to the media, so nobody could accuse her of insider trading. She was only carrying out a personal investigation that she could not foresee would end in blood.
And considering what had happened to her father, she had some good reasons to do so. These mitigating circumstances wouldn't be lost on the jury, should it come to a trial.
Besides, were she ever to come out of her coma, she could have helped the authorities dismantle Orange Hands and therefore ask for a reduced sentence as an informer under protection.
Iorio, on the other hand, was in deep. Legally speaking, he risked his life: were he to be arrested in San Francisco, he would end up on the death row, sentenced to capital punishment according to the laws of California. At a federal level, crimes punishable by death include, among others, multiple homicide, child trafficking and repeated torture on humans. The lethal injection was almost a given, for him.
But could be his real chance at redemption: he would get rid of a heavy weight on his conscience and – possibly for the first time in his life – he would do a good deed and bring justice to innocent victims.
It was the only argument I had to convince him to spill the beans.

The lady behind the counter was side-eyeing me hard.
A quick glance at the time showed me that I had been sitting in that place for about five hours. That one brief pursuit aside, I hadn't even gone out for a breath of fresh air.

I was deep in a flood of words, hastily typed on the computer's keys, with an eye fixed on the street to check if anyone were to stop in front of Iorio's beige house.
Even smoking would stress me out, I hadn't touched a cig since the hamburger on the previous evening.
In those hours, I checked online the details of Mike Curley's death, to see if there was something weird or violent about it. As I suspected, in Monterey, where his corpse was recovered, an orange handprint was also found.
Everything fit, I really was on the right track.
My instincts hadn't betrayed me.
The only detail I could not place was the second corpse found on the scene of the crime, a guy from Seattle. Not a researcher, but a young architect: Jeffrey Cunnigan.
What did he have to do with all this?
I focused my attention back to the woman in front of me, with her yellow and white apron, a smiling donut printed on her chest.
I looked at her sweet round face, she must have weighted some two hundred and twenty pounds and her hair was short, with colored locks framing her face. Purple, fuchsia, green... and yet by looking at her, she can't have been younger than fifty. What an odd character: it really was true that you could find anything and anyone in the States.
I preferred Canada's more bourgeois nature.
I smiled and tried to make some friendly small talk, to make up for the forced cohabitation in the room.
"I'm sorry, I know I'm..."
"You don't know anything, agent."
What a lovely middle-aged punk. I smiled, trying to make a typical cop face, even though I wasn't very good at it. I frowned and grimaced like a hard-boiled detective.
"What's that?"
She snorted and wiped a rag on the counter, staring at me and asking:
"Who are you tailing?"
"A guy, he lives nearby."
"The Italian?"
"That's him. Do you know him?"

"No."
She walked backwards into her kitchen, wiggling her hips against the double doors with a round glass panel in the middle.
Two minutes later, she once again opened the door with her hips and came back inside the shop holding a baking tray.
And went back to talking, just like that.
"I don't know him, but one thing's for sure, he hasn't come out of his home. I think he's still inside or I would've seen him come out."
"And why didn't you tell me earlier?"
"Did you ask, earlier? No you didn't. So..."
I wanted to strangle her, but she was right.
"Fine, but how can you be sure that he's not outside?"
"He's a fine-looking man. I always notice him when he comes out of his courtyard, he's so mysterious... I knew he was a *mafioso*..."
"*Mafioso*?"
"Sure, like in *The Godfather*... Why else would you be looking for him? Besides, aren't all Italians..."
"Sure, sure... But he could've gone out early in the morning, or he could've escaped from a door on the back..."
"No dice on the first hypothesis, I saw a silhouette in the living room's window around eleven in the morning, that was him for sure. Before you arrived, I mean. As for a door on the back, why should I know? You're the cop..."
"So what?"
"So surely you have a partner stationed outside, like in the movie... or what kind of cop are you?"
Well, yes, her reasoning was pretty much flawless. I tried to keep up an air of respectability, nodding and giving for granted that I had a colleague hidden under the bushes.
I decided to wait for two more hours, then I would call him on his cellphone.
The owner gave me the impression that she wouldn't be persuaded to close up shop one minute past her closing time, and judging by the sticker by the entrance, that meant that my deadline was 7.30 PM. By the way, the name of that bizarre cafe was the same as my parents': 'Sweet Capucino'.

Just like our surname, Brigati with a single 't', my father had streamlined the spelling of 'cappuccino' to make it as Italian-Canadian as possible. Which drove me bonkers. As a language purist, having studied them in college, walking into their cafe made my eyes bleed every time.
As expected, at 7.25 the owner started rolling down the shutters, inviting me to pay and get the hell out.
I was anxious, I didn't want to call Paolo.
If he didn't want to meet me, calling him would mean warning him and allowing him to escape, putting an end to all my plans.
So I walked around his courtyard again, walking up the steps and ringing the bell.
No reply.
I tried again, hoping to hear some noise coming from inside.
No reply and not a single noise coming from inside the house either.
I didn't have anything else up my sleeve: I would have to call him on the phone. I would risk blowing up in smoke the only trail that could lead me to him: his home address. Besides, as soon as I'd turn on my phone, a thousand police cars would turn up to arrest me.
I picked up my iPhone, gently pressing the oval power button.
The white apple appeared on the screen's black background.
I pulled out the note where I had written down the phone number that Matteo, Iorio's driver and handyman, had given to me, and dialled it.
“Come on Joe, you have to do this...”
I held my breath and tapped the touch screen to start the call.
It rang and I smiled: finally, the end was in sight.
Truth be told, I didn't know what to tell him, I hadn't exactly prepared a speech. I'd wing it as soon as he picked up.
Except he didn't.
The call was dropped.
As I lowered the phone from my ear, I had a vague feeling that I had heard some noise come from inside the house.
Yes, of course: it was like a strong vibration, was his phone there?
I was standing right in front of the precipice.
“Fuck, I hope not.”
If his phone was there and he was not, I had no way of tracking him down.

My only chance would be to sit outside his home, hoping that some time, possibly before the police found me, he would come back to sleep or to fetch something. Too risky, not too mention too dependent on the whims of fate, and by then I didn't believe in fate anymore. Or rather, I did, but with the keen awareness that mine was definitely not on my side.
I called again, getting the tragic proof that his Blackberry was, indeed, abandoned inside his home: I saw it as I leaned out against the window by the front door. It lay on a walnut table, next to a traditional Chinese vase and to a saucer containing three sealed envelopes. I could see better now compared to a few hours earlier, with the reflected sunlight blocking off everything.
I noticed that a light came from a room at the end of the corridor. Either it wasn't on before or the annoying reflection had prevented me from seeing it.
So I decided to circle the building's perimeter. I checked every window, hoping to see something, anything, I dreamed I would find the owner, scared and crouched down under some table, so that I would somehow be able to convince him to follow me to the police. It was nothing but a flight of fancy, a utopia conceived by my stress-addled mind.
On the back, I could see a light coming from a window.
So I wasn't imagining things... But where could he have come in from?
I dropped my shoulder bag on the ground, careful not to damage the computer, and propped myself up a little to get a clearer view.
I jumped up and held onto the window frame with my arms. Turning my nose up, I could have a good look at the white wooden window with its horizontal glass panes.
Inside the room was a man – I could see his hand on the armrest of a brown leather swivel Chesterfield chair. He gave his back to the window and couldn't see me.
The room was an office, well-furnished with classic taste in dark wooden tones, making a stark contrast with the white walls.
The man was still, but the computer in front of him was turned on. The screen, however, was dark, hibernated after an extended period of inactivity.
I couldn't feel my arms anymore and tried to find a support for my dangling feet, to no avail. As I was about to drop down from the edge of

the window, my gaze went up, toward the room's light ceiling, and I saw red spots.
I fell on the courtyard's grass below like a sack of potatoes.
"What the hell... What were those?"
I once again grabbed a hold of the window frame and lifted myself up to get a clearer view. I held my breath.
There they were: several small red stains on the light ceiling, except for one point where the color was more intense, closer to burgundy. That thicker stain was perpendicular to the chair, just a little to the left.
"But what... Blood?"
I tried to think – it felt like something I should be remembering.
"Of course! The stains are the same as the suicide-homicide in Trezzo sull'Adda two years ago..."
I was sure of it, the spraying pattern was unmistakable. Once again, my experience as a crime journalist was coming in handy. Sadly. I could've done without that grim surprise.
Even though I was collapsing deeper and deeper into the abyss – a homicide was the very last thing I needed – I had to try to go in and check whether that man was still alive.
A shiver ran through my back, from my neck to my ankles: it felt as if a 100 volt electric discharge had gone through my entire body, shocking my heart and lungs.
I had a bad feeling about that.
"Shit, let's hope it's not Paolo... He can't be dead!"
A dead Paolo Iorio would mean that every chance I still had of clearing my name was crumbling down. I could hear police sirens drawing close.
"The police? Have they already localized my GPS signal?"
I understood that I had no time left to lose: I broke the window with a rock and sneaked inside, trying not to get hurt.
I got back up as soon as I hit the ground, my arms still hurting from the effort. I stood in silence and listened: the house's alarm had either been deactivated or never been put on in the first place. Not a single sound came from the house. We were alone, the corpse and I.
I shook off some glass and wooden shards from my pants, careful not to cut my hands. I delicately turned the leather chair around.
The man didn't offer resistance.

I heard something heavy give a thud and instinctively threw myself on the ground, fearing that someone might have been about to hit me, but it was just the victim's gun, falling from his hands to the ground.
Right: the person in front of me was dead, as I imagined.
I carefully observed the corpse and felt like throwing up.
His face was tumid and horrifying, he must have shot himself under the chin. The bullet perforated his jaw and skull, lodging itself in the room's ceiling and tainting the walls with sprayed blood.
It was Paolo.
I was sure of it.
I recognized him from a mole on his neck and from his olive skin. Besides, the physique was also his, it would've been hard not to notice the similarities with the man in the photos I had seen in Jenny's laptop.
I ran my hands through my hair and burst into hysterical tears. It was all over for me.
Adrenaline was leaving my body and the feeling of being lost jumped at me like a ravenous lion.
I could have still told my side of the story to the police, but without Andrea, Jenny and Paolo supporting my thesis, and against the hidden powers of Orange Hands and FourStreet, I would certainly end up in jail. And in all likelihood, I would also be found dead in my cell, hanged without honor.
Who would ever believe a poor, unemployed journalist? It was my word against that of influential personalities in the international business world. Important people, valued by their colleagues as well as by politicians, people whose social profile was spotless.
Last but not least, there was the corpse sitting in front of me. I feared it was all a well-orchestrated scheme, the finale of an unbelievable tale.
Had I fallen into FourStreet's hands, like the protagonist of my biography? Probably. No, certainly. I had given myself in, sparing them any particular effort. I, too, was a victim of the system. So much for playing smart investigative journalist – as they say in Milan, I was a *pirla*, a dickhead.
In front of my eyes, I could see the events of the past two crazy days in San Francisco play out in a flashback.
I had given a false name to the hotel. The lady at the cafe could testify that I was stalking the victim by pretending to be a cop in plain clothes.

Some passer-bies could tell the police that I was a violent man, having witnessed me assaulting Paolo's driver without reason right there on the road. And Matteo himself could confirm that I possessed the fury of a madman as I kept his face pressed on the asphalt and asked him questions that did not make sense to him. Questions that, to add insult to injury, were focused on the victim: Iorio. His studio's window was broken with a stone, a clear sign of my unpredictability and lack of planning, the characteristics of a depraved mind alternating between moments of folly and of delirious clarity. This latter quality would have bestowed upon me the capacity to carefully transform a homicide into a suicide.

The real version of the events? I'd caught Iorio by surprise and shot him at point blank with a gun, maybe an unregistered gun. And he didn't react in time to counter my homicidal fury. Or the weapon belonged to the owner of the place and the shot was accidentally fired during our struggle. At any rate, once I'd killed him, I placed his corpse on the chair.

The cops would say that the gun was still lying on the ground as they arrived because I'd lacked the time to complete the staging of the fake suicide.

Everything was against me and could turn into hard evidence. They couldn't find me on the scene, I had to leave before the police arrived or the would really believe that this was the second corpse in a crime of passion: Jennifer first, now Paolo.

I could already picture the headlines, both in America and in Italy. Maybe the news would travel as far as Canada. I wondered what my parents would think.

I had fled Italy to complete my murderous mission: knowing that Jenny was dead, all that remained to do was to get rid of my rival and finally take my own life.

Like in a novel, a little bit romantic, a little bit splatter. How many times do the news report similar cases?

I would risk ending up on the death row in California, I was sure of it. At least I hadn't touched the murder weapon, even though I knew how good the folks at MAS Security were at faking fingerprints.

Been there, done that.

XXVIII

"They won: deviously,
creating a chain of effects
that slowly killed me.
They wiped out my reputation,
my being alive and, most importantly,
my conviction never to give up."

I knew I had to do it.
I needed to flee, but this time, I didn't have the energy. It wasn't for me.
Joe Brigati was about to raise a white flag, wait for the cops with his hands raised up high and say, "Folks, I'm all yours."
Just like Paolo Iorio before me. He had tested his limits and found out that he couldn't overcome them. It was part of the natural order of things.
So he had decided to put an end to his life, the only, tragic solution to the insurmountable problems he was facing.

I am not a hero, nor will I ever be one.
If this were a movie, I would have jumped out of the house's window, gun in hand, shooting up any agent who would come close.
I would make my way to MAS Security, then to FourStreet and finally MonteForte, bringing down their bosses. And then I would go get my damsel Jennifer, miraculously awoken from her coma. And everything would end with a big, passionate kiss.
But this was no movie. It was life, the hard, sad reality.
My reality, to be precise.
My conscience was looking me in the face with a perplexed expression, saying:
"Enough, Joe, give up. There is nothing left to do."
Fleeing across the globe, with the sole hope that Jenny would one day wake up from her coma and clear my name, almost looked more terrifying than ending up in jail.

Impossible, with my attitude: I need to write in order to survive and believe me, working as a journalist while on the lam is really hard. It's like trying to blend into a crowd and at the same time crying out, “Hey, I'm here!”

I could have tried to reach a non-extradition country such as Mexico. Yet, as close to California as it was, attempting to cross the border would have been too risky. They would try to kill me as I escaped and I did not possess an adventurous soul. It happens, after all. Let's be real: who would attempt it, in my place? I'm your average Joe, I'm part of the crowd. I'm not a hero, nor a movie's lead.

I was compromised, they were right. But I was tired of fighting against ghosts, especially since I hadn't done anything wrong. Yet there I was, in San Francisco, with the absolute certainty that I would never be able to clear my name.

They won, they really did, deviously, creating a chain of effects that slowly killed me. They wiped out my reputation, thrashed my dignity as a man, my being alive and, most importantly, my conviction never to give up. Regardless of the problem.

The system won.

Money won, the economic interests that, in the end, come before anything else.

Even before people's health, people's lives.

I can admit, now, that after being fired I had become depressed, but thanks to that job, the biography, I was starting to pull myself back together. I was going back to being happy again, but then all that mess happened and the worst was yet to come. I, too, was slipping toward the precipice, without realizing what was happening around me.

I had slowly ended up on the bottom of my sea, of my life.

I wasn't experiencing your typical death, but the agony that comes with choking. Slowly, your breath pours out of you, you try to fight back, to struggle. But as the seconds go by, the oxygen in your blood gets lower and lower, you start to realize that you have no way out and your strength leaves you forever.

Darkness inexorably comes to you and the last breath you've got left in your life is a sweet release.

A bitter taste, a mix of sadness and peace.

Maybe that was the way it was meant to be, I had come to my reckoning. Maybe I had gotten it all wrong in my life.

The sirens weren't that far anymore. A few instants left and it would be over.
I sat on the brown leather couch in front of the corpse and once again broke into tears. It was years, maybe decades, since the last time that happened. I felt no shame.
I suddenly remembered that Paolo's computer was still on, I don't know why. Maybe because of the CPU's buzzing, which bothered me as I wept. It was located under his desk, a position which amplified its noise.
I wondered what he had been doing before he took his life. I had to wait for the police, for my destiny to show up.
Might as well check whether there was something interesting in there.
I got up and reached the desk; pressing the 'Enter' key lit up the screen. A Word file was open, called 'TO MATTEO, ONE LAST JOB': obviously, it was meant for his bodyguard.
I scrolled through the text with the keyboard's arrows.

... dear Matteo. I want to thank you for all you have done for me and I ask you to carry out this one last task for me, now that you are reading this letter.
Destiny is, sadly, a cruel master and as you will have noticed, my story has come to its epilogue.
Time for me to exit the stage.
I didn't ask you to come fetch me to drive me to who-knows-where. I called for you so you would find my body.
I killed myself, the memories of the past haunt me and more than anything else, I need silence and peace.
I cannot go on like this anymore.
I want to do this on my own terms, not by someone else's hand.
At any rate, I have one last favor to ask of you: please take care of my funeral and deliver the two letters you will find on my desk to Joe Brigati

and Jennifer Blasquez. The former is the man I had you tail in Milan, the latter you're already familiar with.

Farewell.
Yours truly,

Paolo

I was devastated. It was true, he really had killed himself, Iorio. This really was a suicide note, not like Andrea's.
I leafed through the papers left on the desk and eventually found the two letters hidden under an open magazine. Paolo probably put it there in order to shield the envelopes from blood stains.
I opened mine, noticing that it also included another USB drive.
The letter was hand-written.

... to Joe Brigati.
We do not know each other and we never will. By the time you read these words, I will be dead already, but I felt compelled to leave you my version of the facts.
I don't need to tell you that I am sorry.
My plans were very different, I didn't want you to be involved so openly.
Your role was supposed to be limited to writing, to telling what I did to posterity.
I was forced to do it, I couldn't pull back. I do not think of myself as a murderer – maybe, though, as a coward. I should have stopped a long time ago instead of turning into what I am now.
But if I hadn't complied, I would've been mercilessly killed. I was scared of death, once, yet now I am about to gift it to myself with my own hands in order to escape from the burden I shoulder.
I know that you, too, are risking your life because of me, and for this I am sorry. I think you are the only person I am going to apologize in depths to, for all the wrongs you endured.
I asked Jenny to summon you and ask you to write my biography. Why? Because I wanted to free my conscience from the boulders weighing it

down. Yet nothing went according to plan. I was the one who asked my bodyguard to tail you, I wanted to keep an eye on your safety. I was the one who gave you those Orange Hands files, so...

The letter ended right then and there.
Turning the page around revealed another side, still written in Paolo Iorio's calligraphy. The writing clearly showed more pain there and there were stains on the left side of the page, as if some tears had fallen on the paper.

... I can't do this.
Every time I have a chance to tell the truth, I hide behind pointless lies. But I am ready for death now and lying would not be fair. I want to be honest and sincere, for once.
The purpose of the book you were supposed to write was very different. I wanted an alibi for myself. That's all, creating an alibi and deflecting suspicion. Your role, Joe, was to clear my name, but then things happened and everything went off the rails.
Attached you will find a USB drive, open it. It contains everything you need to frame Natalia Birkman and FourStreet Chemical Ltd.
That way, you will finally be able to write the last chapter of my biography.

Farewell

The man must have been devastated, psychologically wrecked.
Before getting to the files in the drive, I read Jenny's letter, even though it wasn't addressed to me.
A gentleman would never do anything of the sort, but it was such a complex moment that I could not resist.

... My love,

You are lying in a hospital bed because of me.

I hope that you can forgive me after all the harm I have caused you.
I really hope that one day, you will be able to read these words and understand the emptiness I carry inside me, and with that realization consider this extreme gesture of mine as a way of freeing myself from all suffering.
I am fully aware that our first meeting wasn't due to chance, but I do not hold it against you, because I know that in the end, our love was pure. You approached me so you could carry out your mission, the most important in your life. And that was fair... It is for the same reason that I have decided to put an end to all my suffering. My final journey toward eternal peace.

I want you to know that you are the only genuine person I have ever met in my life and I will be forever grateful for how you made me feel loved, for one minute at least.

Yours forever, beyond death...
Paolo.

I couldn't understand what he meant by 'lying in a bed because of me'.
I was sure that the attempt on Jenny's life had been orchestrated by MAS Security, but from his letter, it looked like something else entirely. He certainly wanted to apologize for the trouble he had unwillingly caused to his woman.
I took the USB drive from the envelope and hooked it up to the computer on the desk.
I opened the folder and started reading the .doc file it contained, aptly titled 'LAST CHAPTER'.

XXIX

"So it came to be that,
after I was done burying
the first nineteen human subjects,
I decided to take the game's reins
in my own hands."

... Dear Joe, please consider this text as the last chapter we will have written together. As far as I am concerned, I give you full permission to publish this two-man effort of a book. Now that I have decided to take my life, I have no fears nor resentments. Even though I can't deny that I would like to be there when the people involved will be arrested and, better still, when they will read this text.
I would like you to publish my memoirs and give all profits to charities, so that that money will help the Chinese and Italian families that have been destroyed by the corrupt system I have worked for all these years, in addition to terminal AIDS patients.
You decide how and when to proceed – I trust in the goodness of your heart.
Don't do it in my name, it would be pathetic from me, I would be branded as a no-good lowlife trying to wipe his conscience clean. Do it yourself, under your own name, take all credit, I don't care.
All that matters to me is that you respect this agreement.
Thank you for everything.
And again, I am sorry,

Paolo

LAST CHAPTER

The weight was unbearable.
I felt lost.
Everything seemed compromised when the epiphany struck.
I concocted a depraved plan, one that could save me from death and seal off my past once and for all, some way I could flee with Jenny and share my whole life with her without a care, forever erasing her dark past from her memory.
I had known for months that she worked for Orange Hands.
One day, I saw her casually hide on her laptop a strange link to some server – as soon as she saw me walk into the living room, she hid everything in a rush. I tried to see what she was doing, to no avail: she was determined to resist. I had the keys to her apartment, I didn't think she would react that way to a surprise visit.
I had come in holding a bouquet of roses, but she blew a gasket and threw them in my face, telling me that from that moment onwards, I would have to notify her before any and all visits.
She had never reacted that way.
I was jealous, I thought she was chatting with some lover.
So a few weeks later, I decided to check on her computer while she was busy with a fashion show. I sneaked inside her house and, browsing through her computer, I found out that it was protected by a series of unintelligible passwords. I was no expert and I'd never seen anything like it. I talked to an IT expert at FourStreet and had him install a virus inside her PC that would record, through several videos, everything that happened on screen.
I was then able to decrypt the incredible underground network that hid behind the name Orange Hands.
I found out that Jenny didn't hook up with me for love, but that she had ulterior motives. She was looking for info for her underground organization. I felt betrayed, I was furious.
I wanted to break up with her, but that would alarm the Family and therefore put my life at risk. So I stuck with her, pretending that nothing had happened and constantly checking on her.

Then, one day, I eavesdropped on a secret phone call. I couldn't tell who was on the other end of the phone, but from her words, I understood that she was protecting me. She said that she couldn't talk because I was there at home, taking a shower.
Actually, I was right there, behind the door, spying on her.
She told to the other person that she really loved me and that she couldn't carry on with those investigations anymore. She added that, according to her, I was not aware of all the harm FourStreet was causing.
I cried. Her love was pure and sincere.
As I kept on spying on her, I noticed that several files on the organization's server talked about an upcoming, bloody underground war that wouldn't spare anyone. During those secret phone conversations, she and that person talked at length about it. Jenny maintained that they couldn't spill blood for their cause or Orange Hands would stoop as low as their opponents. I found out that all that insane situation started with her father's death – from what I could tell, he had been killed by the system.
But I couldn't decrypt anything more.
I was pissed off, furious at the entire world.
So it came to be that, after I was done burying the first nineteen human subjects, I decided to take the game's reins in my own hands.
I would kill my torturers, one by one, violently and perversely: that's all they deserved, after all the evil they had caused throughout their existence.
I would annihilate them, murder them with different M.O.s that wouldn't be immediately connected by the authorities, so as to give me enough time to carry out my whole plan.
All the crime scenes would present clear signs that would link them back to FourStreet and to all the evil that reality had caused to humanity. And most importantly, when the time was right, the blame for that bloodshed would fall on Orange Hands. And Jenny would be finally persuaded to leave the organization, to flee with me and hide forever in my arms. She would understand that that world was just as violent as the system it was fighting against.
I stuck notes inside the victims' fists that told of their sins, I painted the palm of their hands orange and next to each of the bastards I left a distinctive handprint.

The first in line was Mark Bongher. I still had no idea how to kill him. In the end, chance would have it that I violently stabbed him nineteen times after setting up a fake appointment with him.
I took it as a sign of fate: it would be my mark.
I planted in the car a map with the location of the mass grave circled. I stole the car from the airport right after Bongher himself had given it back to the rental car lot: he had come back a few days after out first 'shipment' of corpses to mile 26 of the road to San Josè, to check that everything was in order.
Then came professor Jason Wittman. With him, everything was premeditated, every single detail of the murder. And I am satisfied with my work of death.
I caught him by surprise in his home in Sausalito – he was sitting naked in front of the computer watching porn. I tied him up and slowly strangled him. As he tried to wriggle away, I broke his shoulders and hips. With my right hand I tightened the nylon wire around his neck, with my left hand and a foot I hit him hard.
That pig, he had to suffer.
Then, leaving him as naked as I'd found him, I placed him on the floor of his living room and painted a clock with his own blood. I used his legs as the minutes hand and his arms as the hours'. Nineteen was my brand and his time was over: no more tests, the vaccine would not be completed.
Mike Curley's turn came last. I gave him an appointment too, telling him that I needed to talk to him about another job and that in order to speed things up, it would be best if we met at some point midway between Long Beach and San Francisco. We settled on Monterey, early in the morning.
I caught him by surprise on the beach, where he was already waiting for me. I violently choked him with a nylon wire and then decided to cut off his arm with a hacksaw I always carried with me as a safety measure. He would lose the same arm he had used to shake my hand in out mad death pact on Pier 39, not too long ago.
I had the bad luck of running into a busybody who tried to ruin everything; I had to sacrifice him for the cause. I don't even know who he was, he came down from the dock's ladder when I was completing my death display. After killing him, I only managed to draw a number 19 on the sand with the hacksaw and then flee, covering up my tracks.

Of course, in order to frame Orange Hands, I would need someone to investigate on the organization.
I could not turn to the police.
So I picked you, Joe Brigati.
I did my research: you were depressed, out of money and unemployed to boot. An easy prey. That was the reason why I let you have those documents in the USB drive, you would have the right flair for carrying out an investigation and the right contacts to get it published. That way, both Orange Hands and FourStreet would be forever defeated.
While I was in San Francisco, I told Jennifer to contact you and to get the ball rolling by telling you some episodes from my early life. The book would have to paint the moving tale of a man forced to do something against his will. In a pinch, I would also use it as a last attempt to convince the authorities that I didn't want to do what I did, that I was forced to carry out those deeds, under a death threat.
Having completed my plan in the States, I came back to Italy. All that was left was Natalia Birkman, then the circle would be complete and I wouldn't have to kill anymore.
But that wretched biography compromised everything. The family saw you get close to Jenny and got suspicious.
You inadvertently went after the wrong person that day, outside the design studio, and for that reason they decided to kill you.
I had to take out that bodyguard in order to throw everyone off your scent, both the police and the MAS Security people. I hoped that Birkman would worry when she saw that orange hand on the scene of the crime, on the side of that black car.
I really hoped that she would feel hunted. And by putting some fear into her, I hoped to be able to deflect her attention from your relationship with Jenny, allowing you to keep on writing undisturbed.
Paranoid as she is, all she would care about was her safety. The tension was meant to drive her mad, considering that she was already under enormous pressure after the death of professor Wittman: his tests turned out to be a failure.
But they ended up finding something about your work. They figured out that you were writing for me, possibly by looking through your personal

belongings in your flat. At least they didn't find the stuff I had sent you through Jenny.
They feared it would be my confession.
Meanwhile, I was hunted myself: I couldn't stay in Milan, so the last part of my plan was blowing up in smoke. They had already taken out Carmine some time earlier through a weird car accident. I would have to fly back to America and forget about killing Birkman.
So I came back to San Francisco, where the unbelievable happened: Jenny.
Once I figured out that they had attempted to kill her, I stopped fighting. The only light of my life was fading away.
I went back to my home. I knew they would find me sooner or later, there was no point in fleeing...

And now, dear Brigati, everything is in your hands. I only ask one last favor of you, make this story go viral and lock all those FourStreet motherfuckers in jail. They must pay for what they have done, they must be pilloried. Mediatically destroyed.
You have to stop that scientific abomination.
As for the others, the victims of my murders, I am just happy to have dragged them into Hell with me – forever.

The cursor blinked. It was as if, having written those words, Paolo had shot himself. I finished reading that long, depraved confession for the third time and something buzzed in my pants, the vibration coming from the right pocket. It was my iPhone, which I had left on on the assumption that I had surely been located already.
I looked at the screen: it was a text from inspector Mirko Gaudenzi. “Joe, call me! Stop running away, miss Blasquez miraculously woke up from her coma. She told me everything.”
I cried. This time, mine were tears of joy.

XXX

"I soon ended up
chained to a table
in one of those rooms with a mirror on one wall,
so different from what we have in Italy.
Right, like in a cop movie, except this time
it was all horribly real."

The air pockets were ruining what was certainly one of the most comfortable travels of my life. Up until that point, I had never experienced the luxury of a first class flight – as a child, I always ended up in an economy seat, due to issues with the family budget. Squeezed in my seat with my knees against my throat and, usually, the nearby seat occupied by someone who either snored, smelled or talked too much. Was it possible for me to always be that unlucky? At least I could always count on two good allies: a sharp sense of humor and willpower to spare.
But not this time, this time everything had to be perfect.
Because, finally, I was reborn. On Virgin Airlines' leather seat was a different man, the world would see a new Joe Brigati, stronger, more belligerent and most importantly, serene. Right, peace of mind: how much I missed it. I almost couldn't remember what it felt like in full force.
I felt light, to the point that I could have flown by myself.
After more than a year of depression, and more than fifteen days lived on the edge, like in a thriller, my troubles had come to an end. I really needed to blow off some steam and rest. Behind me, so many hours of sleep deprivation, the flight to the States on the hunt for a 'corpse', Jenny's 'almost death' for which I had been framed and lastly the temporary detention after Paolo's death.
I was worn out, in body as well as in mind. Not to mention the haunting feeling of being stalked wherever I went, something I had never experienced before and that I would not wish on my worst enemy. Psychological repercussions were all over the place: feeling tailed, always

feeling compelled to turn around and feeling slightly asphyxiated in a crowd, among others.
So I decided to make myself a present and got a one-way ticket back to Milan – first class.

It was a mandatory payback after almost sixteen hours of difficult, intense, nonstop testimony on the second floor of San Francisco's Police Department.
In a few minutes they arrived at Paolo's home and immediately arrested me. I was sitting on his couch, cellphone in hand and tears in my eyes. I had just read Gaudenzi's text and thought that the nightmare would be over, but I was wrong.
I soon ended up chained to a table in one of those drab rooms with a mirror on one end, so different from what we have in Italy. Right, like in a cop movie, except I wasn't the lead in a procedural. It was all horribly real.
I didn't resist arrest, but got my share of kicks all the same. They got me to lie down on the floor and hit my sides once I was handcuffed. Gratuitous acts, I must have oozed guilt from my very clothes, or so the cops saw me. And they wanted to make it abundantly clear.
I stayed silent. I could imagine how anyone could think I was a murderer, seeing me like that, in front of a corpse, with a broken window right behind me. I also had an international arrest warrant for the same crime, coming from Italy, the very country I had flown out of.
I knew I was innocent, I knew I would soon be released with all due apologies, Gaudenzi had promised me so on the phone.
Yet those moments were terrible. I will never forget that cell's pungent stench and, first and foremost, the humiliation of being brutally arrested.
The cops subjected me to psychological torture, they didn't want to let me sleep. I knew, I believed that everything would be cleared up in the end, but I can't deny that every now and then I felt like I was sinking back in deep shit.
The detectives shouted at me, spat at me, they wanted to put the squeeze on me and I couldn't understand the reason behind such doggedness.
"Who are you covering up for? Huh? We know, we know everything..."
They shook me, as soon as I tried to lower my head to get some rest they threw me on the floor by kicking my chair down. I gritted my teeth – I

was explaining with all my strength that I was innocent, but they weren't listening. They laughed at me, mocked me thinking I was mad. They tormented me for over nine hours. Then, the unbelievable happened.
“Enough with your bullshit, can't you see that you're compromised?”
Right, I was 'compromised'. Hearing that word spat at my face, on the tenth hour of questioning, was too much.
The detective was giving me a sarcastic look, grinning like a bastard. It was fate, coincidence. And he couldn't know it.
Hearing the word 'compromised' hit me straight in the gut.
I fell silent and asked for a lawyer.
The cops grinned, lawyering up read as a guilty verdict to them.
“You giving up, boy? You don't know what to say anymore, do you? Do you want your lawyer? Poor child...”
I stuck to my silence and did not reply to their taunts. But the lawyer never came. They said I wouldn't have to worry, that having a lawyer was my right and that he would come soon but that in the meanwhile, I was free to keep talking to them.
There wouldn't be any consequences, just a friendly chat far from the legally binding testimony. Or so they hinted at, but they never explicitly said it.
Smart guys.
“Get your conscience clean, talk to us, come on, not a worry...”
Suddenly, they were turning into my best friends and confidants: from spits to caresses in less than an hour. I knew it wasn't like that, they were fucking with me.
Anyone who's even a little familiar with procedurals would have thought so.
But I didn't have any choice. Stopping there would have done nothing but prove my guilt. So I testified for six more hours, like a flood, exploiting their fake friendly attitude toward me.
Finally, they were starting to listen to me for real. Of course, I had to use all the best communication techniques at my disposal, I had to act like poor Andrea, bless his soul: go round and round before cutting to the chase and telling all my truth, my version of the facts.
But it wasn't enough to set me free.
It took them five days of custody to verify my claims.

That long, thorough chat, at any rate, at least allowed me to catch some rest, as the officers allowed me to catch a small break.
Right after those sixteen consecutive hours of testimony I felt the first hints of calm and peace, but it was just a small appetizer, too short to taste it in full.
In the two days after the arrest, I was forced to repeat the same story over and over again: first my testimony from start to finish, then from the end to the meeting with Andrea at Sandro's. So we went on for hours on end, stopping just to pee and to sleep. Short naps of course, then a brutal, sudden wake-up call got me back on track and off we went from the beginning.
A detective technique: their goal was to make me err, to find a contradiction somehow and prove that my whole testimony was baloney. They made me repeat everything several times, checking my statements against Iorio's biography and my past versions of my tale.
Because lies come out, sooner or later.
Except they don't, because my story, no matter where it began, was always the same.
The Canadian embassy and Italian consulate even intervened to free me. Interpol gave their full availability to untangle that mess as quickly as possible. But it wasn't enough – I was a prisoner of the very country that made of freedom the banner it shows to the world. Yet another joke.
Unfortunately for me, there were so many details to verify, and putting all the pieces of the puzzle together was all but easy. The biography proved to be a great help, shedding light on some passages the detectives couldn't figure out and lending credibility to my innocence. Most importantly, the last chapter – the words Paolo wrote – were considered proof enough to clear the murder charges to my name.
In order to prove their authenticity, however, the authorities had to analyze the fingerprints on the keyboard, which luckily turned out to be just Paolo's, except for two keys bearing mine – the one I pressed to wake up the computer and the one I used to scroll down.
In order to rule out any possible foul play, however, a legal report was required – both hardware and software on Paolo's computer were analyzed in order to prove that those files had not been uploaded from external

sources nor written with a different USB keyboard. Luckily, the results confirmed my thesis.
Long story short, they proved that every single word really was authentic, unequivocally so. Paolo was the only one responsible for that sad affair. He was the author of all those deaths across California, his own included.
“You threatened him with that gun, didn't you? You made him write everything, eh? You son of a bitch, you think you're getting out scot free? Tell me the truth! Talk!!” These were some of the questions the detectives shouted in my ears during that endless series of testimonies.
Those days were difficult, demeaning and humiliating.
Even in front of a list of decisive evidence, deep down they still thought I was guilty.
They couldn't have arrested the wrong guy, it was inconceivable to them. They wanted to see me crumble and confess to a crime I did not commit. Fortunately, I was stronger than them, but I risked a lot during those hours of psychological torture.
On the third day of detention, the files that proved my innocence finally came in from Italy, voiding the international arrest warrant. Luckily, Jenny had miraculously woken up from her coma and asked for me.
Inspector Gaudenzi knew me a little and did not consider me the kind of guy who would commit a murder out of jealousy, so he immediately jumped at the chance to question her. even though her conditions were still dire, she managed to faintly testify and explain how everything went. Completely clearing my name.
Of course, getting a statement and texting me about it was one thing, but writing the report and informing the American authorities through Interpol was another thing entirely.
So it happened that I was stuck with that disgrace for two more days that I strictly should have. At least I wasn't transferred to jail.
I remained confined to the police station's cell, the one they used for temporary custody. It was no accident, of course: that way, they could torture me without a care.
At any rate, without that international warrant around my neck, the situation definitely took a turn for the better. The US detectives were starting to talk to me in a more relaxed manner, possibly having overcome their preconception that I was a serial killer or a dangerous criminal. The

handwriting analysis on Paolo's two letters and the fingerprints found on his gun – proving that the weapon had been touched by its owner and no-one else – did the rest.

And there was also the lack of gunpowder on my hand. A piece of evidence that the cops initially pretended to ignore.

XXXI

"Every curve was agony,
I felt like a soulless object
carried against its will.
But I was a person
and my soul was pure."

Despite flying on a fancy Virgin Airlines Boeing, in my comfortable first class seat, the voice of my persecutors still echoed in my head. I shivered as I remembered those detectives' faces when they tried every trick in the book to make me confess.
My peace of mind was back, but now and then, the nightmares from my recent past came back to the surface.
I still hadn't had time to digest all that had happened to me.
I was staring at the void when a mellow voice by my side addressed me:
"Beg you pardon, sir... do you want a glass of champagne?"
The flight attendant shot me a dreamy gaze.
It was the first time I got that kind of treatment. I was thrilled.
"Yes, thank you..."
I smiled at her.
She smiled back, gently placing the flute on my tray.
"But you are... Yes, you're that famous journalist! Of course, that Canadian everyone is talking about!"
"Well... yes, that's actually me."
"Congratulations, you were amazing. We are honored to have you on board."
She smiled again and hurried away, probably off to inform the staff that I was on board.
I was excited by those developments, I felt important. A king, a famous personality. A VIP.
Looked like glory and fame could be a valid antidote against depression.

But even that warm feeling was not enough to soothe the memories of those frantic days, the days that transformed my life forever. Not without compromises.

The detectives, my tormenters.
Their eyes were horrible, their memory unsettling and burned in my brain.
But I hadn't hit bottom yet: the worst was yet to come.
Once the files came in from Italy, I thought I was finally safe.
Interpol not only sent over Jenny's testimony, which cleared my name once and for all, but they also transmitted that they had arrested the accomplices of the man who had tried to run over my Vespa in Milan: they were employees of MAS Security, the same people who then went on to sack my house.
While I was still flying toward the States, the police had traced back the ownership of the car that had tried to run me over. Thanks to cctv recordings, they found out that a similar car, also belonging to the same security firm, had parked in front of my house for a couple of hours on the day of the break-in.
An odd coincidence? Not at all.
It was, mostly, Gaudenzi's merit: his intuition had struck gold for the second time in a row. The investigation could proceed at a much quicker pace thanks to his hunch that I was being tapped before the aggression.
They found out that on that day, someone really was listening on me when I was talking with the chief inspector on the phone. And they were probably much closer to my home than I could have imagined. On top of that, the same car was recorded in Piazza San Babila square, outside Andrea's office, a few minutes before his death.
The key to the whole mess turned out to be that black Escalade with its passengers. By joining the dots, Mirko managed to fill the blanks of that incredible tale of blood: my attempted homicide, my altered blood-alcohol tests, the break-in, Orange Hands' sensitive documents, MAS, Andrea's death, Jenny's attempted homicide. All isolated cases, but in his brain, they had common ground.
What common ground? Joe Brigati.
That's right, me. Or, rather, the biography I was writing for Paolo Iorio.

Once he could talk to Jenny at the hospital, it didn't take him long to connect all the pieces of the puzzle.
Lastly, an anonymous tip to the police station allowed them to find the two MAS employees who drove the SUV – former military types, as expected – and arrest them.
They didn't find out the author of that tip. The call came from a phone booth near the central station and the cameras didn't allow them to identify the caller. He was covered in glasses, hat and scarf – with that warm September climate, it was the typical attire of someone who doesn't want to be recognized.
A red herring? Possibly – Gaudenzi initially thought so as well. But the question soon became moot as the two men in custody soon spilled the beans.
They were caught close to the customs in Como, at the border to Switzerland. Which was not exactly clever of them: with all the secondary border crossings, they went for the main one, the one with the strictest checks? Their behavior seemed very strange, especially for two men who used to be part of an elite troop in the army.
They confessed that the former vigilante, the mutilated corpse, was part of the group as well and then confirmed that the man had acted under orders from their boss: Norberto Riesp. They did, however, go back on this last part of their testimony within a few minutes, when Interpol arrived at the station.
“Norberto Riesp didn't know anything, we acted on our own”, was the final version they recounted to the international agents.
Was it a believable one? Not at all. Gaudenzi didn't buy it either and considered it a false testimony, probably changed under fear of backlash. It was all too obvious that they had acted for MAS and its founder.
“Listen, Joe, we're gonna send you all the documents you'll need to get free of all charges. Be strong. I know it's not easy, but we have sorted it all out.”
These were Mirko's last words on the phone after my arrest. I reached out to him with my allotted phone call from the police station and it was during that talk that he updated me on his investigations.

"The two men confirmed everything and that's good. You were right, Joe, it wasn't paranoia. They framed you good, we even found the glass they got your fingerprints from. But..."
There was always a 'but', wasn't there. Every time.
"The bad news is, I was blocked. Interpol halted all investigations on MAS Security. We were about to raid their HQ as well as FourStreet Italia, the same company that had decommissioned Iorio's marketing agency in such a hurry for no apparent reason. We can't proceed, the case is closed. Orders from above. So, Joe, I can't do anything else for you... You're going to have to handle this yourself."
He had saved my life and for that I warmly thanked him: he had done a lot already. I felt such a relief back then. I was free.
A doubt in the back of my mind, however, kept me on alert. It was the same hunch – or intuition – shared by the inspector.
"Anyway, Joe, it all seems fishy to me... There's something missing here. Think about it: as soon as those orange hands appear on the side of the door of the Escalade, Interpol crashes my office demanding to question you. Then, as soon as we get to a turning point in our investigations on MAS... Interpol again... But why? What do they want?"
Fair questions, but there was still one missing link.
"And most importantly, who the fuck are these Orange Hands fuckers? Why did the documents you mentioned on the phone disappear? Your USB drive? The men we arrested claim they gave it to their boss... but then they took that back too!!"
Neither I nor Mirko, then, were convinced that Interpol's intromission and the total freeze it caused was a chance. Who sent them?
"Whatever, Joe. Let's drop this, it's not like we can do anything about it. In the meanwhile, don't you worry, it's all right now. Okay?"
All I could answer was "Yes". And a thank you, again, for what he had done for me.
"When the fire grows under the pot, you need the right lid by your side", my grandfather used to say, and as always, he was right. This fire could obviously end up burning a lot of big names and it was smart to put it out with Interpol's lid before it dangerously spread throughout the world.

It was obvious, it was part of the natural order of things. The way I saw it, the real question was: who the hell ended up with Orange Hands' documents?
A question I would probably never be able to answer. But in the end, little did it matter. I had still solved my problems.
I had managed to dodge two dire charges: attempted murder and murder proper. I had helped the US police solve a whopping four cases of violent deaths and I had proven my status as a victim of that horrible persecution in Italy, which had resulted in two deaths and a third one avoided by an inch. All in all, I was ready to receive all due pats on the back and official thanks for the services rendered to the US and international communities. On top of it all, in those same days, the authorities were starting to investigate Biotech FourStreet Laboratories Inc. and its British parent company, FourStreet Chemical Inc.. That mess with the Chinese immigrants was being uncovered too: their bodies were unearthed and the warehouses were those poor innocents were purportedly tortured in order to get a cure for AIDS were sealed. I say 'purportedly' because those places had been thoroughly cleansed. Only Paolo's testimony in his biography supported that accusation.
At any rate, I could rest easy: it wasn't my problem anymore. I was sure that I had left the worst behind.
At least until the fourth day of detention, when an unexpected visit made my anxiety violently flare up.
They brought me back to the interrogation room for the umpteenth time and I awaited yet another backward confrontation. The reality was very different.
“Joe, dear Joe... Please, take a seat!”
The detective's face was serene, too serene, come to think of it.
“We knew you were up to no good. But a terrorist, of all things...! Who'd have thought!” Not me, in all honesty. I didn't understand.
His face contorted into a mask, drunk with satisfaction. He knew that sooner or later, he would get the chance to see me fold and that he would come out as the winner, sticking it to the colleagues who mocked his insistence with me. I couldn't be a murderer or some lowlife, you could read it all over my face, but he was convinced of the contrary: Joe Brigati was guilty and that was the end of it.

The day of reckoning had come and he would be the one to cheer, I could see it in his eyes: he had won his bet.
I stared at him in distress, unable to parse what he was saying.
“They've come to get you, goodbye honey. A hero! Imagine that.”
A cold shower for my mood, icy even.
In the next room, NSA men were under orders to collect me and bring me in a safe place under their custody.
An NSA agent barged into the room.
“Is he the one?”
The detective, my dear persecutor, nodded and smiled.
I winced.
“Come with us, Joe Brigati. You are under arrest for terrorism and unauthorized possession of strictly classified documents belonging to the United States government.”
They rudely jerked me away from the cold steel chair, covered my view with a hood, cuffed my wrists and ankles and preventing me from fetching the few personal belongings I had back in my cell: a shirt and a rain slicker.
I tried to struggle, to ask questions, but they didn't answer. Nothing.
I couldn't see and I couldn't know.
I was forcefully loaded on a vehicle and driven far from San Francisco's police station. Wearing just my t-shirt, I was cold and shivering.
That trip lasted an eternity. I could feel the truck's wheels spin under my feet, manholes hitting on the bumpers. Every curve was agony, I felt like a soulless object carried against its will. But I was a person and my soul was pure.
The chains dangled against the iron walls of the vehicle's inner cage, which was as cold as it was comforting. Indeed, considering that I didn't know where they were carrying me, being there still felt like an improvement over any other location. I feared that I would be sent to some torture camp, Americans notoriously didn't go easy on terrorists after 9/11.
I tried to get a hold of myself, to stay lucid. I had to. I thought back to the agent's words: “Possession of strictly classified documents”.
Of course! The bag I'd left in the hotel, the one with Jennifer's documents!
I had almost forgotten about it, with everything else going on.
I was fucked. This time, I was truly fucked.

I remembered chief inspector Gaudenzi's words: “You're going to have to handle this yourself.”
But I really didn't know how.

XXXII

"The light was strong and my eyes
weren't accustomed to it anymore.
I was in a cell, grey, with
padded walls. I started to think,
trying to keep my wits about me."

It was all so soft, muffled and delicate.
As I returned from the class bathroom, I slipped back into the happiness of the soft black leather seat, pampered by the flight attendants and spoiled with free sweets and alcohol. I couldn't ask for anything better. Furthermore, the flight assistants serving first class passengers were a lot younger and more attractive.
A newbie's impression or the truth? Good question.
I flew accompanied by the memories of what I had experienced in the past weeks, carried through the air by that Boeing 747, thinking new thoughts. In front of me was a new life, pleasant and luxurious.
I was certain that I wasn't wrong in thinking of myself as stronger, more combative and, most importantly, calmer.
I was stronger because, of course, that experience that I would never be able to forget had forged my personality forever. More combative because, from then onwards, the world would have seen me as a well-respected journalist and I wanted to always prove them right. No-one would ever stop me.
Calmer because, after all, the prospect of a prosperous life, full of privileges, could only put me in a good mood. But there was always a price to pay.
As company, I had those young girl in their red uniforms staring at me from the end of the plane. One of them in particular, and she was very beautiful, had been looking at me for about half an hour.

Her brown hair was very light, almost blonde, her features pleasantly strong, her lips thin and her eyes so blue that they were seductive and glacial at once, in harmonious synchrony.
I was hoping she would come closer and make the first move. Then again, I was never that great with women – I preferred to limit myself to writing and accepting their advances. Except up to that moment, nothing of the sort had happened. I wasn't bad looking, though.
“I'm sorry, may I ask for you autograph?”
The girl was giving me a loving look as she gave me a paper napkin. She popped up from behind me, with her perfumed hair gently falling on my left arm and causing a pleasant, irreverent tickle. I could see her body lean forward from the seat behind mine. I wondered how she did it, up until a few moments earlier she was in front of me along with the other attendants. I hadn't seen her pass by the central aisle.
“Sure. Who is it for?”
“Mary. Add that it's from 'Joe Brigati, the scoop-boy'.”
I put the napkin on the tea cart, turning toward her and crossing my legs, and started signing it.
Mostly, I was drawn by the curves that I could peek at from her slightly unbuttoned white shirt. I wondered if she had approached me like that on purpose.
I would've asked her, if it weren't so rude.
But I couldn't miss that one occasion to flirt after so long.
It was my first autograph.
Behind me, another flight assistant scolded the colleague for her audacity.
“It's no trouble, on the contrary!”
My reply was sudden, as I was feeling very pleased by the developments.
No-one could interrupt that first, meaningful moment of fame.
No-one, not even another flight assistant who was just as good-looking as her colleague.

Hard braking made me hit my head against the truck's side, coming this close to reopening the scar I still had on my neck and which was almost healed.
After untying my chains from an iron ring, two arms grabbed me from the sides and lifted me from my seat. I had noticed the ring during the ride:

there was something, in the middle of the vehicle, that was keeping me hooked. And before we made it to our destination, I stretched my feet to figure out what it was. The side sliding door was forcefully pulled open.
"Get up! We've arrived."
The attitude toward me was very hostile, to the point that it made my arrest look like a pleasant stroll.
All I felt as I got out of the car was a discharge of shivers, spurred by a chilly gust of wind. An electric jolt coursed through my spine.
"Move, piece of shit, and make it quick!"
They shoved me onwards, dragging me violently and against my will.
I was forced to walk for a long time, traversing a series of narrow tunnels. It was hard for me to keep up with my two 'guardian angels' in such a cramped space, every step meant accidentally shoving or being shoved, on my right or on my left. And there was no way they could be persuaded to take the hood off me and let me walk on my own.
At least I could have seen the chains on my ankles and therefore avoided the constant tripping and stumbling. When that happened, those two men supported me.
It took us minutes to get to our destination. Our walk started out in the open, in the cold, then we went inside and I could hear an electric gate and a series of clinky iron doors open. They were probably all armored doors, including the last one, which must have been much heavier than the others: I could hear the wheezing of one of the people at my side as he struggled to open it. As we got inside, they pushed me to the ground and uncuffed both my wrists and ankles as soon as I touched the floor.
I took the hood off myself. Looking around proved to be difficult – the light was strong and my eyes were not accustomed to it anymore. I was in a cell, grey, with no windows and a single neon lamp in the middle of the ceiling.
That small room with padded walls was completely empty: no bed, no toiled, no sink.
I started to think, trying, not without difficulties, to keep my wits about me.
First off, I noticed a detail of no small significance: despite being locked up in a maximum security prison, nobody had stripped me and searched me. As was my habit, I pondered upon it out loud.

"What the fuck kind of place is this? I'm not getting outta this this time... Shit..."
As soon as I was done talking, the armored door came open. It was built like a vault, very thick, with no spy-hole to allow a peek inside. It was opened by a key as well as a rotating handle.
One man came in, then a second one. Finally a woman.
All three of them were dressed with elegant, if anonymous, clothes: gray, black tie, white shirt. The woman wore her shirt buttoned up to her neck, with nothing to adorn it. I couldn't pinpoint their ages, though they were all between forty-five and fifty years old. She might have been the oldest of the bunch.
They cuffed me again and made me sit on the floor.
Behind them stood two US Army soldiers in fatigues, carrying two chairs and a box. They placed everything on the ground and walked back out, closing the cell behind them. One of the two men sat down and took a folder from the box. It was the top secret document Jenny's father compiled, the one I'd read a few days earlier.
"Well then... Joe Brigati. You have no idea of what's about to happen to you."
I looked at them, sitting down with my legs crossed, while the woman paced around me. I felt like Sitting Bull and she a native in a suit.
She started to speak. Her voice was almost masculine.
"You are in deep shit. We found a great deal of classified documents in your hotel room in San Francisco. That's a life sentence waiting to happen, not to mention all the minor felonies: false ID, breaking and entering... shall I go on?"
I offered her a defiant stare, but deep down, I was shaking in my boots.
"Aren't you going to sit down?" I smiled. My question was ironic, seeing how both chairs were occupied by her henchmen.
"Stop trying to be funny and get to answering our questions: how did you get hold of them? Who gave them to you?"
I thought about my answer for about a minute, the longest in my life. I was, indeed, obviously in deep shit, but on the other hand, it was just as obvious that the American government was trembling at the prospect of having those documents go public. They couldn't know how many people were aware of them. "Wanna bet that..."

It was my only chance out, I had to employ the best of my dialectic abilities if I wanted to make a turnabout. Either that or I was finished.
“Wanna bet what?” The man, who had up until then stayed silent, stared at me with unbelievable arrogance and viciousness. I have never seen eyes like those.
“You don't know anything, you're in the dark about all this. Those documents are old news by now, everyone is aware of that stuff. Orange Hands first and foremost.”
“Who?”
“Orange Hands... And don't come tell me you don't know who they are! What a low blow it would be for the NSA! It's that silent enemy you've been fighting for years, the one you don't know how to find, nor where. Because any one of you could be part of them... Because it's like a cancer inside the government: it's there, invisible at first, and when it lashes out, it hurts...”
I coughed twice, I was thirsty. I hadn't drunk in hours and my throat was sore.
“Besides... besides the organization... knows that I've been brought here, so should anything happen to me...”
The trio whispered something to each other, then the woman spoke again.
“Listen up, Joe. Who the hell gave you this information?”
“Nobody.”
She kicked me in the ribs, I would have never imagined I'd suffer this much because of a woman. Then she grabbed me by the hair, lifting my head and bringing my face close to hers.
“Listen up. This is not a movie. Try to give it some serious thought or you're never getting out of here again...”
“And what's my angle, what do I have to gain? What happens if I sing?”
“A much more lenient sentence.”
I fell silent for a while, then smiled again, looking her right in the eyes.
“Mmh... listen, here: let's say these info are about to be made public, uploaded through Orange Hands' networks. And you know how dangerous they can be when they want to, those amiable orange folks... remember WikiLeaks? Made you sweat bricks, didn't it, that one?”
The trio was dumbstruck.

“And let's say I have a way to stop them, a system to avoid the circulation of those documents.”
I paused, in an attempt to create some suspense.
“Go on!”
“If I do that, I want immunity. I want to be driven back to the police station and properly released. Forever. I want immunity and the necessary protection for the person who gave me the info, too, or no dice. And should you try to go back on your word, the world shall know what the US Government did! Touch me and you're finished!”
I paused, then went back to my talk with an even heavier voice.
“We are talking about an unparalleled genocide, ladies and gentlemen! The American government paid a multinational company so as to specifically develop a bacteriological weapon, international conventions be damned – the same conventions it uses as a pretext to attack Arab countries. Remember Iraq? Remember why you attacked it twice in just a few years? And I don't mean the real motive, that is, oil... I mean what you told the media, the cover-up... What would the UN say about you now?”
I felt like in a war tribunal court. As if I could see in front of my own eyes those maimed children, their mothers and fathers dying of consumption in horrible agony because of those chemicals.
“The US used Agent Orange against their own soldiers, on top of ruining the population of Vietnam. Innocent women and children, but also men and soldiers. Do you realize that? You trampled on the civil rights of those people and on your own flag! You spat on it... on the dignity of all those kids who died in war fighting for positive ideals of freedom, which will be proven false as soon as the truth comes out!”
No-one had ever pressed them so hard.
“But if you think you can shit on ideals, think of the economic damage this mess will cause to the nation. Vietnam is going to come back knocking on your door, asking for an enormous reparation. And this time you won't be able to pretend you didn't know, that you were kept in the dark. The stars and stripes economy would collapse: forget about shutdowns, it would come to default proper!”
Checkmate: they couldn't stop my mad rush toward global truth, toward my freedom.

“If you don't want to open Pandora's box, let me go. And stop at least MonteForte Company, forever. You will shut it down and open an investigation on its owners and managers, do it for all the victims weighing on your consciences. If you don't feel like doing it for this reason, because it will remain a state secret, then do it for another one. Tie them to FourStreet Chemical Inc. in Birmingham. You have this trump card, use it! They murdered innocent Chinese people through Biotech here in San Francisco, and they control the international pharmaceutical market through despicable, illegal means. They carry out secret studies by paying doctors and politicians, testing new drugs on unwitting patients... Come on, make something up, but they can't get out scot free... the MonteForte people are the dark puppeteers who govern them! I know this and you know it as well...”

The two men got up from their chairs and moved toward the exit.

Without a word, the woman picked up the cardboard box from the ground and followed them.

“Open up!”, they shouted to the guards outside. They couldn't have heard them, seeing how the walls were covered in layers of soundproof rubbery plastic material. There were microphones inside the room, evidently. Who else might have listened in?

XXXIII

*"Something had stung me,
possibly a syringe.
What did they inject me with?
Then, darkness."*

Three long, endless hours. At least, I thought they were three. Maybe four, maybe two.
It was hard to keep track of the passing of time with no instruments to aid me.
"Hey, can you hear me?", I shouted to the walls. I knew that someone was listening in from the opposite end, just as they were probably watching me through microcameras.
"Hey? I don't have time to lose. You do all your thinking, but you've got minutes left, then the information will be released to the media... Either my people get news from me or there's gonna be hell!"
I was going mad, I wanted to cut through that agony. I wanted to see Jenny, to hug her and hold her tight. Ours could have been a beautiful love story if not for all this mess. I would kiss her, cuddle with her and tell her that from that moment onwards I would be the only one in her life who would protect her.
Wishful thinking: it could never have happened. Especially with the NSA's involvement.
Looking at the facts, how could I ever protect her if I could not protect myself? Besides, I couldn't be so certain that she was feeling the same things that I was slowly starting to feel deep in my heart.
"On the ground."
The voice caught me by surprise, even though it didn't sound very authoritative. Maybe there were loudspeakers hidden in that padding. Seeing how I was alone in the cell.

“Joe Brigati, move the chairs to a corner and lie down on the floor. On your belly, face pressed against the floor, eyes closed, arms crossed behind your back.
I did as they asked and the armored door opened immediately. That noise was unmistakable.
Two men came in, probably uniformed. They were walking fast and their soles hit the rubber floor in a way that revealed very big shoes, such as combat boots.
I tried to peek through my eyelids, but I couldn't see anything before they put the hood back on me.
I was transferred to another room, not too far. Two corridors, one on the right, then one the left. They opened a door, a regular door with a handle, made me sit on a chair, uncuffed me and gently took the hood off me. It felt like a good start.
In front of me was the same woman as earlier, along with one of the two men. The other one, with the unsettling eyes, was gone, and in his stead I saw a distinguished-looking man, thin and going gray.
He wore with class a tailor-made black suit, with a beautiful, elegant gray vest under the jacket. Judging by the cufflinks on his shirt's sleeves, he had to be a big shot of sorts: white gold, with a black stone in the middle.
“I see you've noticed them...”
I met the gaze of the man in front of me. He touched his left cufflink with his right hand.
“Pardon?”, I asked. When stressed out, I sometimes resorted to French – it had its charm.
“Mister Brigati, I mean... I see you've noticed my cufflinks.”
“Yes, they are beautiful. Congratulations.”
“Do you know what this stone is? ...Obsidian. Here, only a few people can appreciate its beauty.”
“Good to know, but if you don't mind – who are you? And what am I doing here right now?”
“Oh, you're right, how rude of me. I am Jefferson Marshall Junior, director of the CIA.”
My astonishment amused him. Talking to such a personality didn't happen every day, I really had gotten the attention of the heavy hitters and the expression painted on my face must have really conveyed the feeling.

"See, your case is quite convoluted. It should be handled by the NSA, considering the documents we found in your hotel room. It's all national security in US territory, so it should be their business, but..."
He stopped to look at the woman.
"But those documents' contents, regarding foreign territories and war zones, are where we come in. Then again, after the Bay of Pigs, everyone knows that the CIA worked side by side with the army in Vietnam. So here we are, up to our necks... Long story short, I won't deny that you are causing quite the stir, Brigati..."
"I can see that, with how quickly you came here..."
Upon further consideration, I wasn't happy to have the big shots here – they could cause yet more problems. But that man seemed good-natured, it felt reassuring in a way.
"Oh, no big deal! Really... I was already listening to your little monologue earlier, comfortably sitting in the room beside yours as a simple spectator, along with the director of the NSA. Then when you involved our government in, let's say, more private matters, I was forced to intervene personally, while my colleague had to step aside..."
To think that just a few weeks earlier, I was a depressed do-nothing who spent his days slouched on the living room's couch drinking and watching TV. Amazing.
"Anyway, I was telling you about the cufflinks... obsidian... do you know why I like it?"
He looked me in the eyes. His face lost any hint of softness and reassurance.
"Because it's rough, but pure. It's volcanic glass and therefore transparent. All these characteristics are part of me: I am pure, possibly a tad rough and transparent when I talk. But I am also hard when the situation calls for it. This is the stone that prehistoric men and pre-Columbian civilizations used to make war weapons and sacrificial knives. Because it is indestructible and sharp... Mister Brigati, I kill when I need to. And I do it silently, with a deep cut that leaves no trace..."
I was having a hard time swallowing.
"Now, let's go back to us. I'll be frank. I have an offer: you can take it and live, or leave it and die... Your pick."
"Let's hear it. It doesn't look so promising from here..."

"The Secretary of Defense is letting you go, even the President believes that it's the right thing to do. You can get away, forget about us... but..."
As they say, in life there is always a 'but'.
"You have to tell us who gave you those documents."
I instinctively replied:
"Hey, who's to say I'll be truly free? That you won't kill me as soon as I walk out of this place, once I've told you what you want to know?"
"Listen well... thanks to you, those documents have finally come back to us after years of absence. Think of it like this, we owe you one. Now tell us who gave them to you and that's it, we are going to stay out of the rest of your life..."
"Yes! I can imagine... But I..."
"I know. You think you have the upper hand on this, don't you? You are wrong. Because, you see... even if you had photocopied every single page of those documents, all you would have would be copies. Not the originals. It's our word against yours, you see? Who would they believe: you, Joe Brigati? Or the President of the United States? WikiLeaks or the US Government? It's one thing to make such bold claims with hard evidence at hand, but copies, counterfeit copies maybe... Do you understand? I am giving you a chance to get out of this, don't pass it up. Besides, as I said, I am ready to kill when the situation calls for it. And had that been my will, you would already be a corpse, believe me."
My heart was beating out of my chest. He'd undermined my claims, turning the situation upside down and leaving me in a cul-de-sac. I didn't have any other choice, no way out.
My only option was selling myself to the enemy.
I remembered another teaching from my grandfather. He said that sometimes, in life, we make compromises with destiny. These are choices we can never forget, that will probably mark us, deep down, for the rest of our lives. We think we don't have any other choice and we follow our base survival instinct. But the truth is that some part of us had already died before we take that step. That was my situation, the first, big compromise of my life.
"I understand, but all those victims? It can't end like this..."

"Wake up, Brigati! That's life... villains live, the good ones die. Truth and goodness are always easy targets of expedience. Don't let this occasion pass you by, be self-serving for once in your life..."
"Fine, fine... But at least MonteForte..."
The graying man burst out laughing. He kept it courteous, it was obvious that he was trying not to offend me, but my almost childish behavior in the face of real injustice was amusing him somehow.
"MonteForte shall not be touched and those victims will remain corpses buried under the rice fields of Laos. No-one cares for the truth, no-one cares for how they died. They are dead and that is that. But all things considered, we could say..."
"What?"
"About FourStreet and their manager Natalia Birkman, should the authorities intend to continue their investigations, we won't oppose them... What do you think? Does this look like a favorable compromise to you? Of course you will need to tell us who gave you those files and erase any sensitive mention of ties between MonteForte and FourStreet from Paolo Iorio's documents... And I don't have to tell you that you won't be mentioning this to anybody, right?"
"Yes, but what will happen to the person who gave me the files?"
"Nothing, if they'll cooperate. Else..."
I blinked. No, I would never sell out Jennifer. Anything but that.
"Listen. Let's settle on this. I will tell you everything, but should the person I name be willing to cooperate, they will need to be put under the European Interpol's protection."
The man laughed again, wildly this time.
"You're something else, Joe, you know that? You're dictating terms now? I've been all too patient with you... You have a few more seconds to make your call, and after those are over, I will walk out of that door and you..."
"Okay, okay... don't move. I'll talk..."
A tear rolled down my cheek and on my lips. I stopped it with the tip of my tongue.
It wasn't salty, but rather bitter. So very bitter.
"It's Jennifer Blasquez. She is the daughter of the Argentinian chemist who created Agent Orange in MonteForte's laboratories. She's part of O..."
A firm voice interrupted my confession.

It was the woman, who had up until that moment maintained a stern silence.
“Fine, we thought it could be her, even though we still lacked evidence. She wanted to avenge her father, for years she's lived under the delusion that his death was caused by the government and by his old company. We were keeping an eye on her, but she isn't dangerous: she just knows too much...”
I couldn't understand what they were driving at.
“But you know, Jef, it might not be such a terrible idea?”
The man gave her a bewildered look: “What are you implying, Paula?”
“If she is the source, should she be willing to cooperate, having her under protection in Europe wouldn't be wrong. With Orange Hands messing around, she wouldn't be safe with us, considering she's living evidence... Don't you think? We can't trust anyone in here anymore, do you understand me?”
The man lowered his eyes, then faintly answered:
“Fine, go on. But make it quick, I want a report as soon as possible. And a constant update on the situation.”
Without saying goodbye, he sprung up and hastened toward the door behind my back, the same door I had come from, hooded, a dozen minutes earlier. Meanwhile, the woman was smiling, as if happy with the results.
“What now?”
“Now it's over, Joe.”
“What do you mean o...”
Behind me, two men burst into the room and pressed me down on my chair.
I felt a strong blow to the neck. It would have been impossible to react.
At first it itched, then the sensation turned into a faint warmth that filled my jaw, rising toward the temples.
Something had stung me, possibly a syringe. What did they inject me with? Then, darkness.

“Oi... Oi! Wake up!”
My face was being slapped, quite vigorously.
I opened my eyes. It was that woman again. I was lying inside a truck, probably the same vehicle that had led me to that gloomy place. This time,

though, I was neither cuffed nor blindfolded. I was free, drowsy and alone with her.
I stared at her as I tried to get up to a sitting position.
"But who the hell are you?"
"My name is Paula, Paula Jackson. I am an analyst at the White House, I work for the president, focusing on critical issues for the country's political security."
"I was afraid I'd been killed."
"I almost went there, Joe. I would have even allowed it... But then I understood..."
"Understood what?"
"That you were one of us."
"Beg your pardon, one of whom?"
"Of Orange Hands. From the way you talked, I could see you were one of us, a pure person. And I tried to dissuade them from hurting you, by trying to make the director of the CIA listen to reason. I told him it would be counterproductive, that you weren't a threat for the government. As it was my own initiative, in theory, I broke protocol. It wasn't an order from my 'introductor', but it was an emergency, I had to protect the organization and the situation was getting out of hand. Were you planning on selling us out to the enemy with all those talks, Joe?"
"Ah..."
I was at a loss. That woman, who up until a few moments earlier was an enemy, had suddenly showed her real face: she was my ally.
"Not at all. It's just that... Listen, I didn't know what to do. I only improvised so I could save my own skin. I have to come clean: I'm not a part of Orange Hands and I've never talked to any of you members. Actually, I only got to know about the orange hands front through Paolo. He presented me with document pertaining to the organization and..."
"Fuck... freeing you was a fucking mistake then. This changes everything, I compromised myself! Shit..."
"Hey... I'm only being honest! What do I have to expect now, are you going to kill me now that you know?"
"No, I can't. And I don't want to. And anyway, after all you've been through, I still consider you one of us. Your soul is orange, Joe: truth matters to you, a lot. Maybe more than life and freedom themselves. And

for me, this is worth everything. At any rate, it's better that we forget about this meeting of ours. You've never seen me and the decision to let you live was the CIA's and the CIA's alone. Not mine, alright?"
"Of course..."
"Perfect. Keep mum and nothing's gonna happen to you. But should you tell anyone what I did, before Orange Hands gets me, I'm gonna get you!"
"Crystal clear."
"Good."
"What now?"
"Now you're free. We're driving you back to the police station. You'll be released and this will be a closed chapter in your past."
"Fine, but what about Jenny?"
"She'll have to cooperate, and if she will, there won't be any trouble. I am sure that she will manage to keep her allegiance to the front secret... Just one thing..."
"I'm listening."
"I would have preferred to have her under American protection, but with how things were going in there, in order to let both you and her live, I had to go along with your requests so you wouldn't keep on talking more than strictly necessary."
Every time I talked to that woman was a wild ride. I could never guess what she wanted to tell me.
"But I..."
"I know, you feared that her life would be in danger with us, but Interpol is a worse danger. Many members of the CIA share the organization's views, Europe on the other hand..."
"On the other hand?"
"There is a lot of corruption, and that's a problem. The men of the Brindeber Foundation, and therefore MonteForte Company, have their hands everywhere. But I promise you that I'm going to keep my eyes peeled, don't worry. We're gonna protect her, she's part of the family."
Those simple words made me understand that I had, albeit involuntarily, sold Jennifer to the devil. I couldn't know at the time.
I could feel that that remorse would stay with me for a long, long time.
"What do I have to do now?"
I looked like a child, scared and alone.

"Nothing. Aid the police in investigating FourStreet and eliminate any mention of MonteForte or Orange Hands from Paolo's documents. There cannot be any more leads except for the ones leading to Birkman and to the murders. The authorities are going to need those. I'll deal with everything else."

"Yes, but..."

"Joe, chill: you will always be protected."

She slammed her hand twice on the truck's side.

The screeching tires made my eardrums jump while my body was shaken by the heavy braking. She opened the vehicle's back door and hurried outside, nodding a salute.

The truck sped up again toward San Francisco's Police Station.

XXXIV

"In life, tragedies aid
the rebirths of people.
From every crooked thing
comes a right one."

"Sir... We are about to land in New York."
The soothing voice reinvigorated me just enough to make me smile at life. I had fallen asleep, like a child in his mother's arms. It was still my favorite flight attendant, smiling at me.
"Thank you. Very kind."
I raised my seat and fastened its belt.
I was, finally, ready to begin again. I was full of energies, I wanted to go back into the fray professionally, and enough with international plots and secret organizations.
I only had pleasant work in front of me.
If nothing else, that misadventure had kicked my career back on track. And indeed, as my grandfather used to say, in life, tragedies aid the rebirths of people, and from every crooked thing comes a right one. And that is what happened here as well.
My return to the police station was amusing; the stares from the cops as I traversed the building, priceless. Especially from that one detective who was dead sure I was guilty of who-knows-what crime against humanity.
He thought he'd sent me to eternal hell, but I was coming back from the flames, stronger that before. I was accompanied by an order to drop all charges to my name, signed by the head of the CIA himself. From suspect number one, I had been promoted to simple person of interest.
I was kept by my jailers for one more day, the fifth day of that endless captivity. But I wasn't scared anymore.
On the contrary: that night in my cell provided a pleasant rest.
The detectives analyzed my notes and my writing in depth. Paolo Iorio's biography was fundamental in concluding the preliminary investigation.

Contrary to protocol, however, those files were not immediately handed over to the agents for the umpteenth checks and controls, but rather given back to me, under the table, for the editing that had been agreed upon with the NSA. It was the last thing I did, early in the morning of the fifth day, a few hours before I was released. A cop blinded the cameras and sneaked me inside a small room with the files and a laptop. I remained there for three hours.
It was there that I committed my first real crime. Justified, in this case.
Of course the editing did not go unnoticed, but they could not figure out how such a thing could have happened, nor who could have broken into a police station under constant, 24/7 surveillance.
At any rate, the accident was soon hushed up. All it took was two hours, especially since the edits did not undercut the primary investigation on FourStreet.
I wondered how many of those agents would have to lower their heads and accept a compromise. The first of their life, or yet another one.
When I was released, outside the police station, an astronomical amount of cameramen, journalists and photographers was lying in wait. That's all the world could talk about in those days: the esteemed British pharmaceutical company that, through its American subsidiary Biotech, tortured poor, powerless Chinese clandestine immigrants, committing a plethora of offenses.
The list was endless: misappropriation of international R&D funding, corruption, abuse of animals in terrifying lab tests. And most importantly, the killing of human test subjects, sacrificed in the name of research. A massacre in the name of money.
Suddenly, in those seized warehouses – the former lager, the evidence necessary to close the loop suddenly reappeared.
Someone up above had decided to stop hiding the truth, at least the part of the truth that could be revealed to the outside world. Consequently, Natalia Birkman and all her staff were arrested on that same day in the States, in a live televised bust that made many a politician puff their chest. She had flown back to California to look for Paolo and take him out. In the end, she and her freedom were the only things that got taken out, forever. And I was the positive protagonist of the news that were spreading worldwide. The story that was passed on – completely unfounded, but that

was good enough for the media – was that I had carried out a secret investigation, going incognito for months and worming my way inside the corrupt international pharmaceutical world. And after days of intense testimony at the San Francisco Police Department central station, I had finally passed on my information to the relevant authorities. The last leg of that crazy adventure.

Daring Joe Brigati, in his hunt for truth, had managed to frame FourStreet all on his own – FourStreet which, in retaliation, had killed two of its employees who had played the role of primary whistleblowers. The murders had been carried out by an employee of Italian origins, whose name had not been made public, and who eventually killed himself.

Suddenly, I was a hero, one of the most famous investigative reporters in the world.

From average Joe to VIP in just five days.

Every piece of the puzzle was finally, magically in place.

Even diplomatic tensions with the Chinese government due to the nature of those crimes were easily allayed by USA and Great Britain. All it took to avoid political repercussions was to create a joint foundation, The Heroes of the Fight Against AIDS, which would cover the medical expenses of both the victims' families and HIV patients in China.

Just a few hours after an agreement was found, the President of the United States and the British Prime Minister broadcast it worldwide.

I smiled when I heard of it: it was part of Paolo's will when he asked me to publish his biography. Maybe there was, after all, some kind of divine justice in some remote corner of the sky.

"Where to?"

The taxi driver stared at me inquiringly. He was black, in his fifties, bright white teeth. He wanted to get moving as soon as possible so as to avoid the 6.30 AM gridlock, when everyone in New York knows that any trip isn't going to last less than two hours.

Which, for him, meant a huge economic loss.

"One Time Warner Center, please."

The car sped away from the taxi stands, leaving the bumbling JFK international airport behind. The skyline was amazing, with the blue sky fading into the sun's red hues, still low on the clouded horizon. Years later,

I was still witnessing the spectacle of New York coming back to life. A pachiderm slowly getting ready ro rise, run and lead America.
“First time here?”
“No, I already came here with my parents, on a holiday.”
“From where?”
“Toronto, but we're Italians.”
“I'm from Eritrea, I can speak Italian if you prefer.”
“No, thank you. Or, whatever suits you best. I'm good with English...”
“That I can see. What brings you in the city?”
“Work.”
“What's your job?”
“I'm a journalist...”
He gave me a look from the rearview mirror, then did a double take, opening his eyes wide for the second time.
“Ah, wait. You're that boy! Yes, the one who got famous for exposing for what was going on behind the scenes of those bastards... You know, the ones who killed those three men and all those immigrants...”
Not quite. But to that man, it didn't matter.
Nor to me.
The news reported by the media were never disproved – on the contrary, politicians bloated it and enshrined it. From that day onwards, I became the investigative reporter who had brought down a corrupt multinational company.
And it made my fortune.
The reason behind the odd number of murders – three instead of five – revealed to the press? Painting Mike Curley, the man paid to smuggle the human subjects in the States, as a member of FourStreet's 'clan' would have caused some degree of embarrassment.
The thing is, Monterey's mayor already painted Curley himself as a poor fool who, in a fit of mad rage, accidentally killed a tourist. Mad to the point that he amputated his own arm before killing himself.
In order to avoid scaring the tourists away from that small former fishermen town – as its economy was so deeply rooted in tourism – the mayor shut down the investigation as soon as possible. By allowing more thorough night patrolling by the local law enforcement, everything soon

went back to normal, the visitors came back with their spending money and the merry town was soon able to prosper.
That was one huge lie he had told and going back on his word would mean a horrible faux pas, ridiculing not just the mayor himself and the town's law enforcement but the President's party as well, as they were all part of the same political faction.
The result was obvious. The facts had to remain buried and in order to facilitate it, the tales about me were backed and given credibility. Paolo Iorio was suddenly transformed from a monster haunted by his demons into a hitman hired by the British multinational company, responsible not for five deaths but for three, two in America, one in Italy.
There was, however, an issue: me. Joe Brigati knew the whole truth.
In exchange for my silence, then, I sealed the deal for an exclusive: I would be the one, the only one, to publish the details of my purported investigation. I would get the chance to write a full reportage on the case, complete with names, surnames and degrees of involvement of everyone responsible. Putting an end to the conjectures and indiscretions of the media.
“We're here, sir, that's One Time Warner Center.”
I raised my eyes to the sky and saw the immense glass building, a gentle giant staring at me, powerful and colossal.
I smiled, thinking back to the Bresso offices of Iorio Farmaceutici. So few days had passed since then.
I also thought about my parents, what they would say about me.
Right, that was it. My destination. In more ways than one.
“Thanks, you can keep the change.”
I got out of the taxi and walked toward the entrance.
I had just arrived at my new office: the *Time*.
It felt like a dream, but it was the simple, gratifying truth.
On the twenty-seventh floor of the building, my new employers were waiting for me, along with my new news editor and colleagues. I was about to sign a million-dollar contract for the exclusive on that story. They were the ones who called me, right outside the police station, on the iPhone the agents had just given back to me along with my other belongings.

How on earth they managed to get my Italian phone number, I never could figure out. But of course I took them up on their offer immediately.
And so I wasn't the 'Canadian protégée' anymore. I was simply Joe Brigati, the 'scoop boy' like the international media liked to call me due to my young age. And in all honesty, it didn't feel half bad.
I could only imagine the faces of my old colleagues at *Repubblica*. Far from being a failure, I was reborn.
As I crossed the sliding door at the entrance, I thought of Jenny, of how I would never see her again. It was the only thing that bothered me. I probably let her down, but then again, she was the one who got me in that mess to begin with. And I didn't have any other choice.
And I didn't want to think sad thoughts anymore.
Away with depression, only positivity, I had to at least make an attempt.
I would finally be able to seriously make a career for myself, or maybe I already had and I still hadn't noticed.
I would be able to tell the truth about the events of those days, by pretending to be the one who took the lid off Pandora's box. The smaller one, of course.
Because as someone once said, "The greatness of a man isn't evaluated by the astonishing deeds he has accomplished in life, but by the amount of compromises he has left behind his back".
No, that wasn't my grandfather.
That was me.
Simply Joe Brigati.

Cit.

“Faber est suae quisque fortunae”

Appius Claudius Caecus (350 a.C. - 271 a.C.)

AFTERWORD

Many people asked and still ask me why I chose to title this novel 'The Orange Hand'.
I know, it's a weird title for the literature market.
It's even difficult to remember, but it is telling of the novel's content.
After reading these pages, you probably have an idea of why.
Let us focus on the word orange.
It's my favorite color and, most importantly, my lucky one, so my hoped that by using it in the title, this book could rapidly rise through the international sales charts.
Superstitious jokes aside, I think that the meaning behind the choice of the color is clear enough: it refers to the use of defoliant chemicals in Vietnam, among which ranked the infamous, dioxin-based Agent Orange.
There can be no denying that thrillers, or novels in general, are often set in nonexistent or invented historical frameworks, because the basis upon which their plot is built is just a fabrication of the author's imagination and not very relevant.
My literary journey, however, is different.
First of all, characters must 'come to life' with their hardships, their anxieties, their fears and joys. The reader must be able to 'experience' them as if they were people, discovering them little by little. This crescendo, aided by a change in tenses as the pages go by, passes through the magnifying lens of the psychological dimension that can be read between the lines. This is the necessary gateway toward immedesimation with the main characters, through a first-person narrative which many deem harder to pull off, but that I consider a priceless tool that allows the reader to experience the story from within.
Besides, following my interest in history, and modern history specifically, for the fictional element of a novel like this I set a personal goal for myself: these pages would absolutely have to convey to the reader a plausible, realistic historical background. "Everything must be possible, nothing left to chance. The plot must be set in history, in real history."
Specifically, my end goal was not to limit myself to entertain the reader for a few hours, but rather to spur them to a reflection.

I wanted my wholly fictive narrative arc to start from real, little-known facts. And when it comes to the Vietnam war, I feel that the talk has always been unilateral, from the point of view of the American soldiers, showing the tragedy of their return from that hell.
The damages caused by Agent Orange were only alluded to a few times: not only did it rain massive destruction upon the country's vegetation, with terrible environmental and agricultural damage, but it generated permanent damage to the people involved in that silent, terrible chemical explosion who had managed to survive it.
The United States mourned 57,685 dead and about 153,000 injured soldiers in the war. The Vietnamese count more than two million dead, three million injured, twelve million refugees.
And the war in Vietnam did not end on April 30th, 1975, either. It is still raging: for the victims of that physical slaughter, the battle lives on.
Day after day, night after night.
Disfigured children, born with unimaginable deformities, now helpless adults, vegetables, growing up without parents, dying of cancer because of the chemicals they inhaled. A tragedy silently slipped between history's pages, but not any less important for this. They wanted to make us forget, but that is wrong.
Besides, not only Vietnamese citizens were harmed by the defoliants' dioxin.
Many American soldiers still carry the brand of Agent Orange on their skin or in their lungs, and many US families were destroyed by this product.
Deep down, then, this book's goal is to encourage reflection. Because 'fiction' can teach too.
Historical books can be something more than simple trivia, because memory and culture are priceless.
Because if by the end of this novel, at least one reader will have turned to the internet to find out exactly what Agent Orange is and what damage it caused, I will have reached my goal as a writer.
I will have won my personal battle as an author as well as a person. Reached this book's real goal.

Tom Bilotta

ACKNOWLEDGEMENTS

It only feels right to dedicate this book to the people who,
in many ways, believed in me.
Writing is a cathartic act,
an inebriating, stimulating profession.
But the start of any work, small or big though it may be,
means the writer will turn into a fickle creature.
The compositional phase brings along a sharp decrease in congeniality,
we often turn into furless bears,
brandishing a keyboard instead of claws.
Or into strange men with our head buried in our thoughts. Because plotting
a novel is constant work, wherever we are.
I dedicate my first thriller to the very people who stuck beside me during these long, difficult months.
They know who they are, there is no need to name them.

www.wh-books.com
www.tombilotta.com
www.emooks.net

Suite LP31588
20-22 Wenlock Road
London, N1 - 7GU
England, UK

Lightning Source UK Ltd.
Milton Keynes UK
UKHW02f1959201217
314841UK00011B/630/P

9 788899 752026